THE LAST
WATCH

SERGEI LUKYANENKO

Translated from the Russian by Andrew Bromfield

WILLIAM HEINEMANN: LONDON

Published by William Heinemann, 2008

2 4 6 8 10 9 7 5 3

Copyright © Sergei Lukyanenko, 2006

English translation © Andrew Bromfield 2008

First published in Russian under the title Последний Дозор by
Издательство ACT, 2006

First published in Great Britain in 2008 by
William Heinemann
Random House, 20 Vauxhall Bridge Road,
London SW1V 2SA

www.rbooks.co.uk

Addresses for companies within The Random House Group Limited can be
found at: www.randomhouse.co.uk/offices.htm

The Random House Group Limited Reg. No. 954009

A CIP catalogue record for this book
is available from the British Library

ISBN HB: 9780434017379
ISBN TPB: 9780434017386

The Random House Group Limited supports The Forest Stewardship
Council (FSC), the leading international forest certification organisation. All our
titles that are printed on Greenpeace approved FSC certified paper carry the
FSC logo. Our paper procurement policy can be found at:
www.rbooks.co.uk/environment

Mixed Sources
Product group from well-managed
forests and other controlled sources
www.fsc.org Cert no. TT-COC-2139
© 1996 Forest Stewardship Council
FSC

Typeset by Palimpsest Book Production Ltd,
Grangemouth, Stirlingshire

Printed and bound in Great Britain by
Clays Ltd, St Ives plc

THE LAST WATCH

In Russia, all volumes of the *Night Watch* series have sold over two million hardcovers between them. *The Night Watch* has been adapted into an internationally successful film, which has been distributed round the world. Sergei Lukyanenko lives in Moscow.

Also by Sergei Lukyanenko

The Night Watch
The Day Watch
The Twilight Watch

Part One

A COMMON CAUSE

PROLOGUE

LERA LOOKED AT Victor and smiled. Inside every man, no matter how grown-up, there was still a little boy. Victor was twenty-five years old and of, course, he was grown-up. Valeria was prepared to insist on that with all the conviction of a nineteen-year-old woman in love.

'Dungeons,' she said straight into Victor's ear. 'Dungeons and dragons. Oo-oo-oo!'

Victor snorted. They were sitting in a room that would have been dirty if it wasn't so dark. Jostling all around them were excited children and adults with embarrassed smiles. On a stage decorated with mystical symbols a young man wearing white make-up and a long flowing black cloak was making frightening faces. He was lit up from below by a few crimson light bulbs.

'Now you are going to learn what real horror is like!' the young man drawled menacingly. 'Aagh! A-a-a-agh! Even I feel afraid at the thought of what you are going to see!'

He spoke with the precise articulation that only drama college students have. Even Lera, who didn't know much English, could understand every word.

'I like the dungeons in Budapest,' she whispered to Victor.

'They have real old dungeons there . . . it's very interesting. And all they have here is one big "room of horror".'

Victor nodded guiltily and said:

'But at least it's cool in here.'

September in Edinburgh had turned out hot. Victor and Lera had spent the morning in the royal castle, a centre of tourist pilgrimage. They had had a bite to eat and had drunk a pint of beer each in one of the countless pubs. And then they had found somewhere to take shelter from the midday sun . . .

'Sure you haven't changed your minds?' the actor in the black cloak asked.

Lera heard someone crying quietly behind her. She turned round and was surprised to discover that it was a grown girl, about sixteen years old. Standing there with her mother and little brother. Several attendants surfaced out of the darkness and quickly led the entire family away.

'There you have the other side of European prosperity,' Victor said didactically. 'Would any grown girl in Russia be frightened by a "room of horror"? Westerner's lives are too calm and peaceful, it makes them afraid of all sorts of nonsense . . .'

Lera frowned. Victor's father was a politician. Not a very important one, but very patriotic, always taking every chance to demonstrate the shortcomings of Western civilisation. But that hadn't stopped him sending his son to study at Edinburgh University.

And Victor, who spent ten months of the year away from his homeland, stubbornly repeated his father's rhetoric. You would have to look very hard to find another patriot like him even inside Russia. Sometimes Lera thought it was funny, and sometimes it made her angry.

Fortunately the introduction was over now, and the slow procession through the 'Dungeons of Scotland' began. Under a bridge beside the railway station some enterprising people had partitioned off the bleak concrete premises into small cages. They had put in weak light bulbs and draped tattered rags and artificial cobwebs everywhere. On the walls they had hung portraits of the maniacs and murderers who had run riot in Edinburgh over its long history. And they had started entertaining children.

'This is the bootikin!' howled a girl dressed in rags – their guide for this room. 'A terrible instrument of torture!'

The children squealed in delight. The grown-ups exchanged embarrassed glances, as if they had been caught blowing soap bubbles or playing with dolls. To avoid getting bored, Lera and Victor stood at the back and kissed while the guides babbled. They had been together for six months already, and they were both haunted by a strange feeling that this romance would turn out to be something special.

'Now we'll go through the maze of mirrors!' the guide announced.

Strangely enough, this turned out to be really interesting. Lera had always thought that those descriptions of mirror mazes in which you could lose your way and run your forehead straight into the glass were exaggerated. How was it possible not to see where there was a mirror and where there was an empty space that you could walk into?

It turned out that it *was* possible. In fact, that it was very possible indeed. They laughed as they jostled against the cold mirror surfaces and waved their arms about as they wandered around in the noisy clamour of the group, which had suddenly been transformed from a handful of people into a crowd. At one point Victor waved in greeting to someone, and when they eventually got out of the maze (the door was slyly disguised as a mirror, too) he gazed around for a long time.

'Who are you looking for?' Lera asked.

'Ah, it's nothing,' Victor said, with a smile. 'Just nonsense.'

Then there were a few more halls with the sombre trappings of medieval prisons, and then – the 'River of Blood'. The hushed children were loaded into a long metal boat that set off slowly across the dark water to the 'Castle of the Vampires'. The darkness was filled with malevolent laughter and menacing voices. Invisible wings flapped above their heads, water gurgled. The impression was only spoiled by the fact that the boat sailed about five metres at the very most – after that the illusion of movement was maintained by fans blowing air into their faces.

But even so Lera suddenly felt afraid. She was ashamed of her fear, but she was afraid. They were sitting on the last bench, there was no one else beside them, ahead of them were actors groaning and giggling as they pretended to be vampires, and behind them . . .

Behind them there was nothing.

But Lera couldn't get rid of the feeling that there was someone there.

'Vitya, I'm afraid,' she said, taking hold of his hand.

'Silly girl . . .' Victor whispered into her ear. 'Just don't cry, all right?'

'All right,' Lera agreed.

'Ha-ha-ha! Evil vampires all around!' Victor exclaimed, imitating the voices of the actors. 'I can sense them creeping up on me!'

Lera closed her eyes and clutched his hand even tighter. Boys! They were all boys, even when they had grey hair! Why was he frightening her like that?

'Ai,' Victor exclaimed very convincingly. Then he said, 'There's someone . . . someone biting my neck . . .'

'Fool!' Lera blurted out, without parting her eyelids.

'Lera, there's someone drinking my blood . . .' Victor said in a mournful, despairing voice. 'And I'm not even afraid . . . It's like a dream . . .'

The fans kept blowing their cold wind, the water slapped against the sides of the boat, the wild voices howled. There was even a smell of something like blood. Victor's hand went limp. Lera angrily pinched him on the palm, but he didn't even twitch.

'I'm not afraid, you blockhead!' Lera exclaimed almost at the top of her voice.

Victor didn't answer, but he tumbled softly against her, and that made her feel a bit less afraid.

'I'll bite your throat out myself!' Lera threatened. Victor seemed to be confused. He didn't say anything. Then Lera surprised even herself by adding: 'And I'll drink all your blood. Do you hear me? Straight after . . . straight after the wedding.'

It was the first time she had mentioned this word in connection with their relationship. She froze, waiting to see how Victor would react. A single man simply had to react to the word 'wedding'! He would be either frightened or delighted.

Victor seemed to be dozing on her shoulder.

'Did I frighten you?' Lera asked. She laughed nervously and opened her eyes, but it was still dark, although the howling had begun to fade away. 'All right . . . I won't bite you. And we don't have to have a wedding!'

Victor still didn't say anything.

A mechanism creaked and the iron boat floated another five metres along the narrow concrete channel. The clamouring kids piled out onto the shore. A three- or four-year-old girl who was holding on to mummy with one hand and sucking one finger of the other kept turning her head and staring straight at Lera. What could have caught her attention? A young woman talking in an unfamiliar language? No, that couldn't be it, they were in Europe . . .

Lera sighed and looked at Victor.

He really was asleep! His eyes were closed and his lips were set in a smile.

'What's wrong with you?' Lera asked and gave him a gentle shove. Victor started slowly slumping over, with his head falling straight towards the iron side of the boat. Lera squealed and managed to grab hold of him (what was happening, why was he so limp and flabby?) and lay him down on the wooden bench. An attendant immediately appeared in response to her cry — black cloak, rubber fangs, cheeks daubed with black and red make-up. He jumped down agilely into the boat.

'Has something happened to your friend, miss?' The boy was very young, probably the same age as Lera.

'Yes . . . no . . . I don't know.' She looked into the attendant's eyes, but he was bewildered too. 'Help me! We have to get him out of the boat!'

'Maybe it's his heart?' The lad leaned down and tried to take hold of Victor's shoulders — then he jerked his hands away, as if he had taken hold of something hot. 'What's this? What kind of stupid joke is this? Light! We need light!'

He kept shaking his hands, and there were drops of something thick and dark falling from them. But Lera was petrified, staring at Victor's pale face. The lights came on, bright and white, burning out the shadows, transforming the frightening tourist attraction into the setting for a sordid farce.

But the farce was over, vanished with the tourist ride. There were two open wounds with raised edges on Victor's neck. Blood was oozing from the wounds slowly, like the last drops of ketchup from an upturned bottle. The thin spurts of blood-drops were even more terrifying because the wounds were so deep. Right above the artery . . . as if they'd been made with two razors . . . or two sharp teeth . . .

And then Lera started screaming. A thin, terrible scream, with her eyes closed, waving her arms around in the air in front of her, like a little girl who has just seen her favourite kitten smeared across the surface of the road by a dump truck.

After all, inside every woman, no matter how grown-up she is, there is still a frightened little girl.

CHAPTER 1

'How come I could do it?' Geser asked. 'And why couldn't you?'

We were standing in the middle of a boundless grey plain. My eyes could not make out any bright colours at all in the overall picture, but I only had to look closely at an individual grain of sand and it would flare up in tones of gold, purple, azure and green. The sky over our heads was a frozen swirl of white and pink, as if a river of milk had mingled with its fruit-jelly banks and then been splashed out across the heavens.

There was a wind blowing too, and it was cold. I always feel cold down on the fourth level of the Twilight, but that's an individual reaction. Geser, on the other hand, was feeling hot: his face had turned red and there were beads of sweat trickling down his forehead.

'I haven't got enough Power,' I said.

Geser's face turned deep crimson.

'Wrong answer! You are a Higher Magician. It happened by accident, but you are still a Higher One. Why are Higher Magicians also known as magicians beyond classification?'

'Because the differences between their levels of Power are so insignificant that they cannot be calculated, and it is impossible to determine who is stronger and who is weaker . . .' I muttered. 'Boris Ignatievich, I understand that. But I haven't got enough Power. I can't get to the fifth level.'

Geser looked down at his feet. He hooked up some sand with the toe of his shoe and tossed it into the air. Then he took a step forward – and disappeared.

What was that, a piece of advice?

I tossed some sand up in front of myself. Took a step forward and tried in vain to raise my shadow.

There was no shadow.

Nothing changed.

I was still where I had been, on the fourth level. And it was getting even colder – the steam of my breath no longer drifted away in a little white cloud, it fell on the sand in a sprinkling of sharp frosty needles. I turned round – in psychological terms I always found it easier to look for the way out behind myself – and took a step forward, emerging onto the third level of the Twilight. A colourless maze of stone slabs corroded by time, lying beneath a low, motionless grey sky. In places the desiccated stems of plants trailed across the stone, looking like oversized bindweed killed by the frost.

Another step. The second level of the Twilight. The stony labyrinth was covered with a carpet of interwoven branches . . .

And another one. The first level. Not stone any longer. Walls with windows. The familiar walls of the Moscow office of the Night Watch – in its Twilight version.

With a final effort, I tumbled out of the Twilight into the real world. Straight into Geser's office.

Naturally, the boss was already sitting in his chair. I stood there, swaying, in front of him.

How on earth had he managed to overtake me? After all, he

had gone on to the fifth level, and then I had started making my way out of the Twilight!

'When I saw you were getting nowhere,' Geser said, without even looking at me, 'I came straight out of the Twilight.'

'From the fifth level into the real world?' I asked, unable to conceal my amazement.

'Yes. What do you find so surprising?'

I shrugged. There was nothing really surprising about it. If Geser wanted to present me with a surprise he always had a huge range to choose from. There's an awful lot that I don't know. And this . . .

'It's annoying,' said Geser. 'Sit down, Gorodetsky.'

I sat down facing Geser, folded my hands on my knees and even lowered my head, as if I felt guilty about something.

'Anton, a good magician always finds his powers when he needs them,' said the boss. 'Until you become wiser, you won't become more powerful. Until you become more powerful, you won't master higher magic. Until you master higher magic, you won't go into places that are dangerous. Your situation is unique. You were affected by' – he frowned – 'the spell of the *Fuaran*. You became a Higher Magician when you weren't ready for it. Yes, you do have the Power. Yes, you do know how to control it . . . and what you used to find hard to do is no problem at all to you now. How long were you down on the fourth level of the Twilight? And now you're sitting there as if it was nothing special. But the things that you couldn't do before . . .'

Geser stopped.

'I'll learn, Boris Ignatievich,' I said. 'After all, everyone says I'm making good progress. Olga, Svetlana . . .'

'You are,' Geser admitted willingly. 'You're not a total idiot, you're bound to develop. But right now you remind me of an inexperienced driver, someone who has driven a Lada around for six months and then suddenly finds himself at the wheel of a

Ferrari racing car! No, worse than that, a dump truck in a quarry. A huge BELAZ truck weighing two hundred tonnes, creeping up round a spiral road on its way out of the quarry . . . with a hundred-metre drop at one side! And there are other dump trucks driving down below it. If you make one false move, turn the wheel too sharply, or let your foot slip on the pedal – then everyone's in trouble.'

'I understand,' I said, with a nod. 'But I never asked to be a Higher Magician, Boris Ignatievich. It was you who sent me after Kostya . . .'

'I have nothing to reproach you with and there are a lot of things I'm trying to teach you,' said Geser. And then he added, rather off the point: 'Although you did once reject me as your teacher!'

I said nothing.

'I don't even know what to do . . .' Geser drummed his fingers on the file lying in front of him. 'Send you out on routine assignments? "A schoolgirl has seen a hobo werewolf," "A vampire has shown up in Butovo," "A witch is casting real spells," "There's a mysterious tapping sound in my basement"? Pointless. With your Power, nonsense like that is no problem for you. You'll never have to learn anything new. Leave you to rot behind a desk? That's not what you want, anyway. Or what then?'

'You know what to do, Boris Ignatievich,' I answered. 'Give me a genuine assignment. Something that will force me to develop and mature.'

Geser's eyes glittered ironically.

'Sure, coming right up. I'll organise a raid on the special vault of the Inquisition. Or I'll send you to storm the Day Watch office . . .'

He pushed the file across the desk:

'Read that.'

Geser himself opened an identical file and immersed himself in the study of several pages from a school exercise book, covered in writing.

Why did we have these old cardboard files with tatty lace bindings in our office anyway? Did we buy several tonnes of them last century, or had we picked them up a little while ago from some charitable organisation providing work to housebound invalids? Or were they produced in some ancient factory that belonged to the Night Watch in the provincial city of Flyshit?

But anyway, it was a fact that in the age of computers, photocopiers, transparent plastic folders and elegant, robust files with convenient clips and pins, our Watch still used flaky cardboard and string . . . What a disgrace – we should be ashamed to look our foreign colleagues in the eye!

'It's easier to apply protective spells that prevent long-distance sensing to files made of organic materials,' Geser said. 'It's the same reason why we only use books for studying magic. When a text is typed into a computer, it doesn't retain any of the magic.'

I looked into Geser's eyes.

'I never even thought about reading your mind,' the boss said. 'Until you learn to control your face, I don't have to.'

Now I could feel the magic that permeated the file. A light defensive spell that caused no problems for Light Ones. Dark Ones could have removed it with no difficulty too, but it would have created a real din while they were at it.

When I opened the file – the Great Geser had tied the laces in a neat bow – I discovered four fresh newspaper clippings that still smelled of printer's ink, a fax and three photographs. The three clippings were in English, and to start with I focused on them.

The first clipping was a brief article about an incident in a tourist attraction that was called the Dungeons of Scotland. This establishment seemed to be a fairly banal version of the standard 'room of horror'. But a Russian tourist had been killed there, 'as a result of technical faults'. The dungeons had been closed and the police were investigating to establish whether the personnel were responsible for the tragedy.

The second article was much more detailed. It didn't mention any 'technical faults' at all. The text was rather dry, even pedantic. I grew more and more excited as I read that the man who had died, twenty-year-old Victor Prokhorov, had been studying at Edinburgh University and was the son of 'a Russian politician'. He had gone to the 'dungeons' with his girlfriend, Valeria Khomko, who had flown from Russia to see him, and he had died in her arms from loss of blood. In the darkness of the tourist attraction someone had cut his throat. Or some*thing* had cut it. The poor guy and his girlfriend had been sitting in a boat that was sailing slowly across the River of Blood, a shallow ditch around the Castle of the Vampires. Perhaps some sharp piece of metal protruding from the wall had caught Victor across the throat?

When I got to this point, I sighed and looked at Geser.

'You've always been good with . . . er . . . vampires,' the boss said, looking up from his papers for a second.

The third article was from the yellow press, one of Scotland's cheap tabloids. And of course, in this case the reporter told a terrible story of modern-day vampires who suck the blood of their victims in the dismal darkness of tourist attractions. The only original detail was the journalist's claim that vampires did not usually suck their victims dry and kill them. But, like a true Russian, the student had been so drunk that the poor Scottish vampire had got tipsy too and then got carried away.

Even though the story was so tragic, I laughed.

'The yellow press is the same everywhere the whole world over,' Geser said without looking up.

'The worst thing is that that's exactly the way it was,' I said. 'Apart from him being drunk, of course.'

'A pint of beer with lunch,' Geser agreed.

The fourth clipping was from one of our Russian newspapers. An obituary. Condolences to Leonid Prokhorov, Deputy of the State Duma, whose son has been killed tragically . . .

I picked up the fax.

As I expected, it was a report from the Night Watch of the city of Edinburgh, Scotland, Great Britain.

The only slightly unusual thing about it was that it was addressed to Geser in person, and not to the duty operations officer or head of the international department. And the tone of the letter was just a little more personal than was normal for official documents.

The contents were no surprise to me, though.

'We regret to inform you . . . the results of a thorough investigation . . . total loss of blood . . . no signs of initiation were found . . . searches have discovered nothing . . . our best men have been put on the case . . . if the Moscow department considers it necessary to send . . . give my best wishes to Olga, I'm very pleased for you, you old co—'

The second page of the fax was missing. Obviously the text on it was personal. And so I didn't see the signature.

'Foma Lermont,' said Geser. 'Head of the Scottish Watch. An old friend.'

'Aha . . .' I drawled thoughtfully. 'And so . . .'

Our glances met again.

'Oh no, you can ask for yourself if he's related to the Russian poet Lermontov,' said Geser.

'I was thinking of something else. "Co" – is that *commander*?'

'"Co" is . . .' Geser hesitated and glanced at the page with obvious annoyance. '"Co" is just "co". That's none of your business.'

I looked at the photographs. A young man, that was the unfortunate victim Victor. A girl, very young. His girlfriend, no need to guess there. And an older man. Victor's father?

'The circumstantial evidence suggests a vampire attack. But why does the situation require intervention by us?' I asked. 'Russians are often killed abroad. Sometimes by vampires. Don't you trust Foma and his men?'

'I trust them. But they don't have much experience. Scotland is a peaceful, calm, cosy country. They might not be up to the job. And you've had a lot of dealings with vampires.'

'Of course. But even so? Is the reason that his father's a politician?' Geser frowned.

'Twenty years ago the young man's father was identified as a potential Light Other. A rather powerful one. He declined initiation, and said he wanted to remain a human being. He sent the Dark Ones packing straight away. But he maintained a certain level of contact with us. Helped us sometimes.'

I nodded. Yes, it was a rare case. It's not often that people reject all the opportunities that Others have.

'You might say that I feel guilty about Prokhorov senior,' Geser said. 'And though I can't help his son any more . . . I won't let the killer go unpunished. You're going to go to Edinburgh, find this crazy bloodsucker and reduce him to dust in the wind.'

That was a direct order. But I hadn't been about to argue in any case.

'When do I fly?' I asked

'Call in at the international section. They should have prepared your documents, tickets and money. And a cover story.'

'A *cover* story? Who for — me?'

'Yes, you'll be working unofficially.'

'*Contacts*?'

For some reason Geser frowned again and gave me a strangely suspicious glance.

'Only Foma . . . Anton, stop mocking me!'

I gave Geser a perplexed look.

'"Co" is the beginning of the word "cocksman",' Geser blurted out. 'We were young then, you know . . . the free and easy morals of the Renaissance . . . All right, off you go! And try to catch the next flight out.' He paused for an instant, and then added: 'If Svetlana doesn't object. And if she does, say that I'll try to persuade her.'

'She will object,' I said confidently.

What was it that had upset Geser like that? And why had he explained to me about that word 'cocksman'?

Svetlana set a plate down in front of me, full of fried potatoes and mushrooms. Then a knife and fork appeared on the table, followed by a salt cellar, a saucer of pickled cucumbers, a little glass and a small carafe with just a hundred grams of vodka. The carafe was straight out of the fridge and it immediately misted up in the warm air.

Bliss!

Every man's dream when he comes home from work. His wife fusses over the stove and puts delicious things that are bad for you on the table. Was there something she wanted to ask me? My daughter was playing quietly with her building set – at the age of five she had already lost interest in dolls. She didn't build little cars and aeroplanes, though. She built houses – maybe she was going to be an architect?

'Sveta, they're sending me to Edinburgh,' I repeated, just to be the safe side.

'Yes, I heard you,' Svetlana replied calmly.

The little carafe on the table lifted into the air. The round glass stopper twisted out of its neck. The cold vodka flowed into the glass in a thick translucent stream.

'I have to get a plane today,' I said. 'There's no flight to Edinburgh, so I'll fly to London and transfer there . . .'

'Then don't drink a lot,' Svetlana said anxiously.

The carafe swerved and moved away towards the fridge.

'I thought you'd be upset,' I said, disappointed.

'What's the point?' Svetlana asked, serving herself a full plate as well. 'Would you not go?'

'No, I would.'

'There, you see, Geser would only start calling and explaining how important your trip is.' Svetlana frowned.

'It really is important.'

'I know,' Svetlana said, nodding. 'This morning I sensed that they were going to send you somewhere far away again. I phoned Olga and asked what had happened in the last few days. Well . . . she told me about that young guy in Scotland.'

I nodded in relief. Svetlana knew all about it, that was great. No need for lies or half-truths.

'It's a strange business,' she said.

I shrugged and drank the forty grams of vodka that I had been allocated. I crunched happily on a pickled cucumber and then asked, with my mouth full:

'What's so strange about it? Either a wild vampire, or one who went loco because he hadn't fed for too long . . . that's pretty normal stuff for them. This one seems to have a distinctive sense of humour, though. Fancy killing someone in a tourist attraction called the Castle of the Vampires!'

'Quiet.' Svetlana frowned and indicated Nadya with her eyes.

I started chewing energetically. I love fried potatoes – with a crispy crust, and they have to be fried in goose fat – with crackling, and a handful of white mushrooms, fresh ones if they're in season, or dried ones if they're not. Everything's all right, mummy and daddy are talking about all sorts of nonsense, about movies and books, vampires don't really exist . . .

Unfortunately, there's no way our daughter can be fooled. She can see them all quite clearly. It had been a struggle to teach her not to mention it in a loud voice in the metro or on the trolley-bus. 'Mummy, Daddy, look, that man there's a vampire!' Never mind the other passengers, they would just put it all down to childish foolishness, but I felt awkward for the vampires somehow. Some of them have never attacked people: they drink their donor blood honestly and lead perfectly decent lives. And then in the middle of a crowd a five-year-old kid jabs her finger at you and laughs: 'That man's not alive, but he's walking around!' There was nothing we could do – she could hear what we were talking about and she drew her own conclusions.

But this time Nadya took no interest in our conversation. She was putting a red tile roof on a little house of yellow plastic bricks.

'I don't think it's a question of anybody's sense of humour,' Svetlana said. 'Geser wouldn't send you right across Europe for that. The Watch in Scotland isn't full of fools, they'll find the blood-sucker sooner or later.'

'Then what is it? I've found out everything about the victim. A decent guy, but no saint. Obviously not an Other. The Dark Ones have no need to kill him deliberately. The boy's father once refused to become an Other, but he cooperated unofficially with the Night Watch. A rare case, but not unique. The Dark Ones have no reason for revenge.'

Svetlana sighed. She glanced at the fridge – and the carafe came flying back to us.

I suddenly realised that she was worried about something.

'Sveta, have you looked into the future?'

'Yes.'

It's not possible to see the future in the way that charlatans and fortune-tellers talk about it. Not even if you're a Great Other. But it *is* possible to calculate the probability of one event or another: will you get stuck in a traffic jam on this road or not, will your plane explode in mid-air, will you survive or be killed in the next battle? . . . To put it simply, the more precise the question is, the more precise the answer will be. You can't just ask: 'What's in store for me tomorrow?'

'Well?'

'There's no threat to your life in this investigation.'

'That's great,' I said sincerely. I took the carafe and poured another glass for each of us. 'Thanks. You've reassured me.'

We drank – and then looked at each other grimly.

Then we looked at Nadya – our daughter was sitting on the floor fiddling with her building set. Sensing our gazes on her, she started trilling: 'La la-la la la-la.'

It was the kind of song grown-ups often use to represent little girls in jokes. Horrid little girls, who are just about to blow something up, break something or say something really nasty.

'Nadezhda!' Svetlana said in an icy voice.

'La-la-la . . .' Nadya said in a slightly louder voice. 'What have I done now? You said Daddy shouldn't drink before he flies away. Drinking vodka's bad for you, you said so! Masha's daddy drank, he drank and he left home . . .'

There was a subtle weepy note in her voice.

'Nadezhda Antonovna!' Svetlana said in a genuinely stern tone. 'Grown-up people have the right . . . sometimes . . . to drink a glass of vodka. Have you ever seen Daddy drunk?'

'At Uncle Tolya's birthday,' Nadya replied instantly.

Svetlana gave me a very expressive look. I shrugged guiltily.

'Even so,' said Svetlana, 'you have no right to use magic on Mummy and Daddy. I've never done that!'

'And Daddy?'

'Neither has Daddy. And turn round immediately. Am I talking to your back?'

Nadya turned round and pressed her lips together stubbornly. She thought for a moment and then pressed one finger against her forehead. I could hardly hold back a smile. Little children love to copy gestures like that. And it doesn't bother them at all that it's only characters in cartoons who put their fingers to their foreheads when they're thinking and real live people don't do it.

'Okay,' said Nadya. 'I'm sorry, Mummy and Daddy. I won't do it again. I'll fix everything!'

'Don't fix anything!' Svetlana exclaimed.

But it was too late. The water that had been in our glasses instead of vodka suddenly turned back into vodka. Or maybe even pure alcohol.

Right there in our stomachs.

I felt as if a little bomb had gone off in my belly. I groaned and started picking up the almost cold potatoes on my fork.

'Anton, at least say something,' exclaimed Svetlana.

'Nadya, if you were a boy you'd get my belt across your bottom!' I said.

'Lucky for me I'm not a boy,' Nadya replied, not in the slightest bit frightened. 'What's wrong, Daddy? You wanted to drink some vodka. And now you have: It's already inside you. You said vodka doesn't taste nice, so why drink it with your mouth?'

Svetlana and I looked at each other.

'There's no answer to that,' Svetlana summed up. 'I'll go and pack your suitcase. Shall I call a taxi?'

'No need. Semyon will take me.'

Even that late in the evening the ring road was packed, but Semyon didn't even seem to notice it. And I didn't even know if he had checked the probability lines or was simply driving with the instincts of a driver who has a hundred years' experience.

'You're getting snobbish, Anton,' he muttered, without taking his eyes off the road. 'You might at least have told Geser: I won't go anywhere on my own, I need a partner, send Semyon with me . . .'

'How was I supposed to know that you like Scotland so much?'

'How? Didn't I tell you how we fought the Scottish at the battle of Sebastopol?'

'Not the Germans?' I suggested uncertainly.

'No, the Germans came later,' Semyon said dismissively. 'Ah, there were real men in those days . . . bullets whistling overhead, shells flying through the air, hand-to-hand fighting by the Sixth Bastion . . . and there we are, flinging magic at each other like fools. Two Light Others, only he'd come with the English army . . . He got me in the shoulder with the Spear of Suffering . . . But I got him with the Freeze – frosted him all the way up from his heels to his neck!'

He grunted happily.

'And who won?' I asked.

'Don't you know any history?' Semyon asked indignantly. 'We did, of course. And I took Kevin prisoner. I went to see him later. It was already the twentieth century then . . . nineteen oh seven . . . or was it eight?'

He swung the steering wheel sharply as he overtook a Jaguar sports car and shouted through the open window:

'Use your brakes, you stupid ass! And he wants to swear at me!'

'He's embarrassed in front of his girlfriend,' I explained, glancing at the Jaguar as it disappeared behind us. 'Letting some old Volga cut him up like that.'

'A car's not the right place for showing off to a girl – the bed's the place for that. The consequences of a mistake there are more upsetting, but less tragic . . . Ah, I tell you what, if things get tight, call Geser and ask him to send me to help. We'll call in to see Kevin, drink some whisky. From his own distillery, by the way!'

'All right,' I promised. 'The moment the pressure comes on, I'll ask for you to come.'

After the ring road the traffic was calmer. Semyon stepped on the gas (I'll never believe that he has the standard ZMZ-406 engine under the hood of his hurtling Volga) and fifteen minutes later we were approaching Domodedovo airport.

'Ah, what a wonderful dream I had last night!' Semyon exclaimed as he drove into the parking lot. 'I'm driving round Moscow in this battered old van, with one of our people sitting beside me . . . Then suddenly I see Zabulon standing in the middle of the road, dressed like a hobo for some reason. I step on the gas and try to knock him down! But he just waves his hand and puts up a barrier. We go flying up into the air, and somersault right over Zabulon. And we drive on.'

'So why didn't you turn back?' I needled him.

'We were in a hurry to get somewhere.' Semyon sighed.

'You should drink less, then you wouldn't be bothered by dreams like that.'

'They don't bother me at all,' said Semyon, offended. 'On the contrary, I enjoyed it. Like a scene out of some parallel reality . . . Oh, hell!'

He braked sharply.

'More like its lord and master . . .' I said, looking at the head of the Day Watch. Zabulon was standing in the parking bay that Semyon was just about to drive into. He gestured for us to come closer. I said, 'Maybe that dream was a hint? Will you have a go?'

But Semyon was not inclined to try any experiments. He drove forward very smoothly. Zabulon stepped aside and waited until we'd halted between a dirty Zhiguli and an old Nissan. Then he opened a door and got into the back seat.

It was no surprise that the door's locking device didn't work.

'Evening, watchmen,' said the Higher Dark Magician.

Semyon and I exchanged glances. Then we looked at the back seat again.

'Almost night,' I said. Semyon might have a thousand times more experience than me, but as the one with the greater Power I would have to do the talking.

'Yes, night,' Zabulon agreed. 'Your time. Off to Edinburgh?'

'To London.'

'And then to Edinburgh, to investigate the case of Victor Prokhorov.'

There was no point in lying. Lying never helps anyway.

'Yes, of course,' I said. 'Do you object, Dark One?'

'I'm all in favour,' Zabulon replied. 'I'm almost always in favour, strangely enough.'

He was wearing a suit and a tie, only the tie knot was lowered slightly and the top button of his shirt was unfastened. He looked just like a man who was in business, or who worked for the state. But the mistakes in that assumption started with the word 'man'.

'Then what do you want?' I asked.

'I want to wish you a pleasant journey,' Zabulon replied coolly. 'And success in investigating the murder.'

'Why are you so interested?' I asked after an awkward pause.

'Leonid Prokhorov, the father of the deceased, was identified as an Other twenty years ago. A powerful Dark Other. Unfortunately,' Zabulon said with a sigh, 'he did not wish to undergo initiation. He remained a human being. But he maintained good relations with us and sometimes helped us in small matters. It's just not acceptable when your friend's son is killed by some petty bloodsucker in a raving fit. Find him, Anton, and roast him on a slow fire.'

Semyon had not been present at my conversation with Geser. But, to judge from the puzzled way he was scratching his clean-shaven chin, he knew something about Leonid Prokhorov.

'I intend to do that anyway,' I said cautiously. 'You have nothing to worry about there, Great Dark One.'

'But what if you need some help?' Zabulon asked, as if it were the most natural thing in the world. 'You never know who you might run up against. Take this . . .'

An amulet appeared in Zabulon's hand. It was a figure carved in bone, a snarling wolf. The little figure had a distinct aura of Power.

'This is contact, help, advice. All together.' Zabulon leaned over the back of the seat and breathed hotly into my ear: 'Take it . . . watchman. You'll say thank you to me.'

'I won't say that.'

'Take it anyway.'

I shook my head.

Zabulon sighed.

'Very well, let us have the foolish theatrical effects . . . I, Zabulon, do swear by the Dark that in presenting my amulet to Light Magician Anton Gorodetsky I do not entertain any evil intent and do not intend to harm his health, soul or mind, nor do I demand anything in exchange. If Anton Gorodetsky accepts my help, this does not impose any obligations on him, the Power of Light or the Night Watch. In gratitude for his accepting this help, I grant permission for the Night Watch of Moscow to make three interventions using Light Magic up to the third level of Power inclusive. I do not demand and shall not demand any gratitude in response. May the Dark be my witness!'

A small dark sphere like a miniature black hole appeared, spinning on his palm beside the carved figure. A direct confirmation of his oath by the Primordial Power.

'Even so, I don't think I would—' Semyon began.

At that moment the cellphone in my pocket rang and switched itself into loudspeaker mode. I never used its multitude of various functions: speaker phone, organiser, games, built-in camera, calculator, radio. I only used the built-in music player. But this time the conference-call function came in handy . . .

'Take it,' said Geser. 'He's not lying about this. We'll work out what he *is* lying about later.'

The connection broke off.

Zabulon laughed and carried on holding out the carved figure. I raked it off the Dark Magician's hand without saying a word and put it in my pocket. I didn't have to swear any oaths.

'Well then, good luck,' Zabulon continued. 'Ah, yes! If it's not too much trouble, bring me a little magnet from Edinburgh for the refrigerator.'

'What for?' I asked.

'I collect them,' Zabulon said, with a smile.

And then he disappeared, dropped straight down to some deep level of the Twilight. Of course, we didn't follow him.

'What a show-off,' I said.

'For the refrigerator,' Semyon muttered. 'Yes, I can just imagine what he keeps in his refrigerator . . . A little magnet . . . Bring him a little jar of strychnine. Mix it into some of that Scottish haggis and bring that back for him.'

'"Haggis" is a brand of nappies,' I said. 'They're good, we used them for our daughter.'

'Haggis is a kind of food too,' said Semyon, shaking his head. 'Although, as far as taste goes, there's probably not much difference.'

CHAPTER 2

IT'S HARD TO get any pleasure out of flying these days. Boeing 737s and Tupolev 154s crashing, Swiss air-traffic controllers getting lost in thought and all sorts of Arab terrorists on the loose don't exactly put you in the right mood to sit back in your comfortable seat and enjoy yourself. And although the duty-free cognac is cheap, the female flight attendant is attentive, and the food and wine are perfectly good, it's not easy for a man to relax.

Fortunately, I am not a man. The probability lines had been checked by Svetlana and Geser. I can feel out the future for a few hours ahead myself if need be. We would get there with no problems, make a nice soft landing at Heathrow, and I would have time to make the connection for the plane to Edinburgh . . .

So I could sit there calmly in my business-class seat (I didn't believe that this was a sudden fit of generosity from my boss, there simply hadn't been any other seats available), sip the decent Chilean wine and glance compassionately at the woman trying to look younger than her real age who was sitting across the aisle from me. She was very frightened. Every now and then she crossed herself and whispered a silent prayer.

Eventually I couldn't stand it any longer. I reached out to her through the Twilight — and stroked her head gently. Not with my hands, with my mind. With the kind of affection that only human mothers can provide, the affection that instantly removes all anxieties. I touched the hair that had been dyed so often.

The woman relaxed and a minute later she fell sound asleep

The middle-aged man beside me was a lot calmer, and he was also pretty drunk. He briskly opened up the two little bottles of gin that the flight attendant had brought, mixed their contents with tonic in the harsh proportion of one to one, drank the result and then started dozing. He looked like a typical Bohemian — jeans, cotton sweater and a short beard. A writer? A musician? A theatre director? London is a magnet for everyone — from businessmen and politicians to Bohemians and rich playboys . . .

I could relax too, look out of the window at the dark expanses of Poland and do a bit of thinking.

Before Zabulon had shown up everything had seemed fairly simple. The boy Victor had run into a vampire who was either hungry or stupid (or both at the same time). He had been killed. Once the vampire had sated his hunger, he had realised exactly what he had done, and he had gone into hiding. Sooner or later, using the old tried and tested police methods, the Night Watch of Edinburgh would check all the local and visiting bloodsuckers, find out if they had alibis or not, put someone under surveillance and catch the killer. Geser, suffering from some kind of guilt complex over Victor's father, who had refused to become a Light Other, had decided to speed up the good work. And at the same time give me a chance to pick up some experience.

Logical?

Absolutely. Nothing odd about it.

Then Zabulon turns up.

And we are shown our noble Leonid Prokhorov, the might-have-been Light Magician, in a different light! It turns out that he is also a might-have-been Dark Magician! He has helped the Day Watch, and so Zabulon is burning with desire to punish his son's killer!

Did such things happen?

Apparently they did. Apparently the man had decided to play for both teams at once. We Others cannot serve the Light and the Dark at the same time. But for people it's simpler. That's the way most of them live anyway.

Then . . . then Victor's killing might not be a coincidence. Zabulon could have found out that Prokhorov was helping us and taken his revenge by killing Prokhorov's son. But not with his own hands, of course.

Or the other way round. It was a sad thought, but Geser could have given the order to eliminate Victor. Not for revenge, of course not! But the Great Magician would always find a morally acceptable form for justifying what he wanted to do.

But stop! Then why would Geser send me to Edinburgh? If he was guilty, then he had to understand that I wouldn't try to conceal his guilt!

And if Zabulon was guilty, then he had even less reason to help me. For all his dainty manners, I would be only too glad to get rid of him!

So it wasn't the Great Ones . . .

I took a little sip of wine and set down the glass.

The Great Ones weren't responsible, but they suspected each other. And they were both relying on me. Geser knew I wouldn't pass up any opportunity to do Zabulon a bad turn. And Zabulon understood that I could even go against Geser.

Excellent − I couldn't have asked to be dealt a better hand. A Great Light One and a Great Dark One, both significant figures in the worldwide struggle between the Light and the Dark, and both on my side. I could get help from them. And Foma Lermont, the Scot with a surname that echoed so sweetly in the Russian heart – he would help me too. And that meant the vampire had nowhere left to hide.

And that made me feel good. Evil goes unpunished far too often.

I got up and squeezed cautiously past the man next to me into the aisle. I looked up at the sign. The toilet at the front of the plane was occupied. Of course, the easiest thing would have been to wait, but I felt like stretching my legs. I moved aside the curtain separating business class from economy and walked towards the tail of the plane.

As that well-known ironic phrase puts it, 'economy-class passengers get there at the same time as first-class passengers, only for a lot less money'. Well, there wasn't actually any first class on our plane, but the business class wasn't bad at all – fine wide seats, lots of space between the rows. And then again, the flight attendants were more helpful, the food was better, the drink was more abundant.

Not that the economy-class passengers were having it tough, either. Some were sleeping or dozing lightly, many of them were reading newspapers, novels or guidebooks. A few people were working on their laptop computers and others were playing games. One highly original individual was piloting a plane. As far as I could see it was a fairly realistic flight-simulator, and the player was actually flying a Boeing 767 from Moscow to London. Maybe that was his own cranky way of fighting his fear of flying?

And, of course, lots of passengers were drinking. No matter how often we're told that alcohol is particularly harmful when flying at altitude, some people are always keen to give their flight above the clouds a little extra lift.

I walked all the way back to the tail. The toilets there were occupied too, and while I stood and waited for a few minutes

I examined the backs of the passengers' heads. Bouffant hairstyles, girlish braids, short crew cuts, gleaming bald patches, amusing kids' punk cuts. Hundreds of heads thinking about their business in London . . .

The door of the toilet opened and a young guy slipped out and squeezed past me. I stepped towards the toilet.

Then I stopped.

And turned round.

The guy was about twenty years old. Broad in the shoulders, a little bit taller than me. Some young men start to grow rapidly and broaden out after the age of eighteen. This used to be attributed to the beneficial influence of the army, which 'made men out of boys'. But in reality, it's simply a matter of the way the hormones work in any particular organism.

Common or garden physiology.

'Egor?' I said uncertainly.

Then I took a hasty glimpse through the Twilight.

Yes, of course. Even if he'd been wearing an iron mask I would still have recognised him. Egor, Zabulon's decoy, who was intercepted and cunningly exploited by Geser. Once he had been a unique boy with an indeterminate aura.★

Now he had grown into a young man. With that same indeterminate aura. A luminous glow that was usually colourless but was sometimes tinted red, or blue, or green, or yellow. Like the sand on the fourth level of the Twilight . . . look closer and you'll see all the colours in the world. A potential Other, still capable, even as an adult, of becoming either kind. Light or Dark.

I hadn't seen him for six years!

What a coincidence!

'Anton?' He was as bewildered as I was.

★ This story is told in the first part of the book *The Night Watch*.

'What are you doing here?' I asked.

'Flying,' he replied stupidly.

But I was up to the challenge, and I asked an even more idiotic question.

'Where to?'

'London,' said Egor.

Then suddenly, as if he had just realised how funny our conversation was, he laughed. As nonchalantly and light-heartedly as if he held no grudges against the Night Watch, Geser, me and all the Others in the world . . .

A second later we were slapping each other on the shoulder and muttering nonsense like 'Well, would you believe it . . .', 'I was thinking just recently . . .', 'What a surprise!' Pretty much the standard response for two guys who have been through something pretty important and rather unpleasant together, quarrelled with each other and then, after years have passed and life has changed, discovered that their memories of those times are basically pretty interesting.

But, at the same time, two guys who don't feel warmly enough about each other to embrace and shed an emotional tear at their meeting.

The passengers nearby looked round at us, but with obvious goodwill. A chance meeting of old friends in such an unexpected place as a plane always arouses sympathy in everyone who witnesses it.

'Is there some special reason why you're here?' Egor asked anyway, with a note of his old suspicion.

'Did you fall out of your tree?' I said indignantly. 'I'm on an assignment!'

'Really?' He narrowed his eyes. 'Are you still working in the same place?'

'Of course.'

Nobody was taking any notice of us any more. And we were left hovering uncertainly, not knowing what to talk about next.

'I see you still haven't been initiated,' I said awkwardly

Egor went tense for a moment, but he answered with a smile:

'Ah, damn the lot of you! Why would I bother with that . . . you know yourself that I'm barely even seventh level. That's pointless, whichever way I go, Light or Dark. So I just sent both sides to hell.'

I felt a sudden tightness in my chest.

Coincidences like this definitely didn't happen!

'Where are you flying to?' I repeated, making Egor burst into laughter again. He was probably regarded as the life and soul of any party – he laughed so easily and infectiously. 'No, I know you're going to London, but what for? To study? A holiday?'

'A summer holiday in London?' Egor snorted. 'Why not in Moscow? One stone jungle is the same as any other . . . I'm going to the festival.'

'In Edinburgh?' I asked, knowing what the answer would be.

'Yes, I graduated from the circus college.'

'What?' Now it was my turn to gape in surprise.

'I'm a conjuror.' Egor chuckled.

Well, would you believe it!

But then, it was an excellent disguise for an Other. Even for an uninitiated one – they still have minor powers that exceed normal human abilities. They're natural stage magicians and conjurors.

'That's just great!' I said sincerely.

'It's a shame you're going to London.' Egor sighed. 'I would have got you into the show.'

And then I did something stupid. I said:

'I'm not going to London, Egor. I'm going to Edinburgh too.'

It's not often that I've seen joy disappear from a face so fast, to be replaced by unfriendliness and even contempt.

'I see. So what do you want from me this time?'

'Egor, you . . .' I hesitated.

Could I honestly say that he had nothing to do with it?

No.

Because I didn't believe it myself.

'I see,' Egor repeated. He turned round and walked to the middle of the cabin. There was nothing left for me to do but step into the toilet and close the door behind me.

There was a smell of tobacco. Even though it was strictly forbidden, passengers who smoked still fugged up the toilets. I looked in the mirror and saw the crumpled face of a man who was short of sleep. Even though I am a lot more and a lot less than just a man . . . I felt like banging my forehead against the mirror, and I did, whispering silently to myself: 'Idiot, idiot, idiot . . .'

I had relaxed. I had believed that I was starting a straight-forward work assignment.

But how could that possibly be, when Geser himself had sent me on my way?

I splashed cold water on my face and stood there for a while, staring angrily at my own reflection. Then I took a leak, pressed the pedal to release the blue liquid disinfectant into the steel toilet bowl, washed my hands and splashed water on my face again.

Whose operation was this? Geser's or Zabulon's?

Who had sent the boy Egor, who never became an Other, on the same route as me? What for?

Whose game was it, whose rules and − most important of all − how many figures would there be on the board?

I took Zabulon's present out of my pocket. The bone was a dull yellow, but somehow I knew that the carver had depicted a black wolf. A large, mature black wolf with its head thrown back in a long, dreary howl.

Contact, help, advice . . .

The figure looked perfectly ordinary – you could find hundreds and thousands like it in souvenir kiosks. But I could feel the magic that permeated it. I only had to take it in my hand . . . and wish. That was all.

Did I want help from the Dark Ones?

I resisted the desire to flush the little figure down the toilet and I put it back in my pocket.

There were no observers to appreciate the pathetic gesture.

I rummaged in my pocket and found a pack of cigarettes. I don't smoke so much that I suffer from withdrawal symptoms during a four-hour flight, but right then I felt like indulging some simple human weaknesses. All Others are like that – the older we get, the more petty bad habits we acquire. As if we are clinging on to the slightest manifestation of our natural being – and there is no anchor more reliable than vice.

But then, having realised that my lighter was in my jacket pocket, without the slightest hesitation I ignited a high-temperature discharge arc between my finger and thumb – and lit up from the magic fire.

Rookie Others try to do everything with magic.

They shave with a Crystal Blade, until they lop off half a cheek or the lobe of their ear. They heat their lunch with fireballs, splashing soup all over the walls and scraping their meatballs off the ceiling. They check the probability lines before they get into a slow-moving trolley.

They enjoy the very process of using magic. They'd use it to wipe their backsides if they could.

Then Others get older and wiser and start getting more economical too. They realise that energy is always energy and it's better to get up out of your chair and walk across to a switch than reach out to the buttons with a stream of pure Power, that electricity will cook your steak a lot better than magic fire, and you should cover a scratch with a plaster and only use the Avicenna spell for serious injuries.

And then later, of course, unless an Other is doomed to stay at the very lowest levels of Power, genuine mastery arrives. And you no longer pay any attention to how you light your cigarette – with gas or with magic.

I breathed out a stream of smoke.

Geser?

Zabulon?

All right, it was useless to guess. I just had to remember once and for all that everything was going to be a lot more complicated than I'd thought at the beginning. And I should go back to my seat – we would soon be landing.

Over the English Channel we were thrown about a bit, as usual. But we landed softly and went through the normal passport control in the blink of an eye. The other passengers moved to collect their luggage (apart from the uninitiated Egor, I was the only Other on the plane) but I dropped back a bit and found my shadow on the floor. I gazed into the grey silhouette, forcing it to assume volume and rise up towards me. I stepped into my own shadow – and entered the Twilight.

Everything here was almost exactly the same. Walls, windows, doors. Only everything was grey, colourless. Ordinary people in the real world drifted by like slow-moving shadows. Without even knowing why, they carefully skirted round an entirely unremarkable section of the corridor, and even started walking faster.

It was best to approach the customs post for Others in the Twilight, in order not to make people nervous. It was shielded by a simple spell, the Circle of Inattention, and people tried very hard not to see it. But they might spot me talking to empty space.

So I approached the desk in the Twilight, and only emerged into the real world when I was protected by the spell.

There were two customs officers – a Light One and a Dark One. Just the way there ought to be.

Monitoring Others when they cross borders doesn't seem very logical to me. Vampires and werewolves are obliged to register with the local branch of the Watch if they stay in a town overnight. The justification for this is that lower Dark Ones too often give way to the animal side of their nature. That's true enough, but any magician, whether he's Dark or Light, is capable of things that would send a vampire running for his coffin in horror. Well, anyway, the tradition exists, and no one anywhere wants to change it . . . despite all the protests from vampires and werewolves. But what's the point in monitoring the movements of Others from one country to another? That's important for people – illegal migration, smuggling, narcotics . . . even spies, if it comes to that. But it's fifty years now since spies used to walk through border control zones with elk hooves tied to their feet, and they don't parachute into enemy territory at night now, either. A self-respecting spy flies in on a plane and moves into a good hotel. And as for Others – we have no immigration restrictions, and even a weak magician can obtain the citizenship of any country without the slightest problem. So what was this absurd counter doing here?

It was probably for the Inquisition. Formally speaking, the customs posts belonged to the local Night and Day Watches. But another copy of the report was sent off every day to the Inquisition. And they probably studied it more carefully there.

And drew conclusions.

'Hello. My name is Anton Gorodetsky,' I said, stopping in front of the counter. We don't use identity documents, and that's a good thing. There are always rumours going round that they're going to start putting a magical tag on everyone, the way they do with vampires now, or else make an invisible entry in the ordinary human passports.

But so far we still manage without bureaucracy.

'A Light One,' declared the Dark Magician. He was a weak magician, sixth level at the very most. And physically very feeble: short, skinny and pale, with narrow shoulders and sparse blond hair.

'A Light One,' I agreed.

My colleague from the London Night Watch was a fat, cheerful black guy. The only things he had in common with his duty partner were that he too was young, and also weak, only sixth or seventh level.

'Hi there, bro!' he said happily. 'Anton Gorodetsky. Serve in a Watch?'

'Night Watch, Russia, city of Moscow.'

'Level?'

I suddenly realised that they couldn't read my aura. They could have read it up to the fourth or fifth level. But after that everything was just a blurred glow to them.

'Higher.'

The Dark One straightened up a bit. Of course, they're all egotists and individualists. But they do admire their superiors.

The Light One opened his eyes wide and said:

'Oh! Higher! Coming for long?'

'Passing through. On my way to Edinburgh. I fly out in three hours.'

'Holiday or business?'

'An assignment,' I said without any further explanation.

Light Ones, of course, are liberal and democratic. But they respect Higher Others.

'Did you enter the Twilight there?' the Dark One asked, with a nod towards the human customs officers.

'Yes. Will it be caught on the cameras?'

The Dark One shook his head.

'No, we monitor everything here. But in town I recommend you should be more careful. There are plenty of cameras. Lots of them. Every now and then people notice us disappearing and re-appearing – we have to cover our tracks.'

'I'm not even leaving the airport.'

'There are cameras in Edinburgh too,' the Light One put in. 'Not so many, but even so . . . Do you have the contact details for the Edinburgh Watch?'

He didn't bother to mention that he meant the Night Watch. That was quite obvious.

'Yes,' I said.

'I have a good friend who runs a little family hotel in Edinburgh,' said the Dark One, joining in the conversation again. 'For more than two hundred years already. Beside the castle, on the Royal Mile. If it doesn't bother you that he's a vampire . . .'

What was all this, nothing but vampires on every side?

'. . . then here's his card. It's a very good hotel. Friendly to Others.'

'I have no prejudices against vampires,' I assured him, taking the rectangle of cardboard. 'Some my friends have been vampires.'

And I sent one of my vampire friends to his death . . .

'There's a good restaurant in Sector B,' the Light One put in.

They were so genuinely eager to help me that I wasn't sure how to get past this solid wall of friendship and goodwill. Fortunately, another plane landed, and several more Others showed up behind me. Keeping a smile on my face all the time – something to which the Russian facial musculature is rather poorly adapted – I went to collect my suitcase.

I didn't go to the restaurant since I wasn't feeling at all hungry. I wandered round the airport a bit, drank a double espresso, dozed for while in a chair in the lounge and walked through into my plane, yawning a bit as I went. As was only to be expected, Egor was on the same flight. But now we ostentatiously ignored each other. Or rather, he ostentatiously ignored me, and I didn't try to impose my company on him.

An hour later we landed at Edinburgh airport.

It was already almost noon when I got into a taxi – one of those remarkably comfortable English taxis that you start to miss just as soon as you leave Great Britain. I greeted the driver and, on a sudden impulse, handed him the card from the 'friendly hotel'. I had a booking in an ordinary human hotel, but the chance of talking to one of Scotland's oldest vampires (two hundred years is no joke, even for them) in informal surroundings was simply too tempting.

The hotel really was in the historical town centre, on a hill close to the royal castle. I lowered the window and gazed around with the curiosity of someone who has just arrived for the first time in an interesting new country.

Edinburgh was impressive. Of course, you could say that any truly old city is impressive if it wasn't flattened sixty years ago by the fiery steamroller of a world war, which reduced ancient cathedrals, castles and houses – large and small – to rubble. But there was something special here. Perhaps it was the royal castle itself, so well sited on a hill and surmounting the city like a crown of stone. Perhaps it was the large number of people on the streets – tourists idly loitering or wandering about with cameras hanging round their necks, looking at the shop windows or the monuments. After all, the king's reputation is always defined by his retinue. Or perhaps it was the lacework pattern of the streets scattered round the castle, with their old houses and cobbled roadways.

Even if he's wearing the most beautiful crown, a king also needs worthy robes. The naked king in Andersen's fairy tale was not saved by the glittering diamonds on his head.

The taxi stopped at a four-storey stone house with a narrow frontage that was squeezed between two shops crowded with customers. The shop windows were hung with colourful kilts and scarves, and there were the inevitable bottles of whisky. What else would you take away from here? From Russia it's vodka and *matryoshka* dolls, from Greece it's ouzo and embroidered table-cloths, from Scotland it's whisky and scarves.

I climbed out of the taxi, took my suitcase from the driver and paid him. Then I looked at the building. The sign above the entrance to the hotel said 'Highlander Blood'.

Right. An impertinent vampire.

I walked up to the door, blinking against the bright sunshine. It was getting hot. The legend that vampires can't tolerate sunlight is just that, a legend. They can tolerate it, they just don't find it pleasant. And on a hot summer day like this I could almost understand them.

The door didn't swing open in front of me – obviously they weren't fond of automatic devices in this hotel. So I pushed it with my hand and walked in.

Well, at least there was an air-conditioner here. The coolness that I felt could hardly have been left over from the night, despite these thick stone walls.

The small entrance hall was rather dark, and perhaps that was why it felt a bit cosy. I saw an elderly, highly respectable-looking gentleman standing behind a counter. A good suit, a tie with a pin, a shirt with silver cufflinks in the form of thistle heads. A plump face with a moustache and red cheeks, a strawberries-and-cream complexion . . . But his aura left no doubt at all – he was human.

'Good afternoon,' I said, approaching the counter. 'Your hotel was recommended to me . . . I would like to take a single room.'

'A single?' the gentleman asked, with an extremely pleasant smile.

'A single,' I repeated.

'We're very short of rooms, it's the festival . . .' the gentleman said, with a sigh. 'You didn't book, then?'

'No.'

He sighed again and started leafing through some papers – as if this little family hotel had so many rooms that he couldn't remember if any were free. Without looking up, he asked:

'Who was it that recommended us?'

'The Dark One at Heathrow customs.'

'I think we should be able to help you,' the man replied, without any sign of surprise. 'Which room would you prefer, light or dark? If you have – er – a dog with you, there is a very comfortable room that even the very largest dog can leave – and come back to – on its own . . . without disturbing anyone.'

'I want a light room,' I said.

'Give him the suite on the fourth floor, Andrew,' said a voice behind me. 'He is a distinguished guest. Very distinguished.'

I took the key that had appeared as if by magic in the receptionist's hand (no, no magic involved, it was simply his dexterity) and turned round.

'I will show you the way,' said the light-haired youth standing in front of the cigarette machine beside the door that led into the small hotel restaurant. Hotels like this one very often do not have a restaurant and they serve breakfast in the rooms, but the guests here had rather exotic tastes.

'Anton,' I said, introducing myself as I examined the owner of the hotel. 'Anton Gorodetsky, Moscow Night Watch.'

'Bruce,' said the youth. 'Bruce Ramsey, Edinburgh. Owner of this establishment.'

He looked just perfect to play Dorian Grey in a film version of Oscar Wilde's novel. Young, graceful and indecently fresh and handsome, he could easily have worn a badge that said 'Ready for debauchery!'

Except only that his eyes were old. Grey and faded, with the uniformly pink whites of eyes that belong to a two-hundred-year-old vampire.

The youth picked up my suitcase – I didn't object – and started walking up the narrow wooden stairs, talking as he went:

'Unfortunately we don't have a lift. It's an old building and too narrow to fit a shaft in. And besides, I am not used to lifts. It seems to me that a mechanical monster would disfigure this wonderful house. I hate those reconstructed houses, old façades hiding boring standard-plan apartments. And we don't often have guests who find it hard to climb the stairs . . . except that werewolves don't like steep steps, but we try to accommodate them on the first floor – there's a special room there – or on the second . . . what wind has blown you into our quiet town, Higher Light One?'

He was not so ordinary himself. A vampire at the first level of Power – not exactly magical Power, not the same as my own, it was vampire Power. But he could definitely be called a first-level Other.

'The incident in the Dungeons,' I said.

'Just as I thought.' The youth walked on in front of me, striding easily up two steps at a time. 'A most unpleasant incident. I appreciate the humour of the situation, of course . . . But it is not good. These are not times when you can simply walk up to someone you like the look of and drink him dry. Not at all!'

'Do you miss the good old days?' I couldn't resist asking.

'Sometimes,' said the youth. He laughed. 'But each age and each time has its own advantages, doesn't it? People become civilised, they stop hunting witches and believing in vampires. And we become civilised. We can't regard human beings as cattle who have no rights. People deserve the right to be respected, if only as our own ancestors. You should respect your ancestors, surely?'

Unfortunately, I couldn't find anything to argue with in all this.

'It's a good room – you'll like it,' the vampire continued as he reached the fourth-floor landing. There were only two doors there and the staircase went on up into the attic. 'On the right is the suite for Dark Ones, also very pleasant. I furnished it to my own taste and am quite proud of the design. And this is your suite.'

He did not need a key – he patted the lock gently with his hand and the door opened. A bit of petty showing-off that seemed rather strange for such an old vampire.

'We have a very good self-taught designer, a Light Other. He is only sixth level, but no magic is needed for this work,' Bruce went on. 'I asked him to decorate three rooms to the taste of Light Ones. Most of the rest of the interior is rather more original, you understand . . .'

I walked into the suite and froze on the spot in astonishment.

I'd never realised that my taste was like this.

Everything around me was white, beige and pink. The parquet flooring was light, bleached wood, the walls were covered with beige wallpaper with pale pink flowers, the furniture was old-fashioned, but also made of light-coloured wood and snow-white satin. The large sofa by the wall was leather. And what colour? White, of course. There was a crystal chandelier hanging from the ceiling. The windows were draped with transparent tulle and the curtains were bright pink.

The sun must really have made this place sizzle in the mornings

One door led into a small bedroom. Cosy, with a double bed. The bed sheets were pink silk. There was a little vase on the dressing table with a fresh scarlet rose in it – the only spot of bright colour in the entire suite. The washroom and toilet were behind another door. The space was tiny, but it was equipped with some kind of hybrid cross between a hydro-massage unit and a shower cabinet.

'Rather vulgar and it doesn't suit the style.' Bruce sighed behind me. 'But many guests like it.'

His face, reflected in the mirror, looked rather pained. Evidently he had not really liked the idea of installing this miracle of modern plumbing in the hotel.

I nodded to the vampire, without turning round. The idea that vampires are not reflected in mirrors is just as false as the tales that they absolutely cannot tolerate sunlight and are afraid of garlic, silver and aspen stakes. They *are* reflected in mirrors, even when they deflect a person's attention.

But if you don't look at them when you're talking to them or, even worse, if you turn your back on them, it really unnerves them. Vampires have a very large number of techniques for which they need to look their opponent straight in the eye.

'I shall be glad to take a wash,' I said. 'But a little later. Do you have ten minutes you could spare me, Bruce?'

'Are you on an official visit to Edinburgh, Light One?'

'No.'

'Then of course I do.' The vampire's face lit up in a broad smile. He sat down in one of the armchairs.

I took a seat facing the youth and forced out a smile in response to his, all the time looking at his chin.

'So what do you think of the suite?' Bruce enquired.

'I think an innocent girl of seventeen would like it,' I replied honestly. 'Only it needs a white kitten.'

'If you wish, we can arrange for both of those,' the vampire suggested politely.

Well, now I could consider the social part of the conversation over.

'I have come to Edinburgh unofficially,' I repeated. 'But at the same time, at the request of the head of the Night Watch – and the head of the Day Watch – of Moscow.'

'How unusual . . .' the youth said quietly. 'The esteemed Geser and the most worthy Zabulon sending the same messenger . . . and a Higher Magician as well – and for such a minor incident. Well, I shall be glad to be of assistance.'

'Does what happened upset you personally?' I asked bluntly.

'Of course. I have already told you my opinion,' Bruce said. He frowned. 'We're not living in the Middle Ages – this is the twenty-first century. We have to break the old patterns of behaviour . . .' He sighed and squinted at the door of the bathroom. 'You can't wash in a basin and go to a wooden privy when water mains and sewers have been invented. Even if you are used to a basin and find it rather more agreeable . . . You know, in recent times there has been a movement growing among us to take a humane atti-tude towards human beings. No one drinks blood without a licence. And even with a licence they try not to kill . . . Hardly anyone drinks children under the age of twelve, even if they are chosen by the lottery.'

'And why twelve?'

Bruce shrugged.

'It's just a matter of history. Do you know, for instance, what the most terrible crime is in Germany? The murder of a child under the age of twelve. If the child is already twelve, it is a completely different crime with different penalties . . . Well, already we don't touch the young growth. And now we are trying to push through a law to exclude children from the lottery altogether.'

'Very touching,' I muttered. 'But why did someone dine on the young man without a licence?'

Bruce thought about it.

'You know, I can only offer hypotheses . . .'

'That's exactly what I'm interested in.'

Bruce paused for a bit longer, then smiled broadly.

'What is there really to discuss? One of the young ones lost control. Most likely a young girl who only became a vampire recently, and she liked the look of the young man. And then there's the setting, so arousing, in the style of the old legends . . . she got carried away.'

'You think it was a woman?'

'It could be a young man. If he's gay. There isn't actually a direct connection.' Bruce turned his eyes away in embarrassment. 'But it's always more pleasant . . . more natural, somehow . . .'

'And the second option?' I asked, struggling to stop myself commenting on what he had said.

'Someone from out of town. Perhaps a tourist. You know, after the Second World War, everything got so jumbled up, everyone started travelling all over the place . . .' He shook his head disapprovingly. 'Certain irresponsible individuals started taking advantage of that.'

'Bruce, I wouldn't like to trouble your Watches,' I said. 'They might get the idea that their Moscow colleagues have doubts about their professionalism Perhaps you could tell me who's the senior vampire in your city? The Elder, the Great . . . what do you call him?'

'I don't call him anything,' Bruce said with a broad smile. And he slowly moved his fangs to demonstrate his status, lowering the two long sharp teeth out of his upper jaw and then drawing them back in again. 'But they call me Master. I don't really like the word, it comes from those stupid books and films. But if that's what they want, let them call me that.'

'You're rather young for a Master,' I said, slightly surprised. 'Only two hundred years old.'

'Two hundred and eight years, three months and eleven days,' Bruce specified. 'Yes, I am young. But this is Scotland. If only you knew what suspicious, stubborn people the highlanders are, absolutely hidebound in their superstitions! In the time of my youth not a year went by without one of us having aspen stakes hammered through his heart.'

Perhaps I was mistaken, but I thought I detected a hint of pride in his fellow countrymen in Bruce's voice.

'Will you help me, Master?'

Bruce shook his head.

'No, of course not! If we find out who killed the Russian boy, we will punish him. Ourselves. We won't destroy him, but we will punish him severely. No one will hand him over to the Watches.'

Well, naturally. I should never have expected anything else.

'Is it pointless to ask: "What if you have already found him and punished him?"'

'It is,' Bruce replied, with a sigh.

'Well then, should I go bustling about trying to find the criminal?' I asked in a deliberately rueful voice. 'Or should I simply take a holiday in your wonderful city?'

A harsh note of irony appeared in Bruce's voice:

'As a Dark One the only thing I can say to you is, "Take a holiday!" Relax, look round the museums, have fun. Who cares about this dead student now?'

That was when I felt I couldn't hold back any longer. I looked into Bruce's eyes. The deep holes of his pupils glittered scarlet. I asked:

'And what if I break you, you bloodsucking carrion? If I break you, turn you inside out and make you answer all my questions?'

'Go ahead,' Bruce replied in a soft, almost tender voice. 'Try it, Higher One. Do you think we don't know about you? Do you think we don't know how you came by your Power?'

Eye to eye.

Pupil to pupil.

A dark, pulsating tunnel, drawing me into emptiness. An eddying vortex of red sparks from the stolen lives of others. An enticing whisper in my ears. The inspired, exalted, unearthly beauty of the youthful vampire's face.

Fall at his feet . . .

Weep in ecstasy at this beauty, wisdom, will . . .

Beg for forgiveness . . .

He was very powerful. After all, he had two hundred years of experience, multiplied by the first level of vampire Power.

And I felt the full brunt of his Power. I stood up on trembling legs that would not obey me. I took an uncertain step forward.

Bruce smiled.

Another vampire once smiled in exactly the same way in a Moscow alleyway when I ran into it, following the boy Egor, who was helplessly following the call . . .

I put so much Power into my mental attack that if I had used it for a fireball, it would have shot straight through about thirty houses and struck the fortress wall of the old Scottish castle.

Bruce's pupils turned white and blank. The alluring dark tunnel was scorched by a white radiance. Sitting there in front of me, swaying backwards and forwards, was a dried-up old man with a young face. But the skin on his face was starting to peel off, flaking away in little scales, like dandruff.

'Who killed Victor?' I asked. The Power continued to flow through me in a fine stream, twisting into a running knot threaded through the vampire's eyes.

He didn't say anything, just carried on swaying in his chair. Maybe I'd burnt out his brain . . . or whatever it was they had instead of a brain. A fine start to the unofficial investigation!

'Do you know who killed Victor?' I asked, reformulating the question.

'No,' Bruce replied quietly.

'Do you have any theories about the matter?'

'Yes . . . two. A young vampire lost control . . . Someone from the outside . . . a visitor . . .'

'What else do you know about this killing?'

Silence. As if he was gathering his thoughts before starting a long speech.

'What else do you know that is not known to the staff of the city Watches?'

'Nothing . . .'

I halted the flow of Power and sank into an armchair.

What should I do now? And what if he submitted a complaint to the Day Watch? An unprovoked attack, interrogation . . .

For about a minute Bruce carried on swaying in his chair. Then he started, and his eyes acquired a meaningful expression again.

Meaningful and pitiful.

'I beg your pardon, Light One,' he said quietly. 'Please accept my apologies.'

It took me a few seconds to understand.

A vampire Master is not simply the most powerful, cunning, clever bloodsucker. He is also the one who has never known defeat.

A complaint from Bruce would mean serious trouble for me. But for him it would mean loss of status.

And this polite old youth was very vain.

'I accept your apologies, Master,' I replied. 'Let what has happened remain between us.'

Bruce licked his lips. His faced turned pink, recovering its former attractive appearance. His voice became slightly stronger – he too had realised that it was not in my interest to publicise what had happened.

'But I would *ask*,' he said, putting emphatic, poisonous hatred into that last word, 'that you do not make any more attacks of that kind, Light One. The aggression was unprovoked.'

'You challenged me to a duel.'

'*De jure*, I did not,' Bruce replied quickly. 'The ritual of challenge was not observed.'

'*De facto*, you did. Are we going to bother the Inquisition with this?'

He blinked. And once again became the hospitable host.

'All right, Light One. Let bygones be bygones . . .'

Bruce got to his feet and swayed slightly. He walked across to the door. Once outside the room, he turned and declared with evident displeasure:

'My home is your home. This room is your dwelling and I shall not enter it without permission.'

This ancient legend, strangely enough, is quite true. Vampires cannot enter anyone else's home without being invited in. No one knows why that is.

The door closed behind Bruce. I let go of the armrests of my chair – there were wet marks left on the white satin. Dark marks.

It's bad not to sleep at night. Your nerves start playing tricks.

But now I knew for certain that the Master of Edinburgh's vampires had no information about the murder.

I unpacked my suitcase and hung a white linen suit and two white shirts on hangers. I looked out of the window and shook my head. I took out a pair of shorts and a T-shirt with the inscription 'Night Watch'. A hooligan's joke, of course, but you can see anything at all written on T-shirts nowadays.

Then my eye was caught by a fancy calligraphic text in a frame on the wall. I had already noticed a frame like it downstairs, and another on the staircase. Were they hanging all over the hotel, then? I walked over and was surprised by what I read:

By oppression's woes and pains,
By your sons in servile chains,
We will drain our dearest veins
But they shall be free!

Robert Burns

'Why, the son of a bitch!' I said, almost admiringly. Even the people who stayed in the hotel would never suspect anything!

Unquestionably, Bruce had the same sense of humour as the vampire who had drained his victim at the Castle of the Vampires. He was an excellent candidate for the role of murderer.

The only trouble was that after the kind of shock he had suffered, Bruce couldn't possibly have lied.

CHAPTER 3

TOURISTS ARE THE most terrible breed of human beings. Sometimes I feel a vague suspicion that every nation tries to send its most unpleasant representatives abroad – the loudest and most clueless, those with the worst manners. But it's probably all much simpler than that. Probably it's just that the secret 'work/play' switch everybody has hidden in their heads clicks and turns off eighty per cent of their brains.

But the remaining twenty per cent is more than enough for play anyway.

I was walking along in a crowd moving slowly towards the castle on the hill. No, I wasn't planning to study the austere dwelling of the proud kings of Scotland. I just wanted to get a feel for the atmosphere of the city.

I liked it. Like any tourist centre, its festive atmosphere was a little bit forced and feverish, encouraged by alcohol. But even so, the people around me were enjoying life and smiling at each other: for the time being they had set their cares aside.

Cars didn't often come in here, and those that did were mostly taxis. Most of the people were walking – the streams moving in the direction of the castle and back intermingled, swirling together in quiet whirlpools around the performers doing their thing in the middle of the street, thin rivulets trickled into the pubs, filtered in through the doorways of the shops. The boundless river of humanity.

A wonderful place for a Light Other. But a tiring one, too.

I turned off into a side street and strolled gently downhill towards the gorge that separated the old and the new parts of the city. There were pubs here too, and souvenir shops. But there weren't so many tourists, and the frantic carnival rhythm slowed down a bit. I checked my map – it was simpler than using magic – and moved in the direction of a bridge over the broad gorge that had once been Loch Nor. The gorge had now passed through its final stage of evolution and had been transformed into a park, a place where local people and tourists who were sick of noise and bustle could take a relaxed stroll.

There were more tourists eddying about on the bridge – boarding the double-decker tour buses, watching the street artists, eating ice cream, pensively studying the old castle on the hill.

And on the grassy lawn there were Cossacks, dancing and waving their swords about.

I gave way to that shamefaced curiosity with which tourists regard their compatriots who are working abroad and moved closer.

Bright red shirts. Broad pants like jodhpurs. Titanium-alloy swords – so that they would give off pretty sparks during swordplay and be easier to wave around. Stiff, frozen smiles.

There were four men squatting down and dancing.

And talking to each other – with Ukrainian accents, but still in my own native Russian. Although you might say they were using the secret version. In more or less printable form it went something like this.

'Up yours!' one pantomime Cossack dancer hissed merrily

through his teeth. 'Move it, you louse! Keep the rhythm going, you tattered condom!'

'Go to hell!' another man in fancy dress answered. 'Quit grousing. Wave those arms about. We're losing money!'

'Tanka, you bitch!' the third man joined in. 'Get out here!'

A girl in a bright-coloured dress started dancing, letting the 'Cossacks' take a short break. But she still found time for a dignified reply with no serious obscenity:

'Bastards, I'm sweating like a pig, and you sit there scratching your bollocks!'

I started making my way back out of the crowd of whirring and clicking cameras. Close beside me I heard a girl speaking to her companion in clear Russian.

'How awful . . . Do you think they always swear like that?'

An interesting question. Always, or just when they're abroad? Everybody? Or just ours, the Russians? In the strangely naive belief that nobody outside Russia knows Russian?

I'd rather believe that's the way all street artists talk to each other.

Buses.

Tourists.

Pubs.

Shops.

A mime artist wandering round a small square, feeling at non-existent walls – a sad man in an invisible maze.

A cool black dude in a kilt, playing a saxophone.

I realised why I was in no hurry to get to the Dungeons of Scotland. I had to breathe this city into my lungs. Feel it with my skin, my body . . . with the blood in my veins.

I decided to wander about in the crowd for a bit longer. And then buy a ticket for the 'room of horror'.

★　★　★

The tourist attraction was closed. The huge sign was still there on the pillars of the bridge. The double doors in the 'entrance-to-ancient-dungeons' style were open, but the opening was roped off at chest height. A handwritten notice on a sheet of cardboard hanging on the rope politely informed me that the dungeons were closed for technical reasons.

To be quite honest, I was surprised. It was five days since Victor had been killed. Long enough for any police investigation. The Edinburgh Night Watch would have examined everything they needed to without advising the human police about it.

But the place was closed.

I shrugged, lifted up the rope, ducked under it and set off down the narrow stairway. The metal-mesh steps echoed hollowly under my feet. Two flights down there were toilets, then a narrow little corridor with ticket offices that were closed. A few lamps were lit here and there, but they were only intended to create a lurid atmosphere for the customers. Standard dim energy-saving light bulbs.

'Is anyone alive down here?' I called out in English, and then realised with a start how ambiguous that was. 'Hey . . . are there any Others here?'

Silence.

I walked through a few rooms. The walls were hung with portraits of people with brutal faces, the kind that would have delighted Lambrozo's heart. Framed texts told the stories of criminals, maniacs, cannibals and sorcerers. There were display cases with crude models of severed arms and legs, retorts full of dark liquids, instruments of torture. Out of curiosity I took a look at them through the Twilight. All newly made – no one had ever been tortured with them; they didn't carry the slightest trace of suffering.

I yawned.

There were strings with rags dangling on them stretched out

above my head – they were supposed to represent cobwebs. Higher up I caught glimpses of a metal ceiling with rather unromantic rivets the size of saucers. The tourist attraction had been built in a strictly utilitarian technical space.

There was something bothering me.

'Is there anyone there? Alive or dead, answer me!' I called out again. And again there was no answer. But what was it that had alarmed me like that? It was something that wasn't right . . . when I looked through the Twilight.

I looked around again, using my Twilight vision.

There it was! That was what was so odd!

There was no blue moss – that harmless but unpleasant parasite that grows on the first level of the Twilight, the only permanent inhabitant of the grey reverse side of the world. In a place like this, where people constantly experienced fear, even if it was only circus fear and not the real thing, the blue moss ought to have flourished with a vengeance. It ought to have been dangling from the ceiling in shaggy stalactites, spread out across the floor in a repulsive wriggling carpet, covering the walls like thick flock wallpaper.

But there wasn't any moss.

Was someone cleaning the premises regularly? Burning the moss off if he was a Light One, or freezing it off if he was a Dark One?

Well, if there was an Other on the staff here, that would be a help to me.

As if in response to my thoughts, I heard the sound of footsteps. They were quite fast, as if someone had heard me shout and was hurrying towards me from a long way away, through the maze of plasterboard partition walls. A few second later the black-painted door from this room into the next one opened.

And in walked a vampire.

Not a real one, of course. He had a normal human aura.

A man in fancy dress.

A black cloak, rubber fangs in his mouth, pale make-up on his face. A good-quality make-up job. Only all this didn't fit too well with the curly ginger hair. He probably had to wear a black wig when he was working. And another thing that didn't fit was the plastic bottle of mineral water that my visitor was just about to drink from.

The young guy frowned when he saw me. His good-natured face turned not exactly angry but strict and reproachful. He reached up to his mouth and turned away for a second. When he looked at me again, the fangs were gone.

'Mister?'

'Do you work here?' I asked. I didn't want to use magic and break his will. There are always simpler ways of coming to terms with someone. Human ways.

'Yes, but the show's closed. Temporarily.'

'Because of the murder?' I asked.

The young guy frowned. Now he certainly wasn't feeling well-disposed.

'Mister, I don't know how you got past . . . This is private property. The place is closed to visitors. Come on, please – I'll show you out.'

He took a step towards me and even reached out one hand to demonstrate that he was prepared to take me out by force.

'Were you here when Victor Prokhorov was killed?' I asked.

'Just exactly who are you?' he asked cautiously

'I'm a friend of his. I flew in from Russia today.'

The young guy's face fell. He started backing away until he came up against the door he'd come in through. He pushed it – but the door didn't open. I must confess that was my fault.

Now he was in a total panic.

'Mister . . . I wasn't to blame for anything! We're all cut up about the way Victor died. Mister . . . Comrade!'

He spoke the last word in Russian. I wondered what old action movie he remembered it from.

'What's wrong with you?' I was the one who was confused now. I moved closer to him. Could I really have been lucky enough to come across someone who knew something, who was involved with the murder somehow? Otherwise, what was all the panic about?

'Don't kill me, I didn't do anything!' the young guy babbled. His skin was whiter than his make-up now. 'Comrade! Sputnik, vodka, *perestroika*! Gorbachev!'

'That last word could certainly get you killed in Russia,' I muttered, and reached into my pocket for my cigarettes.

It was a very unfortunate thing to say. And that movement wasn't the best of ideas, either. The young guy's eyes rolled up and back and he collapsed on the floor. The bottle of mineral water fell beside him.

Out of sheer stubbornness, I dealt with the young man without using any magic. A few slaps to the cheeks and a sip of water soon fixed him up. Then I considerately offered him a cigarette.

'It's all right for you to laugh,' he said morosely, after we had sat down in two fake torture chairs – they had a hole in the seat and lurking in the hole was a menacing stake on a crank and lever mechanism. 'You think it's funny . . .'

'I'm not laughing,' I said mildly

'You're just laughing to yourself.' The young guy drank greedily. Then he held out his hand and introduced himself: 'Jean.'

'Anton. But I thought you were Scottish.'

Jean shook his ginger curls proudly.

'No . . . French. I'm from Nantes.'

'Are you studying here?'

'Just earning a bit of money.'

'Listen, why are you wearing that idiotic costume?' I asked. 'There aren't any customers anyway.'

Jean blushed – quickly, the way only redheads and albinos can.

'The boss put me on guard duty until the show opens up again. I'm just waiting . . . in case the police suddenly decide they want to check something. It's a bit creepy here on your own. I feel calmer in the costume.'

'I almost crapped in my pants,' I complained to him – there's nothing better for easing stress than that kind of low style. 'But what were you afraid of?'

Jean gave me a surly glance and shrugged.

'It's hard to say. That guy was killed here, so it's like we're to blame or something . . . but for what, for what? And he was Russian! You can never tell . . . Everyone knows what that can lead to . . . We started talking about it here, just joking at first . . . Then it got more serious. What if his father comes, or his brother, or a friend . . . and he kills all of us.'

'So that's what you're talking about,' I said brightly. 'Well, let me assure you that blood vengeance isn't really all that common in Russia. But the Scots have it too, by the way.'

'That's just what I'm saying,' Jean agreed, missing the point. 'It's barbaric. Primitive! The twenty-first century, the civilised world—'

'And someone gets his throat cut,' I threw in. 'What actually happened to Victor?'

Jean glanced at me again. He took a drag on his cigarette and shook his head.

'I think you're lying. You're not a friend of Victor's. You're from the KGB. You've been sent to investigate the murder. Right?'

He really must have been overdoing those action movies. This was getting ridiculous.

'Jean, you know yourself,' I said in a low voice, 'that I can't answer that question.'

The young Frenchman nodded very seriously. Then he carefully stubbed his cigarette out on the floor.

'Let's go, Mr Russian. I'll show you the place. Only don't smoke any more, there's nothing but rags and cardboard here, perfect tinder for a blaze – whoosh!'

He pushed the door and, of course, it opened easily. Jean gave it a thoughtful look and shrugged. We walked through a few more rooms.

'There it is, the crappy Castle of the Vampires,' Jean said in a gloomy voice. He fumbled at the wall and clicked a switch. The light became a lot brighter.

Yes, darkness was appropriate here. Without it, the tourist attraction simply looked ludicrous. The River of Blood that people were supposed to sail across to the vampires was a long metal trough about three metres wide. The trough was full of water.

It wasn't deep.

Maybe up to my knee.

The metal barge wasn't actually floating on the water, of course. I rocked the side of the boat with my foot and realised that it was standing on rollers of some kind. And under the water I could see the cable that towed the boat from one 'mooring' to the next. The total length of the trough was no more than fifteen metres. Halfway along it the metal tub crept into a room that was separated off by heavy curtains (they were pulled back now). I saw an impressive-looking fan on the ceiling of the room. On one wall there was a crudely painted picture of a castle standing on a cliff.

I walked to the bow of the barge and glanced into the dark

room. Yes, it was an idiotic sort of place to lose your life. Right . . . in five days any clues could have disappeared, but I would give it a try.

A glance through the Twilight was no help. I spotted weak traces of Others – Light Ones and Dark Ones, but that was the specialists from the Watches who had investigated the crime scene. There were no signs of a 'vampire trail'. But I could sense emanations of death – and they were very clear, as if only an hour or two had elapsed, not five days. Oh, the boy had died a very bad death . . .

'Who does the sound effects?' I asked. 'There must be some kind of gasping and groaning, terrifying howls? Your tourists don't ride in total silence, do they?'

'It's a recording,' Jean said sadly. 'The speakers are over there, and over there . . .'

'And doesn't anyone in here keep an eye on the tourists?' I asked. 'What if someone feels unwell?'

'We watch them,' Jean admitted reluctantly. 'You see that little hole in the wall across there? There's always someone standing there and watching.'

'In the dark?'

'They use a night-vision device,' Jean said, embarrassed. 'An ordinary video camera in night mode. You stand there and watch the screen . . .'

'Aha . . .' I nodded. 'And what did you see when Victor was being killed?'

Either he was feeling calmer now, or he didn't see any point in pretending, but he didn't try to deny anything. He just asked:

'What makes you so sure I was there?'

'Because you're wearing a vampire costume. What if one of the customers is recording in night mode too? That's what the make-up's for, right? I think each one of you has his own role to play, and during the show you were wearing that costume and you were somewhere nearby.'

Jean nodded.

'That's right. I was there. Only I didn't see anything, believe me. They all just sat there. Nobody attacked any of them, no one went anywhere near them.'

I didn't bother to mention that you can't catch a hungry vampire (and he would have to be very hungry to hunt as brazenly as this) on tape in night-video mode. Night mode uses infra-red, and a hungry vampire is no warmer than his environment. There might just be a few slight traces on the tape.

'Was everything being recorded?'

'Of course not. Why waste the tape?'

I squatted down and dabbled my hand in the water. It was cold and musty. It looked as though nobody had bothered to change it . . . but then, if the investigation wasn't over yet, that was only natural . . .

'What do you see?' Jean asked curiously.

I didn't answer. I was looking at the water through closed eyes. Looking with the Twilight vision that pierces through reality to the essence of things.

The trough filled up with hazy crystal forms. There were crimson threads showing through the crystal, and an orange sludge swirling on the bottom of the trough.

There was human blood in the water.

A lot of blood.

About four litres.

That must be where the powerful emanations of death were coming from. Blood preserves its memory longer than anything else in the world.

If the police had only bothered to make a proper analysis of the water they would have realised that all of Victor's blood was simply drained into the channel. And there were no vampires involved in the crime.

But the police hadn't been looking for vampires. And maybe they had carried out an analysis. If they hadn't, it was only because they had no doubt what the result would be. A quick slash of a knife across the throat, and the blood glugs over the side of the boat . . . Only an Other could come up with the idiotic idea of looking for vampires in a tourist attraction!

'The case just opened up,' I muttered, getting up off my knees. 'Dammit . . .'

Yes, it was a vicious killing. And the murderer certainly had a black sense of humour. Only that was no concern of ours. Let the Edinburgh police conduct the investigation.

So just why had the boy been killed? A pretty stupid question. There are far more reasons for death than there are for life. He was a young guy, passionate and keen, his father was a businessman and a politician. He could have been killed for something that he'd done, or for something his father was involved in, or for no reason at all.

Yes, Geser and Zabulon had both been caught out. They'd seen danger where it didn't exist.

'Thanks for you help,' I said to Jean. 'I'll be going now.'

'So you are from the Russian police!' Jean exclaimed happily. 'Did you spot anything?'

I smiled suggestively and shook my head.

Jean sighed.

'I'll show you out, Anton.'

Not far from the Dungeons I found a nice little pub called the Corncrake and Pennant. Three small communicating rooms, dark walls and ceilings, old lamps, glass mugs for the beer, pictures in frames, knick-knacks on the walls. A bar with ten beer pumps and a vast array of bottles – there were at least fifty sorts of whisky. Everything that the phrase 'a Scottish pub' brings to mind, and exactly what the foreign tourist expects when he hears that phrase.

Remembering what Semyon had said, I ordered haggis and soup of the day. And I took a pint of Guinness from the woman behind the bar, who was large and well-built, with muscular arms from constantly working the beer pumps. I walked through to the end room, the smallest, where I found a free table. A group of Japanese were having lunch at the next one. And there was a plump elderly man with a moustache who looked like a local, drinking beer at another table. He looked rather dejected, like a Muscovite who has accidentally found himself in Red Square. There was music coming from somewhere, too – fortunately it was melodic and not too loud.

The soup turned out to be simple meat broth with croutons, and the haggis was nothing more than a local version of liver sausage. But I drank the soup and ate the haggis, with the chips that came with it, and felt that I had fulfilled my obligations as a tourist.

I liked the beer best. As I was finishing off the mug, I phoned home and had a chat with Svetlana. I told her that I wouldn't have to stay away for very long, because everything had been resolved very quickly.

I got myself another pint of beer before calling the head of the Edinburgh Night Watch. I found Foma Lermont's number in the phone book and dialled.

'Hello, how can I help you?' someone answered politely after the phone had rung a couple of times. The interesting thing was that they answered in Russian.

'Good afternoon, Thomas,' I said, deciding not to use the Russian name Foma after all. 'My name is Anton Gorodetsky – I'm a colleague of yours from Moscow. Geser asked me to give you his warmest greetings.'

It all sounded very much like a bad spy story. I pulled a wry face at the thought . . .

'Hello, Anton, I've been waiting for your call. How was your flight?'

'Great. I'm staying in a very nice little hotel. It's a bit dark, but it is right in the centre. I've had a stroll round the old town and some of the surroundings.' I was getting carried away – it seemed highly amusing to speak in Aesopian language. 'Could we get together?'

'Of course, Anton, I'll just come across. Or perhaps you might join me? I have a nice cosy spot here.'

I raised my eyes and looked at the elderly gentleman sitting by the window. A high forehead, pointed chin, intelligent and ironic eyes. The gentleman put a mobile phone away in his pocket and gestured towards his table.

Yes, he and Geser had a lot in common, all right. Not in the way they looked, but in the way they behaved. Thomas Lermont was probably just as good as Geser at putting his subordinates in their place.

I picked up my glass and joined the head of Edinburgh's Night Watch at his table.

'Call me Foma,' he said. 'I'll enjoy remembering Geser.'

'Have you known him for long?'

'Yes. Geser has older friends, but I don't . . . I've heard a lot about you, Anton.'

I let that pass. There was nothing I could say. I hadn't heard of the head of the Edinburgh Night Watch before yesterday.

'You've been talking to Bruce. What do you make of our vampire Master?'

I paused to formulate my impression precisely:

'Spiteful, unhappy, ironic. But they're all spiteful, unhappy and ironic. Of course, he didn't kill Victor.'

'You put pressure on him,' Lermont said, not asking but stating.

'Yes, that was just the way it worked out. He doesn't know anything.'

'No need to make excuses,' said Lermont, taking a sip of his beer. 'It worked out just fine. His own vanity will make sure that he keeps quiet, and we have the information . . . All right, what did you see in the Dungeons of Scotland?'

'Scary stories for children. The show's closed, but I managed to speak to one of the actors. And take a look at the crime scene.'

'Well?' Lermont asked keenly. 'So what did you find out, Anton?'

I'd learned a lot from all those years dealing with Geser. Nowadays I could tell when the boss's hand was poised to swat down a young magician who had overreached himself.

'That River of Blood where Victor's throat was cut . . .' I glanced at the impassive Lermont and corrected myself: 'Where Victor was killed. There's blood in the water. A lot of human blood. It doesn't look as if it was a vampire who sucked the boy's blood out. Someone opened his artery and held him while his blood spilled out into the trench. But we need an analysis of the water. We could bring in the police, they could do a DNA analysis . . .'

'Oh, what great faith you have in technology,' Foma said with a frown. 'It's Victor's blood in the trench. We checked the very first day. Simple similitude magic, no more than fifth-level Power required.'

But I wasn't about to give in. Dealing with Geser had also taught me the art of wriggling out of things.

'It's no help to us, but the police ought to be given the idea too. Let them know that the blood was drained into the trench, and that will put an end to any rumours about vampires.'

'The police here are good,' Foma said calmly. 'They checked

everything too, and they're conducting an investigation. But putting an end to stupid rumours is none of their business. Who takes any notice of the yellow press?'

I felt encouraged. I had gone straight to the right conclusions after all.

'I don't think any more intervention will be required from us,' I said. 'Murder is evil, but let people fight their own evil themselves. It's a pity about the boy, of course, but . . .'

Foma nodded once or twice and took another sip of beer. Then he said:

'Yes, a pity about the boy . . . But Anton, what are we going to do about the bite?'

'What bite?'

Foma leaned forward across the table and whispered:

'It wasn't a knife wound on Victor's neck, Anton. There's absolutely no doubt that the marks were left by a vampire's fangs. Now, that's an unfortunate problem, isn't it?'

I felt my ears burning.

'Is that definite?'

'Ab-so-lute-ly. Just how would a hit man know so much about the way a vampire's fang is structured and how it works? The lateral grooves, the tapping point, Dracula's fissure, the corkscrew twist on entry . . .'

By this time my entire face was blazing red. I could see the classroom where I had once been taught, and my teacher Polina Vasilievna with her pointer, and the huge rubber model on the desk: a pointed, twisted object like a corkscrew and a white fibreglass board with black letters: 'Vampire's right canine (operational) tooth. Model, scale 25:1.' It had been a working model at one stage: when a button was pressed it had elongated and begun to rotate. But the electric motor had burnt out long ago, and nobody had taken the trouble to repair it, so the fang was permanently frozen in a position between concealed and operational.

'I was too hasty with my conclusions,' I admitted. 'It's my fault, Mr Lermont.'

'It's nobody's fault, you simply didn't want any Others to be involved,' Foma said generously. 'If you'd familiarised yourself with the results of the autopsy, you'd have realised that your version was wrong. So now what do you say?'

'If the vampire was very hungry and he sucked the man dry' – I frowned – 'he could have puked up afterwards. But not all the blood. Were there any traces of anaesthetic serum in the water?'

'No, there weren't,' Foma said, with a nod of approval. 'But then, that doesn't mean anything, the vampire could have been in such a hurry that he didn't bother with the anaesthetic.'

'He could have been,' I agreed. 'So either he puked or he bit and then held the victim until he bled out. But what for?'

'To confuse us all and mislead the investigation.'

'That doesn't make any sense,' I said, shaking my head. 'Why confuse things? Why leave the marks of a vampire's bite and drain away the blood? They're very careful with it, they wouldn't just pour it away. Our vampires even have a saying for novices: "Blood spilt on the ground is mother's milk wasted".'

'You can always find a way to make sense of anything,' Foma declared didactically. 'For example – the killer vampire needed to make us suspect a young, hungry vampire. So he bit the boy but he didn't drink, just poured the blood away, hoping that it wouldn't be found. Or the vampire was hungry, but as soon as he bit he realised what he'd done and decided to pour the blood away, to create the impression of falsified evidence . . .'

Completely carried away now, I fluttered my hands in the air, as if I was talking to Geser.

'Oh, come on, Bo— Foma! You can come up with lots of theories, but I've never met a hungry vampire who would leave the blood once he had his fangs in. This argument isn't getting us anywhere. What's far more important is why the boy was killed. Was he a random victim? Then we really do have to look for a tourist or a novice. Or did someone have a special reason for killing Victor?'

'A vampire can kill a man with a single blow,' said Foma. 'And without even touching him. Why would he leave any clues behind? Victor could have died from a heart attack, and no one would have suspected a thing.'

'Agreed,' I said, with a nod. 'Then . . . then your Master is right. It's some vampire from out of town, and the boy just happened to be in the wrong place. He bit him, then got frightened and puked up the blood.'

'It looks that way,' Foma agreed. 'But there's still something bothering me, Anton.'

We finished our beer without another word.

'Have you tried testing traces from the body?' I asked.

I didn't have to say that I meant traces left by an aura.

'A dead aura from a dead body?' Foma said, with a sceptical shake of his head. 'That's never been much help. But we did try. No traces were found . . . Tell me, watchman, what else did you see that was unusual in the Dungeons?'

'There are Others working there,' I said. 'There's no blue moss, although the place is overflowing with emotions. Someone cleans it out regularly.'

'There are no Others working there,' Foma snapped. 'The blue moss just doesn't grow there.'

I looked at him uncertainly.

'Out of interest, we tried bringing it in from outside. It withers and falls off in an hour. A sort of natural anomaly.'

'Well . . . it happens, I suppose,' I said, making a mental note to check in the archives.

'It does,' Foma agreed. 'Anton, I'd like to ask you not to leave the investigation just yet. There's something here that really bothers me. Try having a word Victor's girlfriend.'

'Is the girl still here?'

'Of course. The police asked her not to leave town. The Alex City hotel, not far from here. I think it will be easier for you to make contact with her.'

'Do you suspect her of something?'

Foma shook his head.

'She's just an ordinary person . . . It's something else. She's taking her lover's death very hard, cooperating willingly with the police. But maybe a fellow Russian will find it easier to get through to her. A gesture, a glance, a word – any little thing. I really don't want to close this case and leave everything to the police, Anton.'

'And it would be a good thing to meet the owner of the Dungeons of Scotland, too,' I said.

'That won't get you anywhere,' Foma said dismissively.

'Why not?'

'Because those stupid Dungeons belong to me!' Foma said with loathing.

'But—' I broke off. 'Well . . . but then . . .'

'What then? I have a small holding company – Scottish Colours – that works in the tourist business. Our Night Watch is a shareholder in the company, and the profits go to finance its activities. We organise musical events and circus performances, we have shares in a few hotels, four pubs, the Dungeons of Scotland, three tour buses and an agency that takes tourists to the Scottish lochs. How else would you like us to earn our money?' He laughed. 'The whole of Edinburgh lives off the tourists. If you go to Glasgow and you find yourself in the suburbs, you'll see a frightening sight – buildings on the point of collapse, hotels boarded up, factories closed down. Industry is dying. It's not profitable to produce goods in Europe any longer, but it *is* profitable to produce services. What else should an old bard do but run concerts and tourist attractions?'

'I understand, it was just unexpected . . .'

'There aren't any Others working there,' Foma repeated. 'It's a strange place – the blue moss doesn't grow there – that was why I bought the land in the first place. But I didn't find anything unusual.'

'Then could the murder have been intended as a blow against you?' I asked. 'Against you personally and the Night Watch of Edinburgh? Does someone want to compromise Light Ones?'

Foma smiled and stood up.

'That's what I need you for, Anton. To have a powerful magician from the outside involved in the investigation. Have a word with Valeria, all right? And don't put it off.'

But I had to put off the meeting with Valeria for a little while after all.

When I was already almost at the hotel I saw yet another crowd of tourists gathered in a circle around a performing street artist. There was a whole rainbow of tiny little coloured balls flying up in the air above the people's heads, and somehow I knew who I was going to see. Even though Egor had called himself an illusionist and not a juggler.

In actual fact, there were five performers there. Three young guys in bright 'circus' clothes were taking a break. A young girl in a flowing semi-transparent dress was going round the spectators with a tray, and they were gladly putting in coins and notes.

At the moment, only Egor was performing. He was wearing a black suit and white shirt, with a bow tie – looking very well-groomed and quite different from the crowd in their summery clothes.

Egor was juggling with the coloured balls. But not simply

juggling . . . His right hand was shooting red, blue and green balls no bigger than a cherry high up into the air. The open palm swivelled with emphatic slowness, demonstrating that there was nothing in it. Then the fingers folded together and the whole hand swung rapidly – and another ball went soaring upwards. His left hand caught the falling balls and crumpled them into his fist, breaking off the rainbow, and then immediately opened again – empty.

The little balls came from nowhere and disappeared into nowhere. There were more and more of them all the time – as if Egor didn't have enough time to take back out of the air everything that he had thrown up into it. The coloured parabola kept growing brighter and brighter, denser and denser, turning into a gleaming, glittering rope of colour. It was dazzling. The movements of his fingers became so fast that they exceeded the ability of any prestidigitator. The spectators held their breath. The sounds of the street rolled up to that motionless circle of people and died, like the murmuring waves of a distant sea. The coloured cord fluttered through Egor's hands,

The tension grew and grew. The girl stopped collecting money – nobody was looking at her now in any case. She turned towards Egor and looked at him with eyes filled with love and delight.

Egor suddenly jerked both his hands – and he was left holding a fluttering brightly coloured ribbon.

The spectators applauded as if they had just woken up.

I recalled the hoary old joke about the conjuror who came to a circus looking for a job. 'I go out onstage and juggle with different-coloured fish, get it? And then they fly up into the big top and disappear. The only thing is, I haven't figured out how to do it yet . . .'

Poor stupid conjuror. To do that, you have to be an Other. Even an uninitiated one.

In actual fact, even without being initiated, or having made that first entry into the Twilight, an Other is capable of far more than an ordinary human being. And in Egor's case everything was far more complicated. He had entered the Twilight when he was a child. He had even broken through into the second level – although he was fed Power by someone else, since his own abilities were minimal.

But he had avoided going through with initiation, and remained what he was – an indeterminate Other who did not know how to control his abilities and had not turned either to the Light or the Dark. His Book of Fate had been rewritten, returning him to his initial condition and giving him the chance to choose again – but he had refused to make a choice.

And he had decided that he was an ordinary human being.

Egor himself did not understand how he performed his act. He was certain that he was controlling the little balls very deftly, skilfully transferring them from one hand to the other before launching them into the air again, and then adroitly replacing them with a special kind of ribbon that was evidently weighted at several points to make it all easier.

In actual fact a trick like that is impossible.

But Egor was quite certain that he performed his act without any magic. Like a very dexterous ordinary human being.

The spectators applauded with expressions of lively, genuine delight on their faces, the kind of delight that you only see in the faces of children at the circus. For a moment the world had become magical and wonderful for them.

They didn't know that that's the way the world really is – our world . . .

Egor bowed and walked round the circle quickly – not collecting money, although they were holding out notes to him, but simply looking in the eyes of the spectators.

He was drawing Power from them, feeding! Without even realising it, he was feeding on the emotions of his spectators!

I started hastily making my way out of the crowd, but the spectators behind me were pushing forward, there were children jumping about at my feet, and a semi-naked girl with studs in her pierced lips was breathing hotly in my ear. I was too slow, Egor had spotted me. And he stopped.

There was nothing left to do but open my arms wide.

Egor hesitated for a second, then whispered something to the girl with the tray, who was following him. He squirmed his way into the crowd. People made way for him, but they also slapped him enthusiastically on the back and made delighted comments in various languages.

'I'm sorry, I just happened to be passing,' I said guiltily. 'I wasn't expecting to see you at all.'

He looked at me for a second, then nodded.

'I believe you.'

Ah yes, he was at the peak of his Power right then. He could sense a lie intuitively.

'I'll be going,' I said. 'That was a great performance, I was fascinated.'

'Wait, I need to wet my throat,' said Egor, setting off beside me. 'I've been streaming with sweat . . .'

Some curious little boy grabbed hold of his sleeve. Egor politely stopped and unbuttoned his shirt to show that there was nothing in it. Then he took a light, silvery little ball out of the air and handed it to his suspicious spectator. The kid squealed in delight and dashed across to his parents, who were standing nearby.

'Really great,' I said appreciatively. 'Do you perform in Moscow? I could take my daughter to the circus.'

'No, not in Moscow,' Egor said, frowning. 'Do you know how hard it is to get into the circus back home?'

'I can guess.'

'If you're not from a circus family, if you haven't been jumping around the circus ring since you were five years old and you haven't got any contacts . . . And if you get an offer to perform abroad . . .' Egor frowned. 'To hell with them! Next year I'll be performing in a French circus, I'm just negotiating the contract, then they'll really be jealous . . .'

We sat down at a table outside the nearest café. Egor ordered a glass of juice and I asked for a double espresso. I was feeling sleepy again.

'So are you here because of me or not?' Egor asked abruptly.

'I had no idea that you were flying to Edinburgh. My assignment here has nothing to do with you!'

Egor looked into my face suspiciously. Then he sighed and relaxed.

'Then I apologise. I got a bit heated in the plane. I don't like the outfit you work for . . . I have no reason to like it.'

'That's OK,' I said gesturing with my open palms towards him. 'No offence taken. You don't have to like our outfit, it doesn't deserve it.'

'Uh-huh,' said Egor, staring pensively at his glass of orange juice. 'Well, how are things there? Still Geser, is it?'

'Of course. He was, he is, he always will be.'

'And how about Tiger Cub and Bear?' Egor asked with a smile, as if he'd just remembered something good. 'Did they get married?'

'Tiger Cub was killed, Egor.'★ I actually started when I realised he didn't know about it. 'It was a very bad business . . . we all suffered.'

'Killed,' Egor said thoughtfully. 'A pity. I liked her a lot. She was so strong, a were-tiger . . .'

'A shape-shifting magician,' I corrected him. 'Yes, she was strong, but very emotional. She attacked a Mirror.'

'A Mirror?'

★ This story is told in the second part of the book *The Day Watch*.

'Yes, well, that's a type of magician. A very unusual type. Sometimes, if some Watch starts winning, a Mirror Magician appears to help the other side. They say they're created by the Twilight itself, but no one knows for sure. A Mirror Magician can't be defeated in ordinary battle, he absorbs his opponent's Power and parries every attack. We really took a beating that time – and Tiger Cub was killed.'

'What about the Mirror? Did you kill him?'

'Vitaly Rogoza was his name . . . He dematerialised. Of his own accord, that's their destiny. A Mirror is originally a weak, indeterminate magician who loses his memory, then travels to the place where one Power is gaining a serious advantage over the other and takes the side of the one that's losing. And afterwards the Mirror disappears, dissolves into the Twilight.'

I said all this automatically, thinking about something else.

There was a painful cold lump growing in my chest.

A weak, indeterminate magician?

'Serves him right,' Egor said vengefully. 'I feel sorry for Tiger Cub – I often used to think about her. And you, sometimes.'

'Really?' I asked. 'I hope you weren't too angry with me.'

To be quite honest, I really couldn't have cared less right then just who Egor used to remember and how.

A weak, indeterminate magician.

He travels to the place where . . .

He dissolves into the Twilight . . .

'I was a bit angry,' Egor admitted. 'But not too much. It wasn't really your fault. That's the way your job is . . . lousy. But I resented it, of course. I even dreamed once that you were really my father. And I was going to become a Dark Magician and work in the Day Watch in order to spite you. ★

★This story is told in the movies *Night Watch* and *Day Watch*.

But he hadn't lost his memory, had he! I couldn't draw such a simple comparison between Rogoza and Egor after all.

'That's a funny dream,' I said. 'They say some dreams are an alternative reality breaking through into our consciousness. Maybe somewhere, somehow, that's the way it was. You shouldn't have gone over to the Dark Ones, though . . .'

Egor said nothing for a moment. Then he snorted.

'Oh, no. A plague on both your houses. I don't like the Dark Ones, and I don't like the Light Ones. But you come round any time, Anton! I'm staying just near here. In the Alex City hotel. I'll introduce you to the rest of our crew, they're all great guys!'

He put a few coins on the table and stood up.

'I'll go back to work. My number's the highlight of the show – the lads won't take much money without me.'

He had hardly even touched his juice.

'Egor!' I called to him. 'How did you happen to come to Edinburgh? Was it your own idea?'

The young man looked at me in surprise.

'No, it wasn't. A company invited me – Scottish Colour. Why do you ask?'

'I thought I could give you a hand, if necessary,' I lied without a moment's hesitation. 'Find you an agent.'

'Thanks,' said Egor, and the warmth in his voice made me wish the earth would open up and swallow me. 'No need, but thanks anyway, Anton.'

I sat there, looking at the dregs in the bottom of my cup. Was that still not enough coincidences for me? Maybe I should use the coffee grounds for a bit of fortune-telling?

'Scottish Colour,' I muttered.

My chest was feeling so cold now that it didn't hurt any more.

CHAPTER 4

THERE'S NOTHING MORE absurd than to arrive in a new city and spend your time in a hotel room. That's okay for the red-hot after-noon of the Spanish siesta. Or for newly-weds on honeymoon, when the size of the bed is far more important than the view out of the window.

But then, Valeria was caught in a hopeless situation. The police had told her not to leave the city. And she simply didn't have the strength to go out into that crowd of merrymakers, that swirling mass of tourists.

She opened the door immediately, as if she had been waiting just behind it. Although, of course, no one could have warned her, since I'd walked past the receptionist under the protection of a Circle of Inattention.

The girl was wearing nothing but shorts and a bra. Well yes, it was quite hot, of course. Even the good hotels here didn't have air-conditioning, the climate didn't really require it. As I said, it was quite hot – especially if you were drinking.

'Yes?' Lera challenged me drunkenly.

Her black hair was styled in a square cut. She was attractive, thin, quite tall.

One of her hands was on the handle of the open bathroom door. I had arrived just as she was on her way to the toilet.

'Hello, Lera,' I said politely. I wasn't exactly looking super-respectable, just shorts and a T-shirt, but I still chose the 'representative-of-the-authorities' tone of voice. 'Can I come in?'

'Why not?' Lera asked in surprise. 'Come . . .' She hiccupped. 'Come on through. Only . . . I'll just be a moment.'

She went into the bathroom without even bothering to lock the door behind her. I shook my head, walked past the unmade bed and sat in an armchair by the window. It was a small room, quite comfortable in a formal sort of way. There was a bottle of Glenlivet whisky on the coffee table. It was more than half empty. Glancing at the door of the bathroom I sent a simple spell in Lera's direction.

I heard the sound of coughing in the bathroom.

'Need any help, Lera?' I asked, pouring myself two fingers of whisky.

Lera didn't answer. She was being sick.

I found some cold mineral water in the mini-bar and rinsed out Lera's glass – it smelled strongly of whisky. Then I poured in a little bit of water and splashed it out straight on to the carpet. And then I poured in more water.

'I'm sorry . . .' said the girl, as she emerged from the bathroom, looking a lot livelier. 'I . . . I'm sorry.'

'Have a drink of water, Lera,' I said, holding out the glass.

A good-looking girl. Very young. And with very sad eyes.

'Who are you?' she asked and drained the glass avidly. 'Hell – my head's splitting.'

She sat down in the other armchair and took her head in her hands.

We'd never be able to make conversation like that.

'Can I help?'

'Do you have any aspirin? Something for a headache . . .'

'Ancient Chinese massage,' I said, standing up and going round behind her. 'The pain will soon be gone.'

'Oh sure, I believe in massage, all the guys say they can do massage, anything to get their paws on you . . .' Lera began, and then stopped talking the moment my hands started taking away the pain.

Of course, I don't really know how to do massage. But I can disguise healing magic as massage.

'That's really good . . . you're a magician . . .' Lera murmured.

'Yes, I am,' I agreed. 'A fully qualified Light Magician.'

Right . . . stop the blood vessels cramping . . . draw the alcohol out of the blood . . . okay, pass it through the kidneys . . . neutralise the metabolites . . . balance the serotonin and adrenalin . . . restore the pH of the blood to normal . . . okay, and at the same time we'll reduce the output of hydrochloric acid in the blood . . .

Of course, I'm nowhere near as good as Svetlana. She could have done all this with a single touch. I laboured away for about three minutes. I had the Power, but I lacked the skill.

'Miracles like that don't happen,' Valeria said nervously. She turned round and looked at me.

'Oh yes, they do,' I said. 'You'll want to go to the toilet now. Don't be embarrassed and don't wait, you'll pass water every fifteen minutes. Until you get all the garbage out of your system . . . Stop. Wait a moment . . .'

I looked at her closely. Well, would you believe it . . .

'Don't drink any more,' I told her. 'Not at all.'

I went to the bathroom to wash my hands. The running water carried away the fatigue from my fingers and the imprint of an aura distorted by suffering. I could have used Power to clean myself, but the old folk methods are still the best.

'Why are you ordering me about?' Lera said darkly when I got back. 'But thank you, the massage was good . . . I'll just be a moment!'

I waited for her to come back from the toilet, clearly shocked by the speed and efficiency with which her organism was being purged. Once she had sat down, I explained.

'You're pregnant. You shouldn't drink now.'

'My period is due to start tomorrow,' Lera retorted so furiously that I realised she could sense it. Through sheer feminine intuition, without any outside help, she had realised she was pregnant. Then she had rejected the idea and started binge-drinking.

'It won't start.'

She didn't argue. She didn't even ask how I knew. Probably she put it down to the wonders of oriental medicine. She asked:

'Why would I want a child without a husband?'

'That's for you to decide,' I said. 'I'm not going to try to persuade you either way.'

'Who are you?' Lera finally asked.

'Gorodetsky. Anton Gorodetsky. I'm from Moscow. I . . . I was asked to investigate the circumstances of Victor's death.'

Lera sighed and said bitterly:

'Vitya's father using his contacts . . . What's the point now . . .'

'To find out the truth.'

'The truth . . .' The girl poured herself some water and drained the glass in one. Her body was driving her blood through her kidneys at a furious rate, removing the alcohol and its metabolic products. 'Victor was killed by a vampire.'

'Vampires don't exist, Lera.'

'I know. But what do you do when a guy says "There's someone drinking my blood", and then they find him with a bite mark on his throat and no blood left in his body?'

There was a subtle note of hysteria in her voice.

'I checked the channel that the boat was sailing in,' I said.

'There's blood in it. A lot of blood. Calm down, Lera. Vampires really don't exist. Someone killed your friend. He bled to death. That's terrible, it's cruel, but vampires don't exist.'

She said nothing for about a minute. Then she asked:

'Why didn't the police tell me that?'

'They have their reasons. They're afraid of leaks of information. Perhaps they even suspect *you* of something.'

That didn't frighten her at all – in fact, it seemed to make her angry.

'The bastards. I can't get to sleep, I get sloshed on whisky in the evenings. Yesterday I almost dragged some guy into bed . . . I'm afraid to be alone, understand? Afraid. And they don't tell me anything . . . Excuse me, I'll just be a moment.'

I waited for her to come back from the toilet, then said:

'I must have overdone it a bit with the massage. But I'm not a professional, I've just picked up a few moves.'

'The things they teach your crowd,' Lera said, and I realised she was as certain that I worked for the KGB as the young Frenchman in the Dungeons had been. We're all children of mass culture. We all believe in its clichés. You don't even need any documents if you behave like a secret agent in an action movie.

'Lera, I want to ask you to make an effort to recall all the circumstances of Victor's death,' I said. 'I know you've said it all over and over again. But please try.'

'We got into that stupid boat,' Lera began. 'I almost fell over, it was a very awkward step down, a long way, and I couldn't see the bottom of the boat in the darkness.'

'Tell me everything from the very beginning. Start from the moment when you got up that morning. Every detail.'

Lera's eyes glinted mischievously.

'Well . . . we woke up at ten, we missed breakfast. Then we had sex. Then we went into the shower, and we got a bit carried away in there . . .'

I nodded and smiled benevolently as I listened to the girl's story, which really did include all the details. And when she broke into tears, I waited for a few minutes without saying anything. The tears stopped and Lera shook her head. She looked into my eyes.

'We went into a pub, the Oak and Ribbon, and had something to eat. We drank a pint of beer each. It was hot, and then we saw the sign for that damned tourist show. Victor thought it would be interesting. Or at least that it would be cool inside. So we went in.'

Nothing. Not a single clue. I realised that Lera had been questioned by professionals before me: they had drained her, forced her to remember, asked the same questions ten times. What else could she possibly remember out of the blue now?

She started describing the boat again, the awkward step down into it, and I raised my hand.

'Stop there, Lera. That mirror maze – you said it was the most interesting thing. Didn't anything odd happen in there?'

I didn't know why I'd asked that question. Perhaps because I was still thinking about Egor. Perhaps I'd remembered the old wives' tale that vampires have no reflections in mirrors.

'In the hall of mirrors . . .' Lera knitted her brows. 'Ah! There was something. Victor started waving to someone. As if he'd seen someone he knew. Afterwards he said he must have imagined it.'

'How about you, Lera? Did *you* see anybody you knew?'

She shook her head.

'No. There are mirrors on all sides in there. You really get lost among all those faces, all those people. And it gets a bit annoying after a while . . . I tried not to look.'

'Can't you even make a guess at who he might have seen?'

'Could that be important?' Lera asked seriously.

'Yes,' I replied with no hesitation.

It was very important. It was a clear clue. If there was a vampire in the Dungeons and he was diverting people's eyes, he could have been seen in the room of mirrors. And Victor hadn't just seen someone – he had recognised him.

So what was dangerous about being recognised? Someone had gone into the Dungeons – what of it? Why had the vampire panicked and killed the unsuspecting student?

I didn't know. Not yet.

'I think Victor thought he had seen a friend of his . . . not someone from here,' Lera said after thinking for a moment. 'Because he was very surprised. If he'd seen someone from the university, he would have waved to him and shouted "Hi." But he just waved and didn't say anything. You know, the way you do when you're not quite sure if you've seen a friend or made a mistake. And afterwards, when he couldn't find anyone, he really seemed quite upset. And he said it was all nonsense. As if he'd persuaded himself that it couldn't have happened. Anton, did Vitya see his killer?'

'I'm afraid he did,' I said, nodding. 'It's possible that was why he was killed. Thank you. You've been a great help.'

'Should I tell this to the police?' Lera asked.

'Why not? Only, if possible, don't mention that I was here, okay? But you can tell them what you've remembered.'

'Will you tell me if you find the killer?'

'Definitely.'

'You're lying,' Lera said, shaking her head. 'You're lying – you won't tell me anything.'

'I'll send you a postcard,' I said after a pause. 'With a view of Edinburgh. If you get a postcard, it means that Victor has been avenged.'

Lera nodded. I was already at the door when she asked:

'Anton, if I . . . What should I do about the child?'

'That's for you to decide. You must understand that nobody else will ever decide anything for you. Not the president, not your boss, not even a kind magician.'

'I'm nineteen,' Lera said in a quiet voice. 'I loved Vitya. But now he's gone. Twenty years old, with a child and no husband . . .'

'You have to make up your mind. But please don't drink in any case,' I said.

And I closed the door behind me.

Evening arrived, and I hadn't slept the night before, which had been divided between airports and aeroplanes. I had another coffee and glanced regretfully at the beer pumps: one pint would be enough make me completely dozy now. I phoned Geser and gave him a summary of what I'd found out during the day.

'Look for a vampire in Victor's circle of Moscow acquaintances,' Gesar mused thoughtfully. 'Thank you, Anton, all his Moscow contacts have been checked already . . . All right, we'll look a little bit harder. We'll start digging as far back as the kindergarten. What are you going to do now?'

'Go and catch up on my sleep,' I said.

'Any provisional conclusions?'

'There's something going on here, Geser. I don't know what it is, but it's something big.'

'Do you need any help?'

I was about to say no, but then I remembered Semyon.

'Boris Ignatievich, if Semyon isn't too busy . . .'

'Is he missing Scotland?' Geser chuckled. 'All right, I'll send him over. If he gets a move on you'll meet in the morning. Get some rest.'

I didn't tell Geser anything about Egor. I put my cellphone away, with a quick glance at the charge indicator. Well, well – the battery was almost full. In Moscow my phone went flat in a single day, even though I didn't talk very much. But abroad, it worked quite happily for a week. Were the pylons here planted closer together, or something?

Now for another part of the job. An unpleasant part.

I took out the carving of the wolf and set in on the table.

Contact, advice, protection?

I grasped the figure with both hands and closed my eyes. Perhaps that wasn't how it worked?

'Zabulon!'

Was that someone's gaze I seemed to sense?

As far as I could recall, Zabulon never responded immediately. Not even when his lover called.

'Zabulon!'

'Why are you shouting like that, Gorodetsky?'

I opened my eyes. There was no one there, of course.

'I need some advice, Dark One.'

'Ask.'

It was a good thing that almost no emotion at all is transmitted in this kind of conversation. Zabulon was probably chuckling to himself. A Light One coming to him for help!

'Zabulon, when the Mirror Magician came to you, did you summon him?'

That obviously wasn't the question he'd been expecting.

'The Mirror? Vitaly Rogoza?'

'Yes.'

A pause. No, he knew the answer all right: he was deciding whether to tell the truth or to lie.

'A Mirror cannot be summoned, Light One. They are children of the Twilight.'

'Then what has to happen for a Mirror Magician to appear?'

'One Power has to acquire a significant advantage over the other. And it has to be a sudden imbalance, acquired too quickly.

The Mirror came because Geser was raising Svetlana's level too rapidly, he brought Olga back into play and . . . and he rewrote your future daughter's destiny to make her the Greatest of the Great.'

'Is it possible to foresee who will be the next Mirror Magician?'

'It is. He is an Other whose own fundamental Power is minimal. He must have no love for the Light or for the Dark. Or, on the contrary, he must love the Light and the Dark. A human being, and an Other, who stands at the fork in the road and makes no distinction between Light and Dark. There are individuals like that, but they are rare. In Moscow there are two of them – Victor's father and . . . your little friend Egor. But then, he's already grown-up now, isn't he?'

'Why did Rogoza come from Ukraine?'

'Because we're not the ones who decide who's going to be a Mirror. I was rather hoping that he would show up, but nobody ever knows anything in advance. A Mirror Magician might come, or he might not. He can appear straight away, or he can take days, even months, to reach the place where the equilibrium has been disrupted. Have I satisfied your curiosity?'

'Yes.'

'Then I expect a courtesy in return. Who killed Victor? And what have Mirror Magicians got to do with it?'

'You won't like this information, Zabulon. I think that Victor was killed in order to discredit the Scottish Night Watch. They own the tourist attraction. And as for the Mirror . . . I'm afraid that the situation here might be destabilised. So badly that a Mirror Magician will turn up. Are there any candidates for the role in Edinburgh?'

He believed me. At least, I thought he believed me. He answered thoughtfully:

'I don't know. I've never tried to find out.'

'Then that's all for the time being. If you do find out, please let me know, if you would be so kind.'

Without bothering to wait for his mocking chuckle, I opened my hand and cut off the contact. The figurine was gleaming with sweat, which made it seem almost alive.

That was it: time to go back to the hotel. To that cosy de luxe apartment for Light Ones, that kingdom of white and pink and beige, those lace curtains and silk sheets.

My phone jangled.

'Hello?' As I pressed the phone to my ear, I caught the waiter's eye and ran one finger across my open palm, as if I was writing out a bill. The waiter gave a laboured smile, glanced at the solitary cup standing in front of me and scribbled '£2' on a piece of paper.

'Anthony, my friend,' Lermont said in English. That 'Anthony' told me immediately that there was someone there who was not supposed to know that I was Russian. 'How was my employee feeling when you left the Dungeons?'

'Just fine.'

'He's been killed, Anthony. Do you think you could come over?'

I hissed something unprintable and scooped the small change out of my pocket. Right – the castle was there, the ravine and the bridge were there . . .

'If I can catch a taxi straight away, I'll be there in five minutes.'

'Make it quick,' Lermont told me.

I found a free taxi immediately – I didn't need to resort to magic in order to get someone out of a cab that was already occupied. Edinburgh was remarkably good for taxis in general. I got in, took out a cigarette and lit it. The driver looked at me rather disapprovingly, but didn't say anything. I wound the window all the way down. Of course, his next passengers would be non-smokers . . .

But I felt like smoking.

Idiot. What an idiot I was! I'd felt alarmed for Egor, concerned for Valeria . . . But I hadn't bothered to use my head for what it was really meant for. My visit to the Dungeons had been observed. And now poor Jean, the nervous French student, would never go back home to Nantes . . .

It was my fault.

But what about Lermont — closing the place down and only leaving one man on duty to watch it? Not an Other, not a Battle Magician who could fight vampires on equal terms, but a frightened kid in make-up and fancy dress.

I imagined the young red-headed guy with his face pale from loss of blood instead of make-up, lying there surrounded by those appalling instruments of torture. 'It's a bit creepy here on your own.' And I started swearing wildly under my breath.

'I'm a fool, a fool . . .'

Lermont was waiting for me at the entrance to the Dungeons. He looked dark-faced and angry, the way only a Light One can be angry.

'Let's go,' he said and tramped off without even looking round. We walked quickly through a string of empty rooms and came out at the River of Blood. This place again?

But Foma got into the boat without saying a word. I followed him in. He waved his hand, the mechanism creaked, and the boat moved forward.

'Haven't you called the police yet?' I asked.

'Not yet. Only our own people — and observers from the Dark Ones.'

'Where are they?

'I asked them to wait a few rooms away. I said I wanted to bring in an independent expert to examine the body. An ordinary human being. No point in anyone knowing about you at this stage . . .'

The boat crept across the small dark space and docked at the other mooring.

'There,' Foma said morosely.

I clambered out of the boat and followed Foma into the next room, which contained an exhibition of methods of execution. There was a dummy hanging in a noose from the ceiling, and over there on the guillotine – it wasn't a dummy on the guillotine. The killer had demonstrated his sense of humour once again.

To cut a man's head off with the sham blade of the fake guillotine must have taken superhuman strength – the kind of strength that a vampire has, for instance.

The white plastic bucket under the guillotine was half full with blood. The severed head was lying beside it. I squatted and picked the head up cautiously. I felt like screaming at the helpless awareness of my own stupidity.

'I wish I knew what bastard did this,' said Foma. 'That man worked for me for seventeen years.'

'The bastard was a young red-headed guy,' I said. 'He pretended to be French and spoke with a slight accent. He looked twenty years old. And he had a liking for theatrical effects. Very quick-witted, a remarkable actor.'

Carefully laying the severed head back down on the floor, I looked at Lermont's dumbfounded face and explained.

'He made a total fool of me. I was talking to the killer only two steps away from the body. And I didn't suspect a thing. Not a thing!'

The head of the murdered guard – black-haired, but with a sprinkling of grey quite appropriate for a man over fifty – stared up blindly at me from the floor.

'You can only mask your true nature from someone who's very weak,' said Lermont, drilling into me with his mistrustful eyes. 'That's axiomatic. Try to define my aura.'

A strange conversation over a dead man whose head has been severed. A strange place, a strange crime, strange conversations . . .

Lermont's aura — a blaze of bright yellow-green discharges, a prickly hedgehog of Power — dimmed. The pointed discharges were drawn in and faded. A few seconds later Lermont was surrounded by the smooth multilayered aura typical of a human being.

A ragged open aura is a sure sign of an Other. It can have sharp needles and prickles, swirling vortices, gaping holes. All these are indications of an open-energy pattern and the ability to absorb energy, not just give it out like human beings. To absorb, process and perform miracles.

A human aura is smooth, multilayered, integrated. People only give out Power, they don't absorb it. And the smooth membrane of their aura is an attempt to protect themselves, to halt the slow, implacable draining away of life.

Yes, now Lermont looked like a human being.

Almost like a human being . . .

I looked a bit more carefully and saw the pale needles of his aura. Foma had disguised himself very well, but I had broken through his defence

'I see it,' I said, 'but I didn't look at that young guy so carefully. He could have masked himself.'

'In that case, your red-headed companion is a Higher Vampire. Or a Higher Magician pretending to be a vampire.' Foma nodded in satisfaction. 'And he was not able to put on a mask while disguising his aura at the same time. This is good, Anton, this is already good. We know his physical appearance: young, red-haired — there aren't all that many Higher Others in the world.'

'He must have got the cloak from somewhere here,' I said. 'And the false fangs. He heard me coming and instead of running away he came out calmly to meet me — and invented a cover story on the spot.'

'I think I can guess why he needed the cloak,' Foma said gloomily, glancing at the blood-spattered floor. 'He must have got blood on himself . . . Send me his image, Anton.'

I closed my eyes and tried to remember the Frenchman as clearly as possible. Then I sent the mental picture to Lermont.

'Aha,' said the Scot. 'Excellent. I'll check out all the files.'

'Perhaps we ought to inform the Inquisition?' I asked.

Lermont shook his head.

'No, not yet. The events have not exceeded the limits of a crime committed by a solitary Dark One. The Day Watch of Edinburgh has not lodged any protests. We'll manage without the Inquisition, Anton. For as long as we can.'

I didn't argue. There's not much fun in calling the Inquisition in to help.

'Is my help still required here?'

'No – go and catch up on your sleep,' said Lermont. 'We won't inform the police: this is purely our business. My lads will try to find some clues, and I'll start checking the Higher Others.'

He grunted as he bent down over the severed head, as if he was hoping to spot some kind of clues carelessly left by the criminal. Lermont could do with losing that belly.

'Foma,' I asked in a quiet voice. 'What is there in here, in the Dungeons of Scotland?'

'Eh?' he asked without even turning round.

'What are the Dark Ones looking for here?'

'It's a tourist attraction, Mr Gorodetsky,' Foma said coolly. 'Just that, and nothing more.'

'Well, all right,' I said and left.

The killer had not needed to come back. If he had left any clues, they would already have been found – both the ordinary ones and the magic ones.

But he had come back and killed again. In order to anger the Night Watch even more? Nonsense. In order to put pressure on Lermont? Total nonsense.

So there was something he hadn't managed to do the first time around. And he had had to come back again.

What could Lermont be hiding? This place wasn't as straight-forward as it seemed. For example, the blue moss didn't grow here. That was already a significant anomaly. The structure of the Twilight is heterogeneous. For instance, in some places it is harder to enter than in others. I had even heard about zones where it is quite impossible to enter the Twilight. But the blue moss was a universal parasite . . .

I walked about a hundred metres away from the place and looked through the Twilight.

Aha.

Where I was standing, the moss was flourishing. There were thick garlands of it outside the pubs and cafes. It was thicker on the houses where people lived and thinner on the offices and shops. And there was more moss on the crossroads, where drivers get nervous.

All perfectly normal.

But when I looked towards the bridge, the closer to the entrance to the Dungeons, the more blue moss there was! It was drawn in that direction . . . And no wonder! The moss got thicker and thicker and then suddenly, ten metres from the doors, it started to dry up, as if it had hit some invisible boundary line.

Strange. If there was some factor that was harmful to the moss, it ought to have thinned out gradually. This had to be something else . . .

I reached out one hand to the closest colony of moss – a luxuriant blue clump on the asphalt. I said:

'Burn!'

The Power flowed through me, only I held back the pressure. The moss didn't burn up immediately. It swelled up and started growing, trying to process this free dose of energy. But the Power increased, and the moss couldn't cope. It started turning grey and drying up . . . and finally it burst into flames.

Now I could see it. When you know exactly what to look for, everything becomes extremely clear.

The Power scattered through space, the vital energy given out by human beings, drained into the twilight unevenly. Yes, it constantly seeped through the fabric of the universe, down to the first level, the second, the third . . . but somewhere in the region of the Dungeons there was a gaping hole – and there was a constant stream of Power gushing down into it. As if someone had cut a hole in a piece of cloth through which water normally filtered slowly . . .

Too much food for a brainless parasite. The moss crept towards the tourist attraction, attracted by both the stream of Power and the emotions of the frightened customers. It crept up close – and then dried up.

I thought I could understand why Foma Lermont had chosen this precise spot to open his attraction. All this energy flowing into one place had to be concealed from rank-and-file Others. The excessive free Power here could be attributed to tipsy tourists, frightened children, the endless carnival that was Edinburgh . . .

I wouldn't have been surprised to learn that Foma had put a lot of effort into popularising Edinburgh for just one reason: to conceal this spot.

Even Light Ones sometimes have dark secrets. It can't be helped.

I walked slowly uphill along one of the streets leading to the Royal Mile. It wasn't a very touristy kind of street. Dark, with the only light coming from the windows. All the shops on it were closed. But it had to lead straight to my hotel. I was feeling desperately sleepy. Maybe I ought to take a taxi after all? But it was only a ten-minute walk . . .

I turned in to a narrow street between the houses and found myself in something between a small square and a large court-yard. I walked over to a small monument, only one metre high, in the roadway. There was a bronze parrot sitting on a stone chalice with a thin stream of water flowing from it – it was either an undersized street fountain or a drinking-water fountain. Lighting my cigarette lighter to examine the plaque below the parrot, I learned that this fountain had been erected by the inhabitants of the city in memory of a beloved parrot who had died of pneu-monia at a very advanced age . . .

Something clicked behind me and I felt a powerful jolt in my shoulder. So powerful that I had to take several steps forward to avoid falling face down in the chalice of water.

Something hot trickled down my back

What the hell?

There was another click and something ricocheted loudly off the bronze bird. The hot bullet hissed as it fell into the water, finally convincing me that I had almost been killed beside the parrot fountain.

Someone was shooting at me!

At me, an Other!

A Higher Magician.

Who could destroy palaces and raise up cities with a wave of my hand!

Well, all right, the cities are a bit of an exaggeration – breaking down is always easier than raising up.

Squirming in my hiding place behind the fountain, I looked hard into the darkness. No one. Okay, how about through the Twilight?

The result astounded me.

The shots had clearly come from the side street next to the one that had led me to the fountain. But I couldn't see anyone, either human or Other!

At least it was only a flesh wound. The bullet had passed straight through the soft tissues. I had stopped the bleeding in a reflex response, within a second. Now I could recall a couple of good healing spells to knit the damaged muscles back together.

Another shot – the bullet passed over the top of my head and a wave of heat tousled my hair. The soft sound suggested that the gun must have a silencer. The fact that they hadn't killed me yet suggested that they were firing from a pistol, and firing very well, or from a sniper's rifle, and extremely badly.

But why couldn't I see the gunman?

I waved my hand and spread a five-minute Morpheus spell over the entire street. Then, after a moment's hesitation, I spread it across all the windows. And the roofs of the buildings, and the nearby side streets. Morpheus is a gentle spell, it gives a man about five seconds before it puts him out altogether: if he's standing, he can sit down, mothers holding children can put them down, drivers can slow down. There wouldn't be any casualties. Or probably not.

Silence.

Had I got him?

I got up and looked through the Twilight again. Well now, whoever you might be, if you've fallen asleep, your camouflage will fail—

A click. A faint flash in the side street. And another bullet went flying into my poor right shoulder! In exactly the same spot!

Well, I could take some comfort in the fact that I already had a wound there in any case. But it was really painful! Why did it hurt so badly if there was already a hole there?

I squatted down so that the fountain shielded me from the gunman. Now there was no doubt that the shots really were coming from the side street.

What was I going to do? Hurl fireballs into the darkness and try to get the camouflaged gunman that way? Scorch everything around me with the White Mirage? Put on a Magician's Shield and go into open battle . . . but if I couldn't see my enemy, then I was facing a magician more powerful than I was!

Or call for help, ring the police, call in Geser and Foma?

Stop.

It didn't have to be Geser and Foma.

What was that Zabulon had said? Contact, advice, protection?

A bit of protection wouldn't come amiss right now.

I took the little figure out of my pocket and set it down on the cobblestones of the roadway. I touched it gently with Power and shouted:

'I! Need! Help!'

It all happened in a split second. The air struck my face so hard that for a moment I thought the invisible gunman had switched to grenades, But it was the figure being transformed – swelling up and softening and turning into a shaggy grey shadow. White fangs glinted in the darkness, yellow wolf's eyes glittered, and the werewolf leapt straight over the fountain, then immediately jumped to the right. There was the click of a shot, but obviously it missed. Skipping from side to side as precisely as only a creature that is targeted by gunfire can, the beast went dashing into the side street. I heard growling, then there was a rumble and a metallic clang. The clicks of the shots carried on sounding in the same way, at regular intervals of a second or two, but something told me the bullets were going astray, and the gunman was not dangerous any more.

I jumped up and ran after the wolf, covering myself with a Shield just in case. And I finally did what it would have been a very good idea to have done in the first place: I created light. A simple spell that any Light Magician can manage. An appeal to the primordial Power — and there was a bright white light swaying in the air above me.

And I immediately saw the one who had nearly killed me. The one who had not been visible in the Twilight.

A fancy metal tripod similar to a professional stand for a video camera. Standing on a rotating disc on the tripod — a cylinder with gleaming lenses. Attached to the disc by a spring-recoil clamp — a short rifle with a round magazine like that of the old Soviet PPSh and a long ridged silencer on the barrel. A metal-clad cable ran up to the trigger, ending in a clamp with a wire that ran round the trigger.

The robot was still functioning. The cylinder was twitching with a quiet buzzing sound, the clamp was pressing the trigger — and the rifle, now pointing upwards, was firing into the sky. I leaned down, feeling the blood flowing over my shoulder. I put my good hand on the cylinder. On the side I found a little lid with an inscription in Chinese characters — 'Shooter I' — followed by a number: '285590607'. Below the hieroglyphs a round, smiling child's face was sketched in a few simple lines.

Humorists.

I prised open the little lid with my fingernail and turned the power switch to 'off'.

'Shooter I' gave a quiet whir of its servomotors and then fell silent.

'Greetings from the Heavenly Kingdom,' I said and sat down beside the robot. I looked at the short rod of the aerial, protruding from the cylinder. Yes, the real gunman could be absolutely anywhere. I had been fighting a robot.

And it was very lucky for me that its sights had been slightly off-centre.

'Would you believe it?' I said, examining the robot. 'What are we going to do about this sort of thing? Start inventing spells against technology?'

The wolf walked out of the darkness. He sat down facing me and started licking his paw. I couldn't see any wound – he had probably burned himself on the hot gun barrel when he knocked the tripod over.

'If Martian tripods had fleas, they'd look like this,' I said to the wolf. 'Have you read *War of the Worlds*?'

At first I didn't think he would answer. Not all werewolves are capable of speech when they change into animal form. But the wolf looked up at me gravely and barked:

'On-ly-seen-the-mo-vie.'

'Then you know what I mean,' I said. 'Thanks.'

'Lick-the-wound.'

'I'm no shape-shifter to go licking my wounds . . .' I said, pressing my palm to my right shoulder and concentrating. I felt sick and the pain pulsed in my hand. A gun wound is a nasty business. Even for a magician. Sveta, now – she'd have healed me in a couple of minutes . . .

'Whose-tail-have-you-stepped-on?' Words were coming more easily to the werewolf now. 'The-Ei-ffel-Tow-er's?'

I didn't realise immediately that he was joking. I shook my head.

'I see you're as witty as Petrosian. Thanks for your help. Were you hurt?'

'My-paw,' the wolf said indistinctly, starting to lick himself again. 'The-ma-chine-burned-it.'

'Change to human form and I'll heal it,' I said, standing up. I wasn't bleeding any more. Casting a camouflage spell on the disabled tripod (everyone would see something quite ordinary and un-interesting in its place), I put it under my left arm. It was heavy, with a strong smell of hot metal, sour gunpowder smoke and something oily. But I'd have to carry it, I couldn't just leave a weapon lying in the centre of the city.

'La-ter,' the wolf said evasively. 'In-a-safe-place. Where-are-you-stay-ing?'

'In a hotel. You'll like it. Let's go. Only stay by my leg all the way and try to look like a good dog.'

The wolf growled, but then immediately hid his fangs. He wasn't really such a big beast. In the darkness he could pass for an Alsatian.

To be honest, I wasn't expecting that to be the end of the day's unpleasantness. But we reached the hotel with no problems. There was a new receptionist looking bored behind the counter, but he didn't ask any questions: he'd obviously been given instructions and guidance about me. He gave the werewolf a curious look, but didn't make any comment about him either. I walked up to the desk and said:

'The key to the Dark suite upstairs, please.'

The receptionist didn't argue, but he did enquire:

'Could you not spend the night in a single suite?'

'I have an allergy to animal hair,' I replied.

I could hear voices and glasses clinking in the restaurant. Guests relaxing. But I didn't really feel like joining in a party at which a Bloody Mary was the most popular drink, and its name was taken quite literally.

CHAPTER 5

FIRST I UNLOCKED the wolf's door, and then mine. The wolf darted into the dark room, turned round and slammed the door shut with his muzzle. Immediately I heard a damp tearing sound, as if someone was ripping wet foam rubber into pieces. The werewolf had begun transforming back into a human.

I walked into my suite, switched on the light and closed the door. I put Shooter I, still smelling of gunpowder smoke, in the corner. I pulled off my bloody T-shirt and threw it in the rubbish bin. I took a look at myself in the mirror.

A handsome devil. One shoulder caked with blood and a terrible crimson scar where the bullets had entered.

But never mind. The important thing now was to patch up the wound. I'd apply an Avicenna spell now, and by morning there wouldn't be a single trace left. What was a bullet wound to us magicians? Pah! A mere trifle. But I closed the curtains across the windows anyway and switched off the ceiling light. If I got another bullet in the head, no magic would save me.

I stood under the shower, washing away the sweat and blood, and simply luxuriating in the warm streams of water, trying to fit all the pieces together.

The Dungeons of Scotland was an anomalous zone through which Power drained out of our world . . . to where? To the lower levels of the Twilight, obviously. That was clear enough.

Egor had been invited to Edinburgh as a potential Mirror Magician. That is, as a magician who would take the side of the Night Watch – Foma wouldn't work against his own interests! And so Foma was afraid of a serious battle in which the Dark Ones would get the upper hand. He was so afraid that he was trying to cover himself in every possible way. And Geser had apparently sent me to Scotland at his request. That was clear enough too.

But after that, things were a bit less clear!

Victor's blood had been sucked out – only a vampire, with his throat built like a vacuum pump, could drain a man dry like that in three or four minutes. But the vampire had immediately puked the blood into the trough. Why? Was he not hungry? But a vampire is never well enough fed to turn down another helping. Blood is not so much food as energy in the only form that vampires can absorb. A vampire can digest the blood he has drunk in fifteen minutes. Why pour it away? So they wouldn't think it was a vampire? But people don't believe in vampires anyway, and the form of the wound would make everything clear to the Watch.

Why had the watchman been killed? And in such a cruel manner? Was he getting under somebody's feet in the Dungeons? But there were plenty of ways to put a man out of action without doing him any harm. That Morpheus spell, for instance. The vampire Call. If it came to it, a blow across the head with a club – cruel, but not fatal! An incomprehensible, unnecessary murder . . .

And then everything really got tied into knots with the robot shooter! Sometimes we and the Dark Ones do use firearms. It's particularly common among young Others – a serious faith in heavy pistols, machine guns loaded with silver bullets, powerful grenades. But who could have brought a remote-controlled robot shooter to peaceful Edinburgh? I hadn't even known that such devices had already got past the prototype stage and been put into mass production in China. There was nothing complicated about them, of course – a rotating turret, a TV camera and a night-vision device. Whoever had set up the robot on my route had been hiding somewhere far away, staring into the screen of a control panel, twirling a joystick, pressing the 'fire' button. Any magician – or any vampire – could do it. Or any human being, come to that.

What was going on? Why was there so much aggression directed against me? Attacking a Higher Light One, and a member of the Night Watch, was a very serious step to take. Whoever had taken it must have nothing to lose . . .

As if someone had read my thoughts there was a knock at the door. I groaned, closed my dressing gown and went to open up.

Standing outside on the doorstep was a girl, or a very young woman – she was about fifteen, the age that can be interpreted in different ways. The girl was barefoot, her short black hair glistened and the black-and-red dressing gown seemed to be the only thing that she was wearing.

'May I come in?' she asked in the voice of an exemplary schoolgirl.

'I ought to have guessed straight away,' I said. 'Yes, come in.'

'And how ought you to have guessed?' the girl asked, lowering her eyes. 'By taking a better look at the figurine?'

'I didn't have a microscope with me. But a male wolf would certainly have pissed on the gun.'

'Oh, how crude you are – and a Light One, too!' the girl said with a frown. She walked over to an armchair, sat down and crossed her legs. 'Not pissed on it, marked it! You don't mind me coming in? I won't compromise you?'

'Unfortunately no, my child, you won't compromise me,' I said, opening the mini–bar. 'Would you like something?'

'Warm milk with honey.'

I nodded.

'All right, I'll just call the restaurant.'

'There isn't any room service here.'

'They'll make an exception for me,' I said confidently.

'Don't worry, pour me some wine. Red.'

I poured myself a whisky with ice. Then I spotted a fifty-gram bottle of Drambuie and poured that into the whisky. Just what I needed for a sound night's sleep – a large serving of 'rusty nail'. If the girl could do without her milk and honey, that was no reason for me to do without my honeyed whisky . . .

'So whose tail have you stepped on so hard?' the girl asked. 'That's the first time I've seen a robot rod blazing away like that . . .'

'It isn't a rod . . .'

'What's the difference?' My guest snorted. 'I'm a girl, I'm allowed to get it wrong.'

'You're not a girl, you're a werewolf.' I looked closely at her face. 'And I remember you.'

'You do?' All her bravado suddenly evaporated. 'You remember?'

'Of course. Your name's Galya. You were the one who noticed the witch Arina when she kidnapped my daughter.★

'You do remember,' the girl said, with a smile. 'And I thought you must have forgotten a long time ago.'

'No.' I handed her the glass of wine. 'Thank you. You really helped a lot that time.'

'You have a fine daughter.' She took a bold gulp of wine and frowned slightly. 'And your wife is very beautiful.'

I nodded and asked:

★This story is told in the second part of the book *The Twilight Watch*.

'What are you going to do now?'

'I don't know. Zabulon told me this is a very important assignment. He said I have to help you, even though you're a Light One. Protect you against everything.'

'But why you?' I asked. 'Pardon me for saying so, but you are very young. And you're only fifth level.'

'Because I . . .' Galya hesitated. 'Was I some help? Even though I am only fifth level?'

'Yes, you were.' I downed my cocktail in a single gulp. 'I'm sorry, I'm terribly sleepy.'

'So am I. But I feel so afraid in there. It's all red and black. Can I stay with you?' She looked at me and lowered her gaze in embarrassment.

I put down my glass and nodded.

'Of course. Will the sofa be all right for you? I'll give you a pillow and a blanket.'

'Light One . . .' the girl said slowly in an offended voice. 'All right, I'll leave these heavenly halls and go back to my anteroom in hell. It will probably feel more cheerful in any case!'

She walked proudly out of the room, clutching the glass of wine in her hand. I glanced into her doorway – her suite really was decorated in crimson and black. On the floor I saw scraps of black wool – the girl had transformed so quickly that she hadn't given her skin time to change completely.

As she closed her door, Galya stuck her tongue out at me.

And after I closed mine, I started laughing quietly.

Acceleration, emancipation and the sexual revolution! No, I won't lie, I liked the idea that this girl had fallen for me four years earlier. Or maybe not four years earlier, maybe she had fallen in love afterwards. Retrospectively, so to speak. When the flood of hormones brought the time for romantic emotions and vague desires.

And how hard she'd tried to seduce me! Crossing her legs like that, allowing her dressing gown to slip, making those eyes at me.

Yes, sometimes I felt it was a great shame that I was a Light One . . .

But I wanted to sleep so badly that I felt absolutely no desire to indulge in exciting fantasies about sex with a young female werewolf. I posted a few guardian and defence spells entirely automatically — it was the same kind of ritual as cleaning my teeth. Then I climbed into bed and listened to the sounds outside the windows — the city was still enjoying itself, the city was in no hurry to get to sleep. I took my cellphone, switched it to the music function and closed my eyes. The age of cassette players had gone the same way as gramophone records, the age of minidiscs had never happened, and now the age of CDs was on the way out. Now there was just the cold code name MP3. But we'd got used to that. It didn't bother us any more.

This how the light begins
A dark night with no special signs.
But someone has entered into that gloom.
You still don't realise it will be the same way for you.
Yes, this sounds crazy, yes, it sounds like a pipe dream.
But this is exactly how the light begins, how the fear ends,
How the sound is born.

This is how the fear ends.
And you have drunk the potion of poisoned herbs
From the carefully hidden books.
Now each shout you make is also a clue.
So much unhappiness and misfortune. So much meaningless
    suffering.

But this is the only way the light begins, the only way the
    fear ends,
The way the sound is born.

Soon is the day of funerals,
So dig that trench to the roaring of thieves and cawing of
    ravens.
Bury your own death,
Tell yourself a fortune of life and of light.
The first trace left. The last friend lost.
This is how the light begins, how the fear ends,
How the sound is born . . .*

I fell asleep. And in my dreams there was no one shooting.
There was no one cutting off heads with a blunt guillotine. And
there was no one chasing anyone else.

There wasn't a young girl in a silk dressing gown, either. There
wasn't even any room for Sveta. Just someone's curious, hostile
gaze that was fixed on me and never moved.

It's never nice to be woken by a phone call. Not even if it's the
woman you love or an old friend who's calling.

It was already light outside. I lifted my head up off the pillow
and looked round the bedroom – everything was fine, except that
I'd kicked the blanket off onto the floor during the night. I reached
out for my phone and looked at the number.

Instead of a number, the screen on the phone simply said
'Zabulon', even though the Dark One's number was not in my
address book, of course.

'Hello, Dark One.'

*Kirill Komarov, 'This is how the sound is born'.

'How's your health, Anton?' Zabulon enquired sympathetically. 'Has the shoulder healed up?'

'Everything's fine, thank you.' I touched the place where there had been a wound the day before. The skin there was pink and it itched.

'I'm glad my gift was of some use,' Zabulon continued in the same polite tone. 'I'd like to share a bit of information with you. There are no candidates for the role of Mirror in Great Britain. There is one in France, one in Poland, two in Italy . . . I can't imagine why Thomas chose to drag Egor all the way to Edinburgh.'

Clear enough. My naive attempt at cunning had failed. Zabulon had dug up the truth after all.

'I hope that he won't be required,' I said.

'Of course, of course,' Zabulon agreed. 'It really is quite disgraceful to exploit the poor boy again in the interests of the Light . . . Anton, my dear fellow, what is actually going on there? I heard there was another murder yesterday. Has someone else has his blood drained?'

'Yes,' I said, sitting up in bed. 'Another one. He was beheaded with a model guillotine.'

'And what did they do with the blood?' Zabulon enquired.

'Drained it into the bucket used for washing the floor.'

'I see.'

'I'm glad you understand something at least,' I said.

'Don't be so modest, Anton . . .' Zabulon said and paused. 'Ask Foma how long it is since he visited his neighbour in the grave.'

'What's that?' I said, thinking that I must have misheard. 'His neighbour's grave?'

'How long is it since he visited his neighbour in the grave?' Zabulon said with a chuckle and cut the connection.

Swearing under my breath, I got up and set out for the bathroom. I tidied myself up and took a cold shower, then put on a short-sleeved shirt and a pair of jeans. Somehow I wasn't in the mood any more for frivolous shorts and a T-shirt – if the weather had allowed, I would have put on a sweater or a jacket.

My phone rang again.

'Hello, Geser,' I said after glancing at the display.

'How are you getting on?'

'The shoulder's healed,' I said, absolutely certain that Geser knew everything.

'Which shoulder's that?'

'Yesterday someone shot at me.' I told him in brief what had happened. And there was such a deadly silence that I blew into the microphone, as if it was an old-style telephone.

'I'm thinking,' Geser said drily. 'Thinking . . .'

'Maybe I should go and get some breakfast first?'

'Yes, do,' said the boss. 'And then find Foma. Tell him there's no time left for half-truths and dissembling. He has to check the Rune.'

'Which one exactly?' I asked in the tone of someone who checks Runes every day of the week.

'Merlin's Rune.'

'Ah . . .' I said, slowly beginning to understand something. 'Merlin's Rune . . . isn't that in the grave?'

It was a shot in the dark, but from Geser's silence I realised that I'd hit the bull's eye.

'Anton, how do you . . .' He swore briefly. 'Find Foma and have a completely frank talk with him! I'll get in touch with him too.'

'Yessir!' I rapped and put the phone away my pocket.

Well, how about that!

So there was a Rune. A Rune in a grave. The grave of Merlin.

But Merlin was a mythological character, wasn't he? King Arthur, the Knights of the Round Table, Merlin . . . None of them had ever existed!

Aha. But the Great Geser and Thomas the Rhymer didn't exist, either. Neither did crazed vampires and young girl werewolves, Light Healers and obstinate young magicians who had acquired the Higher level of Power by some oversight . . .

Strangely enough, my mood was rapidly improving. Maybe because things had finally started moving? I ran down the stairs, said good morning to the previous day's receptionist and opened the door of the restaurant.

There wasn't a single human being in there. Only two young vampires and a girl werewolf.

The vampires were eating carpaccio. Galya was eating an omelette. That was surprising – usually after two consecutive transformations werewolves eat meat by the kilogram.

'Good morning,' I greeted my fellow guests.

The vampires smiled crookedly and nodded. Galya began prodding at the omelette with her fork. It was obvious why: the hormonal rush had receded, and now she was feeling embarrassed. She'd managed to get some clothes from somewhere – black trousers, a white blouse, a little jacket with short sleeves. Something like the things that schoolgirls wear in Japanese cartoons.

'Hi,' I said, sitting down beside her. 'Had a good rest?'

'Uh-huh.'

'Not bothered by any nightmares? That's a frightening kind of room you've got – I'm not surprised you didn't want to stay in it. The designer tried a bit too hard, don't you think?'

Galya gave me a thoughtful look. She put a piece of omelette in her mouth, chewed it and said:

'Thank you, Light One. But I don't really fancy you, honestly. Would you like me to bring you some food? Look after you a bit?'

'Yes, do,' I agreed.

The girl went over to the smorgasbord – omelettes and fried eggs in heated containers, bread, salami, cheese, meat, a bunch of green herbs. In the corner by the door into the kitchen there was a small refrigerator. I wondered if the vampire's blood was kept in there? Or did the barman pour it for them in the evening? The bar counter was empty now: even the beer pumps were draped with colourful coverings.

My phone rang again.

'Oh, let me get something to eat,' I groaned, taking the phone out of my pocket.

'Anton?'

'Hello, Foma.'

'Are you up already, Anton?'

'Yes, I'm just having breakfast.'

'I'll send a car round for you. Can you be outside your hotel in about five minutes?'

'Er . . .' I said, gaping at Semyon, who had appeared in the doorway. He looked radiant and he waved to me gleefully. 'All right if I bring a friend?'

'That Dark One? The girl werewolf? Better not.'

'No. A friend of mine has just arrived from Moscow. A Light Magician.'

Foma sighed.

'All right. Both of you come. The driver knows where to go.'

'There's something I have to ask you,' I warned him.

Lermont sighed again.

'I'm afraid there's also something that I have to tell you. Get a move on, I'm waiting.'

I put the phone away and smiled at Galya, who had just reached me with the plates and the coffee pot. At the same time Semyon started moving towards me from the door.

'Oh! Galya Dobronravova!' Semyon exclaimed, breaking into a broad smile. 'I remember, I do . . . How's school going? How's Marina Petrovna?'

The little girl's face came out in red blotches. She put the dishes down on the table.

'Can you imagine?' Semyon told me in a confidential voice. 'Galya took a dislike to her chemistry teacher and started harassing her. She would transform and then wait for her outside the house in the evenings, snarling and showing her teeth. Can you believe it? But the husband of this modest teacher of chemistry turned out to be a modest police patrol officer. And on the third evening, the way it always happens in fairy tales, he came out, rather concerned about aggressive dogs, to meet his wife on her way home from work. He saw our little Galya snarling in the bushes, realised that she wasn't a dog but a wolf, grabbed his pistol and fired at her, emptying the entire clip. Two bullets, by the way, got Galya in her little backside as she was hightailing it away from the infuriated guardian of law and order. There a was great fuss, we worked out what was going on, paid Galya a visit at home and had a little chat . . . It was okay, though, we managed without the Inquisition. The whole business was played down.'

The girl turned and ran out of the dining room. The vampires watched her go, with thoughtful expressions on their faces.

'You shouldn't be so hard on her,' I said. 'Yesterday she faced bullets to save my life.'

Semyon grabbed a piece of salami and chewed it. He sighed.

'Pure soya . . . It's good that she faced up to the bullets. But what about persecuting her teacher?'

'That's bad,' I said gloomily

We piled into the taxi that was waiting for us, taking the robot shooter wrapped up in a dressing gown. The metal tripod stuck out, but that didn't concern us too much.

The driver was a human being. It looked as if the Edinburgh Watch made much greater use of paid human staff than we did.

We drove quickly out of the tourist centre and set off in the general direction of the bay.

'Thanks for calling me over,' said Semyon, gazing out of the window with undisguised delight. 'I'd been stuck in Moscow too long . . . So tell me, what's going on?'

I started telling him. At first Semyon listened with the condescending interest of an experienced old soldier listening to a raw recruit's horror stories. But then he turned serious.

'Anton, are you sure? I mean that Power flows down there?'

'Shall I ask the driver to turn back and drive past the Dungeons?'

Semyon sighed and shook his head. He said just two words:

'A vault.'

'Meaning?'

'A hiding place. Where something very important is hidden.'

'Semyon, I don't really understand . . .'

'Anton, imagine that you are a very, very powerful magician. And, for instance, you can stroll around on the fifth level of the Twilight.'

'I can't.'

'Imagine it?'

'Stroll around down there. I can imagine it easily enough.'

'Then imagine it. You can go deeper than any of the Others that you know. You suddenly need to hide something that's very valuable. A magical artefact, a powerful spell – even a sack of gold, if you like. So what do you do? Bury it in the ground? It will be found. Especially if you're hiding a magical object: it would create a disturbance in the Power around itself, no matter how you covered it up. Then you take this thing and go down deep into the Twilight . . .'

'And I leave it there, say on the fifth level,' I said and nodded. 'But an object from our world would be pushed back up . . .'

'That's why you need a constant stream of Power. Well . . . it's like putting an object that floats on the bottom of a bath of water. Left on its own, it will surface. But of you keep it pressed down with a stream of water . . .'

'I understand, Semyon.'

'Do you have any ideas about who hid what down there?'

'Yes,' I said. 'Only first I'll ask Foma about it.'

The phone in my pocket rang again. Would it never give me any peace . . .

'Yes?' I said, without looking at the screen.

'Anton, this is Geser.'

The boss's voice sounded strange somehow. As if he was bewildered.

'Hello.'

'I've had a word with Foma, and he's promised to be frank with you. And with Semyon, now it's come to that . . .'

'Thank you, Boris Ignatievich.'

'Anton . . .' Geser began and paused. 'There's another thing . . . We've dug back into Victor Prokhorov's past. And we've found something.'

'Well?' I asked, already sure that I shouldn't expect anything good.

'Did his photo look familiar to you?'

'An ordinary-looking young guy. A statistically average Moscow face.' I caught myself starting to get rude, the way I always do when I get agitated. 'Every second guy in every college looks like that.'

'Try to picture Victor a bit younger. As a teenager.'

I made an honest effort. And answered;

'You get a statistically average Moscow schoolboy. In every school . . .'

'But you've almost certainly seen him, Anton. And not just once.

He was in the same class at school as your neighbour Kostya Saushkin. He knew him very well – you could say they were friends. He probably dropped in to see him at home quite often. I think sometimes he must have run into you, waving his brief-case about and laughing for no reason at all.'

'It's not possible,' I whispered. Geser's story had flabbergasted me so completely that I wasn't even amazed by the untypically colourful way he'd told it. Waving his briefcase about and laughing? Yes, more than likely. If there are children living on your stairwell in the apartment building you're bound to stumble over their briefcases, hear them laughing and step in little patches of chewing gum. But who remembers the faces . . . ?

'Anton, it's true. The only vampire Victor ever knew was Kostya Saushkin.'

'But Geser, Kostya was killed.'*

'Yes, I know,' said Geser. 'At least, that's what we all thought.'

'He couldn't have survived,' I said. 'There's no way he could have. Three hundred kilometres above the Earth. There isn't any Power there. He burned up in the atmosphere. He burned up, you understand, Geser? Burned up!'

'Stop shouting,' Geser told me calmly. 'Yes, he burned up. We watched his spacesuit on radar right to the very end. But what we don't know, Anton, is if Kostya Saushkin was still in that space-suit. The altitude was quite different by then. We have to think. We have to calculate.'

He cut off the call. I looked at Semyon, who shook his head sadly.

'I heard, Anton.'

'Well?'

'If you haven't seen the body, don't be in a hurry to bury it.'

*   *   *

---

* This story is told in the third part of the book *The Twilight Watch*.

Foma Lermont lived in the suburbs. In a quiet, wealthy district of cosy cottages and well-tended gardens. The head of the Edinburgh Night Watch met us in his own garden. He was sitting in a wooden arbour entwined with ivy, setting out a game of patience on a coffee table. In his crumpled grey trousers and polo shirt he looked like a typically placid gentleman of pre-pension age. Surround him with a crowd of grandsons and granddaughters and he would have been the elderly head of a large family. When Semyon and I arrived, Lermont politely got to his feet and greeted us. Then he swept the cards up into a heap and muttered:

'It's not working out . . .'

'Foma, I think the time has come for straight talking,' I said, and glanced at Semyon. 'You don't object if my friend is present?'

'Not at all. Geser has vouched for him.'

'Foma, today I got a call from Zabulon of the Moscow Day Watch.'

'I know who Zabulon is.'

'He told me . . . he *asked* me to ask you when was the last time you visited your neighbour in the grave.'

'Last night,' Lermont replied in a low voice.

'And Geser . . . he asked about the Rune. Merlin's Rune.'

'The Rune's not in the grave,' Lermont said. He looked across at Semyon and asked, 'What do you know about Merlin?'

'There was a magician of that name,' said Semyon, scratching the back of his head. 'A Great Light Magician. A long time ago.'

Lermont looked at me and asked:

'How about you?'

'I always thought Merlin was a mythological character,' I replied honestly.

'You're both half right,' Lermont said, smiling. 'The Great Light Magician Merlin really is a mythological character. The real Merlin was . . . not so nice. Yes, of course, he did help the young Arthur to draw the sword out of the stone and become king. Although Arthur had no right to the throne at all . . . that's just between you and me. Merlin was not a thoroughly black-hearted villain. He simply used any means available to achieve his ends. If he needed to put a king who would listen to him on the throne, then he did. If the king had to inspire respect and love in his subjects – and of course he had to, why suffer unnecessary complications? – then he educated the king to be noble and high-minded. And the king could have his own royal toys to play with: a beautiful round table and brave knights. And did you know that Arthur's ruin at the hands of a child born on a certain day was predicted even before Mordred was born? And do you know what the noble Arthur did?'

'I'm afraid to imagine.'

Lermont laughed. And then he recited off by heart:

'"Meanwhile did King Arthur order to be brought to him all the infants born to noble ladies and noble lords on the first day of May, for Merlin had revealed to King Arthur that the one who would destroy him and all his lands had been born into the world on the first day of May. And therefore did he order them all to be sent to him on pain of death, and many sons of lords and knights were sent to the king. Mordred was also sent to him by the wife of King Lot. He did put them all in a ship and launched it to sea, and some were four weeks from birth, and some younger still. And by the will of fate the ship was driven ashore where a castle stood, and shattered, and they were almost all killed, only Mordred was cast up by a wave and picked up by a good man and raised until he did reach the age of fourteen years from birth, and then he brought him to the court, as is told hereafter, at the end of the book *Morte d'Arthur*.

'"And many lords and barons of Arthur's kingdom were outraged that their children had been taken away and killed, but they laid the blame for this more on Merlin than on Arthur. And either out of fear or out of love, they did keep the peace.'"

'A worthy successor to the good King Herod,' Semyon murmured.

I didn't say anything. I was remembering a cartoon film that my little Nadya was very fond of. About the young King Arthur. About the funny, forgetful magician Merlin. I imagined the sequel, about how Arthur, egged on by Merlin, orders wailing, screaming infants who can't understand what's going on to be loaded into an old, useless ship . . .

So this was the symbol of purity and nobility? The much-vaunted King Arthur of glorious legend?

'Not much like that fine young boy in the warm-hearted Disney cartoon, is it?' Lermont asked, as if he had read my thoughts. 'Or like that eccentric magician who took him under his wing? But you mustn't blame Arthur. It was his destiny. That was the kind of teacher he had.'

'How did Mordred survive?' I asked.

Lermont's eyes glinted ironically.

'That's hard to say. How did the boy Arthur become heir to the throne? Perhaps Mordred didn't survive. But there were people who told some boy that he was Arthur's son and his father had tried to kill him when he was a baby. What does it matter who he really was by birth? The important thing was who he thought he was.'

'Is he still alive?'

'Mordred? Of course not. He was only a human being. And so was Arthur. He departed this world a long time ago.'

'And Merlin?'

'He withdrew into the Twilight for ever . . .' Lermont said, with a nod. 'But Merlin was a genuinely great magician. I think he was the greatest magician of all time. I think,' he said with a sideways glance at Semyon, 'that Merlin was a *zero-point* magician.'

I nodded. I understood that. A magical 'temperature' of zero. Merlin didn't contribute a single drop to the streams of Power that permeate the world, he had absolutely none of it. And that was precisely why he was a great magician. He absorbed the Power of others, the Power that was diffused in space – and used it to work miracles.

No other magician so powerful had been born in the world since then.

But one such enchantress had been born. My daughter, Nadya.

'Merlin didn't leave many artefacts,' Lermont continued. 'He created them playfully, as if it cost him no effort at all. Excalibur, of course. Merlin's cloak. Merlin's chalice. Merlin's crystal. Merlin's staff.'

'He didn't bother himself too much about finding names for them, then?' Semyon said, with a laugh. Then he suddenly fell silent.

'Merlin's Rune?' I asked.

Lermont shook his head.

'Merlin's Rune is only a key, kept in Merlin's grave, twenty-two miles from . . . from what is believed to be the grave of Thomas the Rhymer. Naturally, Merlin himself is not in the grave, but some traces of the great magician are preserved there. You may think me sentimental, but I often visit my own grave. Although I have never liked going to Merlin's. I simply relied on the protective spells. But that was a mistake. The grave has been robbed.'

'I thought Merlin's grave was in Brittany,' said Semyon.

'No, it lies to the south of Edinburgh. Near the little town of Peebles, at the confluence of the Tweed and the Powsel. It's not very far from here.'

'And what does this Rune consist of?' I asked.

'A stone. Charged to the hilt with magic and scratched all over with almost illegible signs. Merlin's Rune . . .' Lermont hesitated and looked round us all, but continued nonetheless '. . . is the key, or rather, the main part of the key that allows access to a hiding place that Merlin once set up on the bottom of a lake. The lake has vanished long ago, but the hiding place, of course, is still there.'

'A hiding place in the Twilight?' I asked.

'Yes.'

'Fifth level?'

Lermont sighed.

'I could get down to the fifth level myself, my young friend. Or I could call in Geser. Or Andrew. Higher Ones can be found who are capable of reaching the fifth level. But this hiding place was made by Merlin. It's right down at the very bottom. Which means it's on the seventh level.'

'Oh, my sainted aunt!' Semyon exclaimed in delight. 'The seventh! So the seventh level *does* exist! It's not a fairy tale, then?'

'It exists all right. Only I don't know anybody alive on this planet who is capable of getting there . . .' Lermont shrugged and spread his hands wide.

'What about the key? And the Rune?'

'As for the Rune . . . I've read the inscription – it gives instructions on how to get past a sentinel on the fifth level. But after that you have to go further. I can't do that.'

'Have you at least tried?' I asked.

'What for?' Lermont asked, throwing his hands up. 'Why go down into the Twilight for Merlin's heritage? Anton, you must have some idea now of what he was like . . . do you think there's anything good down there?'

I shrugged.

'The hiding place is believed to contain the Crown of All Things,' said Lermont. 'Sounds tempting, doesn't it? But somehow I think that the Crown of All Things is really the End of All Things.'

Semyon opened his mouth to say something, but then changed his mind.

'And what are the other parts of the key?' I asked. 'Merlin's Crystal Mace? Or perhaps Merlin's Old Shoe?'

Lermont shook his head.

'That's the most unpleasant part of the story. You've already realised that Power goes pouring down out of our world to the lowest level of the Twilight from the spot above the hiding place, haven't you?'

'Yes.'

'Well then, if you try to enter the Twilight when you're inside the Dungeons you can only get as far as the third level. After that there's a barrier, a whirlpool of Power. It's simultaneously a load that holds the hiding place down at the bottom of creation and a defence against the curious.'

'Not too many of the curious would even be able to get down to the third level . . .' Semyon mumbled, scratching the back of his head. 'Sorry, I'll keep quiet!'

'Well, Merlin's Rune won't help you get past the third level,' Foma went on. 'I was certain that no one, apart from me, knew the secret, and I only discovered it by chance when there was an accident beside the bridge: a young woman fell and ruptured an artery on a sharp metal rod . . .'

'Blood,' I said.

'Yes,' Foma said. 'If someone dies from loss of blood, then the Twilight is temporarily saturated with energy. The whirlpool on the third level calms down and you can get past it and go on deeper.'

'Does the person have to die?' I asked.

'I don't know. I haven't checked, as you can understand. Preserved blood is no use, we know that for certain. That's why the killing in the Dungeons put me on my guard. But the protective spells on Merlin's grave hadn't been touched. No one had approached the grave, no one had tried to open it. And I relaxed, I put it all down to coincidence. But last night I decided to go to the grave.'

'And you found it had been opened using a remote-controlled device?' I said. 'Right? Something like those robots they use at nuclear power stations.'

'How did you know?' Lermont asked.

'Yesterday someone shot at me with that,' I said, nodding towards the tripod with the rifle, which Semyon had leaned against the outside of the arbour. 'An automatic radio-controlled shooting device.'

Lermont glanced at the weapon without the slightest interest. He smiled bitterly.

'We've got old, Anton. We pride ourselves on having got old . . . Geser, Al-Ashaf, Rustam, Giovanni, me – all the other ancient ones who remember the world without electricity, steam trains and gunpowder. The oldest magicians who know the most and are almost the most powerful. We have underestimated the new generation. Rockets, robots, telephones . . .' He chewed on his lips and looked at his neat little house, with the same melancholy expression that I had sometimes seen in Geser's eyes.

It's probably that melancholy look that allows me to forgive Geser for everything he does in his job as head of the Night Watch.

'One of the young generation,' Foma went on. 'One of the young generation, who know how to use technology and are not afraid of it.'

'I think I know who it is,' I whispered. 'Kostya Saushkin.'

'The Higher Vampire who took the *Fuaran*?' Lermont asked with a frown. 'I know that story. But he was destroyed!'

'Nobody saw the body,' I said. 'In any case, he wouldn't be afraid to go down after Merlin's legacy. And he'd use technology without the slightest hesitation. And as well as that, he must hate me. Enough to try to shoot me. It was my fault! I sent him off to die. He survived – and decided to take his revenge.'

'Anton, don't be in such a hurry,' Semyon said reasonably. He explained apologetically to Foma: 'Please don't be angry, Mr Lermont! Anton is still young and hot-headed. Yesterday he thought that Kostya was dead. Now all of a sudden he's changed his mind. But what we have to worry about is something else. What do you think, Mr Lermont? Has the villain of the piece already found Merlin's hiding place?'

'Merlin was a magician of the old school,' Lermont answered after a moment's thought. 'A key has to have three elements. Three is a magic number, a number of Power. Three, seven and eleven.'

'Yes, prime numbers,' Semyon agreed, 'That's clear enough. But what about the third part of the key?'

'I discovered the second part by accident,' Lermont said. 'I don't know anything about the third. I can only assume that it must exist. I don't even know what it is – an object, an incantation, a sacrifice, a time of day. Perhaps you have to enter the Twilight naked on the night of the full moon, holding a thistle flower between your teeth. Merlin was a great joker.'

We said nothing for a while. Then Lermont gave a forced smile.

'All right, my friends. I have revealed all the secrets that I had. I can't see any point in panicking ahead of time. Merlin's hiding place will surrender its secret to a Higher Other of immense power who spills someone else's blood in the Dungeons and gets his hands on the third part of the key. But what that third part is, no one knows. Let's all calm down, go inside and have a cup of tea.'

'The English tradition of tea-drinking!' Semyon said respectfully.

Foma gave him a mocking glance and corrected him.

'Not English. Don't forget that you're in Scotland now. You are welcome guests in my home—'

'I have just one more question,' I said, interrupting Lermont. 'Why did you invite Egor to Edinburgh?'

'You mean the young illusionist?' Lermont asked, with a sigh. 'I decided to take out an insurance policy. If there's a serious conflict, then the first to suffer will be our Night Watch. I don't have that many battle magicians. A Mirror is the best thing that can be used to oppose—'

'Oppose whom?' I asked, when Lermont broke off in mid-phrase

The distant forefather of the Russian poet Lermontov gave me a look of annoyance so intense that I felt the full force of the same hot temper that brought a premature end to the Russian poet's life.

'Merlin! Now are you satisfied?'

'You believe that he . . .'

'The one thing that Merlin always valued above all others was himself. And he could have given the name of the Crown of All Things to the means for bringing him back from oblivion. It would be his kind of joke.'

'Nothing of the sort has ever happened,' said Semyon, shaking his head.

'No, it hasn't. But there have never been any other magicians like Merlin. His essence — his soul, if you like — could be slumbering somewhere down there, on the seventh level . . . until a sufficiently powerful magician can reach it. To put it crudely, until a stupid body arrives to provide Merlin's black soul with a new receptacle! Would you be glad to see the Great Merlin back in the world? I certainly wouldn't! And that's the reason I need a potential Mirror Magician close at hand. Perhaps that might do the trick. He might possibly become a Mirror and destroy Merlin. What don't you like about that, Gorodetsky?'

'But you can't do that!' I exclaimed with a feeling of anguish that surprised even me. Everything was muddled together in my head – Kostya, whom I had killed and who might still be alive; the Dark Magician Merlin, thirsting for resurrection, the totally unsuspecting Egor . . . 'Ever since he was a child we've exploited him for our operations! And now are we going to throw him into hell, use the lad to protect ourselves against Merlin? He's nothing but a boy!'

'All right!' said Lermont, also raising his voice. 'You've advanced a convincing argument! Now let me lay out in front of you the personal files of all the potential Mirror Magicians. Will you point the finger? Choose a different candidate? There's a girl of nine, a boy of fifteen, a young husband and father, a pregnant woman . . . they never live to old age in an indeterminate state, sooner or later they choose the Light or the Dark! They're all young, all of them almost children! Will you take the choice on yourself and relieve me of this appalling responsibility?'

'Yes!' I shouted, leaping to my feet. 'Yes, I will! I'll relieve you. Bring out your files, Mr Foma Lermont!'

'I'll bring them this very moment!' he said, also getting to his feet. 'You choose, you choose!'

We stood there, glaring angrily at each other, and it was a while before we realised that both of us had tears running down our faces.

CHAPTER 6

I DON'T KNOW if Lermont really would have brought the files or
not. And I have even less idea what I would have done if he had.
Probably I would have chosen a different candidate for the role
of the Mirror Magician.

But we weren't given a chance to do any of that.

First I noticed Lermontov's face change. He was looking away
from me, in the direction of the road.

Then I heard the roar of an engine and turned round.

A little white van hurtling along the road suddenly turned and
broke easily though the symbolic wooden fence surrounding
Lermont's cottage. It braked to a halt with a wild squeal, throwing
up earth and gravel from under its wheels.

The rear doors of the van had been removed earlier. Two men
jumped out of it and a third, left inside, opened fire from a machine
gun mounted on a swivel.

The first to react was Foma. He had put up a shield as soon as
the van came flying into his garden. Or maybe he hadn't put it
up? Perhaps it was just a guard spell that had been installed a long
time ago in order to deal with this kind of invasion?

The machine gun roared and rattled, the sound resonating in

the back of the van and reaching us as if it had been amplified by a huge tin megaphone. The sound was accompanied by a stream of lead. But the bullets didn't reach their target. They halted gently, hung in the air for a second like some special effect in an action movie, and then fell to the ground.

The two who had jumped out, both masked in black hoods, dropped to the ground and opened fire with sub-machine guns. As yet, no one had got out of the front of the van.

Were they idiots, or what?

Semyon waved his hands a few times. I noticed the harmless Morpheus, which would give the attackers about ten seconds to carry on playing at soldiers, and the instantly acting Opium. But the spells didn't work and the firing continued, with the bullets getting stuck in mid-air halfway between us. I looked closely – no, they weren't Others. Just ordinary people. But each of them had the gentle glow of a protective amulet on his chest.

'Just don't kill them!' Lermont cried out when I raised my hand.

I only had two Triple Blades ready and waiting for instant action – I hadn't been expecting to wind up in a shoot-out like this. I flung both, aiming at the large machine gun. The first charge missed, but the second struck home, reducing the weapon to a heap of shredded metal. The racket quietened down a bit – now only the men with sub-machine guns were firing, but rather uncertainly, as if they had just discovered the invisible barrier. That was good. Every defence has its limit of saturation and the machine-gun fire would have put it out of action fairly quickly.

We had been attacked by men! Ordinary men, equipped with protective amulets. An act that was not only absolutely unheard of but also stupid. It's one thing to shoot a magician from ambush, using a remote-controlled weapon. But like this, face-to-face, three gunmen against three magicians . . . what were they hoping to achieve?

Simply to distract our attention!

I swung round just in time to see the white smoke trail heading in our direction. The rocket had been launched from the roof of a high-rise building standing almost a kilometre away. But it was clearly controllable, and it was coming straight for the arbour.

'Foma!' I shouted, throwing a Freeze in the direction of the rocket on the off chance. But the temporal stasis spell either missed its target, or the rocket had also been protected against magic – nothing happened.

'Into the Twilight!' Lermont shouted.

Sometimes it's better to do as you're told than to think up your own original moves. I stepped into the Twilight, sinking down to the second level almost immediately. Lermont was there beside me – he too considered the first level an insufficiently secure defence. But to my surprise, he didn't stop on the second level – he waved his hand and went down deeper. Perplexed, I followed him down to the third level. What need was there for this? A powerful explosion in the real world might be felt on the first level, but it wouldn't reach the second . . . and if Foma suspected the unthinkable, the most terrible thing possible, then a nuclear blast scorched through the material of all levels of the Twilight . . .

The grey gloom was lit up by a white flame. The ground under our feet trembled slightly. Only slightly – but it trembled!

'Where's Semyon?' I shouted.

Lermont merely shrugged. We waited a few more seconds for the splinters to stop flying, the flame to die away and the smoking fragments of the arbour to stop falling in the real world.

And then we went back out.

Lermont's neat and tidy cottage had lost all the glass in its windows and was covered with a fine sprinkling of debris. A hefty branch torn off the nearest tree by the explosion was protruding from a window on the second floor.

The small van was lying where it had been tossed on to its side. There were two motionless bodies beside it. A third man, the machine-gunner or perhaps the driver, who had prudently stayed put in his cabin, was slowly crawling away towards the fence, dragging his useless legs behind him.

I didn't feel any particular pity for him. He was an ordinary bandit who had been used to distract our attention from the rocket attack. He'd known what he was getting into.

Where the arbour had stood there was a small crater, strewn with white scraps of wood. The playing cards were soaring and circling above our heads – a capricious chance had tossed them up into the air instead of incinerating them.

We found Semyon right beside the van. He was inside a transparent glowing sphere that looked as if it had been carved in crystal. The sphere was slowly rolling along and Semyon, with his arms and legs held out, was turning over and over with it. His pose was such a hilarious parody of the picture *The Golden Section* that I giggled stupidly. Squat and short-legged, Semyon looked nothing like the muscular athlete drawn by Leonardo da Vinci.

'A very uncomfortable spell,' Lermont said in relief. 'But then, it is reliable.'

The crystal sphere cracked all over and disintegrated in a cloud of steam. Semyon, who was upside down at that moment, nimbly swung round and landed on his feet. He stuck a finger in his ear and asked:

'Do they always do that round here on Saturdays, Mr Lermont? Or is it just in honour of our arrival?'

Lermont took no notice of this simple piece of wit. He inclined his head to one side, as if he were listening to someone's voice, and frowned. And his frown became deeper and deeper.

Then, with just a couple of gestures, he created the glowing frame of a portal in front of himself, and said:

'Follow me, gentlemen. I am afraid all this was merely a diversion.'

I didn't get time to ask what he intended to do about the over-turned van, the demolished arbour and the crawling bandit who was already out in the street, where the neighbours could see him. A second portal opened beside the first, and Others began jumping out of it, one after another.

They weren't simply Light Ones from the Night Watch – they were dressed in police uniforms, with bulletproof vests and helmets, and they were holding their machine pistols at the ready!

Well now, Thomas the Rhymer, aren't you a fine one for the blather! We have underestimated technology! I can see just how badly you underestimate it . . .

Lermont stepped into the first portal. I hung back for a moment, waiting for Semyon, but he suddenly stopped, with his stare fixed on a gaunt man with red hair.

'Kevin! You old fogey!'

'Simon, you old blockhead!' the redhead shouted in delight. 'Where are you going? Hang on!'

They put their arms round each other and started hammering each other on the back with all the enthusiasm of those crazy rabbits in the advert for electric batteries.

'Later, we'll catch up on everything later,' Semyon muttered, freeing himself from Kevin's embraces. 'Look, the portal's getting cold. I brought you some wine from Sebastopol – remember it? Sparkling muscat, here!'

I spat and shook my head. What sort of thing was that to say – 'later, later . . .' In the movies any character who said that to an old friend was irrevocably doomed to die soon.

I could only be glad that we weren't characters in an action movie.

I stepped in through the frame of the portal.

A dense white glow all around. A feeling of lightness that could only be compared with what cosmonauts experience. Mysterious paths inaccessible to human beings.

What were those others in police uniforms going to do there? Wipe clean the memories of any chance witnesses, remove all traces of the explosion, interrogate the attackers if they survived? The basic day-to-day routine work of the Watches.

But who had dared to do it? Attacking a member of a Watch was already an act of insanity. But to attack the head of a Watch, plus two foreign magicians, was absolutely unheard-of. And to use human beings to do it . . .

I suddenly realised quite clearly that the Frenchman I had met in the Dungeons had also been a human being. Not a Higher Magician who had concealed his true nature from me. Just an ordinary man. But incredibly cunning and cool, a brilliant actor. Not the same sort of pawn as these bandits who had been sent to their death. Perhaps it was him who had fired the rocket at us?

And then the vampire. Was it really Kostya? Had he really survived after all?

And to top everything off there were the protective amulets on the bandits, which had won them time. Vampires weren't capable of creating amulets. That was the work of a magician, an enchantress or a witch!

Just who were we up against here? Who was trying to break into the Twilight to get his hands on Merlin's legacy?

And was he capable of going down to the seventh level?

As always, the portal came to an end suddenly. The white glow contracted into a frame, I stepped through it – and I was immediately grabbed by the shoulder and jerked sharply down to the left, onto the floor behind the cover of an improvised barricade consisting of several overturned tables.

Just in time. A bullet went whistling over my head.

I was in the Dungeons of Scotland. In one of the first rooms.

Lermont was beside me, sheltering behind the barricade, and I had been dragged to the floor by a dark-skinned Other. Judging from the number of spells that he had 'teed-up' on his fingers, he was a battle magician.

Another shot rang out. The shooting was coming from the open door leading into the next room.

'Foma, what's happened?' I asked, looking at him in bewilderment. 'Why are we lying on the floor? We should put up a Shield . . .'

Lermont didn't stir a finger, but a barrier appeared at the door, sealing it off. Before I even had time to feel amazed at the Scottish magician's stupidity and delighted with my own astuteness, there was another shot, and the bullet whistled by over our heads. The barrier hadn't held it back.

'I beg your pardon, I was a bit hasty there . . .' I muttered. 'How about going through the Twilight?

'The same problem as with the rocket,' Lermont explained. 'The bullets are enchanted down to the second level.'

'Let's go through the third.'

'There's a barrier on the third!' Lermont reminded me. I felt ashamed and said no more.

The dark-skinned magician half-stood and hurled several spells into the corridor. I spotted Opium, Freeze and Bugaboo. The reply was another shot. With that same precise, mechanical rhythm . . .

'It's a machine!' I said quickly. 'Lermont, it's the same kind of machine that fired at me!'

'So what? It's protected against minor spells. Do you suggest blazing away with fireballs, starting a fire and bringing the bridge down on top of us?'

No, Thomas the Rhymer wasn't panicking or falling into despair. He was clearly trying to think of something. And he had to have some kind of plan. Only I didn't want to hang about.

Semyon stepped out of the portal that was still hanging in mid-air. He immediately squatted down and scrambled towards the barrier. Yes: sometimes experience is more important than Power . . .

Somewhere far away, behind the walls and the doors, there was a scream that broke off on a high note.

. . . And sometimes fury is more important than experience.

I slipped into the Twilight.

First level. The decor seemed to have become real. The walls of plasterboard and plastic were now stone and there were dried stalks of some kind rustling under my feet. In the Twilight the interior of the building must have been constructed by human fantasy — too many people had passed this way who sincerely believed in the rules of the game and had made themselves believe in dungeons.

Dungeons and dragons.

There was a little dragon with bristling red scales standing in the stone archway and blocking my way. The beast came up to my shoulder: he was supporting himself on his back legs and a long tail that was twisted into a corkscrew. His webbed wings were flickering nervously behind his back. The glowing faceted eyes glared at me, and then the mouth opened and spat out a gobbet of flame.

So that's what you look like in the Twilight, Shooter I . . .

I jumped to one side, tossing a fireball at the little dragon. A very small fireball, so as not to cause any shocks in the real world.

Then I went down to the second level.

The dungeon hadn't changed. But the dragon here was black and a little bit taller. His eyes were bigger, rounder and darker, and he had acquired pointed ears that stuck up. The scales had changed into either coarse fur or chitin spines that were pressed tight against his body. The jaws were extended forwards. The wings had been transformed into small, trembling legs.

The mouth opened wide and a bundle of blue sparks flew out in my direction.

I dodged and took a few more steps. And then, forgetting once again about the barrier, I stepped down onto the third level of the Twilight.

At first it felt as if I had run into a wall — a flexible, springy, but impenetrable wall. But that sensation only lasted for a second.

An instant later I found myself on the third level.

And I realised immediately that this was connected with that scream of a dying human being.

Someone had opened the barrier again. Opened it with someone's living blood.

But there wasn't any little dragon here.

I ran along the corridor without bothering to destroy the robot shooter. Lermont could handle that himself. The machine wasn't going anywhere. It was more important for me to catch the killer. Whoever he might be — vampire, magician, sorcerer. A stranger or a former friend . . .

This was clearly the central section of the Dungeons. The focus of the Power, the centre of the vortex, the keyhole. The River of Blood — only here it looked like a ditch filled with bubbling black liquid as thick as pitch. A gleaming black table. And lying on it — a motionless body in a bloodstained white robe.

It looked as if this time the person who had lost his life was one of the hired human personnel who worked for the Edinburgh Night Watch. One of the pathologists who did jobs for Lermont.

Could Lermont really have left the Dungeons with no reliable guards? Without anyone to ambush raiders? Had he abandoned the people who trusted him to the whim of fate?

A single glance at the real world told me everything.

He had left guards. And had set up an ambush.

But he had underestimated the strength of his enemy.

I counted six bodies in the room. Three of the dead were raiders – in semi-military uniforms that didn't belong to anyone's army, with automatic weapons – and the magazines of the guns glittered with the spells applied to the bullets. One of the dead was a first-level Light Magician, almost torn in half by bursts of machine-gun fire at point-blank range. The magician's unexpended Power was slowly oozing out of him in a cloudy white glow. The other two who had been shot were human – employees of the Night Watch. The protective amulets that had failed to save them sparkled brightly on their chests. They too had died with guns in their hands – they were still clutching pistols.

How many attackers had there been? And how many had gone on past the third level?

Before I had time to complete the thought, a grey shadow came flitting down through the Twilight from the first level to join me on the third. And Bruce appeared in front of me.

The Master of Vampires looked in pretty poor shape. His chest had been ripped to shreds by bullets. He was breathing heavily, and his fangs glittered in his mouth.

'Aha!' I exclaimed with such obvious delight that Bruce understood me straight away.

'Stop, Light One!' he howled. 'I'm on your side! I came at Lermont's request!'

'And who shot you?'

'The robot in the corridor!'

I screwed up my eyes, tracing the 'vampire trail'. Yes, the traces of the undead feet passed through the corridor, from the entrance to the Dungeons. He wasn't responsible for the bloodbath.

So this was who Lermont was counting on to defeat the automated gunman. It's hard to kill someone who's already dead, even with charmed bullets.

'Who is he?' I didn't specify who I meant, but Bruce understood.

'I don't know! Not one of us! A stranger! He had about twenty people with him, but they're all dead. And Lermont's guards are dead!'

'Let's go after them,' I ordered.

Bruce hesitated. He glanced at the body oozing blood – unlike all the others, this man had died very recently, and his body existed on all levels of the Twilight at once. Death is very strong magic . . .

'Don't even think about it,' I warned him.

'He doesn't need it any more,' Bruce muttered. 'He doesn't need it, but who knows who I still have to fight?'

It was disgusting, and it was also true. But to hand a dead employee over to a vampire to feed on . . .

'If you drink the blood, the barrier will appear again,' I said, finally finding an argument in my favour. 'Let's go. You can hold out.'

Bruce pulled a face, but he didn't object. He hung his head low, as if he was about to butt against some barrier, and went to the fourth level.

I slipped down after him.

Bruce was standing there, holding his chest. He was shaking and there was naked fear in his eyes. There was no one there apart from Bruce. Nobody and nothing – the dungeons had disappeared. Just sand, grey and coloured at the same time, just black boulders scattered about here and there . . . And a pink and white sky with no sun.

'Anton – I can't go any deeper.'

'Have you been on the fifth level?'

'No!'

'Neither have I. Let's go!'

'I can't!' the vampire howled. 'Damn it, can't you see that I'm dying!'

'You've been dead for a long time!'

Bruce shook his head so furiously that it seemed as if he wanted to screw it off his neck.

If I'd had even the slightest suspicion that he was faking, I would have forced him to go down. Or finished him off for ever.

But going to the fourth level had clearly exhausted his final reserves of strength.

'Go and get Lermont!' I ordered him.

Clearly relieved, Bruce went dashing back the way he had come. The way a diver who is choking for breath hurtles upwards out of the fatal depths.

And I started looking for my shadow on the sand.

It had to be there. I had to cast a shadow. I was going to find it.

Otherwise something terrible was going to happen.

For instance – Merlin would rise from the dead. And a Mirror Magician would come to the assistance of the Edinburgh Night Watch, which had already suffered heavy losses. And he would maintain the equilibrium come what may.

The conjuror Egor.

And that would be his blinding moment of glory – before he self-destructed, dissolved into the Twilight and was cast into emptiness by the remorseless will of the primordial Powers.

We had used plenty of people before, surely?

I growled, taking a step forward. I shouldn't be looking for this shadow on the sand. This shadow was inside me.

I was lashed by an icy wind – and I fell through to the fifth level of the Twilight.

And landed face down in green grass.

There was a cold, fitful wind blowing. The sunlight filtered through the purple clouds, as heavy as snow clouds, that were drifting across the sky. The rolling plain, covered with tall, prickly grass, extended all the way to the horizon. Somewhere in the

distance there was thunder rumbling and lightning flashing –
flashing the wrong way, from the earth up into the sky, up into
those purple clouds.

I stood up and swallowed hard – my ears were blocked. The
usual oppressive sensation of the Twilight, the creeping weariness,
the desire to get back out into the real world as quickly as possible,
had disappeared. The fifth layer turned out to be energetically
balanced. When my eyes had adjusted and I looked more closely,
it was obvious that the colours around me were not entirely alive
after all. The grass was green, but pale. The clouds were more
dove-grey than purple. Even the flashes of lightning were strangely
subdued: they didn't sear the retinas of my eyes.

But even so . . . It looked as if it was possible to live here.

I looked around me. And I saw the Guard in the flattened grass.

It was a golem – a creature made of clay and brought to life
by magic. A rare sort of thing: nobody has made them for a long,
long time. A medieval robot that they sometimes tried to put to
work, but more often created to guard things.

Only the classic golem looked like a clay man and he was
brought to life by means of Runes inserted in a special opening.
(When it came to this the magicians' sense of humour usually
plumbed the depths.)

But this golem was a snake. Something like a clay anaconda ten
metres long, as thick as the torso of a grown man, and with two
rapaciously grinning heads – one at each end of its body. Its skin
was reddish-grey, like a badly fired brick. The golem's eyes were
open – and it was the eyes that frightened me most of all. They
were absolutely human.

But then, why shouldn't they be, if the golem had been made
by Merlin?

Exactly halfway along the snake's trunk there was a slim section
with a small hollow in it, about the size of an open hand. And

lying in that hollow was a square grey stone, covered with half-effaced Celtic writing.

Yes, a strange golem. The Rune hadn't brought it to life, it had killed it.

Or rather, it had rendered it motionless – if the baleful glint in its eyes was anything to go by.

I looked round again. There was no one there apart from me and the motionless golem. The grave-robber had already gone deeper.

Right, then!

I summoned the battle spells up out of my memory, all the most powerful things that I had learned and had sufficient Power for, and teed them up for rapid use. I had to be ready to go into battle at any moment. Provided, of course, that I managed to get any deeper . . .

'Wait, Anton!'

Three figures materialised out of the air: Lermont, Semyon, and a black man I didn't know. Lermont had literally dragged Semyon and the black man after him, holding them by the arms. Oh, he was powerful, all right . . .

'What a lovely place!' Semyon said in delight, gazing around. 'Ooh . . . So this is where . . .'

He spotted the golem and stopped. Then he walked across and gave it a cautious kick. He shook his head.

'Ooh . . . what a massive beast . . . Did you bring it down, Anton?'

'I'm afraid it's not that simple to bring down,' I said, pointing to the Rune. Then, turning to Foma, I said, 'Shall we move on, Mr Lermont?'

'Can you manage it?'

'I'll give it a try.'

Lermont shook his head doubtfully. He glanced at his subordinate and said:

'You can't go any further. I brought you along because of this . . . ugly brute. But there's no way you can go on. Wait for as long as you can and then go back.'

He heaved a deep sigh – and dissolved into thin air.

I took a step forward.

Nothing.

Another step. And another, and another.

'It's not working, then?' Semyon asked sympathetically.

What was this? I'd broken through to the fifth level, and it was absolutely calm here, but I couldn't get any lower!

A step. Another step. Where's that shadow?

'Anton . . .' said Semyon, shaking me by the shoulder. 'Anton, stop. You're just wasting your strength.'

'I'll get through,' I whispered. 'I have to . . .'

'You don't have to do anything. Lermont's got the experience. He'll handle everything.'

I shook my head, trying to relax. I'd got to this level using my anger . . . maybe I could get to the next one if I was calm, peaceful? All I was facing was a kind of watershed. A thin film of surface tension between worlds, a borderline beyond which the vital Power began to increase. The first level was practically dead, dried out, sterile. The second was a little more alive. The third and fourth already began to resemble our world. The fifth . . . the fifth was almost fit to live in. There were already colours here and although it was cold it wasn't so cold that you would freeze, grass grew here, there was rain, and strange violent storms. What would there be on the sixth level? I had to understand the place I was trying to break into. Was it a glacial world, a dying world? A place where it would be hard to breathe, difficult to walk or talk?

No. The sixth level wouldn't be like that. It would be even more colourful than the fifth. Even more alive. Even closer to the real world.

I nodded to my thoughts.

And stepped from the fifth level to the sixth.

It was night there. Perhaps not a summer night, but it was still warm. I couldn't see a single star in the sky above my head, but there was a moon. Not a strip of grey dust in the sky, like on the first level. Not the three tiny coloured moons that shone on the second level. An absolutely normal moon, perfectly familiar to the human eye.

But not a single star. The stars are not for Others.

Under the white spotlight of the moon the world seemed completely real. The trees were real, alive, with leaves that rustled in the wind. There was a smell of grass and burning . . . I suddenly realised that this was the first time I had ever smelled anything in the Twilight. No doubt, if I chewed on a grass stalk I would actually taste the bitter juice . . .

Burning?

I turned round, and saw Lermont. But I didn't see him as a stout middle-aged gentleman. I saw him in his Twilight form.

Thomas the Rhymer had become a white-haired giant almost three metres tall. His skin radiated a murky white light. He was grabbing bunches of white and blue light out of the air, mixing them together in his gigantic hands as if he was making snow-balls, and throwing them off into the far distance. I followed the trajectory – the hissing bundles of flame went flying over the flat plain, sweeping aside the rare trees in their path, and fizzled out in a dark cloud that was moving rapidly away. Burning trees marked the shots that had missed.

'Foma!' I shouted. 'I'm here!'

The giant mixed up a truly immense sphere in his hands and grunted as he hurled it after the dark cloud. He turned round.

He had an amazing face. Kind and harsh, beautiful and fright-ening, all at the same time.

'The young magician has passed the barriers,' Thomas rumbled. 'The young magician has hastened to come to our aid . . .'

He was little bit crazy just at that moment – like all Others who take on their deep Twilight forms in the heat of battle

Thomas covered the distance between us in just a few steps. It seemed to me that the very ground shook under his feet.

'They didn't manage it, my friend . . .' The ancient bard lowered a hand as big as a shovel onto my shoulder. 'They only got as far as the sixth level. Thomas drove them away, he did. Thomas drove them away, like cowardly little puppy dogs.'

Lermont leaned his face down to me and whispered confidentially:

'But only because his enemies didn't fight. They'd been here long enough to realise that they couldn't get to the seventh level of the Twilight.'

'How many of them were there, Thomas?'

'Three, my friend, three. The right number.'

'Did you get a look at them?'

'Only a short one,' Thomas said with a shake of his head. 'You can't read an aura properly here, but Thomas managed. A Dark Other – an undead vampire. A Light Other – a sorcerer-healer. An Inquisitor Other – a battle magician. Three came together for the legacy of Merlin. Three almost got through. Three Higher Others. But even Higher Ones cannot get though to the seventh level of the Twilight.'

'A Dark One, a Light One and an Inquisitor?' I asked in amazement. 'All together?'

'The legacy of Merlin is enticing to all. Even Light Ones. Why else do you think, young magician, that Thomas wished to keep your arrival secret from his Watch?'

'Are they all men?' I asked.

'All men. All women. How should Thomas know? Thomas didn't touch them. Thomas just saw a little bit of their auras.'

'Thomas, we have to go,' I said, looking into the giant's eyes. 'Thomas, it's time to go back. Time to go home.'

'Why?' the giant asked in surprise. 'It's good here, young magician. You can live here. A magical land, a kingdom of fairies and magicians . . . Thomas can settle here, Thomas can find his haven . . .'

'Thomas Lermont, you are the head of a Night Watch! The whole of Scotland is under your protection! Witches, vampires, ghouls – you're not going to let them all run riot, are you?'

Thomas said nothing, and for a moment I thought he would refuse to go, that he really had found the fairy kingdom to which, legend said, he had withdrawn four hundred years earlier.

Of course, the Dark Ones wouldn't have run riot. Help would have come – from England, from Ireland, from Wales. And Light Ones would have been found in Europe and America to come to the aid of the orphaned Scottish Watch.

But would Lermont's disappearance be the final drop that triggered Egor's transformation into a Mirror Magician?

'Let's go, my young friend,' Lermont said. 'You're right, you're right, and I am in too much of a hurry . . . it is not yet time . . . But listen, young magician! Listen to the ringing of the silence, to the singing of the crickets in the grass, to the night birds beating the air with their wings . . .'

Either he made me hear it, or it was all real, but through the giant's noisy breathing I heard the silence and the sounds.

'See how hotly the fire blazes, how the silvery leaves catch the moonlight, how dark the grass is beneath our feet . . .' Lermont whispered. 'You could live here . . .'

And I saw.

'Not many Others have been here when they were still alive . . .'
Lermont said and sighed. 'We only come here after we die, do
you understand? We come here for ever . . .'

I felt a cold shiver run down my spine. I remembered the
members of our Watch who had died: Igor, Tiger Cub, Andrei . . .

'Did you know that? Did you know that earlier?'

'All Higher Ones who have managed to reach the fifth level
know it,' Thomas said in a sad voice. 'But this knowledge is too
dangerous, young magician.'

'Why?'

'It is not good to know what awaits you after death. Thomas
knows – and it is a burden to him. Thomas wishes to come here.
Far away from cruel and greedy people. Far away from human
evil and human good. It is so sweet . . . to live in a world of
Others . . .'

'Live?'

'Live, young magician . . . Here even vampires have no need of
blood. Here everything is different, otherwise. Everything is the way
it should be. Here is the real world . . . on the fifth and sixth levels,
and the seventh – the very greatest. Here the towers of wise men
studying the world of creation soar up to the heavens; cities full of
Light and Dark seethe with vital life; unicorns roam through virgin
forests and dragons guard their mountain caves. We shall come
here . . . I sooner, and you later . . . and our friends will come out
to greet us. I too shall be glad to greet you, young magician . . .'

A gigantic arm hugged me round the shoulders as if I were a
child. Foma heaved a deep, heavy sigh and continued:

'But it is not yet time. Not yet time. If I had been able to
reach the seventh level . . . I would not have come back. But my
Power is not sufficient for that. And yours will not be either,
young magician . . .'

'I'm in no hurry for the time being,' I muttered. 'I have . . .'

What did I have? A wife and daughter? They were Others, Higher Others. We could all depart together. For the cities of Light and Dark . . . where Alisa and Igor were happy together, where no one remembered about those stupid little people . . .

I shuddered. Was I dreaming, or had I become taller too? Or had Lermont started to shrink?

'Foma, let's get going!'

'Wait. Look at this!'

A white light had started dancing above our heads. Foma reached out his hand and pointed to a slab of transparent red stone hidden in the grass under our feet. What was this, a ruby the size of a large tea tray?

I squatted down, ran my hand across the smooth surface and looked at the lines and dashes of the Celtic Runes.

'What's written here, Foma?'

'Merlin wrote that,' Lermont said, with a thoughtful note in his voice. 'Merlin wrote that, it is the keyhole and the final key, both at the same time. It says here in Coelbren . . .' He paused. 'If we say it in high style . . . then . . .'

'Say it in any style!' I exclaimed, feeling the time slipping away.

'The Crown of All Things is here concealed. Only one step is left.
But this is a legacy for the strong or the wise —'

Foma declaimed in a strange voice, one that was higher and more tuneful. And at the first words he spoke the letters carved in the stone started to glow, as if someone had lit up a powerful lamp underneath it. One after another the letters were transformed into slim columns of light, shooting up into the sky.

'You shall receive all and nothing, when you are able to take it.
Proceed, if you are a strong as I;

> *Or go back, if you are as wise as I;*
> *Beginning and end, head and tail, all is fused in one,*
> *In the Crown of All Things. Thus are life and death inseparable.'*

The final letter flared into white brilliance just as Lermont spoke the final word.

'I hate karaoke,' I said. 'What does all this mean?'

'Thomas knows no more than you do, young magician,' said the giant, clutching me in his arms. 'And now, let's be leaving!'

I thought Lermont was going to step straight into the real world. But no, he went to the fifth level first and waved to Semyon and the black guy.

'Leave!'

They didn't have to be asked twice. Then Lermont winked at me, leaned down over the golem – and jerked Merlin's Rune out of the snake's body.

The beast's eyes flashed in fury, its trunk swirled up into the air, and both mouths opened wide in unison.

But we were already out of the Guard's reach. In the ordinary human world. In a room full of dead bodies.

Overweight, ageing Lermont put me down and collapsed on the floor. His face was covered with sweat – there were even beads of it hanging on the ends of his moustache.

We were surrounded by a familiar hustle: Light Others were taking prints of auras, studying the bodies, collecting small pieces of flesh and drops of blood for analysis. When I arrived, and Semyon straight after me, we were immediately met with wary glances, and I felt the probes of spells slipping over my body. When they discovered that we were Light Ones, and high-ranking, the embarrassed watchmen withdrew their probes.

I saw Bruce off to one side. The Master of Vampires no longer looked like a walking corpse, the rosy bloom had even returned to his cheeks. He was squatting in the corner, drinking something from a glass. I didn't try to see exactly what it was.

'Well, I never!' said Semyon, shaking his head. He looked absolutely happy. 'I never even imagined I'd see the fifth level some day, like the Great Geser or Thomas the Rhymer. Oh . . . now I can die happy . . .'

He winked at me.

'I'll sew your mouth shut,' Lermont declared in a very familiar tone of voice. 'The fifth level of the Twilight is no subject for idle talk.'

'Aha,' Semyon agreed quickly. 'It's just my stupid way of nattering.'

'Foma . . .' I reached out one hand to help the magician up. 'Thank you . . . for coming back. And for showing me – thank you for that.'

'Let's go,' said Foma, walking quickly through to the next room and the 'mooring', where the metal boat was swaying on the dark water. I followed him. Lermont hung an umbrella of silence over us and the noise immediately died away. 'Did you want to ask something?'

'Yes. Who are they?'

'I don't know.' Foma took out a handkerchief and wiped the sweat off his face. 'Several attempts have already been made to reach the legacy of Merlin. But I'm not certain it was these Others who tried . . . the last attempt was more than a century ago. And in particular, no one has ever made such wide use of people before . . . This is all very serious, Anton. But we've been lucky – Merlin has puzzled everybody with the third key.'

'What does that poem mean?'

'It's a riddle. In those days they were very fond of riddles, Anton. It was considered good form to give your opponent a chance to beat you. Even if it was only the bare ghost of a chance.'

'One thing is clear: apart from simply going head-on trying to break through into the seventh level, there's an alternative route,' I said.

'It looks that way. But I don't know what to say to you about that. And if I did, I wouldn't say it.'

'Are you going to guard Merlin's hiding place until the end of time?'

'For as long as I can,' said Lermont, turning the Rune of Merlin over in his hands. He sighed. 'At least now the Guard is watching over the fifth level again. Next time the enemy will have to subdue it again.'

'Destroy the Rune, Foma!'

He shook his head.

'There aren't any simple answers, Anton. If the Rune is destroyed, the Guard will disappear too. I'll hide it as securely as I can. You don't need to know how. And . . . thank you for your help . . .'

'Meaning "Now get lost"?' I asked, smiling.

'Meaning "Thank you for your help." The more outsiders there are here, the more fuss there will be over everything that has happened. I'm grateful to you, and to Semyon. Your tickets will be delivered to your hotel.'

'Fair enough. And thank you, Foma.' I bowed. 'May the Light be with you!'

'Wait,' Thomas said in a gentle voice. He walked up to me and embraced me. 'I mean "Thank you." Don't take offence. We're going to have a lot of problems here, and a lot of visitors from the Inquisition. Do you really want to get stuck here for a month?'

'Guard the Crown well, Foma,' I said after a pause.

'Think about what you've seen, Anton. I'm sure that one of your compatriots is involved in what has happened. Approach the mystery from your side – and we'll meet again.'

'If I find whoever it is from our side, I'll tear his legs off and stick them in his ears. Goodbye, Thomas the Rhymer!'

When I had already reached the door, I added:

'Oh yes, by the way, we're used to flying first class!'

'Be grateful if I don't send you as baggage,' Foma replied in the same tone of voice. Then he turned and walked back to his colleagues.

EPILOGUE

'YOU KNOW, THAT'S a really bad sign, to tell someone you fought side by side with that you'll meet again later,' Semyon declared sombrely. 'He hasn't got a single free moment to see me. And we're flying back home, like real ninnies. If we had just a week . . . we could have gone to the lochs, done a bit of fishing . . .'

'Semyon, the Inquisition will arrive any minute – we'd be stuck here for a month.'

'So what's wrong with that?'

'I'm a family man.'

'Oh, that's right . . .' Semyon said with a sigh. 'With a little daughter . . . Is she walking yet?'

'Semyon, stop playing the fool!'

We stopped in front of the hotel entrance. Semyon chuckled and rubbed the bridge of his nose.

'Er . . . how much time have we got?'

'Five or six hours. If there are tickets for the evening flight.'

'I'll just drop into a shop and buy a few souvenirs. Shall I get some for you?'

'What, exactly?'

'What sort of question's that? Whisky and scarves. Whisky for the men and scarves for the women. I usually get five of each.'

'Go on, then,' I said, waving him away. 'Only get me a child's scarf too, if you see one. Something bright and cheerful.'

'Definitely.'

I walked into the vestibule. The receptionist was not at his desk, but there was an envelope lying there with the name 'Anton Gorodetsky' written on it in large letters. Inside there were three first-class tickets – for me, Semyon and Galya Dobronravova. Foma had acted with incredible efficiency, and he hadn't even forgotten about the wolf-girl.

I knocked on the door of the Dark suite on the fourth floor. No response. I listened, and heard the sound of water flowing somewhere inside. I took Galya's ticket out of the envelope and pushed it under the door.

I found the key in my pocket went into my own suite.

'Slowly-slowly-go-over-to-the-armchair-and-sit-down,' gabbled the young red-haired guy who had introduced himself to me as Jean in the Dungeons of Scotland.

He had positioned himself perfectly. At the window, with the blinding sunlight pouring in through it. My shadow was behind me – there was no way I could plunge into it.

'Start-moving-towards-the-armchair-slowly-slowly,' the young guy rattled off.

He was accelerated, enveloped in the green glow emanating from the amulet on his arm: it looked like an ordinary woven bead trinket, the kind that hippies make. His reflexes now were many times faster than those of a normal human being. And since he was holding an Uzi automatic rifle and its magazine of charmed bullets was glowing bright red, it would have been unwise to object.

'Speak more clearly,' I said, walking to the chair and sitting in it. 'Since you didn't kill me straight away, there must be something to talk about.'

'You're-wrong-wizard,' the young guy said, and I noted that funny, childish 'wizard'. 'I-was-ordered-to-kill-you-but-there's-something-I-want-to-ask-you.'

'Ask away.'

I needed my shadow. I needed to turn my head, see my shadow and dive into the Twilight. I would be faster than him there.

'Don't-turn-your-head! If-you-look-at-your-shadow-I'll-shoot-straight-away. How-many-of-you-are-there?'

'What?'

'How-many-brutes-like-you-are-there-walking-the-earth?'

'Well . . .' I thought for a moment. 'Do you mean Light Ones or Dark Ones?'

'It-doesn't-matter.'

'Approx . . . imate . . . ly . . . one . . . in . . . every . . . ten . . . thousand . . .' I drawled slowly. Not to be smart, but to try to convince this young guy that he was speeded up too far. But then, was he able to control the effect of the charm?

'Bastards-I-hate-them,' he said. 'I-was-told-to-say-you-betrayed-a-friend-and-deserve-to-die . . .'

There was a knock at the door. The young guy's glance darted to the door and then back to me. In a single movement he pulled the tablecloth off the table and covered his automatic rifle, which was still trained on me. He said:

'Open-it!'

'Who's there? It's open!' I shouted.

If it was Semyon, we'd have a chance.

The door opened and Galya walked in. The way she looked simply took my breath away. A short little black skirt, an almost transparent pink top – she had Lolita smoking nervously in the corner.

Jean was dumbstruck too.

'Hi.' The girl was chewing something. She concentrated and blew out a huge bubble of gum. The bubble burst and Jean started. I was afraid he would start blasting away, but the moment passed safely. 'And who are you?' she asked.

She gave Jean a look that made him blush bright red. He managed to jabber and mumble at the same time:

'I'm-just-visiting.'

'Well, friends of Anthony's get a discount,' Galya said, and winked at the young guy. She walked up to me, swaying her hips, and said, 'I left my knickers in your place – did you find them?'

All I could do was just shake my head.

'Ah, screw them anyway,' Galya declared. And she began slowly leaning down, reaching out for my lips with her own, giving Jean a chance to stare . . . I dared not even think at what!

But he stared.

'Get ready,' Galya whispered. The girl's stare was serious and tense. But she still touched my lips – and sparks of mischief glinted in her eyes.

She transformed herself instantly into a she-wolf. Crudely, horribly, scattering drops of blood and scraps of skin around her, wasting no time on morphing properly. And she flung herself round and leapt at the killer like a shaggy black shadow.

He started to shoot at the same moment that I flung two Triple Blades, one after another.

The first cut off the hand holding the gun and gouged out a chunk of his body. I didn't realise where the second one had gone at first. I leapt to my feet and jumped towards the she-wolf writhing on the floor. Her body had taken all the bullets intended for me. Not very many – only five or six. If only they hadn't been charmed.

Jean stood up, swaying on his feet. He looked at me with wild, insane eyes.

'Who sent you?' I shouted, hitting him with a Domination, the spell of absolute obedience.

Jean shuddered and tried to open his mouth — and his head flew apart into three pieces. My second shot had hit him in the head.

The body swayed and slumped to the floor beside the wolf-girl. Blood pulsed out of its arteries.

If she had been a vampire, and not a werewolf . . .

I leaned down over her, and saw that she was transforming back into a human being.

'Don't you dare! You'll die!'

'I'll die anyway,' she said in a clear voice. 'I don't want to die as an animal . . .'

'You're not . . .'

Instantly there was note of irony in her voice.

'Silly . . . Light One . . .'

I stood up. My hands were covered in blood and there was blood squelching under my feet. The killer's headless body was shuddering convulsively.

'What's happening here?' Semyon froze in the doorway. He ran his hand over his face and swore.

His other hand was holding two plastic bags. One had bottles in it. The other probably had scarves

'What's happening? Nothing,' I said, looking at the dead girl. 'It's all over.'

I bought the magnet for Zabulon in Edinburgh airport, while Lermont and Semyon were rebooking the tickets. We now only needed two seats in the cabin of the plane and one ticket for an item of non-standard freight — a long wooden box that had been treated with spells. One of them was to protect the contents against decomposition. Another was to persuade the customs men that there was no need to check the box, since it was being used to transport harmless skis.

The magnet was banal but beautiful: a Scotsman in a kilt, with bagpipes. I put it in my pocket, then stood in front of the display of postcards for a while. I chose one with a photograph of the castle and put it in my guidebook to Great Britain. I didn't have any reason to send it to the girl Lera as yet. But I hoped very much that sooner or later I would be able to keep the promise I had made to Victor's girlfriend.

Semyon was unusually quiet. He didn't reminisce about the way aeroplanes used to look at the dawn of the aviation industry, he didn't crack any jokes. We walked through the customs and passport checks, and took our seats in the plane. Semyon took out a flask of whisky and glanced at me enquiringly. I nodded. We each took a mouthful straight from the flask, earning ourselves a disapproving glance from the flight attendant. She immediately went off to her little cubbyhole and came back with glasses and a few little bottles, which she handed to Semyon without saying a word.

'Don't feel sorry for her,' Semyon said gently. 'Dark Ones will always be Dark Ones. She would have grown up into a monster. Most likely.'

I nodded. He was right, of course. Even a silly Light One like me had to understand that . . .

I leaned back in my seat and closed my eyes. I realised that I'd even forgotten to check the probabilities to see if the plane was in any danger of crashing. Ah . . . what difference did it make? People flew all the time without worrying if anything bad was going to happen. I could try that too . . .

'I checked the reality lines,' Semyon said. 'We leave ten minutes late, but we arrive on time. There's a tail wind. Lucky, that, isn't it?'

I opened the little plastic bag, put the disposable earphones in my ears and stuck the jack into the socket hidden in the arm of

my seat. I pressed the buttons to select a channel and stopped
when I heard a familiar song:

> Do not lose what has been given,
> Do not regret what has been lost.
> This boy at the doorway to heaven
> Is weary of sighing and tears.
> But he can see straight through you,
> And he won't sing us any psalms.
> He will ask us only one question —
> Did we live and did we love . . .
> Did we live and did we love . . .
> Did we live and did we love . . . *

* Kirill Komarov, 'At the Doorway to Heaven'.

Part Two

A COMMON ENEMY

PROLOGUE

THE FIRE-SAFETY inspector jabbed his finger in the direction of the aromatic joss stick smoking in its stand.

'And what's that?'

'Opium,' the young woman replied dreamily.

There was a sudden silence in the accounts office. The inspector's face broke out in red blotches.

'I'm not joking. What is it?'

'A joss stick, it's Indian. It's called opium.' The young woman looked round at her colleagues and added self-consciously, 'But that's only a name, you mustn't think . . . There isn't really any opium in it!'

'At home you can smoke opium or cannabis, or anything else you like,' said the inspector, ostentatiously nipping his fingers together and extinguishing the small smouldering stick. 'But here . . . you're surrounded on all sides by nothing but paper.'

'I keep an eye on it,' the young woman objected resentfully. 'And it's in a special stand, see? The ash falls on the ceramic base. It's a nice smell, everyone likes it . . .'

She spoke in a gentle, reassuring voice, in the same tone as adults use when they're talking to a little child. The inspector was about to say something else, but just then the middle-aged woman who was sitting facing all the other bookkeepers intervened.

'Vera, I'm sorry, but the inspector is quite right. It's a very sickly smell. By the time evening comes it gives you a headache.'

'In India the windows are probably always kept wide open,' a third woman put in. 'And they burn their fragrances all the time. It's terribly dirty there, there are always cesspits some-where close by, and everything rots very quickly because of the climate. They have to smother the stench somehow. But what do we need it for?'

A fourth girl, the same age as Vera, giggled and pressed her face towards the screen of her computer.

'Well, you should have said!' Vera exclaimed. Her voice sounded tearful. 'Why didn't you tell me?'

'We didn't want to offend you,' the older woman replied.

Vera jumped to her feet, covered her face with her hands and ran out into the corridor. Her heels clattered on the parquet flooring, and the door of the restroom slammed in the distance.

'We had to tell her sooner or later,' the middle-aged woman said with a sigh. 'I'm really sick of smelling those sticks of hers. It's always opium, or jasmine, or cinnamon . . .'

'Do you remember the chillies and cardamom?' the young girl exclaimed. 'That was really horrible!'

'Don't make fun of your friend. You'd better go and bring Vera back, she's much too upset.'

The young girl willingly got to her feet and left the room.

The inspector gazed round at the women with a wild expres-sion. Then he glanced at the man beside him – a plump young, individual wearing a T-shirt and jeans. Beside the inspector in his respectable uniform, he looked very untidy.

'This is a madhouse,' the inspector declared. 'Nothing but

breaches of the fire-safety code everywhere I look. Why haven't you been closed down yet?'

'I'm surprised at that myself,' the other man agreed. 'Sometimes when I'm walking to work, I wonder: What if it's all over now? What if they've put an end to the whole mess, and from now on we're going to work according to the fire-safety regulations, without breaking a single rule . . .'

'Show me the fire-safety board on the second floor,' the inspector interrupted, looking at his plan of the building.

'Gladly,' said the man, opening the door for the inspector and winking at the women they were leaving behind in the office.

The inspector's indignation was lessened a bit by the sight of the board. It was brand new and very neat and tidy, painted red. Next to it were two fire extinguishers, a bucket of sand, an empty conical-shaped bucket, a spade, a gaff and a crowbar.

'Well, well. Well, well, well,' the inspector murmured as he glanced at the buckets and checked the date when the extinguishers were last refilled. 'The good old-fashioned kind. I didn't really expect that.'

'We make an effort,' said his guide. 'When I was still in school, we had one just like that on the wall.'

The inspector turned his plan round and thought for a moment.

'And now let's take a look at . . . at your programmers.'

'Yes, let's,' the other man said brightly. 'That's upstairs – follow me.'

At the foot of the stairs he stepped aside to let the inspector go first. He turned back and glanced at the fire-safety board, which faded and then dissolved into thin air. Something fell to the floor with a quiet sound. The man smiled.

The visit to the programmers gave the inspector another reason to be indignant. The programmers (two young women and one young guy) were blithely smoking at their workstations and the wires from the computers were twisted into terrible tangles. (The inspector even crawled under one desk and checked that the sockets were earthed.) When they came back down to the first floor fifteen minutes later, the inspector walked into an office that had the strange title 'Duty Pointsman' on the door and laid his papers out on the desk. The young man acting as his guide sat down facing him and watched with a smile as the inspector filled in his report form.

'What sort of nonsensical title is that you have on the door?' the inspector asked, without looking up from what he was doing.

'"Duty Pointsman"? He has to deal with anything that turns up. If some inspector or other calls, if the drains burst, if someone delivers pizza or drinking water – he has to handle everything. Something between a receptionist and an office manager. It's a boring job, we take turns to do it.'

'And just what is it that you do here?'

'Is that really any business of the fire-safety service?' the man asked thoughtfully. 'Well . . . we guard Moscow against manifestations of evil.'

'You're joking!' said the inspector, giving the 'duty pointsman' a dour look.

'Not at all.'

A middle-aged, eastern-looking man walked in without knocking on the door. The duty pointsman quickly got to his feet as he entered.

'Well now, what have we got here?' the newcomer asked.

'One item left in the accounts office, one in the toilet, one in the fire-safety board on the second floor,' the duty pointsman replied eagerly. 'Everything's in order, Boris Ignatievich.'

The inspector turned pale.

'Las, we haven't got a fire-safety board on the second floor,' Boris Ignatievich observed.

'I created an illusion,' Las replied boastfully. 'It was very realistic.'

Boris Ignatievich nodded and said:

'All right. But you didn't notice the other two bugs in the programmers' room. I think this is not the first time our guest has combined the duties of fire inspector and spy – am I right?'

'What do you think you're—' the man began, and then stopped.

'You feel very ashamed of carrying out industrial espionage,' said Boris Ignatievich. 'It's disgusting! And you used to be an honest man . . . once. Do you remember how you went to help build the Baikal–Amur railroad? And not just for the money, you wanted the romantic dream, you wanted to be part of some great effort . . .'

Tears began running down the inspector's cheeks. He nodded.

'And do you remember when you were accepted into the Young Pioneers?' Las asked cheerfully. 'How you stood in line, thinking about how you would devote all your strength to the victory of communism? And when the group leader tied your tie for you, she almost touched you with her big bouncy tits . . .'

'Las,' Boris Ignatievich said in an icy voice. 'I am constantly amazed at how you ever became a Light One.'

'I was in a good mood that day,' Las declared. 'I dreamed I was still a little boy, riding a pony . . .'

'Las!' Boris Ignatievich repeated ominously.

The duty pointsman fell silent.

The silence that followed was broken by the fire-safety inspector's sobbing.

'I . . . I'll tell you everything . . . I went to the Baikal–Amur railroad to avoid paying alimony . . .'

'Never mind that,' Boris Ignatievich said gently. 'Tell us about being asked to plant bugs in our office.'

CHAPTER 1

'I THINK YOU can guess why I've gathered you all together,' Geser said.

There were five of us in the boss's office. Geser himself, Olga, Ilya, Semyon and me.

'What's to guess?' Semyon muttered. 'You've gathered all the Higher and First-Level Others. Svetlana's the only one missing.'

'Svetlana's not here because she's not on the staff of the Night Watch,' Geser said and frowned. 'I've no doubt that Anton will tell her everything. I won't even attempt to forbid it. But I won't connive at breaches of the rules, either . . . this is a meeting of the Night Watch top management. I have to warn Ilya straight away that some of what he hears will be new to him, and under normal circumstances he would never have heard it. So he must not talk about it. Not to anyone.'

'What exactly is that?' Ilya asked, adjusting his spectacles.

'Probably . . . probably everything that you are about to hear.'

'A bit more than just "some of it",' Ilya said, with a nod. 'Whatever you say. If you like, I'm willing to accept the mark of the Avenging Fire.'

'We can dispense with the formalities,' said Geser. He took a small metal box out of his desk and began rummaging in it. Meanwhile I carried on looking round with my usual curiosity. What made the boss's office so interesting was the huge number of little items that he kept because he needed them for his work or simply as souvenirs. Something like Pliushkin's bins in *Dead Souls*, or a child's box in which he keeps his most cherished 'treasures', or the apartment of some absent-minded collector who's always forgetting what it is that he actually collects. And the most amazing thing was that nothing ever disappeared, even though there was almost no space left in the cabinets: new exhibits were added all the time.

This time my attention was caught by a small terrarium. It didn't have a lid, and there was a piece of paper glued to its side, with the letters OOO (or the numbers 000). Standing inside the terrarium was a stupid little toy made in China – a small plastic toilet, with a tarantula squatting on it in a regal pose. At first I thought the spider was dead or made of plastic, but then I noticed its eyes glinting and its mandibles moving. There was another spider crawling across the glass walls: fat and round, looking like a hairy ball with legs. Every now and then the spider stopped and spat a drop of green venom onto the glass, clearly aiming at something outside. At the same time something showered down off the spider into the terrarium. There were some other spiders moving around on the bottom, greedily reaching out their legs to catch the treat. The fortunate ones who managed to grab something began jumping up and down for joy.

'Interested?' Geser asked, without looking up.

'Uh-huh . . . what is it?'

'A simulation. You know I like to study self-contained social groups.'

'And what does this simulation represent?'

'A very interesting social structure,' Geser said evasively. 'In its basic form it should have become the traditional jar of spiders. But here we have two principal spiders, one of whom has taken up a dominant position by climbing onto a high point, while the other is acting as if he is providing protection against external aggression and caring for the members of the community. As long as the dominant spiders remain active, this simulation can continue to function with minimal internal aggression. I just have to spray the inhabitants with beer every now and then to relax them.'

'But doesn't anyone ever try to climb out?' Ilya asked. 'There's no lid . . .'

'Only very rarely. And only the ones who get fed up of being a spider in a jar. In the first place, the illusion of conflict is constantly maintained. And in the second place, the experimental subjects regard being in the jar as something out of the ordinary.' Geser finally took some object out of his box and said, 'All right, that's enough of the small talk. Here is the first thing for you to think about. What is it?'

We stared in silence at the grey lump of concrete that looked as if it had been chipped out of a wall.

'Don't use magic!' Geser warned us.

'I know,' Semyon said guiltily. 'I remember that incident. A radio microphone. They tried to put it in here in the 1950s . . . or was it the 1960s? When we were the "Non-Ferrous Mining Equipment Assembly Trust". Some bright guys from the KGB, wasn't it?'

'That's right,' said Geser. 'Back then they were very keen on looking for spies, and on a sudden impulse they decided to check us . . . we had provoked certain suspicions in the "organs" . . . It was a good thing that we had our own eyes and ears in the KGB. We organised a campaign of misinformation, certain vigilant comrades managed to get others rebuked for the pointless squandering of expensive equipment . . . And what about this?'

A huge steel screw glinted in Geser's hands. To be quite honest, I didn't even know that they made screws that large.

'I doubt if you know about this,' Geser told us. 'It's the only attempt — at least, I hope it is — ever made by the Dark Ones to spy on us using human means. In 1979 I had a very difficult conversation with Zabulon, and afterwards we signed an appendix to the agreement on prohibited methods of conflict.'

The screw was put back in the box. In its place two tiny brown 'tablets' were taken out.

'That was when they wanted to take our building away!' Ilya said brightly. 'In 1996, wasn't it?'

Geser nodded.

'Absolutely right. A certain ambitious young oligarch got the idea that the former state enterprise which had become the "Non-Ferrous Metal Mining Company" looked like a very tasty and absolutely defenceless little morsel of property. However, when their listening devices and external observation revealed the kind of people who simply dropped in for tea and a chat with the old director, the oligarch cut his ambitions back sharply.'

'That was misinformation as well, of course?' Olga asked curiously. It seemed that the boss's unusually complicated introduction was intended for her, because she had missed all these old events.

Semyon giggled and drawled in a voice like Yeltsin's:

'You un-der-stand, my friend, you decide important matters at the city level, and you don't ask for any help . . . Call round if anything happens.'

Geser smiled and replied:

'"Call round if anything happens", is putting it a bit strongly.

But never mind, no one judges the victors . . . Right, those were cases from the past. But here is today's catch . . .'

He took something that looked like a Band-Aid out of the box. A thin white square, slightly sticky on one side – it was not easy for Geser to pull it off his finger.

'Technology is always developing,' I said, impressed. 'A microphone and transmitter?'

'You'll be surprised to know that there's a recorder here too,' Geser told me. 'Everything is recorded and then shot off in a three-second coded burst once a day. A fine little toy. Expensive. And you can't buy it just anywhere.'

'Get to the point, Boris,' Olga said.

Geser tossed the 'toy' back into the box, and glanced round keenly at all of us.

'A week ago Anton and Semyon spent some time in the city of Edinburgh. Something rather unpleasant happened there: without going into too much detail, a group of Others, including at least one Light One, one Dark One and an Inquisitor, tried to steal one of the most ancient magical artefacts in existence, with the help of paid human assistants who were equipped with magical amulets. The artefact is the so-called "Crown of All Things", created by the Great Merlin shortly before he withdrew into the Twilight.'

Ilya whistled. Olga said nothing – either she had already heard about this from Geser, or she didn't think any display of emotion was required.

'I should add that the three Others were all Higher Ones,' Geser continued. 'Well . . . perhaps not all of them. Perhaps two of them. Together they could have taken the third one down to the sixth level of the Twilight.'

To my surprise, Ilya didn't say anything. He must have been stunned. I didn't think he had ever gone any deeper than the third level.

'This is already unpleasant,' said Geser. 'None of us knows what kind of artefact Merlin hid on the seventh level of the Twilight, but there are serious grounds for believing that this artefact is capable of destroying all civilisation on Earth.'

'Another "Fuaran"?' Semyon asked.

'No, Merlin didn't have the knowledge to transform people into Others,' said Geser, shaking his head. 'But it is something very powerful indeed. Security measures to keep the artefact safe have been tightened up: the Inquisition is guarding it now, as well as the Night Watch of Scotland. But the situation is too serious. I have learned that attempts have been made to spy on Watches in Moscow, New York, London, Tokyo, Paris, Beijing . . . in short, at all the key points on the planet. Everywhere the people involved have no idea who hired them. So far all attempts to find the instigators have produced nothing.'

'Geser, what's down there, on the seventh level of the Twilight?' Ilya asked. 'I know it's not done to talk about the deeper levels to anyone who hasn't been there, but—'

'Semyon will tell you what he saw,' Geser replied. 'He's been to the fifth level. And ask Anton if you like – he'll tell you about the sixth level. I give my permission. But as for the seventh level . . .'

Everybody gazed curiously at Geser.

'I haven't been there. And I can't answer your question,' Geser concluded firmly.

'Ha,' said Olga. 'I was certain you had been there, Boris.'

'No. And before you ask – Zabulon hasn't been there either. Nor have any of the Others I know. I believe that only a *zero-point* magician is capable of it. Someone who possesses absolute Power. Merlin was such a magician. Nadya Gorodetskaya will become such an enchantress . . .'

Everybody turned to look at me.

'I won't let her into the Twilight before she's grown up,' I said firmly.

'Nobody's asking you to,' Geser assured me. 'And . . . don't start objecting before I finish. I want to put your Nadya under guard. Continuous guard, round the clock. At least two battle magicians. Second or third level of Power. They won't hold out long against Higher Ones, but if we provide them with good artefacts, they'll be able to drag things out long enough to call help.'

Ilya held his head in his hands.

'Boris Ignatievich! Where will I get that many second- and third-level Others from? Are we going to take our entire fighting force off the street?'

'No, not all of it,' Geser replied. 'We have four second-level Others, after all. And nine third-level. Alisher and Alexander can be raised to third level.'

'Which Alexander? Korostilyov?' Ilkya asked in amazement.

'No, Malenkov.'

'Sasha can be raised,' Olga put in. 'I'm prepared to do it in three days. Even two.'

'Wait!' I exclaimed. 'Wait! Would you like to hear my opinion?'

Geser looked at me curiously.

'Yes, I would. Only bear in mind that sooner or later the individuals who failed to obtain the artefact will come to the conclusion that they need an absolute magician. And there is only one in the whole world. One. Your daughter. So will you agree to her being guarded?'

'But what will Svetlana say?'

'Svetlana is a mother,' Olga said in a gentle voice. 'I think she remembers how her daughter was kidnapped once already. And she understands that she herself cannot guard her daughter twenty-four hours a day.'

'Sveta will agree, Anton,' Semyon said, with a nod. 'No need for any crystal ball there.'

'But Boris Ignatievich, what am I supposed to do with the streets?' Ilya objected. 'I protest officially as your deputy for the patrol service! Am I supposed to send out fourth- and fifth-level magicians to work on their own? The Dark Ones will walk all over us!'

'They won't,' Geser said, frowning. 'Zabulon is also allocating his second- and third-level magicians to guard Nadya Gorodetskaya.'

It was my turn to clutch my head in my hands. But Ilya immediately calmed down.

'Then we only need to supply half of the bodyguards? In that case, I—'

'No, not half. It's two of ours and two Dark Ones.'

'Geser!' I protested.

'Anton, this is being done for the sake of your daughter's safety,' Geser replied in a firm voice. 'That's all – the matter's closed! Let's get on with other business. Ilya, you stay behind after the meeting, we'll discuss who to use as bodyguards and how to equip them.'

I said nothing. I was seething inside, but I said nothing.

'So far we have only spoken about defence,' Geser continued. 'I charge Olga with developing the measures for protecting the Watch against spy technology and a possible attack by human mercenaries. Involve Tolik from the computer service. And Las from the operations side.'

'But he's a weak magician,' Olga snorted.

'But he has a non-standard way of thinking,' said Geser. 'And you know pretty much all there is to know about battles between Others and human beings. You've certainly had plenty of experience.'

I gave Olga a curious glance. So she had a interesting background, then . . .

'What I need from all of you now is something else,' Geser went on. 'How are we going to attack?'

'Attack whom?' I protested. 'If only we knew who it is that's muddying the water . . .'

'To attack doesn't necessarily mean to go rushing into battle,' Olga stated didactically. 'To attack also means to take actions that the enemy isn't expecting, to disrupt his plans.'

Geser nodded in approval.

'Then there's only one thing we can do,' I said. 'That is, apart from trying to find the traitors . . . but I expect the Inquisition is breaking its back on that one already. We have to break through to the seventh level. But if we can't . . . the chain of Power?'

'Zabulon suggested a Circle of Power,' Geser said, with a nod. 'But it won't help, not even if we try, by accumulating each other's power, or the Dark Ones try, by sucking each other dry – not even with a human sacrifice . . . The strength of barriers between the levels of the Twilight increases exponentially. We have calcu-lated it.'

'Not even a human sacrifice?' Semyon asked in amazement.

'Not even,' Geser said drily.

'That little poem . . . on the sixth level . . .' I said, looking at Geser. 'Remember, I told you about it?'

'Recite it,' Geser said, nodding.

'The Crown of All Things is here concealed. Only one step is left.
But this is a legacy for the strong or the wise –
You shall receive all and nothing, when you are able to take it.
Proceed, if you are as strong as I;
*   Or go back, if you are as wise as I;*
Beginning and end, head and tail, all is fused in one,
In the Crown of All Things. Thus are life and death inseparable.'

I recited the poem from memory.

'And what does that give us?' Geser asked almost jovially.

'Go back, if you are as wise as I,' I repeated. 'There is some kind of detour, an alternative route to the seventh level. You don't have to go head-on at the barrier.'

Geser nodded again.

'That's right. And I wanted you to say that.'

Semyon gave me a look of sympathy. It was clear enough. In the Watch, things work like in the army: you suggested it, now you do it.

'Just don't overestimate my intellectual capabilities,' I muttered. 'I'll think about it, of course. And I'll ask Svetlana to think about it too. But so far nothing comes to mind. Maybe we should delve into the archives?'

'We will,' Geser promised. 'But there is another way to go.'

'And I'm the one who has to go there,' I said. 'Am I right?'

'Anton, your daughter's in danger,' Geser said simply.

I shrugged.

'I surrender. Okay, I'm ready. Where do I go? Into the mouth of a volcano? Under the Arctic ice? Out into space?'

'You know very well that there's nothing we can do out in space,' Geser said, frowning. 'There is one hope – not a very big one. Perhaps one of Merlin's associates might guess what he had in mind.'

'We'd have to find a living contemporary . . .' I began.

'I'm his contemporary, more or less,' Geser said in a bored voice. 'But unfortunately I was not acquainted with Merlin. Neither when he was a Light One, nor when he was a Dark One. Why are you looking at me like that? Yes, it is possible. Sometimes. For Higher Ones. That's not the point . . . I hope none of you are planning to change colour?'

'Boris Ignatievich, don't drag it out,' I said.

'Merlin was friendly – insofar as that was possible – with an Other whom I knew by the name of Rustam.'

I exchanged glances with Semyon. He shrugged. Olga looked puzzled too.

'He had many names,' Geser continued. 'He used to be in the Watch too. A very, very long time ago. He and I were friends once. We helped each other in battle many times . . . saved each other's lives many times. Then we became enemies. Even though he was and still is a Light One.'

Geser paused. It seemed as if he didn't really want to remember all this.

'He is still alive, and he lives somewhere in Uzbekistan. I don't know exactly where – his strength is equal to mine and he can camouflage himself. He hasn't served in the Watch for a very long time. He is most probably living as an ordinary human being. You will have to find him, Anton. Find him and persuade him to help us.'

'Uh-huh,' I said. 'Uzbekistan? Easy as ABC. A – comb the whole place. B – winkle out a magician in hiding who's more powerful than I am . . .'

'I'm not saying it's simple,' Geser admitted.

'And C – persuade him to help us.'

'That part's a bit easier. The point is that he saved my life six times. But I saved his seven times.' Geser chuckled. 'He owes me. Even if he still hates me as much as he used to. If you find him, he'll agree . . .'

There was no confidence in Geser's voice, and everyone could sense that.

'But it's not even certain that he knows anything!' I said 'And is he still alive?'

'He was alive ten years ago,' said Geser. 'My assistant, the devona, recognised him. And he told him about his son.'

'Magnificent,' I said, with a nod. 'Absolutely wonderful. I suppose I have to follow tradition and set out unarmed and completely alone?'

'No. You will set out fully equipped, with a thick wad of money and a bag full of useful artefacts.'

It was several seconds before I realised that the boss was being perfectly serious.

'And not alone,' Geser added. 'Alisher will go with you. In the East, as you know, there are more important things than power and money. It is far more important for someone who is known and trusted to vouch for you.'

'Alisher too . . .' Ilya sighed.

'I'm sorry,' Geser said, without even the slightest note of apology in his voice. 'We must regard this as a military emergency. Especially since that's just what it is.'

I don't often get to go back home in the middle of the day. If you've been out on Watch duty, then you come home early in the morning. If you have an ordinary working day to get through, you won't get back before seven. Even with the ability to foresee traffic jams on the roads – what good is that if the jams are everywhere?

And naturally, even without the help of magic, any wife knows that a husband doesn't come back early from work without good reason.

'Daddy,' Nadya announced. Naturally, she was standing by the door. She can tell I'm coming just as soon as I approach the entrance to the building – that's if she happens to be busy with some important childish business of her own. If she's feeling bored, she knows from the moment I leave the office.

I tried to pick my daughter up. But she was clearly far more interested in the cartoons on TV: I could hear a squeaky 'La-la-la, la-la, la-la-la' coming from the sitting room. She had done her duty as a daughter: Daddy had been met when he came back from work and nothing interesting had been discovered in his hands or his pockets.

So little Nadya deftly slipped out of my arms and made a dash for the TV.

I took off my shoes, tossed the *Autopilot* magazine that I had bought on the way home onto the shoe stand and walked through into the sitting room, patting my daughter on the head along the way. Nadya waved her arms about – I was blocking her view of the screen, on which a blue moose with only one antler was hurtling downhill on skis.

Svetlana glanced out of the kitchen and looked at me intently. She said, 'Hmm!' and disappeared again.

Abandoning any attempts to fulfil my paternal functions until better times, I walked into the kitchen. Svetlana was making soup. I've never been able to understand why women spend so much time at the cooker. What does it take so long to do there? Toss the meat or the chicken into the water, switch on the hotplate, and it boils itself. An hour later drop in the macaroni or potatoes, and a few vegetables – and your food's ready. Well, you mustn't forget to salt it – that's the most difficult part.

'Will you pack your own suitcase?' Svetlana asked, without turning round.

'Did Geser call?'

'No.'

'Did you look into the future?'

'I promised you I wouldn't do that without permission . . .' Svetlana paused for a moment, because I had gone up to her from behind and kissed her on the neck. 'Or unless it's absolutely necessary . . .'

'Then why did you ask about the suitcase?'

'Anton, if you come home from work during the day, then I go to bed alone in the evening. They're either sending you out on watch or away somewhere on an assignment. But you

were on watch two days ago, and the city's calm at the
moment . . .'

In the sitting room Nadya laughed. I glanced in through the
door – the moose on skis was hurtling wide-eyed straight towards
a line of small and obviously young animals, who were walking
along the edge of a precipice. Oh, this was going to be a real
disaster . . .

'Sveta, are you sure Nadya should be watching cartoons like
that?'

'She watches the news,' Svetlana replied calmly. 'Don't avoid the
issue. What's happened?'

'I'm going to Samarkand.'

'Your assignments do take you to some interesting places,'
Svetlana said. She scooped up a spoonful of soup, blew on it and
tasted it. 'Not enough salt . . . What's happened out there?'

'Nothing. Nothing yet.'

'The poor Uzbeks. Once you get there, something's bound to
happen.'

'Geser held a meeting today. With the Higher Ones and the
first level . . .'

I told Svetlana briefly about everything we had discussed. To
my surprise, there was no reaction to the idea that from now on
Nadya would be guarded in secret by two Light and two Dark
magicians. Or rather, the reaction was exactly what Olga had fore-
cast it would be.

'Well, good for Geser! I was thinking about ringing him
myself . . . to ask for protection.'

'You're serious? You'll allow it?'

Svetlana looked at me and nodded. Then she added:

'While I'm with her, Nadya's in no danger. Believe me, I'll make
mincemeat of any three Higher Ones. But it's best to take precau-
tions. When's your flight?'

'In five hours. From Sheremetievo.'

'Semyon will get you there in an hour. So you still have two hours left. You can have something to eat, then we'll pack your things. How long are you going to be there?'

'I don't know.'

'Then how much underwear and how many pairs of socks shall I put in?' Svetlana asked reasonably. 'I can't imagine you washing anything while you're away.'

'I'll buy new ones and throw the old ones away. Geser promised to give me heaps of money.'

'I wonder how much "heaps" is for him,' Svetlana replied doubtfully. 'I'll pack five sets of underwear. Sit down at the table – I'm serving the soup.'

'Daddy!' Nadya called from the sitting room.

'What, my little daughter?' I answered.

'Daddy, will Uncle Afandi give me the beads for a present?'

Svetlana and I looked at each other, then walked quickly into the sitting room. Our daughter was still watching the cartoons. The screen showed a group of different-coloured animals gathered round a campfire.

'What uncle's that, Nadya?'

'Uncle Afandi,' said our daughter, without looking away from the screen.

'What Afandi?' Svetlana asked patiently.

'What beads?' I asked.

'The man Daddy's going to see,' Nadya told us, with that 'How stupid you grown-ups are!' intonation. 'And the beads are blue. They're beautiful.'

'How do you know who Daddy's going to see?' asked Svetlana, continuing the interrogation.

'You were just talking about it,' Nadya replied calmly.

'No, we weren't,' I objected. 'We were talking about me going on an assignment to Uzbekistan. That's a beautiful country in the East – Geser used to live there once. Do you remember Uncle Geser? But we didn't say anything about Afandi.'

'I must have misheard, then,' Nadya replied. 'There isn't any uncle.'

Svetlana shook her head and looked at me reproachfully. I shrugged – okay, I'm sorry, I shouldn't have butted in. Mummy would have got a lot more out of her . . .

'But the beads are real anyway,' Nadya suddenly added inconsistently. 'You bring them, all right?'

There was no point in asking any more about Uncle Afandi. Nadya had had 'fits' of clairvoyance ever since she was three, if not two. But she was absolutely unaware that she was prophesying, and as soon as you started asking 'How do you know that?' she clammed up.

'My fault,' I confessed. 'Sorry, Sveta.'

We went back to the kitchen. Svetlana poured me some soup without saying a word, sliced the bread and handed me a spoon. It sometimes seems to me that she plays the role of a perfectly ordinary housewife with emphatic irony. But after all, it was her choice. Geser would be absolutely delighted if Svetlana came back to the Watch.

'Rustam has had a lot of names . . . is that what Geser said?' Svetlana asked thoughtfully.

'Uh-huh,' I said, slurping my soup.

'We can assume that now he's called Afandi.'

'Anything's possible.' I wasn't exactly counting on it, but in my situation I couldn't afford to ignore even the slimmest lead. 'I'll ask around.'

'It's good that Alisher will be with you,' Svetlana observed. 'You let him do the asking as often as possible. The East is a subtle business.'

'Now there's an original thought . . .' I said sourly. 'Sorry, I've been hearing wise thoughts about the East all day long today. The rivers of eloquence have already flooded the lake of my awareness, oh Turkish delight of my heart!'

'Daddy, bring back some Turks and some delight!' my daughter responded immediately.

I didn't meet Alisher often at work. He preferred working 'in the field' – he was always out on patrol and usually only appeared in the office in the morning, with his eyes red from lack of sleep. I once heard that he was having an affair with some girl from the accounts department, and I knew he was a seventh-level Other, but apart from that I knew very little about him. He was naturally reserved, and I don't like to force my friendship on anyone.

However, Semyon seemed to be on friendlier terms with him. When I went down and got into the car, Semyon was just finishing telling a joke. As I sat beside him, he was leaning back over his seat and saying:

'All right, Daddy, let's go the long way round. Bring me a little scarlet flower, please!'

Alisher laughed first and then held his hand out to me.

'Hi, Anton.'

'Hi, Alisher.' I shook his hand and passed my bag back to him. 'Dump it on the back seat, I don't want to bother with the trunk.'

'How's Sveta? Did she scold you?' Semyon asked as he drove off.

'No, of course not. She wished me luck, fed me a delicious dinner and gave me heaps of useful advice.'

'A good wife even keeps her husband happy,' Semyon declared cheerfully.

'You're in a good mood today,' I remarked. 'Is Geser sending you to Samarkand too?'

'As if he would,' Semyon said, with a histrionic sigh. 'Listen, lads, why are you going to Samarkand? The capital's Binkent, I remember that for certain!'

'Tashkent,' I corrected him.

'Nah, Binkent,' said Semyon. 'Or isn't it? Ah, I remember! The town's called Shash!'

'Semyon, you're not old enough to remember Binkent,' Alisher scoffed. 'Binkent and Shash were ages ago – only Geser remembers that. But we're flying to Samarkand because that's where the oldest Light Other who works in a Watch lives. The Watch in Tashkent is bigger, they have all the swank of a capital city, but most of them are young. Even their boss is younger than you are.'

'Would you ever . . .' said Semyon, shaking his head. 'Incredible. The East – and everyone in the Watches is young?'

'In the East the old men don't like to fight. The old men like to watch beautiful girls, eat pilaf and play backgammon,' Alisher replied seriously.

'Do you often go home?' Semyon asked. 'To see your family and friends?'

'I haven't been there even once in eight years.'

'Why's that?' Semyon asked in surprise. 'Don't you miss your home at all?'

'I haven't got a home, Semyon. Or any family. And a devona's son doesn't have any friends.'

There was an awkward silence. Semyon drove without speaking. Eventually I just had to ask:

'Alisher, if this isn't too personal a question . . . Your father, was he a man? Or an Other?'

'A devona is a servant whom a powerful magician creates for himself.' Alisher's voice was as steady as if he were giving a lecture. 'The magician finds some halfwit who has no family and fills him with Power from the Twilight. He pumps him full of pure energy . . . and the result is a stupid but very healthy man who possesses magical abilities . . . No, he's not quite a man any more. But he's not an Other, all of his power is borrowed, inserted into him by the magician at some time. A devona serves his master faithfully, he can work miracles . . . but his head still doesn't work any better than it did before. Usually the magician chooses people who are mentally retarded, or have Down's syndrome – they're not aggressive and they're very devoted. The power inserted into them gives them good health and a long life.'

We didn't say anything. We hadn't expected such a frank answer from Alisher.

'The common people think a devona is possessed by spirits. And that's almost true . . . it's like taking an empty, cracked vessel and giving it new content. Only instead of intelligence it is usually filled with devotion. But Geser's not like all the others. Not even like other Light Ones. He cured my father. Not completely – even he can't do absolutely anything. At one time my father was a total idiot. I think he suffered from imbecility – obviously owing to some kind of organic damage to the brain. Geser healed my father's body, and in time he acquired normal human reason. He remembered that he had once been a complete imbecile. He knew that if Geser didn't fill him with fresh Power in time, his body would reject his reason again. But he didn't serve Geser out of fear. He said he would give his life for Geser because he had helped him to become aware. To become a man. And also, of course, because a mindless fool like him now had a family and a son. He was very afraid that I would grow up an idiot. But it was all right. Only . . . only the people remember everything. That my father was a devona, that he had lived too long in this world, that once he was an imbecile who couldn't even wipe his own nose – they remembered all that. My mother's family rejected her when she left to join my father. And they didn't acknowledge me, either. They forbade their children to play with me. I am the son of a devona.

The son of a man who should have lived the life of an animal. I have nowhere to go back to. My home is here now. My job is to do what Geser tells me to do.'

'Well, well . . .' Semyon said quietly. 'That's a tough deal – really tough. I remember how we drove back those counter-revolutionary bandits, the *basmaches*. You don't mind me saying that, do you?'

'What's wrong with it?'

'Well, maybe now they're not bandits any longer, but national heroes . . .'

'When Geser was a commissar in Turkestan my father fought in his detachment,' Alisher said with pride.

'He fought there?' Semyon asked excitedly. 'What year was that in?'

'The early 1920s.'

'No, I was there later . . . In Garm, in 1929, when the *basmaches* broke through from abroad.'

They launched into a lively discussion of events from days of long ago. From what I understood, it seemed that Alisher's father and Semyon had almost crossed paths – they had both fought alongside Geser when he'd been on active military service in the Red Army. To be quite honest, I didn't really understand how Geser could have taken part in the events of the Civil War. The Great Light One couldn't possibly have bombarded the White Guards and the *basmaches* with fireballs! Apparently not all Others had been indifferent to that revolution. Some of them had taken one side or other in the struggle. And the great Geser and his comrades had gone dashing about the steppes of Asia to fight the other side.

And I also thought that now I could probably guess why Geser and Rustam had quarrelled.

CHAPTER 2

EARLY IN THE morning is the right time to arrive in a new city. By train, on a plane – it makes no difference. The day seems to start with a brand new leaf.

In the plane Alisher became taciturn and thoughtful again. I half-dozed almost all the way through the flight, but he looked out of the window as if he could see something interesting on the distant ground, enveloped in night. Then just before we landed, when we flew out into the morning and the plane started its descent, he asked:

'Anton, would you mind if we separated for a while?'

I gave the young magician a curious look. Geser's instructions hadn't involved anything of the kind. And Alisher had already told me everything about his family and friends, or rather, about the fact that he didn't have any.

But then, it wasn't hard to guess what a young guy who had left his homeland at the age of just over twenty might be thinking about.

'What's her name?' I asked

'Adolat,' he replied without trying to deny anything. 'I'd like to see her. To know what happened to her.'

I nodded and asked:

'Does that name mean something?'

'All names mean something. Didn't you ask Geser to give you knowledge of the Uzbek language?' Alisher asked in surprise.

'He didn't suggest it,' I mumbled. But really, why hadn't I thought of it? And how could Geser have goofed so badly? We Others learn the major languages of the world as a matter of course – naturally, with the help of magic. Less common languages can be lodged in your mind by a more powerful or experienced magician. Geser could have done it. Alisher couldn't . . .

'That means he didn't think you needed it,' Alisher said thoughtfully. 'Interesting . . .'

It looked as if Alisher couldn't imagine Geser making a mistake.

'Will I really need the Uzbek language?' I asked.

'It's unlikely. Almost everyone knows Russian . . . And anyway, nobody would take you for an Uzbek,' Alisher said, with a smile. 'Adolat means justice. A beautiful name, isn't it?'

'Yes,' I agreed.

'She's an ordinary human being,' Alisher murmured. 'But she has a good name. A Light name. We went to school together . . .'

The plane shuddered as the undercarriage was lowered.

'Of course, go and see her,' I said. 'I think I can find the way to the Watch office on my own.'

'Don't think it's only because of the girl,' Alisher said, and smiled again. 'I think it would be best for you to talk to the members of the local Watch yourself. You can show them Geser's letter and ask for their advice . . . And I'll get there an hour or an hour and a half later.'

'Weren't you on very friendly terms with your colleagues, then?' I asked quietly.

Alisher didn't answer – and that answered my question.

★   ★   ★

I walked out of the airport terminal building, which had clearly been reconstructed recently and looked absolutely new. The only things I was carrying were my hand baggage and a small plastic bag from the duty-free shop. I stopped and looked around. The sky was a blinding blue and the heat was already building up, although it was still early in the morning . . . There weren't many passengers – our flight was the first since the previous evening, and the next one wasn't expected for about an hour. I was immediately surrounded by private taxi drivers, all offering their services in their own particular way:

'Come on, let's go, dear man!'

'I'll show you the whole city, you'll see the sights for nothing!'

'Where are we going, then?'

'Get in, my car's comfortable, it has air-conditioning!'

I shook my head and looked at an elderly Uzbek driver who was waiting calmly beside an old Volga with the black-and-white checkerboard squares of a taxi stencilled on its side.

'Are you free, Father?'

'A man's free as long as he believes in his own freedom,' the taxi driver replied philosophically. He spoke Russian very well, without any accent at all. 'Get in.'

There you go. I had barely even arrived, and already I'd called someone 'Father', and the taxi driver had replied with the typical florid wisdom of the East. I asked:

'Did one of the great ones say that?'

'My grandfather said that. He was a Red Army soldier. Then an enemy of the people. Then the director of a Soviet farm. Yes, he was great.'

'Did he happen to be called Rustam?' I enquired.

'No, Rashid.'

The car drove off and I turned my face to the breeze from the window. The air was warm and fresh, and it smelled quite different

from how it did in Russia. And the road was good, even by
Moscow standards. A wall of trees along the side of the highway
provided shade and created the impression that we were already
in the city.

The taxi driver said thoughtfully:

'An air-conditioner. Nowadays everyone promises their
passengers coolness. But what did out grandfathers and great-
grandfathers know about air-conditioners? They just opened
the windows in their cars and they felt fine!'

I looked at the driver in bewilderment.

'It's just my joke. Have you flown in from Moscow?'

'Yes.'

'No suitcase. . . Ai-ai-ai!' He clicked his tongue. 'Don't tell me
they lost it!'

'An urgent business trip. There was no time to pack.'

'Urgent? Nothing's urgent in our city. There was a city standing
here a thousand years ago, two thousand years ago, three thousand years ago. The place has forgotten what urgent means.'

I shrugged. The car was certainly taking its time, but it didn't
bother me.

'So where are we going? There's the Hotel Samarkand, the
Hotel . . .'

'No, thanks. I didn't come here to sleep. I need the market
place. The Siabsky Market, in the Old City.'

'That's the right way to do it!' the driver said warmly. 'The man
knows where he's going and what for. The moment he lands he
goes straight to the market. No luggage, no wife, no problems –
that's the right way to live! But did you bring money to go to
the market?'

'I did,' I said, nodding. 'How can you go to the market with
no money? How much will I owe you? And what do you take –
soms or roubles?

'Even dollars or euros,' the driver replied nonchalantly. 'Give me as much as you think you can spare. I can see you're a good man, so why haggle? A good man is ashamed not to pay a poor taxi driver enough. He pays more than my conscience will allow me to ask.'

'You're a good psychologist.' I laughed.

'Good? Yes . . . probably. I did a Ph.D. in Moscow. A long time ago . . .' He paused and then said, 'But no one needs psychologists nowadays. I earn more as a taxi driver.'

He paused again, and I couldn't think of anything to say in reply. But we were already driving through the city, and soon the driver began listing all the places I had to visit in Samarkand. Three madrasahs that made up the Registan, a single architectural ensemble; the Bibi-Khanum mosque . . . All this, as it happened, was right beside the finest market in Samarkand, the Siabsky, which, as the driver now realised, was famous even as far away as Moscow. And I also had to visit the market, even before anything else. It would be a sin not to see it. But a good man like me wouldn't make a mistake like that . . .

The driver would probably have been very disappointed to see me walk straight past the entrance to the market. No, of course I was planning to visit it. There was work to do, but I still had to gather some impressions to take away with me.

Only not right now.

And so I elbowed my way out of the noisy crowd outside the entrance to the market, walked past a herd of Japanese (they'd even found their way here!) who all had the usual tiny cameras and video cameras dangling from their necks and their shoulders, then set off to walk round the Bibi-Khanum mosque. It really was impressive. The ceramic tiling of the huge dome glinted a bright azure blue in the sunlight. The doorway was so huge that I thought

it looked bigger than the Arc de Triomphe in Paris, and the absence
of any bas-relief work on the wall was more than made up for
by the intricate patterning of blue glazed bricks.

But the place I was headed for was no glamorous tourist spot.

Every city has streets that were built under an unlucky star. And
they don't have to be located in the outskirts, either. Sometimes they
run along beside gloomy factory buildings, sometimes along the
railway lines or main highways, sometimes even beside a park or
ravine that has survived through some oversight by the municipal
authorities. People move in there reluctantly, but they don't leave
very often either – they seem to fall under the spell of a strange
kind of drowsiness. And life there follows quite difference laws and
moves at a quite different pace . . .

I remember one district in Moscow where a one-way street
ran alongside a ravine overgrown with trees. It seemed like a
perfectly ordinary dormitory suburb – but it was under that spell
of drowsiness. I found myself there one winter evening on a false
alarm – the witch who was making love potions had a licence.
The car drove away, leaving me to draw up a report noting the
absence of any complaints on either side, then I went out into
the street and tried to stop a car – I didn't want to call a taxi and
wait for it in the witch's apartment. Although it wasn't very late,
it was already completely dark and there was thick snow falling.
There was absolutely no one on the street, everyone took a
different way home from the metro station. Almost all the cars
had disappeared too, and the ones that did drive by were in no
hurry to stop. But right at the edge of the ravine there was a small
amusement park, surrounded by a low fence: a little hut for the
ticket-seller, two or three roundabouts and a children's railway –
a circle of rails about ten metres in diameter. And in the total
silence, under the soft snow falling from the sky, against the background of the empty, lifeless blackness, the tiny locomotive was

running round the circle, jingling its bell and blinking its little coloured lights as it pulled along two small carriages. Sitting absolutely still in the first one was a boy about five years old, dusted with snow, wearing a large cap with earflaps and clutching a plastic spade in his hand. He was probably the ticket-seller's son and she had no one to leave him with at home . . . It didn't seem like anything special, but it gave me such a bad feeling that I made the driver of a passing truck stop and took off to the city centre.

Allowing for the difference between the cities, that was pretty much the kind of street where the Night Watch office was located. I didn't need a map, I could sense where I needed to go. And I only had to walk for ten minutes from the market place, which was right at the centre of town. But I seemed to have entered a different world. Not the bright world of an eastern fairy tale, but a kind of ordinary, average place that you can find in the Asian republics of the former Soviet Union, and Turkey, and the southern countries of Europe. Half European, half Asian, with far from the best features of both parts of the world. A lot of greenery, but that's the only good part – the two- or three-storey houses were dusty, dirty and dilapidated. If they'd been less monotonous they might at least have rejoiced the eye of some tourist. But even that variety was lacking here. Everything was dismally standard: paint flaking off the walls, dirty windows, entrance doors standing wide open, washing hanging on lines in the courtyards. The phrase 'frame-and-panel housing construction' surfaced from somewhere in the depths of my memory. Its bleak bureaucratic tone made it the perfect description of these buildings that had been meant to be 'temporary' but had already stood for more than half a century.

The Night Watch office occupied a small, dilapidated single-storey building that was surrounded by a small garden. I thought a building like that looked just perfect for a small kindergarten, filled with swarthy, dark-haired little kids.

But all the children here had grown up long ago. I walked round a Peugeot parked by the fence, opened the gate, went past the flower beds in which withering flowers were struggling to survive, and shuddered as I read the old Soviet bureaucratic-style sign on the door.

NIGHT WATCH
Samarkand branch
Business hours:
20.00 – 8.00

At first I thought I must have gone crazy. Then I thought I must be looking through the Twilight. But no, the inscription was absolutely real, written in yellow letters on a black background and covered with a cracked sheet of glass. One corner of the glass had fallen off, and the final letter of the word 'watch' was tattered and faded.

The same text was written alongside in Uzbek, and I learned that 'Night Watch' translated as '*Tungi Nazorat*'.

I pushed the door – it wasn't locked, of course – and walked straight into a large room. As usual in the East, there was no entrance hall. And that was right: why would they need a hallway here? The weather was never cold in Samarkand.

The furnishings were very simple, reminiscent in part of a small militia station and in part of an old office from Soviet times. There was a coat rack and several cupboards full of papers by the door. Three young Uzbek men and a plump middle-aged Russian woman were drinking tea at an office desk. There was a large electric samovar, decorated in the traditional Khokhloma folk style, boiling on the desk. Well, how about that – a samovar! The last time I'd seen one in Russia had been at the Izmailovo flea market, with all the *matryoshka* dolls, caps with earflaps and other goods for the foreign tourists. There were several other desks with no one sitting at them. An ancient computer with a massive monitor was clattering away on the farthest desk – its cooling fan ought to have been changed ages ago . . .

'*Assalom aleikhum*,' I said, feeling like a total idiot who was trying to look intelligent. Why on earth hadn't Geser taught me Uzbek?

'*Aleikhum assalom*,' the woman replied. She was swarthy-skinned, with black hair – quite clearly Slav in origin, but with that remarkable change in appearance that happens without any magic at all to a European who spends a long time in the East or is born and lives there. She was even dressed like an Uzbek woman, in a long, brightly coloured dress. She looked at me curiously – I sensed the skilful but weak touch of a probing spell. I didn't shield myself, and she gathered her information with no difficulty. Her expression immediately changed. She got up from the desk and said:

'Boys, we have a distinguished visitor . . .'

'I'm here entirely unofficially!' I said, raising my hands in the air.

But the fuss had already begun. They greeted me and introduced themselves: Murat, sixth level; Timur, fifth level; Nodir, fourth level. I thought they looked their real age, about twenty to thirty. According to Geser, there were five Others in the Samarkand watch . . . and according to Alisher, the members of the Watch in Tashkent were younger. How much younger could they be? Did they take on children from school?

'Valentina Ilinichna, Other. Fourth level.'

'Anton Gorodetsky, Other, Higher,' I said in turn.

'I run the office,' the woman went on. She was the last to shake my hand and in general she behaved like the most junior member of the Watch. But I estimated her age as at least a hundred and fifty, and her Power was greater than the men's.

Another peculiarity of the East?

But a second later any doubt about who was in charge here was dispelled.

'Right, boys, get the table set out quick,' Valentina commanded. 'Murat, you take the car, run round the route quickly and call into the market.'

And so saying, she handed Murat the key to the huge old safe, from which the young guy took out a tattered wad of banknotes, trying his best to do it inconspicuously.

'Please, there's no need!' I implored them. 'I'm only here for a brief, entirely unofficial visit. Just to introduce myself and ask a couple of questions . . . And I have to call in to the Day Watch too.'

'What for?' the woman asked.

'There were no Others at the border check. There was just a notice in the Twilight, saying that Light Ones should register with the Day Watch on arrival, and Dark Ones should register with the Night Watch.'

I wondered what she would have to say about such a flagrant piece of incompetence. But Valentina Ilinichna merely nodded and said:

'We don't have enough members to maintain a post in the airport. In Tashkent they do everything properly . . . Nodir, go and tell the ghouls that Higher Light One Gorodetsky is here on a visit from Moscow.'

'I'm here unofficially, but not exactly on personal—' I began, but no one was listening to me any longer. Nodir opened an inconspicuous door in the wall and walked through into the next room, which I was surprised to see was equally large and half empty.

'Why the ghouls?' I asked, struck by an unbelievable suspicion.

'Oh, that's the Day Watch office, they haven't really got any ghouls, that's just what we call them – to be neighbourly . . .' Valentina Ilinichna laughed.

I followed Nozdir into the next room without saying anything. Two Dark Others – one young and one middle-aged, fourth and fifth level – smiled at me amicably.

'*Assalom aleikhum . . .*' I muttered and walked through the large room (everything was just the same, even the samovar was standing in the same place) and opened the door to the street running parallel to the one from which I had entered the building.

Outside the door there was an identical garden and on the wall there was a sign:

DAY WATCH
Samarkand branch
Business hours:
8.00 – 20.00

I closed the door quietly and walked back into the room. Nodir had evidently sensed my reaction and cleared out.

One of the Dark Ones said good-naturedly:

'When you finish your business, come back to see us, respected guest. We don't often get visitors from Moscow.'

'Yes, do come, do come!' the other one said emphatically.

'Some time later . . . thank you for the invitation,' I muttered. I went back into the Night Watch office and closed the door behind me.

It didn't even have a lock on it!

The Light Ones appeared slightly embarrassed.

'The Night Watch,' I hissed through my teeth. 'The forces of Light . . .'

'We've cut back on space a bit. Utilities are expensive, and there's the rent . . .' said Valentina Ilinichna, spreading her hands and shrugging. 'We've been renting these premises for two offices like this for ten years now.'

I made a simple pass with my hand and the wall separating the Light Ones' office from the Dark Ones' office lit up with a blue glow for an instant. The Dark Ones of Samarkand were not likely to have a magician capable of removing a spell cast by a Higher One.

'There's no need for that, Anton,' Valentina Ilinichna said reproachfully. 'They won't listen. That's not the way we do things here.'

'You are supposed to keep a watch on the powers of Darkness,' I exclaimed. 'To monitor them!'

'We do monitor them,' Timur replied judiciously. 'If they're right next door, it makes them easier to monitor. And we'd need five times as many members to go dashing around all over town.'

'And the signs? What about the signs? Night Watch? Day Watch? People read them!'

'Let them read them,' said Nodir. 'There are all sorts of offices in the city. If you try to hide and don't put up a sign, you're immediately suspect. The militia will come round, or bandits working the protection racket. But this way everybody can see this is a state organisation, there's nothing to be got out of it, let it get on with its work . . .'

I came to my senses. After all, this wasn't Russia. The Samarkand Watch didn't come under our jurisdiction. In places like Belgorod or Omsk I could criticise and lay down the law. But the members of the Samarkand Watch didn't have to listen to me, even though I was a Higher Light One.

'I understand. But in Moscow it could never happen . . . Dark Ones sitting on the other side of the wall!'

'What's the harm in it?' Valentina Ilinichna asked in a soothing voice. 'Let them sit there. I expect their job's not too much fun either. But if anything happens, we won't compromise on our principles. Remember when the *zhodugar* Aliya-apa put a hex on old Nazgul three years ago, boys?'

The boys nodded. They livened up a bit and were obviously quite ready to reminisce about this glorious adventure.

'Who was it she put the hex on?' I asked, unable to resist.

They all laughed.

'It's a name – Nazgul. Not those nazguls in the American movie,' Nodir explained, and his white teeth flashed as he smiled. 'He's a man. That is, he was – he died last year. He took a long time to die, and he had a young wife. So she asked a witch to sap her husband's strength. We spotted the hex, arrested the witch, repri- manded the wife, did everything the way it's supposed to be done. Valentina Ilinichna removed the hex, everything worked out very well. Although he was an obnoxious old man, a very bad char- acter. Malicious, greedy and a womaniser, even though he was old. Everybody was glad when he died. But we removed the hex, just like we're supposed to do.'

I thought for a moment and sat down on a squeaky Viennese chair. Yes, knowledge of the Uzbek language wouldn't have been much help to me. It wasn't a matter of language. It was a matter of a different mentality.

The rational explanation had calmed me down a bit. But then I spotted Valentina Ilinichna's glance – kindly, but condescendingly sympathetic.

'But even so, it's not right,' I said. 'Please understand, I don't want to criticise, it's your city, you're responsible for maintaining order here . . . But it's a bit unusual.'

'That's because you're closer to Europe,' Nodir explained. He obviously didn't think that Uzbekistan had nothing at all to do with Europe. 'But it's all right here: when there's peace we can live beside each other.'

'Uh-huh,' I said and paused before I went on: 'Thank you for the explanation.'

'Have a seat at the desk,'Valentina Ilinichna said amicably.'Why are you sitting over in the corner like a stranger?'

I actually wasn't sitting in the corner at all. Timur was finishing setting the table in the corner. The bright-coloured tablecloth that had instantly transformed two office desks into one large dining table was already covered with plates of fruit: bright red and luscious green apples; black, green, yellow and red grapes; huge pomegranates the size of a small melon. And there was very appetising-looking home-made salami, meat cut into slices and hot bread cakes that must have been heated using magic. I remembered how in one rare moment of nostalgia Geser had started singing the praises of the bread cakes in Samarkand – how delicious they were, how they didn't turn stale even after a week, all you had to do was warm them up, and you just kept on and on eating them, you couldn't stop . . . At the time I had taken what he said as the standard old man's reminiscences of the sort 'the trees were bigger then, and the salami tasted better'. But now I began drooling at the mouth and I suddenly suspected that Geser hadn't been exaggerating all that much.

And there were also two bottles of cognac on the table. The local kind – which frightened me a bit.

'Forgive us for laying such a simple table,' Nodir said imperturbably. 'Our junior member will be back from the market soon, and we'll dine properly. Meanwhile we can make a light start.'

I realised there was no way I was going to escape a gala dinner with abundant alcohol. And I suspected it was not only Alisher's entirely understandable interest in his old girlfriend from school that had made him dodge an immediate visit to the Watch. It was many years since a visit by someone from Moscow had also been a visit from a superior, but even so, Moscow was still a very important centre for the members of the Samarkand Watch.

'I've actually come here at Geser's request . . .' I said.

I saw from their faces that my status had soared from simply important guest to quite unimaginable heights. Somewhere way out in space, where Others could not go.

'Geser asked me to find a friend of his,' I went on. 'He lives somewhere in Uzbekistan . . .'

There was an awkward pause.

'Anton, are you talking about the devona?' Valentin Ilinichna asked. 'He went to Moscow – in 1998. And he was killed there. We thought that Geser knew about it.'

'No, no, I'm not talking about the devona!' I protested. 'Geser asked me to find Rustam.'

The young Uzbeks exchanged glances Valentina Ilinichna knitted her brows.

'Rustam . . . I've heard something about him. But that's a very, very old story. Thousands of years old, Anton.'

'He doesn't work in the Watch,' I admitted. 'And, of course, he has a different name. I think he has changed his name many times. All I know is that he is a Higher Light Magician.'

Nodir ran a hand through his coarse black hair and said firmly:

'That's very difficult, Anton-aka. We do have one Higher Magician in Uzbekistan. He works in Tashkent. But he's young. If an old and powerful magician wishes to hide, he can always manage it. Finding him doesn't just require someone who is powerful, it requires someone who is wise. Geser himself should search for him. *Kechrasyz*, apologies, Anton-aka. We will not be able to help you.'

'We could ask Afandi,' Valentina Ilinichna said thoughtfully. 'He is a weak magician and not very . . . not very bright. But he has a good memory, and he has lived in this world for three hundred years . . .'

'Afandi?' I asked cautiously.

'He's the fifth member of our Watch.'Valentina Ilinichna seemed a little embarrassed. 'Well, you understand, seventh level. He mostly takes care of the office and grounds. But he just might be able to help.'

'I'm almost certain he will,' I said, with a nod, remembering what Nadya had said. 'But where is he?'

'He should be here soon.'

There was nothing else I could do. I nodded again and walked towards the 'empty' table.

Murat got back half an hour later carrying several full bags, and some of their contents immediately migrated to the table. He carried the rest into the small kitchen attached to the main premises of the Watch. My culinary knowledge was sufficient for me to realise that pilaf was about to be made.

And meanwhile we drank the cognac, which unexpectedly turned out to be quite good, and tried the fruits.Valentina Ilinichna let Nodir lead the conversation. And I listened politely to the history of the Uzbek Watches from ancient mythological times to Tamerlaine, and from Tamerlaine to our own time. I won't lie – the Light Ones here had not always lived in perfect harmony with the Dark Ones. There were plenty of grim, bloody and terrible events. But I got the feeling that the flare-ups of hostility between the Watches in Uzbekistan were governed by laws that I knew absolutely nothing about. People could fight wars and kill each other, while the Watches maintained a polite neutrality. But during Khrushchev's time and the early years of Brezhnev's rule, Light Ones and Dark Ones had fought each other with quite incredible ferocity. Three Higher Magicians had been killed at that time – two from the Day Watch and one from the Night Watch. And that war had also decimated the ranks of first- and second-level Others.

Then everything had gone quiet, as if the 'stagnation' of the

1980s also extended to the Others. And since then relations between Dark Ones and Light Ones had consisted of a rather half-hearted stand-off: more jibes and taunts than genuine enmity.

'Alisher didn't like that,' Timur observed. 'Is he still in Moscow?'

I nodded, delighted by this opportune change of subject.

'Yes. He's in our Watch.'

'How is he getting on?' Nodar asked politely. 'We heard he's already fourth level.'

'Practically third,' I said. 'But he can tell you himself. He flew down with me, but he decided to visit some friends first.'

The members of the watch were clearly not pleased by this news. Timur and Nodir both looked not exactly annoyed but uncomfortable. Valentina Ilinichna shook her head.

'Have I said something to upset you?' I asked. The bottle we had drunk together obliged me to speak frankly. 'Do explain to me what the problem is. Why do you feel that way about Alisher? Is it because his father was a devona?'

The members of the Watch exchanged glances.

'It's not a question of who his father was,' Valentina Ilinichna said. 'Alisher is a good boy. But he's very . . . categorical.'

'Really?'

'Perhaps he has changed in Moscow,' Timur suggested. 'But Alisher always wanted to fight. He was born in the wrong time.'

I thought about that. Of course, in our Watch, Alisher had always preferred to work on the streets. Patrols, confrontations, arrests – there wasn't much that happened without him being involved . . .

'Well . . . that's a bit more natural in Moscow,' I said. 'It's a big city, life is more stressful. But Alisher misses his homeland a lot.'

'But we're glad that Alisher's here, of course we are!' Valentina Ilinichna said, changing her tune 'It's been such a long time since we saw him. Hasn't it, boys?'

The 'boys' agreed with feigned enthusiasm. Even Murat declared from the kitchen that he really missed Alisher.

'Will Afandi be here soon?' I asked, turning the conversation away from an awkward subject.

'Yes, indeed,' said Valentina Ilinichna, concerned. 'It's after two already . . .'

'He's been here for a long time,' Murat commented from the kitchen again. 'He's wandering round the yard with a broom – I can see him through the window. He probably decided we'd ask him to cook the pilaf . . .'

Nodir walked across quickly to the door and called out:

'Afandi, what are you doing?'

'Sweeping the yard,' the fifth member of the Samarkand Watch replied, with a dignified air. To judge from his voice, not only had he been born three hundred years earlier, his body was far from young too.

Nodir turned back to us and shrugged apologetically. He called again:

'Afandi, come in – we have a guest!'

'I know we have a guest. That's why I'm sweeping!'

'Afandi, the guest is already in the house. Why are you cleaning outside?'

'Eh, Nodir! Don't you teach me how to receive guests! When the guest is still outside – everybody cleans and tidies the house. But if the guest is in the house, you have to clean outside!'

'Have it your own way, Afandi.' Nodir laughed. 'You know best, of course. But meanwhile we're going to eat grapes and drink cognac.'

'Wait, Nodir!' Afandi replied agitatedly. 'It would be disrespectful to the guest not to dine at the same table with him!'

A moment later Afandi was standing in the doorway. He looked absolutely ridiculous. A pair of trainers with the laces unfastened on his feet, a pair of blue jeans held up with a Soviet Army belt and a white nylon shirt with big broad buttons. Nylon is a durable material. The shirt was probably twenty or thirty years old. Afandi himself was a clean-shaven old man (the scraps of newspaper stuck to the cuts on his chin suggested that this cost him a serious effort) with a balding head. He was about sixty years old. He cast an approving glance at the table, leaned his broom against the door-post and skipped briskly across to me.

'Hello, respected guest. May your Power increase like the fervour of a man undressing a woman! May it rise to the second level and even the first!'

'Afandi, our guest is a Higher Magician,' Valentina Ilinichna put in. 'Why do you wish him the second level?'

'Quiet, woman!' said Afandi, letting go of my hand and taking a seat at the table. 'Do you not see how quickly my wish has come true and even been exceeded?'

The members of the Watch laughed, but without the slightest malice. Afandi – I scanned his aura and discovered that the old man was on the very lowest level of Power – was regarded as the jester of the Samarkand Watch. But he was a well-loved jester: they would forgive him any foolish nonsense and never let him come to any harm.

'Thank you for the kind word, Father,' I said. 'Your wishes really do come true with remarkable speed.'

The old man nodded as he threw half a peach into his mouth with evident relish. His teeth were excellent – he might not take much care of his appearance, but he obviously attached great importance to that particular part of his body

'They're all young whippersnappers here,' he muttered. 'I'm sure they haven't even welcomed you properly. What's your name, dear man?'

'Anton.'

'My name's Afandi. That means a sage,' said the old man, looking round sternly at the other members of the Watch. 'If it weren't for my wisdom, the powers of Darkness, may they wither in agony and burn in hell, would long ago have drunk their sweet little brains and chewed up their big stringy livers!'

Nodir and Timur chortled.

'I understand why our livers are stringy,' said Nodir, pouring the cognac. 'But why are our brains sweet?'

'Because wisdom is bitter, but foolishness and ignorance are sweet!' Afandi declared, washing down his peach with a glass of cognac. 'Hey! Hey, you fool, what do you think you're doing?'

'What?' said Timur, who was about follow his cognac with a few grapes. He looked at Afandi quizzically.

'You can't follow cognac with grapes!'

'Why?'

'It's the same thing as boiling a kid in its mother's milk!'

'Afandi, only Jews don't boil young goat meat in milk!'

'Do you?'

'No,' said Timur, abashed. 'Why use milk—'

'Then don't follow cognac with grapes!'

'Afandi, I have only known you for three minutes, but I have already tasted so much wisdom that I shall be digesting it for an entire month,' I put in to attract the old man's attention. 'The wise Geser sent me to Samarkand. He asked me to find his old friend, who once went by the name of Rustam. Do you happen to know Rustam?'

'Of course I do,' Afandi said, with a nod. 'But who's Geser?'

'Afandi!' Valentina Ilinichna exclaimed, throwing her hands in the air. 'You must have heard of the Great Geser!'

'Geser,' the old man mused. 'Geser, Geser . . . Wasn't he the Light Magician who worked as a night-soil man in Binkent?'

'Afandi! How can you confuse the Great Geser with some night-soil man?' Valentina Ilinichna was shocked.

'Ah, Geser!' said Afandi, nodding. 'Yes, yes, yes! At Oldjibai, the vanquisher of Soton, Lubson and Gubkar. Who doesn't know old man Geser?'

'But who knows old man Rustam?' I butted in again, before Afandi could start reciting Geser's great and glorious deeds.

'I do,' Afandi declared proudly.

'Please don't exaggerate, Afandi,' Timur said. 'Our guest really needs to meet Rustam.'

'That's not easy,' said Afandi, suddenly shedding all his buffoonery. 'Rustam has cut himself off from people. He was seen in Samarkand ten years ago, but since then no one has spoken to Rustam, no one . . .'

'How do you know about Rustam, Afandi?' I couldn't resist asking. If it wasn't for what my daughter had said, I would have believed the old man was simply stringing me along.

'It was a long time ago,' Afandi said, with a sigh. 'In Samarkand there was an old man, a complete fool, just like these young whippersnappers. One day he was walking through the town, complaining that he didn't have anything to eat. And suddenly a mighty hero, a *batyr,* with eyes that glowed and a high, wise forehead, came out to meet him. He looked at the old man and said: "Grandad, why are you so sad? Do you really not know the power that is concealed within you? You are a *Boshkacha*! An Other!" The *batyr* touched the old man with his hand, and the old man acquired power and wisdom. And the *batyr* said: "Know that the Great Rustam himself has been your teacher." That was what happened to me two hundred and fifty years ago!'

As far as I could tell, the members of the Watch were as astonished by this story as I was. Murat froze absolutely still in the doorway of the kitchen and Timur spilled the cognac he was just about to pour into the glasses.

'Afandi, you were initiated by Rustam?' Valentina Ilinichna asked.

'I'll tell everything to a person wise enough,' Afandi answered, taking his glass from Timur. 'But you can tell a stupid person a hundred times, and he won't understand a thing.'

'Why didn't you tell us this story before?' Timur asked.

'There was no reason to.'

'Afandi, a pupil can always call his teacher,' I said.

'That is true,' Afandi confirmed pompously.

'I need to meet Rustam.'

Afandi sighed and gave me a cunning look.

'But does Rustam need to meet you?'

How sick I was of that florid Eastern style! Did they really talk to each that way in their daily lives? 'My wife, have you warmed a bread cake for me?' – 'Oh, my husband, will not my warm embraces take the place of your bread cake?'

I realised I was on the point of giving way and saying something unworthy of a guest who had been met with such great hospitality. But fortunately there was a quiet knock at the door and Alisher walked in.

I didn't like the look on his face at all. I wouldn't have been surprised to see Alisher looking sad. After all, he could have discovered that his school sweetheart had married, had five children, got fat and completely forgotten about him – more than enough reason for feeling sad.

But Alisher was alarmed about something.

'Hi,' he said to his former colleagues, as if he had only left them yesterday. 'We've got problems.'

'Where?' I asked.

'Right outside the fence.'

CHAPTER 3

AFTER EDINBURGH I ought to have been expecting something like this.

But instead I had relaxed. The streets smothered in greenery, the splashing of the water in the irrigation ditches, the noisy eastern market and the severe outlines of the domes of the mosque, the Dark Ones on the other side of the wall and the overwhelming hospitality of the Light Ones – it was all so completely different from Scotland. I thought the only problem I'd have to deal with would be finding the old magician – I wasn't expecting any more cunning tricks involving human beings. The building was surrounded by about a hundred men. I could see militiamen among them, and well-equipped soldiers from the Special Forces, and young soldiers – skinny, pimply kids, awkwardly clutching automatic weapons. All sorts of forces had been brought together to capture us. Everything that had been close at hand.

That wasn't a problem. Even without my help, Alisher could brainwash a hundred or two hundred attackers. Unfortunately, every man in the cordon was protected by magic spells.

Every Other is capable of shielding himself against the influence of magic and of shielding others. He doesn't even have to be at a very high level in order to apply protective spells to a hundred people. To put it simply: magic that is controlled by reason is more like a knife than a grenade launcher. And what you need to protect yourself against is not the heavy armour plate of a tank, but a light bulletproof vest made of Kevlar. By striking with raw Power in the form of a Fireball, a White Lance or a Wall of Flame, I could burn out an entire city block. And equally powerful amulets and spells would have been required to protect anyone against the strike. But in order to subordinate the attackers to my will and scatter them, first I would have to strip each one of them of his protection. And that was far from simple. There are dozens of different kinds of mental Shields, and I didn't know which kind had been used. Most likely (at least, this was what I would have done) each individual Shield was made up of two or three spells chosen at random. One soldier, for instance, has the Shield of Magic and the Sphere of Calm. Another has the Sphere of Denial, the Crust of Ice and the Barrier of Will.

Just try finding the right approach for each one! And from a distance!

'They followed me,' Alisher explained while I, protected by my own Sphere of Denial, stood at the window and studied the warriors who had surrounded us. 'I don't know how, but they followed me all the way from the airport. I always had the feeling I was being followed, but I couldn't spot anything. And then, when I was leaving my acquaintances' house . . . they tried to arrest me. About twenty men. Not a single Other. I tried to shield myself from them, but they could see me!'

They could see me too. Not all of them, but a few soldiers had clearly spotted me despite the magic. That meant that they had been charged with search spells as well as protective spells. Glance of the Heart, Clear Gaze, True Vision – the magical arsenal is quite extensive. Light Ones and Dark Ones have been thinking up ways to deceive each other for thousands of years.

And now it had all been turned against us.

'How did you get away from them?' I asked, moving away from the window.

'Through the Twilight. Only . . .' Alisher hesitated. 'They were waiting for me there, too. There was someone keeping watch on the second level . . . I got out as fast as I could.'

'Who was it on watch? A Light One? A Dark One?'

Alisher gulped and smiled awkwardly.

'I think it was a deva.'

'Nonsense,' I exclaimed, suppressing the urge to swear. 'Devas don't exist.'

'They don't exist in Moscow, but we have them here,' Timur stated with absolute certainty. He caught my gaze where it focused on the door leading to the Dark Ones. 'Anton, believe me. It's not them! They have no reason to attack us, and to involve people as well! The Inquisition would have their heads!'

I nodded. I wasn't even thinking of suspecting the Samarkand Day Watch.

'Get in touch with the top management in Tashkent. Tell them to stop these men!'

'How?' asked Timur, puzzled.

'By human methods! Phone calls to the ministers of defence and internal affairs! And get on to the Inquisition, quick!'

'What shall I say?' Valentina Ilinichna asked, taking out an old mobile phone.

'Tell them we have a critical situation here. An alpha-prime violation of the Great Treaty. The provision of information concerning Others to human beings, the involvement of human beings in confrontation between the Watches, the illegal use of magic, the illegal dissemination of magic, violation of the agreement on the separation of powers . . . in brief, violations of clauses one, six, eight, eleven and fourteen of the Basic Appendix to the Treaty. I think that will be enough.'

Valentina Ilinihcna was already making the call. I looked out of the window again. The soldiers were waiting, sitting on the picket fence. What were the walls made of here? If they really were compressed reeds, bullets would go straight through them . . .

'Ah, what beautiful words!' Afandi suddenly exclaimed. He was still sitting at the table and chewing with relish on a piece of sausage. His glass was full, and the cognac bottle on the table was empty. 'A violation of the Basic Appendix! That makes everything clear all right, clear as day. Keep giving the orders, Commander!'

I turned away from Afandi. It was just my luck – the person all my hopes rested on was as half-witted as the devona before he met Geser . . .

'Time to be going, lads,' I said. 'I'm sorry things turned out this way.'

'Anton, can you disperse them?' Nodir asked, with timid hope in his voice.

'I can kill them, no problem. But not disperse them.'

Someone began hammering on the door that led to the Dark Ones' office. Timur walked over, asked something and opened it. The two Dark Ones who were on duty there came running in. Judging from their bewildered expressions, they had only just discovered the cordon and were desperate for explanations.

'What are you doing, Light One?' howled the one who was a bit older. 'Why did you bring these men here?'

'Quiet,' I said, raising my hand. 'Shut up!'

He had enough wits to do as I said.

'This situation comes under point one of the Appendix to the Great Treaty,' I said and Afandi grunted loudly. I gave him an angry sideways glance, but the old man had just swallowed an entire glass of cognac, and now he was breathing rapidly and pressing his hand to his mouth. I continued: 'In this situation, under the terms of the Convention of Prague, as the most powerful magician here, I assume general command of all Others here present. *All Others here present!*'

The young Dark One looked at his elder, who frowned, nodded and said:

'We await your orders, Higher One.'

'Total evacuation of the Watches,' I said. 'All documents and artefacts to be destroyed. Get to it.'

'How are we going to get out?' the young Dark One asked. 'Put up shields?'

I shook my head.

'I'm afraid they have charmed bullets. We have to leave via the Twilight.'

'Oh, Afandi has been in the Twilight!' the old man declared loudly. 'Afandi can walk in the Twilight!'

'Afandi, you will go with me and Alisher,' I ordered. 'The others . . .'

Alisher looked at me in alarm and moved his lips soundlessly. 'The deva . . .'

'The others will cover us,' I ordered.

'Why should we?' the young Dark One protested. 'We—'

I waved my hand, and the Dark One squirmed and squealed in agony, pressing his hands against his stomach.

'Because I order it,' I explained, removing the pain. 'Because I am a Higher Magician and you are fifth level. Do you understand?'

'Yes.' Appallingly enough, there wasn't even a hint of indignation in the Dark One's voice. He had tried to throw his weight about, been punished and accepted my right to command because I was more powerful. Later, of course, he would write a whole bunch of complaints to the Inquisition. But for now he would obey.

Meanwhile the other Watch members were destroying their offices. The older Dark One was working alone, but he seemed to have everything under control. The destruction spells had been applied to the safe in advance – there was smoke pouring out of the keyhole – and they had been applied to all the documents too: the ones on the desk were curling up, turning yellow and crumbling to pieces. The Light Ones were burning everything by hand, and they were doing it with real enthusiasm: I watched as Timur drove a deftly rolled fireball straight through the metal wall of the safe and it exploded inside.

'They've gone very quiet,' Alisher said anxiously, glancing out of the window. 'They'll see the smoke any minute . . .'

They saw it all right. A voice with a strong accent addressed us in Russian through a megaphone:

'Terrorists! Lay down your weapons and leave the building one at a time! You are surrounded! If you do not comply, we will storm the building!'

'What crazy nonsense . . .' Valentina Ilinichna exclaimed indignantly. 'Terrorists – would you believe it!'

A second later Alisher leapt back from the window and the glass shattered with a tinkling sound. A small metal cylinder fell to the floor, spinning around its axis.

'Let's leave!' I shouted, diving into the Twilight. After the heat of Samarkand, the coolness of the first level was actually quite pleasant.

That very moment the grey gloom around me was lit up brightly. I didn't even want to think about how blinding the flash must have been in the human world. Fortunately, from down there in the Twilight I couldn't hear the ear-splitting screech.

I'd never thought that the Special Services' light-and-sound grenades could be so devastating against Others. Only Valentina Ilinichna had managed to withdraw into the Twilight with me — in here she looked like a slim young woman no more than thirty years old.

The other Watch members were blundering helplessly around the room. Some were rubbing at their eyes, some were holding their ears. A light-and-sound grenade blinds you for ten to twenty seconds, so they couldn't withdraw into the Twilight.

'Help the boys!' I shouted to Valentina and rushed to the doors. I flung them open in the Twilight, not the ordinary world, and looked outside.

Yes, of course, they were already storming us. Clumsily and stupidly, en masse — there were dozens of Special Services men running towards the entrance, and the soldiers on the other side of the fence had started firing at the windows. The assault was uncoordinated, as it always is whenever somebody gets the clever idea of creating a joint unit of militiamen, common soldiers and Special Services. I saw one of the Special Services men throw his hands up and fall — he had taken a bullet in the back. But he probably wouldn't have anything worse than bruising — the troops in the assault wave were wearing bulletproof vests.

But the fact that several marksmen started aiming their shots at me was very bad news. That was either Clear Gaze or True Vision. Which was very, very serious indeed. And the bullets really were charmed up to the hilt. Not only did they exist in the real world and the first level of the Twilight at the same time, they were packed with deadly magic!

I ducked — fortunately, our enemies had not been accelerated and the advantage of speed remained with me. I waved my hand, allowing the Power to flow from my fingertips. A rain of fire fell on the earth and a wall of smoke and flame sprang up in front of the attackers. Right — now, lads, are you ready to jump into the fire?

They weren't. They stopped (one was moving too fast and he stuck his face into the flames and jumped back with a howl), then they drew back and started raising their automatic rifles.

Naturally, I didn't wait for them to fire. I burst back into the house, on the way reducing the dubious Night Watch sign to cinders with a fireball. The adrenalin was coursing through my veins.

War games? All right, then, let's play war games!

Hang the Absolute Lock spell on the door (actually there are two of these spells, but the other one wouldn't have had any effect if it was applied to an inanimate object). Hang a Light Shield right across the walls, one that would hold against automatic fire for about five minutes. Of course, the attackers would notice that something was wrong. But there was no way that we could leave secretly now.

The two Dark Ones entered the Twilight one after the other – they had been standing with their backs to the grenade when it exploded. The older one was about to strike the window with something, but I caught hold of his arm.

'What have you got there?'

He bared his long, crooked teeth in a grin. Well, well, an ordinary weak Dark Magician, but what a jaw he had sprouted now!

'They'll shit themselves. Just a little bit.'

'Go ahead,' I agreed. 'Only not here. Cover your side!'

Timur entered the Twilight, followed by Alisher, who was dragging Murat after him. Only Nodir was still rubbing his eyes, unable to recover his senses: he had been blinded worst of all.

'Alisher, let's get Afandi!' I shouted.

We walked over to the old man who was still sitting at the table, trying to suck on the mouth of a fresh bottle of cognac.

'On the count of two,' I said. 'One, two . . .'

We leapt out of the Twilight, grabbed Afandi under the arms and lifted him off his chair. With my free hand I managed to grab the bag with all my bits and pieces and throw the strap across my shoulder. The bursts of automatic fire thundered in my ears and the bullets jangled as they ricocheted off the Shield. The crimson flames flickered outside the windows. With a deft movement, the old man managed to get one suck at the bottle – just at the moment when we dragged him into the Twilight.

'Ai!' he exclaimed in disappointment. The bottle had been left behind in the normal world, and Afandi's hand closed on emptiness. 'Ai, the drink's disappearing!'

'Grandad, we haven't got any time for drink,' Alisher told him with quite incredible patience. 'Enemies have attacked us – we're leaving!'

'No surrender to the enemies!' Afandi exclaimed gleefully. 'Into battle!'

At long last Nodir too entered the Twilight. I looked round at my improvised army: four weak Light Ones, two weak Dark Ones, Alisher, who had been tested on the streets of Moscow, and Afandi as ballast. Well, if could have been worse. Even if those Higher Ones who had been in Scotland were hiding somewhere around here, we could give them a fight for their money.

'Let's leave!' I commanded. 'Alisher, you take Afandi! Valentina, Timur – you go first! Everybody erect the Magician's Shield!'

We left straight through the wall. On the second level of the Twilight it wouldn't have existed at all. On the first level it did exist, and it even seemed to slow down our movements. But if you took a run, it was possible to pass through almost any material object down here.

And we did pass through it. Only Afandi got one leg stuck, and he jerked it about in the wall for a long time before he broke free, leaving one trainer behind. It would stay hanging there on the first level of the Twilight, slowly fading away over a period of several months. A few particularly sensitive people would even notice it out of the corner of their eye – provided, of course, that the building survived

On the side we broke out through, the cordon was thinner. Five men with sub-machine guns were staring at the blank wall, obviously puzzled about why they had been stationed there. But two of them turned out to be charmed and they saw us. I don't know what we looked like – ordinary people who leapt out through the wall or spectral shadows. In any case, there was no goodwill evident in the soldiers' faces, only fear and the readiness to shoot. Valentina did the right thing – her spell had no visible effect, but the foolproof Kalashnikov in one soldier's hands refused to fire. And then Timur hurled a fireball through the Twilight and burned off the barrel of the other soldier's automatic rifle.

That was a mistake!

Sure, those two couldn't shoot any more. But their comrades, who couldn't locate us themselves, saw the ball of flame come flying out of nowhere – and they started firing. Either out of sheer fright or because they had been trained to do it.

At first I thought Timur hadn't put up a Shield. The burst of fire literally cut straight through him – I saw the bullets leave holes in his back, one after another. He fell over on to his back, and then I saw that he did have a Shield after all. A weak one, only at the front, but it was there.

The enchanted bullets had pierced straight through his magical armour. It was the very same technique as in Edinburgh!

'Tim!' Nodir shouted, bending down over his friend.

That was what saved him – several bursts of fire from the soldiers blazing away erratically with their automatic weapons went right over his head.

The next moment, before I could do anything to stop him, Murat struck back.

They didn't have a very wide choice of spells. As provincial magicians unused to combat and not naturally very powerful, they were quite unprepared for this skirmish with human beings who could kill Others.

Murat used some version of the White Sword that I didn't know. In theory this spell should only kill Dark Others and people who are totally given over to evil. In practice, you have to be a monk who spends his days in prayer and self-mortification for the remorseless blow not to cause you any harm. Any trace of aggression or fear makes a man vulnerable to the blade of pure Light.

Those young Uzbek lads in military uniform had any amount of fear and aggression in them.

The white blade cut straight through four soldiers like a sharp scythe mowing down wheat. It literally sliced them in half. With fountains of blood and other unmentionable sights. The fifth soldier dropped his automatic weapon and took to his heels, screaming wildly. Even seen from the Twilight he seemed to be moving fast, he put on such a burst of speed!

Murat was frozen to the spot. I walked round in front of him. The white blade was still fading away in his hand and he looked very calm, almost sleepy. I looked into his eyes and found the answer to my question.

It was over. He was already withdrawing.

I squatted down beside Nodir and shook him by the shoulder: 'Let's go.'

He turned his face towards me and said in a surprised voice: 'They killed Timur. They shot him!'

'I can see. Let's go.'

Nodir started shaking his head.

'No! We can't leave him here . . .'

'We can and we will! Our enemies won't get their hands on the body; it will dissolve in the Twilight. We'll all go that way sooner or later. Get up.'

He shook his head again.

'Get up. The Light needs you.'

Nodir groaned, but he got up. And then his gaze fell on Murat. He shook his head again, as if he was trying to shake out the sudden overload of dark impressions. He dashed over to Murat and tried to grab hold of his arm.

His fingers clutched nothing but air. Murat was melting away, dissolving into the Twilight. Far more quickly than Timur's dead body would disappear. A Light Magician has to have a lot of experience of life in order to convince himself that he has the right to kill four people. I could probably have held out. Murat couldn't.

'Let's go!' I ordered, giving Nodir a slap across the face. 'Let's go!'

Somehow he managed to pull himself together and plod along behind me – away from the office, which was still being stormed, away from two comrades, one dead and one dying. Valentina walked in front, with the Dark Ones beside her. Alisher was dragging along Afandi, who had sobered up and calmed down. Nodir and I brought up the rear of the procession.

They started firing after us again – the screams of the soldier who had survived had attracted attention. I raised another Wall of Flame and, unable to resist, flung a small fireball at the old Peugeot by the fence. The car flared up in a jolly blaze, adding a little French charm to the Central Asian landscape.

The confusion that had set in made it easier for us to retreat. Moreover, in the Twilight there were gaping holes in the low fence, and the next building didn't exist at all. We ran down the deserted street as far as the crossroads and turned on to another narrow street that led to the market. It seemed that sooner or later every street here led to the market . . . Nodir was sobbing and swearing by turns. Afandi kept looking back, gazing in amazement at the battle raging around the empty building. It looked as if the attackers had started firing at each other in their confusion.

The Dark Ones were holding up better. Valentina Ilinichna was walking in the centre, and they were providing perfectly competent lateral protection. I actually thought that we had already escaped pursuit. And that was an unforgivable mistake for a Higher Magician to make. Or almost unforgivable.

After all, I had never really believed that devas existed.

The European tradition is golems – creatures created out of clay, wood, or even metal. In Russia the wooden ones are known affectionately as pinocchios, although the last actual operational pinocchio rotted away sometime in the eighteenth century. We don't know what their contemporaries used to call them. We were taught to create pinocchios in our classes and that was both amusing and instructive – the wooden doll that came to life could walk, perform simple work, even talk . . . and it crumbled into dust after only a few minutes. For a wooden golem to last even a few days, the magician has to be very powerful and very skilful, and experienced magicians don't really have much use for dim-witted pinocchios. Bringing metal to life, making a creature of metal, is even harder: I remember that Sveta once made a walking doll out of paper clips for little Nadya, but it took exactly three steps and then froze for ever. Clay is remarkably malleable and amenable to animation – it holds the magic for a long time – but even clay golems are only made very rarely nowadays.

In the East, though, there were devas. Or rather, it was believed that there were. Essentially, they're golems too, only without any material basis – animated clumps of the Twilight, intertwined vortexes of Power. According to legend, creating such a deva (the Arabs usually called them genies) was regarded as an examination that a magician had to pass to be acknowledged as higher level. First you had to create the golem, then you had to subordinate it to your will. Some were eliminated at the first stage, but a far sadder fate awaited those who screwed things up at the second.

I thought devas were creatures of legend. Or, at the very most, an extremely rare experiment that one of the greatest magicians of antiquity had managed to pull off once or twice. And even less did I imagine that devas still existed in our own times. However, the members of the local Watches seemed to believe in them

Only they didn't have the Power to spot a deva approaching.

The young Dark One – I never did learn his name – screamed and started flailing his arms about, as if he was trying to fight off something invisible. He was lifted up off the ground and carried through the air until he stopped, shouting and squirming, at the height of a two-storey house. I shuddered as I watched the Dark One's sides collapse as if from the pressure of a gigantic hand, and his clothes start to char. His scream became a feeble wheeze.

And then a bloody streak appeared on the Dark One's body in the form of an arc. A moment later the dead body fell to the ground, cut – or rather bitten – right through.

'Shields!' Alisher shouted.

I didn't increase the strength of my own shield. In the first place, I didn't know if it would be any use to me against the deva. And in the second – I was the only one who could stand up to the creature.

I instantly sank down to the second level of the Twilight.

And immediately I saw the deva.

The flexible body woven out of plumes of fire and smoke really did resemble a mythical genie. The predominant colour was grey – even the petals of flame were blackish-grey, with just the faintest hint of crimson. The deva didn't have any legs: its torso narrowed and became a snake's body that writhed as the deva moved along. The ground underneath it steamed, like damp laundry under an iron. The head, the arms and even the genitals that protruded absurdly from the serpentine half appeared completely human. But they were huge – the deva stood five or five and a half metres tall – and they were made of smoke and flame. The eyes blazed with a scarlet fire – the only bright detail on the deva's body, and in the entire second level of the Twilight.

The deva saw me too – just at the moment when it was reaching its hand out for Valentina. The monster howled in glee and came skidding towards me with surprising agility. What was this crazy fashion for reptiles? A two-headed snake in Scotland, and now a half snake, half man in Uzbekistan . . .

Just as a test, I threw a fireball at the deva – it had absolutely no effect: the bundle of flames simply dissolved in the monster's body. Then I tried a Triple Blade – the deva winced, but it didn't slow down.

All right, then . . .

I allowed the Power to flow through my arm and created a White Sword. I was probably influenced by Murat's final action, but it was a mistake to follow the Uzbek magician's example – the white blade easily sliced through the deva's body, but without causing it any harm. There was no time to ponder the reasons for this failure. The deva swung its arm back and struck out with its hand. I managed to jump back, but a cunning thrust with the tail caught me by surprise and I was sent tumbling across the ground. The deva advanced on me, laughing triumphantly, but I couldn't get up. Strangely enough, I didn't even feel afraid – all I felt was revulsion at the sight of the monster's penis rising into an erection. The deva clutched his penis in one hand and began waggling it about, either masturbating or preparing to use it as a club of fire to splat me with.

What was this? Was I supposed to die of a blow from some brainless monster's dick? I didn't try to create another white blade. I gathered Power into the palm of my hand and struck out at the deva with the sign of Thanatos.

The deva flinched and, with his free hand, scratched his chest where the blow had landed. Thin streams of smoke curled and twisted like hairs behind his open palm. Then the deva started roaring with laughter, still clutching his male member, which had grown to the size of a baseball bat by now. The deva radiated heat – not living warmth, but hot air, the same as a blazing bonfire gives off.

He wasn't so brainless after all. I was far more stupid, striking with the sign of death at a being that wasn't even alive.

'Ai, you Satan, you mangy dog, vicious offspring of a sick tapeworm!' I heard someone shout from behind the deva. Old man Afandi had somehow managed to enter the second level of the Twilight! And not only that – he had taken a firm grip of the deva's tail and was trying to drag it away from me!

The monster turned round slowly, as if it couldn't believe that anyone would dare to treat it with such contempt. It stopped scratching, and raised its massive hand above the old man's head in a clenched fist. It would drive him into the ground up to his ears!

I sifted frantically through the clutter that had accumulated in my head. Everything to do with golems, from the first classes to the tall stories I'd heard from Semyon. The deva was just another golem. Golems could be destroyed! Golems . . . golems . . . cabbalistic golems, golems with goals and free will, golems for fun and amusement, wooden golems . . . the impossibility of creating a plastic golem . . . Olga had once told me . . . a skill that no one needed any more . . . the spell wasn't that difficult in principle, but it took a lot of Power . . .

'Dust and Ashes,' I shouted, throwing out one hand towards the deva.

Now everything depended on whether I'd made the sign correctly. The standard position widely used in magical passes, with the thumb gripped between the next two fingers, but with the little finger extended forward, parallel to the thumb. That month of training in stretching our fingers had certainly been well spent. We would be the envy of any pianist . . .

The monster froze and then slowly turned round to face me. The red light in its eyes went out and the deva began whining shrilly, like a puppy dog when someone steps on its paw. It opened its hand and the penis fell off and shattered in a heap of sparks, like a firebrand that had flown out of a bonfire. Then the fingers on its hands started crumbling away. The deva had stopped whining now: it was sobbing, reaching its fingerless hands out towards me and shaking its blind-eyed head.

That was how the great magicians of the East used to subdue them . . .

I held the position with the sign of Dust and Ashes, allowing the Power to flow through me, on and on, for about three minutes in second-level Twilight time, until the deva was finally reduced to a handful of ash.

'Cold, isn't it?' said Afandi, hopping up and down. He walked up to the remains of the deva, held out his hands and rubbed them together as he warmed them. Then he spat on the ash and muttered, 'Ugh, you son of evil and father of abomination . . .'

'Thank you, Afandi,' I said as I got up off the frosty ground. It really was terribly cold on the second level. At least by some miracle I'd managed not to lose the bag with my things – it was still hanging on my shoulder. Although . . . perhaps the miracle in question was an affinity spell cast by Svetlana? 'Thank you, Grandad. Let's get you of this place. It's hard for you to stay down here for very long.'

'Ai, thanks, O mighty warrior,' said Afandi, beaming. 'You thanked me? I shall take pride in that for the rest of my pointless life! The vanquisher of a deva has praised me!'

I took him by the elbow without saying a word and dragged him up to the first level. I'd put so much Power into destroying the deva that even I was finding it hard to stay in the Twilight.

CHAPTER 4

THE *CHAIKHANA*, OR tea hall, was gloomy and dirty. Fat bluebottles buzzed as they circled round the weak light bulbs in fly-spotted shades hanging from the ceiling. We were sitting on greasy bright-coloured cushions or small mattresses around a low table, only about fifteen centimetres high. The table was covered with a brightly patterned tablecloth, and it was dirty too.

In Russia a café like this would have been closed down in a moment. In Europe they would have put the owner in prison. In the USA the proprietor would have been hit with an absolutely massive fine. And in Japan the boss of an establishment like this would have committed *seppuku* out of a sense of shame.

But never before had I come across smells as delicious as those in this little *chaikhana* that was absolutely unfit for tourists.

Once we'd got away from our pursuers we had split up. The Dark One had gone to find his colleagues and report on what had happened. Valentina Ilinichna and Nodir had set out to gather together the Light Ones who were reserve members of the Watch and to call Tashkent and request reinforcements. Alisher, Afandi and I had caught a taxi and made our way to this *chaikhana* beside a small market on the outskirts of Samarkand. I had already begun to suspect that there were at least a dozen markets in Samarkand, and there were certainly more than all the museums and movie theatres taken together.

On the way I cast a masking spell on myself and became Timur's double. For some reason young magicians think it's a bad sign to assume the appearance of a dead man. There are all sorts of beliefs attached to this superstition, from 'You'll die soon' to 'You'll pick up someone else's habits.' Anybody would think that habits were fleas that scatter after their host dies and look for someone who resembled him as closely as possible . . . I have never been super-stitious, so I didn't hesitate to adopt Timur's appearance. I had to disguise myself as a local in any case. Even in this *chaikhana* a visitor with a European appearance would have looked as much out of place as a Papuan at the haymaking in a Russian village.

'The food here is very good,' Alisher explained in a low voice after he had ordered. Since I didn't know a word of Uzbek, I had kept quiet while the young waiter was with us. Fortunately, so had Afandi: he only croaked every now and then as he rubbed his bald patch and glanced proudly at me. The meaning of that glance was quite clear: 'We showed that deva what-for, eh?' I nodded amiably in reply.

'I believe you,' I said. There was a massive Chinese music centre standing by the wall, with huge hissing speakers and blinking coloured lights. The cassette that was playing featured some Uzbek folk music that had originally been very interesting but had been hopelessly spoiled by the pop-music rhythms introduced into it and by the quality of the music centre. But at least the volume was set so high that I could speak Russian with no worries about attracting glances of surprise from the people nearby. 'It certainly smells delicious. Only, I'm sorry, but it is rather dirty in here.'

'That's not dirt,' Alisher replied. 'At least, it's not that kind of dirt. You know, when people come to Russia from Western Europe they frown too, at how dirty it is everywhere! But it's not dirty because no one ever cleans anywhere! In Russia the soil is different and there's more ground erosion. That fills the air with dust and it settles everywhere. Wash the sidewalk with soap, and in Europe it will stay clean for three days. But in Russia you can lick it clean with your tongue, and the dust will settle again in an hour. In Asia, there's even more dust, so the Europeans and the Russians say: "Dirt, ignorance, savagery!" But that's not true! It's just the way the land is. But when you find good smells in Asia, that's not the dirt. In Asia you have to trust your nose, not your eyes!'

'That's interesting,' I said. 'I never thought about it like that before. That must be why people in the East have narrow eyes and big noses, then?'

Alisher gave me a bleak look. Then he forced a laugh.

'Okay, that's one to you. It's funny. But that really is what I think, Anton. In the East, everything's different.'

'Even the Others,' I said, with a nod. 'Alisher, I didn't believe in the deva. I'm sorry.'

'You know, from your description, it wasn't the same one who followed me,' Alisher said in a serious voice. 'He wasn't so tall, but he was very agile. He had legs. More like a monkey with horns.'

'Curses on them, foul belches of creation, creatures of feckless magicians!' Afandi put in. 'Anton and I defeated that licentious, depraved deva! You should have seen the battle, Alisher! Although a young boy shouldn't really watch pornography . . .'

'Grandad Afandi . . .' I said. 'Please!'

'Just call me Bobo!' said Afandi.

'What does it mean?' I asked warily.

'It means 'grandad',' said the old man, slapping me on the shoulder. 'You and I defeated those devas, and now you're my grandson!'

'Afandi–Bobo,' I said. 'Pleaase, don't remind me of that fight.

I feel very embarrassed that I couldn't overcome the deva straight away.'

'Devas!' Afandi repeated firmly.

'Deva?' I suggested naively.

'Devas! There were two of them. The big one was holding the little one in his hand and waving him about, left and right, left and right!'

Afandi got halfway to his feet and gave a very graphic demonstration of the behaviour of the 'devas'.

'Hai, great warrior Afandi,' Alisher said quickly. 'There were two of them. Anton was so afraid he didn't notice the second one. Sit down, they're bringing our tea.'

We spent ten minutes drinking tea and eating sweet pastries. I recognised halva, Turkish delight and something like baklava. All the other sweet miracles of the East were new to me. But that didn't stop me enjoying the way they tasted. There were different-coloured sugar crystals (I preferred not to think about what they had been coloured with), skeins of very fine, very sweet threads, something that looked like halva, only it was white, and dried fruit. They were all delicious. And they were all very sweet, which was particularly important for us. A serious loss of Power always leaves you with a yearning for something sweet. Even though we operate with Power that isn't our own and simply redistribute it in space, it's not easy by any means. Your blood-sugar level falls so low that you can easily slip into a hypoglycaemic coma. And if that happens in the Twilight, it will take a miracle to save you.

'Next there'll be *shurpa* broth and pilaf,' Alisher said, pouring himself a fifth bowl of green tea. 'The food here is simple. But it's the real thing.'

He paused, and I realised what he was thinking.

'They died in battle. The way watchmen are supposed to die,' I said.

'It was our battle,' Alisher declared in a low voice.

'It is our common battle. Even for the Dark Ones. We have to find Rustam, and no one is going to stop us. But I feel sorry for Murat . . . he killed those men, and then he couldn't live any more.'

'I could have,' Alisher said morosely.

'And so could I,' I admitted. We looked at each other with understanding.

'Humans against Others,' Alisher sighed. 'I can't believe it! It's a nightmare! They were all enchanted – that's a job for a Higher One.'

'At least three Higher Ones,' I said. 'A Dark One, a Light One and an Inquisitor. A vampire, a healer and a battle magician.'

'The End of Time has arrived,' said Afandi, shaking his head. 'I never thought the Light, the Dark and the Fear would all join together . . .'

I glanced at him quickly – and just managed to catch the brief instant before the stupid expression reappeared on his face.

'You're not nearly as stupid as you pretend, Afandi,' I said quietly. 'Why do you act like some senile old man?'

Afandi smiled for a few seconds, then became more serious and said:

'It's best for a weak magician to appear like a fool, Anton. Only a powerful one can afford to be clever.'

'You're not so very weak, Afandi. You entered the second level and stayed there for five minutes. Do you know some cunning trick?'

'Rustam had a lot of secrets, Anton.'

I carried on looking at Afandi for a long time, but the old man's face remained absolutely impassive. Then I glanced at Alisher. He was looking thoughtful.

I wondered if he and I were thinking the same thing.

I was sure we were.

Was Afandi Rustam? Was the simple-minded old man who had meekly cleaned a provincial Watch's office for decades one of the oldest magicians in the world?

Anything was possible. Absolutely anything at all. They say that the passing years change every Other's character and he becomes less complicated: a single dominant character trait overshadows everything else. The cunning Geser had wanted intrigues, and he was still intriguing to this very day. Foma Lermont, who dreamed of a quiet and comfortable life, was now tending his garden and working as an entrepreneur. And if Rustam's dominant character trait was secretiveness, after living so long he could quite easily have become totally paranoid and disguised himself as a weak and dim-witted old man . . .

But if that was so, he wouldn't open up to us, even if I told him what I suspected. He would laugh in my face and sing an old song about his teacher . . . After all, he hadn't actually said that Rustam initiated him! He had told the story in the third person: Rustam, a foolish old man, an initiation. We were the ones who had set Afandi in the role of the foolish old man!

I looked at Afandi again, with my inflamed imagination ready to see cunning and morbid secretiveness and even malice in his gaze.

'Afandi, I have to talk to Rustam,' I said, choosing my words carefully. 'It's very important. Geser sent me to Samarkand, he asked me to seek out Rustam and ask for his advice, in the name of their old friendship. Advice and nothing more!'

'It's a fine thing, old friendship,' Afandi said, nodding. 'Very fine! When it exists. But I heard that Rustam and Geser quarrelled, that Rustam spat after Geser as he walked away and said he never wanted to see him on Uzbek ground again. And Geser laughed out loud and said that in that case Rustam would have to put out his own eyes. At the bottom of a bottle of fine old wine there can be a bitter sediment, and the older the wine, the more bitter the sediment gets. In the same way an old friendship can produce very, very great pain and resentment!'

'You're right, Afandi,' I said. 'You're right about everything. But Geser said one other thing. He saved Rustam's life. Seven times. And Rustam saved his life. Six times.'

The waiter brought our *shurpa*, and we stopped talking. But even after the young lad had gone away Afandi sat there with his lips firmly clamped shut. And the expression on his face suggested that he was figuring something out in his head.

Alisher and I exchanged glances and he nodded very slightly.

'Tell me, Anton,' Afandi said eventually. 'If your friend was distressed when the woman he loved left him – so distressed that he decided to leave this world – and you came to him and stayed with him for a month, drinking wine from morning until night, making him go to visit friends and telling him how many other beautiful women there are . . . is that saving his life?'

'I think that depends on whether the friend really was prepared to leave this life because of love,' I said cautiously. 'Every man who has ever gone through something like that has felt that there was nothing left to live for. But only very, very rarely have they ever killed themselves. Unless, of course, they were foolish, beardless young boys.'

Afandi said nothing again for a while.

And then, as if it had been waiting for the pause, my phone rang.

I took it out, certain that the caller was either Geser, who had been informed about what had happened, or Svetlana, who had sensed that something was wrong. But there was no number or name on the display. It was simply glowing with an even grey light.

'Hello,' I said.

'Anton?' It was a familiar voice, with a slight Baltic accent.

'Edgar?' I exclaimed in delight. No normal Other would ever be glad to get a call from an Inquisitor. Especially if that Inquisitor was a former Dark Magician. But this was a highly unusual situation. Better Edgar than someone I didn't know, some zealous devotee of equilibrium hung from head to toe with amulets and ready to suspect anyone and everyone of being a criminal.

'Anton, you're in Samarkand.' Edgar wasn't asking, of course, he was stating a fact. 'What's going on there? Our people are putting up a portal from Amsterdam to Tashkent!'

'Why Tashkent?' I asked, puzzled.

'It's easier. They've used that route at least once before,' Edgar explained. 'So what's up down there?'

'Do you know about Edinburgh?'

Edgar snorted derisively. Right, what a question to ask. There probably wasn't one single trainee in the Inquisition who hadn't heard about the attempt to steal Merlin's artefact. So what could I expect from the experienced members of staff?

'Everything indicates that it's the same team. Only in Scotland they used paid mercenaries, but here they mesmerised local soldiers and policemen. Loaded them up with amulets and spells, charmed bullets . . .'

'I can see this is the end of my vacation,' Edgar said gloomily. 'I wish you hadn't stuck your nose into this! They pulled me back in off the beach! Because I have experience of working with you!'

'I'm very flattered,' I said acidly.

'Is all this very serious?' Edgar asked after a pause.

'A hundred men sent to attack both the local Watches. As we withdrew two Light Ones were killed. And then we were attacked by a deva, who bit a Dark One in half. It took me three minutes to beat it down!'

Edgar swore and asked:

'What did you beat it down with?'

'Dust and Ashes. It was lucky I just happened to know it . . .'

'Tremendous!' Edgar said sarcastically. 'By sheer chance a young Moscow magician happens to remember a spell against golems that hasn't been used in a hundred years!'

'Are you trying to stitch me up already?' I laughed. 'Come and join me, you'll like it here. And by the way, swot up on those spells against golems – the word is that there's another one on the loose.'

'This is an absolute nightmare . . .' Edgar muttered. 'I'm in Crete. Standing on the beach in my swimming trunks. My wife's rubbing suntan lotion on my back. And they tell to be in Amsterdam in three hours and set out immediately for Uzbekistan! What do you call that?'

'Globalisation, sir,' I answered.

Edgar groaned into the phone. Then he said:

'My wife will kill me. This is our honeymoon. She's a witch, by the way! And they summon me to lousy Uzbekistan!'

'Edgar, it doesn't become you to say "lousy" like that,' I said, unable to resist another jibe. 'After all, we all lived in the same state once upon a time. Consider it your deferred patriotic duty.'

But Edgar was obviously not in the mood for sarcasm or exchanging jibes. He heaved a sigh and asked:

'How will I find you?'

'Call me,' I replied simply, and cut the connection.

'The Inquisition,' Alisher said with a understanding nod. 'They've caught on at last. Well, they'll certainly find a few things to do here.'

'They could start by cleaning out their own backyard,' I said. 'They've got someone beavering away on the inside.'

'Not necessarily,' said Alisher, trying to intercede for the Inquisition. 'It could be a retired Inquisitor.'

'Yes? Then how did anyone find out that Geser had sent us to Samarkand? He only informed the Inquisition!'

'One of the traitors is a Light Healer,' Alisher reminded me.

'Are you saying it's a Higher Light One from our Watch? A Healer? Working for the enemy?'

'That could be it!' Alisher said obstinately.

'There has only ever been one Higher-level Light Healer in our Watch,' I reminded him calmly. 'And she's my wife.'

Alisher stopped short and shook his head.

'I beg your pardon, Anton! I didn't mean anything of the kind!'

'Ai, that's enough quarrelling!' Afandi said in his foolish old voice. 'The *shurpa's* gone cold! And there's nothing worse than cold *shurpa*. Apart from hot vodka!'

He looked around stealthily and passed his hands over the bowls of *shurpa*. The cold broth started steaming again

'Afandi, how can we talk to Rustam?' I asked again.

'Eat your *shurpa*,' the old man muttered. And he showed us how.

I broke off a piece of a bread cake and started on my broth. What else could I do? The East is the East, they don't like to give a straight answer here. The best diplomats in the world come from the East. They don't say 'yes' or 'no', but that doesn't mean they abstain . . .

It was only after Alisher and I had finished our *shurpa* that Afandi sighed and said:

'Geser was probably right. He probably can demand an answer from Rustam. One answer to one question.'

Well, at least that was one small victory!

'Coming right up,' I said, nodding. Of course, the question had to be formulated correctly, to exclude any possibility of an ambiguous answer. 'Just a minute . . .'

'Why are you in such a hurry?' Afandi asked in surprise. 'A minute, an hour, a day . . . Think.'

'In principle, I'm ready,' I said.

'So what? Who are you going to ask, Anton Gorodetsky?' Afandi laughed. 'Rustam's not here. We'll go to see him, and then you can ask your question.'

'Rustam's not here?' I asked, struck almost dumb.

'No,' Afandi replied firmly. 'I'm sorry if anything I said might have misled you. But we'll have to go to the Plateau of the Demons.'

I thought I was beginning to understand how Geser could have quarrelled with Rustam. And I thought that Merlin, for all his evil deeds, must have been a very kind soul and an extremely patient Other. Because Afandi was Rustam. No crystal ball was needed to see that!

'I'll just be a moment . . .' Afandi got up and went towards a small door in the corner of the *chaikhana* that had the outline of a male figure stencilled on it. It was interesting that there wasn't any door with a female silhouette. Apparently the women of Samarkand were not in the habit of spending time in *chaikhanas*.

'Well, this Rustam's a real character,' I muttered while he was gone. 'As stubborn as a mule.'

'Anton, Afandi's not Rustam,' Alisher said.

'You mean you believe him?'

'Anton, ten years ago my father recognised Rustam. At the time I didn't think anything of it – the ancient Higher One was still alive, so what? Many of them have withdrawn from the active struggle and live unobtrusive lives among ordinary people . . .'

'So?'

'My father knew Afandi. He must have known him for fifty years.'

I thought about that.

'But what exactly did your father say to you about Rustam?'

Alisher wrinkled up his forehead. Then, speaking very precisely, as if he was reading from the page of a book, he said:

'Today I saw a Great One, whom no one has met anywhere for seventy years. The Great Rustam, Geser's friend, and then his enemy. I walked past him. We recognised each other, but pretended that we hadn't seen anything. It is good that an Other as insignificant as I has never quarrelled with him.'

'But what of it?' I asked – it was my turn to argue now. 'Your father could finally have recognised Rustam, disguised as Afandi. That's the point.'

Alisher thought about that and admitted that yes, it could have happened like that. But he still thought his father hadn't meant Afandi.

'But anyway, that doesn't get us anywhere,' I said, gesturing impatiently. 'You can see how obstinate he is. We'll have to go to the Plateau of the Demons with him . . . By the way, what is that? Only don't tell me that in the East there are demons who live on some plateau!'

Alisher laughed.

'Demons are the Twilight forms of Dark Magicians whose human nature has been distorted by Power, the Twilight and the Dark. They teach us that in one of our very first lessons. No, the Plateau of the Demons is a human name. It's a mountainous area where there are boulders that have fantastic shapes – just like petrified demons. People don't like to go there. That is, only the tourists go . . .'

'Tourists aren't people,' I agreed. 'So it's just common or garden superstition?'

'No, it's not all superstition,' Alisher said in a more serious voice. 'There was a battle there. A big battle between Dark Ones and Light Ones, almost two thousand years ago. There were more Dark Ones, they were winning . . . and then the Great White Magician

Rustam used a terrible spell. Nobody has ever used the White Haze in battle again since then. The Dark Ones were turned to stone. And they didn't dissolve into the Twilight, but tumbled out into the ordinary world, just as they were – stone demons. What people say is true, only they don't realise it.'

I felt my heart suddenly seared by a cold, clammy, repulsive memory. I was standing facing Kostya Saushkin. And from far away Geser's voice was whispering in my head . . . *

'The White Mist,' I said. 'The spell is called 'the White Mist'. Only Higher Magicians can work it: it requires total concentration and the bleeding of all Power from within a radius of three kilometres . . .'

It was as if Alisher's words had broken open some lock in my memory. And the door of a closet had creaked open to reveal an ancient skeleton, with its teeth bared in a bony grin . . .

Geser had not simply given me bare knowledge. He had transferred an entire piece of his memory. A generous gift.

. . . The stone burns your feet through the soft leather shoes, because the stone is red-hot, and even the spells applied to your clothes lose their effect. And up ahead someone's body is smoking, half sunk into the softened stone. Not all of our comrades' charms have withstood the Hammer of Fate.

'Geser!' a broad-shouldered man shouts in my ear. His short black beard has turned frizzy in the heat, his red-and-white clothes are dusted with black ash. Lacy black-and-grey flakes are falling on us from above, crumbling into dust as they fall. 'Geser, we have to decide!'

I say nothing. I look at the smoking body and try to recognise who it is. But then his defence finally collapses, and the body

---

* This story is told in the third part of the book *The Twilight Watch*.

explodes into a column of greasy ashes that shoots up into the sky. The streams of dispersing Power waft the ashes about and for a moment they assume the spectral form of a human figure. I realise what it is that is falling on us, and a lump rises in my throat.

'Geser, they're trying to raise the Shade of the Rulers.' The voice of the magician dressed in red and white is full of panic and horror. 'Geser!'

'I'm ready, Rustam,' I say. I reach out my hand to him. Magicians do not often work spells in pairs, but we have been through a lot together. And it's easier for two to do it. Easier to take the decision. Because there are hundreds of Dark Ones and tens of thousands of men in front of us.

And behind us there are only a hundred people who have put their trust in us and about ten apprentice magicians.

It's not easy to convince yourself that a hundred and ten are worth more than a hundred and ten thousand.

But I look at the black-and-grey ash, and suddenly I feel better. I tell myself what powerful and benign individuals will always tell themselves in a situation like this, in a hundred, a thousand, or two thousand years.

These are not people facing me!

These are raging beasts!

The Power flows through me, the Power floods my veins with an effervescent broth, emerging onto my skin as bloody perspiration. There is so much Power all around: flowing out of the dead Others; dissipating from the spells that have been pronounced; flooding out of the men running into the attack. The Dark Ones knew what they were doing when they brought an entire army with them. Others do not fear the weapons of men, but the arms waving swords, the screaming mouths set in fierce grins and the eyes craving death belong to living wineskins filled with Power.

And the more this filthy human rabble – driven together under the banner of the Dark by cruel rulers or the thirst for gain – hates and fears, the stronger are the Dark Magicians walking amongst them.

But we have one spell in reserve, a spell that has never yet been uttered beneath this sun. It was brought back by Rustam from an island far away in the north, where it was invented by a cunning Light One called Merlin: but even he, who stood so dangerously close to the Dark, had been horrified by it . . .

The White Mist.

Rustam pronounces strange, coarse-sounding words. I repeat them after him, without even trying to understand their meaning. The words are important, but they are only the hand of the potter, giving shape to the clay, shaping the clay mould into which the molten metal will be poured, creating bronze manacles that allow no freedom to the hands. There are words at the beginning and end, words provide the form and the direction, but it is Power that decides everything.

Power and Will.

I can no longer hold back the force that is pulsing within me, ready to tear my pitiful human body apart with every beat of my heart. I open my mouth at the same time as Rustam. I shout, but I shout without words.

The time for words is over.

The White Mist surges out of our mouths in a murky, billowing wave – and it rolls on towards the advancing army and the circle of Dark Magicians, who are weaving the cobweb of their spell . . . no less terrifying, but slower . . . just a little bit slower. The grey shadows that are just beginning to rise out of the stone are swept aside by the White Mist.

And then the White Mist reaches the Others and the human warriors.

The world in front of us loses its colours, but not in the same way that this happens in the Twilight. The world turns white, but it is the whiteness of death, not life, a displacement of colours that is as sterile as their absence. The Twilight shudders and collapses, layer upon layer adhering to each other, pulling the men screaming in pain and the Others struck dumb by fear in between its icy millstones.

And the world congeals.

The white gloom disperses. The ash falling from the sky is still there. The red-hot ground beneath our feet is still there. And there too are the petrified figures of the Others – freakish and bizarre, often entirely unlike human forms. They have been turned to granite and sandstone, coarsened and warped. A shape-shifter who was transforming into a tiger, a vampire who had fallen to the ground, magicians with their hands raised in a vain attempt to protect themselves . . .

There is not a trace left of the humans. The Twilight has swallowed them, digested them and reduced them to nothing.

Rustam and I are shaking. We have torn and bloodied each other's skin with our nails. Well, we had been thinking for a long time of becoming blood brothers.

'Merlin said that Others would be cast out on the final level of the Twilight, the seventh . . .' Rustam says in a quiet voice. 'He was wrong. But this is not a bad result either . . . This battle will live down the ages . . . It is a glorious battle.'

'Look,' I say to him. 'Look, my brother.'

Rustam looks – not with his eyes, but in the way that we Others know how to look. And he turns pale.

This battle will not live down the ages. We shall never glory in it.

To kill the enemy is valorous. To condemn him to torment is infamous. To condemn him to eternal torment is eternal infamy.

They are still alive. Turned to stone. Deprived of movement and
Power, touch, vision, hearing and all the senses granted to men
and Others.

But they are alive and they will remain alive – until the stone
is reduced to sand, and perhaps even longer than that.

We can see their auras quivering with life. We can see their
amazement, fear, fury.

We shall not glory in this battle.

We shall not talk about it.

And we shall never again pronounce the prickly, alien words
that summon up the White Mist . . .

Why was I looking up at Alisher? And what was the ceiling doing
there behind his head?

'Are you back with us, Anton?'

I lifted myself up on my elbows and looked round.

The East is subtle. The East can be sensitive. Everyone in the
chaikhana had pretended that they hadn't seen me faint. They had
left Alisher to get on with bringing me round.

'The White Mist,' I said.

'All right, all right,' said Alisher, nodding. He was seriously
alarmed. 'I made a mistake: not haze, but mist. I'm sorry. But what
reason is there to faint?'

'Rustam and Geser used the White Mist,' I said. 'And three years
ago . . . anyway, Geser taught me that spell. He taught me it very
thoroughly. Shared his memories. Anyway . . . now I can remember
how it all was.'

'Is it really so very grim?' Alisher asked.

'Yes, very. I don't want to go to that place.'

'But it was all a long time ago,' Alisher said reassuringly. 'It's all
over now, it's been forgotten for ages . . .'

'If only . . .' I said, but I didn't try to explain. If Alisher was unlucky enough, he would see it and understand for himself. Because we would have to got to the Plateau of the Demons in any case. The Rustam in my borrowed memories was nothing at all like Afandi.

Just at that moment Afandi came back from the toilet. He sat down on his cushion, looked at me and asked:

'Decided to take a rest, did you? It's too soon for resting – we'll have a rest after the pilaf.'

'I'm not so sure,' I muttered as I sat down.

'Ah, what a fine thing civilisation is!' Afandi went on, as if he hadn't heard me. 'You're both young, you don't know what blessings civilisation has brought to the world.'

'Was the light bulb in there actually working, then?' I murmured. 'Alisher, ask that waiter to get a move on with the pilaf, will you?'

Alisher frowned.

'You're in a hurry . . .'

He got up, but just at that moment a young man appeared bearing a large dish. Naturally, one plate for everyone, just as it should be: reddish, crumbly rice, orange carrots, a generous amount of meat, a whole head of garlic on the top.

'I told you the food here was good,' Alisher said delightedly.

But I looked at the man who had brought the pilaf and wondered where the young boy had got to. And why this waiter was acting so nervous.

I took a handful of rice and raised it to my face. Then I looked at the waiter. He started nodding and smiling eagerly.

'Mutton in garlic sauce,' I said.

'What sauce?' Alisher asked in amazement.

'I was just remembering the wise Holmes and the naive Watson,' I replied, no longer concerned that my Russian might seem out of place. 'The garlic is to cover the smell of the arsenic. You told me yourself – in the East you have to trust your nose, not your eyes . . . My dear fellow, take a little pilaf with us!'

The waiter shook his head and backed away slowly. Out of curiosity I took a look at him through the Twilight – the predominant colours in his aura were yellow and green. Fear. He was no professional killer. And he, instead of his younger brother, had brought the poisoned pilaf himself, because he was afraid for him. It's amazing what abominable things people will do out of love for their nearest and dearest.

Basically, it was all pure improvisation. Some filthy substance with arsenic had been found in the *chaikhana*, some kind of rat poison. And someone had given the order to feed us poisoned pilaf. It's not possible to kill a powerful Other that way, but they could easily have weakened and distracted us.

'I'll make *lagman* noodles out of you,' I promised the waiter. 'And feed them to your little brother. Is the *chaikhana* being watched?'

'I . . . I don't know . . .' The waiter had realised that, despite the way I looked, he ought to speak Russian. 'I don't know, they ordered me to do it!'

'Get out!' I said, standing up. 'There won't be any tip.'

The waiter dashed for the door of the kitchen. And the customers started leaving the *chaikhana*, deciding to take the opportunity not to pay. What had frightened them so badly? What I said, or the way I said it?

'Anton, don't burn a hole in your trousers,' said Alisher.

I looked down – there was a hissing fireball spinning in my hand. I had got so furious that the spell had slipped off the tips of my fingers into the launch stage.

'I ought to burn down this nest of vipers, just to teach them a lesson,' I hissed through my teeth.

Alisher didn't say anything. He smiled awkwardly and frowned by turns. I understood exactly what he wanted to say. That these people were not to blame. They had been ordered to do it, and they couldn't refuse. That this modest *chaikhana* was all that they had. That it fed two or three large families with little children and old grandparents. But he didn't say anything, because in this case I had a right to start a little fire. A man who tries to poison three Light Magicians deserves to be shown what's what, to teach him and other people a lesson. We're Light Ones, not saints . . .

'The *shurpa* was good . . .' Alisher said quietly.

'Let's leave via the Twilight,' I said, transforming the fireball into a thin plume of flame and directing it at the dish of pilaf. The rice and meat were reduced to glowing ashes, together with the arsenic. 'I don't want to show myself in the doorway. These bastards work too quickly.'

Alisher nodded gratefully and got up, stamped on the embers in the dish and emptied two teapots on them just to be sure.

'The green tea was good too,' I agreed. 'Listen, the tea looks pretty ordinary. Pretty poor stuff, to be honest. But it tastes really good!'

'The important thing is to brew it right,' Alisher replied, relieved by the change of subject. 'When a teapot is fifty years old and it hasn't been washed once . . .' He paused, but when he didn't see an expression of disgust on my face, he went on. 'That's the cunning part! This clever crust forms on the inside – tannins, essential oils, flavonoids . . .'

'Are there really flavonoids in tea?' I asked in surprise, hanging the bag over my shoulder again. I'd almost forgotten it. The underwear wouldn't have mattered, but the bag also contained the selection of battle amulets that Geser had given me and five thick wads of dollars!

'Well, maybe I'm confusing things . . .' Alisher admitted. 'But it's the crust that does it, it's like brewing tea inside a shell of tea . . .'

Taking Afandi under the arms in the way that had already

become a habit, we entered the Twilight. The cunning old man didn't argue: on the contrary, he pulled up his legs and dangled between us, giggling repulsively and crying out: 'Hup! Hup!' I thought that if, despite what Geser's memories told me, Afandi really was Rustam, I wouldn't let his age prevent me from giving him an earful of good old vernacular.

CHAPTER 5

To BE QUITE honest, I would have preferred a Russian 'Uaz' or 'Niva'. Not out of patriotic considerations, but because the Toyota jeep was by no means the most common car in Uzbekistan and disguising it with magic would have been like unfurling a flag over my head and howling: 'Here we are. Come and get us!'

However, Afandi had told me very definitely that the road ahead was bad. Very bad. And the only Niva we had come across near the *chaikhana* had been in such terrible condition that it would have been shameful to subject the old lady to such mockery and humiliation.

But the Toyota was new and kitted out with all the gear, the way they do things in Asia – if you can afford to buy an expensive car, then let it have the works! A sports silencer, a bicycle rack (although the pot-bellied owner had never got up on a bike since he was a child), a CD-changer, a tow-bar and facings on the door-sills – pretty much all the glittering trash that the manufacturers invent to hike up the basic price by an extra fifty per cent.

The owner of the car was apparently also the owner of the local market. He looked like a standard Uzbek *bey*, the way they're always shown in the cartoons. In other words, about as credible as the fat capitalist with the eternal cigar clutched in his teeth. The irony of the situation was that this young man had probably derived all his ideas about how a rich man ought to look from children's cartoons and fashionable European magazines. He was fat. He had an Uzbek skullcap embroidered with gold thread on his head. He was wearing a very expensive suit that was clearly too tight. And an equally expensive tie that had definitely been splattered with fatty food more than once and then run through a washing machine. He wore a pair of polished shoes that were quite out of place in the dusty street. And gold rings with huge artificial gemstones or 'dopealines' as the jewellery traders spitefully refer to them. The skullcap was supposed to symbolise his closeness to the people, and all the rest symbolised his European gloss. He was clutching a cellphone in one hand – an expensive one, but the kind that ought to belong to a rich young dope, not to a respectable businessman.

'Will this car be okay for us?' I asked Afandi.

'It's a good car,' Afandi said.

I glanced around once again – there were no Others to be seen anywhere nearby. No enemies, no allies, no ordinary Others living among the ordinary human beings. So that was fine.

I emerged from the Twilight and looked hard at the owner of the four-by-four. I touched him gently with Power and then waited until he turned to face me, knitting his thick brows in bewilderment. I smiled and sent him two spells with names that are much too flowery to bother with here. They're usually referred to as 'Haven't Seen You for Ages' and 'Bosom Buddies'.

The modern-day *bey*'s face dissolved into a broad smile.

The two young guys accompanying him – either bodyguards or distant relatives – stared at me suspiciously. In the Twilight my hastily applied Timur mask had fallen away, and this unfamiliar Russian who was walking towards their boss with his arms held out wide naturally made them suspicious.

'Ah, how long it's been!' I shouted. 'My father's old friend!'

Unfortunately, he was about twenty years older than me. Otherwise I could have got away with the 'old-school-friend' line, or 'Remember our times in the army, brother!' But then, recently, the 'times in the army' approach had failed to work more and more often – the mark was simply unable to figure out how he could possibly have served in the army with you when he had honestly bought his way out of military service with a bundle of greenbacks from the good old USA. Some people had even developed a serious neurosis as a result.

'Son of my old friend!' the man howled, opening his arms wide to embrace me. 'Where have you been all this time?'

The important thing at this point is to give the other person just a little bit of information, He'll invent the rest for himself.

'Me? I've been living in Mariupol with my grandmother!' I told him. 'Oh, how glad I am to see you! You're such a big man here now!'

We hugged each other. The man had about him a delicious smell of *shashlik* and eau de cologne. Except that there was rather too much eau de cologne.

'And what a fine car you have!' I added, with a glance of approval at the Toyota jeep. 'Is that the one you wanted to sell me?'

A melancholy expression appeared in the man's eyes, but 'Bosom Buddies' gave him no choice. Never mind – he ought to have been happy that Geser had equipped us so generously for our journey. Otherwise I would have asked him to *give* me the Toyota.

'But . . . it's . . .' he exclaimed sadly.

'Here!' I opened my bag, took out four wads of dollars and thrust then into his hand. 'Now the keys, please, if you don't mind – I'm really in a hurry!'

'It . . . it's worth more than that . . .' the man said in a wretched voice.

'But I'm taking it second-hand!' I explained. 'Right?'

'That's right,' he admitted, speaking slowly.

'Uncle Farhad!' one of the young men exclaimed in bewilderment.

Farhad gave him a strict glance, and the youth fell silent.

'Don't interrupt when your elders are talking. Don't shame me in front of the son of my old friend!' Farhad barked. 'What will the son of my old friend think?'

The young guys were in a panic, but they kept quiet.

I took the keys out of the man's hands and got into the Toyota's driving seat. I breathed in the fresh smell of the leather upholstery and glanced at the dashboard. Yes, the car was definitely second-hand. According to the odometer, it had only travelled three hundred kilometres.

I waved to the three men who had been left with forty thousand dollars instead of their means of transport. Then I drove out onto the road and said: 'Everybody leave the Twilight!'

Alisher and Afandi appeared on the empty back seat.

'I would have given him a little more happiness,' said Alisher. 'So he wouldn't suffer too much afterwards. He looks pretty spiteful, not a very good man, but even so.'

'More spells only make a screw-up all the more likely,' I said, shaking my head. 'It's all right. I paid him fair and square. He'll survive.'

'Are we going to wait for Edgar?' Alisher asked. 'Or look for the Light Ones?'

But I'd already thought about these choices and rejected them.

'No, there's no point. Let's make straight for the hills. The further we are from people, the quieter it'll be.'

Alisher took my place at the wheel when it started getting dark. We had been driving south from Samarkand, towards the Afghan border, for three hours. Just as twilight fell the asphalt-surfaced road had given way to an appallingly bad dirt track. I moved to the back seat, where Afandi was snoring peacefully, and decided to follow the old man's example. But before I dozed off I took several battle amulets out of my bag.

Novices are often fond of all sorts of magical wands, crystals and knives, either made by themselves or charged by a more powerful magician. Even a weak and inexperienced magician can achieve a quite astounding effect if he prepares an artefact with loving care and pumps it full of Power. The problem is that this effect – powerful, prolonged and precise – is a one-off. You can't attach two different spells to the same object. A magic wand intended to belch out flame will cope magnificently with its task, even in the hands of a weak Other. But if his opponent guesses what is happening and raises a defence against fire, the wand and its miraculous flames are useless. It can't freeze, dry, or stand someone on his head. You can either use the fire that's available, or hammer away with the wand like a club. It's no accident that weak magicians who have dealings with people (and it's precisely the weak magicians who interfere in human affairs or involve people in their own) have always used a magical staff – a hybrid of the usual wand and a long club. Some of them, to be honest, have been far more skilful with the club than at using magic. I remember how all of us in the Watch went to the 'Pushkin' movie theatre for the premiere of *The Lord of the Rings*. Everything was fine until the Light Gandalf and the Dark Saruman started fighting each other with their magic staffs. The two rows filled with Others broke into genuinely Homeric laughter. Especially the trainees, who had it drilled into them every day that a magician who relied on artefacts was simply an idle show-off, more interested in appearances than efficiency. A magician's true power lies in his skill in using the Twilight and spells.

But, of course, there are exceptions to every rule. If an experienced magician has managed to foretell the future, no matter how – by skilful analysis of the lines of probability, or simply from his own experience – then a charged artefact is quite indispensable. Are you certain that your opponent is a werewolf, who cannot manipulate power directly and relies on physical strength and speed? One accelerating amulet, one pendant with a Shield that is activated at close quarters, one simple wand (many prefer to charm an ordinary pencil – wood and graphite make an excellent accumulator for Power) with a freezing spell. And there you are! You can quite confidently send a seventh-level magician off to hunt down a Higher Werewolf. The Shield will repulse the attack, the amulet will lend the magician's movement quite incredible speed, and the Temporal Freeze will transform the enemy into a motionless bundle of fur and fury. Call for transport, and he's ready for shipping to the Inquisition.

The artefacts in my bag were far more valuable than the money lying beside them. And they had been prepared by Geser in person . . . well, perhaps not prepared, but at least selected from the special stores in the armoury. I could be sure that they were powerful, and that they would be useful. I suddenly remembered an old Australian cartoon film that I had seen when I was a kid, *Around the World in Eighty Days*. In that cartoon, the cool-headed English gentleman Phileas Fogg, who was attempting to set a new speed record for travelling round the world, seemed like a cunning fortune-teller who always knew what he would need in the hours ahead. If he took a spanner, a stuffed opossum and a bunch of bananas with him in the morning, then by the time evening came the stuffed animal had plugged a leak in the side of a ship, the spanner had braced shut a door that his enemies were trying to break down, and the bananas had been given to a monkey in exchange for a ticket on a steamship. All in all, it was very much like a computer game in the same genre as *Quest*, where you have to find an effective use for every item that you collect.

Artefacts from Geser could be used for their designated purpose or in some entirely unexpected way. But whatever happened, some use was usually found for them.

I laid the twelve items out on the seat between myself and the snoring Afandi and studied them carefully. I should have done this earlier, but I hadn't taken them out at home because I hadn't wanted to attract Nadya's attention. I hadn't felt like fiddling with magical artefacts in the plane either, and after that there simply hadn't been time. Wouldn't it be annoying if I found one of the amulets was a weapon against golems!

Two portable battle wands, each no longer than ten centimetres. The first made out of ebony – fire. The second made out of a walrus tusk – ice. Well, they were both commonplace and useful. I'd managed without them so far, but anything could happen.

Four silver rings with protective spells. That was a very strange set! The standard magician's Shield protected against everything: you just had to feed it with energy. An Other didn't often need protective rings. And here I had specific protection against fire, ice, acid . . . and vacuum. At first I couldn't believe what I'd seen through the Twilight. I studied the last ring carefully. No, I was right! If the pressure suddenly dropped, the ring started to work and held the air around the person wearing it.

That was strange. Of course, there were several battle spells that suffocated the enemy, some by removing the air from around him. The things that had been thought up in thousands of years of warfare! But nobody actually used these whimsical and slow spells in battle.

Four bracelets. At least it was quite clear what they were for! Four different spells that forced a man or an Other to tell the truth. If Rustam got really stubborn, all I had to do was say 'Tell me the truth' and the ancient magician would be struck with a blow of absolutely monstrous power. The truth, the whole truth and nothing but the truth.

The last two amulets were rather less ordinary, both in appearance and content, and had quite clearly been prepared by Geser himself for this mission of ours. The first was a cellphone SIM card in a little plastic box. An ordinary card, but pumped full of magic. I studied it for a while, but I couldn't figure it out. Then I decided to experiment – I took my own card out of my phone and put the one charged with magic in its place.

It didn't make any sense! It was a copy of my own SIM card! But what for? So I wouldn't have to waste money on calls to Moscow? What raving nonsense . . .

I thought for a while and then asked Alisher to call my number. Strangely enough, the phone still worked there.

My phone rang immediately. Everything was okay, it really was a copy of my SIM, but it had been treated with magic for some reason . . . I shrugged and decided to leave the card in my phone. Maybe it coded the calls in some cunning magical way? But I'd never heard of any magic like that before.

The final amulet was a small stone rolled smooth by the sea. It had a hole in it, so it was one of those so-called 'chicken gods' that human superstition believes bring good luck. A cunningly woven silver chain that looked like a thick twisted thread ran through the hole.

In itself, of course, a 'chicken god' doesn't bring any good luck, but that doesn't stop children searching enthusiastically for them on the seashore and then wearing them on a string round their necks. This stone, however, had been enchanted with a complex spell that partially resembled the Dominant. Was that for the conversation with Rustam too? I thought about it for a while and then hung the chain round my neck. It couldn't do any harm . . .

All I still had to do was distribute the rings and the wands. I didn't think about that for too long, either. I nudged Afandi awake and asked him to put on the rings. He exclaimed 'Ah!' in delight, put the rings on his left hand, admired them – and nodded off again.

I gave the wands to Alisher, and he put them in the breast pocket of his shirt without saying a word. They stuck out like Parker or Mont Blanc ballpoint pens, no less elegant and almost as deadly. Almost – because a single stroke of a boss's pen could kill more people than those battle wands could.

'I'll get some sleep,' I told Alisher.

He didn't say anything for a while. The jeep was slowly making its way up the rocky track, which had been climbed by donkeys far more often than by anything on four wheels. The beams of the headlights swung from side to side, alternately picking out a steep rocky cliff and a sheer drop with a river roaring at the bottom.

'Sleep,' said Alisher. 'But take a look at the probability lines first This road's really bad.'

'I wouldn't even call it a road,' I said. I closed my eyes and looked into the Twilight. Into the immediate future, where the sinuous interwoven lines of probability led.

I didn't like the picture that I saw. There were too many lines that broke off abruptly and ended at the bottom of the ravine.

'Alisher, stop. You're too exhausted to drive through the mountains in the dark. Let's wait until morning.'

Alisher shook his head stubbornly.

'No – I can sense that we have to hurry.'

I could sense that too, so I didn't argue.

'Shall I drive?' I suggested.

'I don't think you're any wider awake than I am, Anton. Give me a blast, will you?'

I sighed. I don't like using magic to drive away sleep and tired-ness, to sharpen the senses. Not because of the negative conse-quences: there aren't any — get a good sleep afterwards and you're fine. That's not the problem. The problem is that very soon you stop relying on your usual senses and start using a constant feed of magical energy, walking around hyped up all the time, like a manic-depressive in the manic phase. Everything you do goes well, and you're a welcome guest in any company, a bright spark, a jester. But sooner or later you get used to it, you want to be even livelier, even wittier, have even more energy. You increase the flow of Power stimulating your nerves. And so it goes on, until you discover that you're spending all the Power that you are capable of processing on maintaining an artificial level of vivacity. And you are simply afraid to stop.

Addiction to magic is no different from ordinary drug addic-tion. Except that only Others suffer from it.

'Give me a blast,' Alisher asked me again. He stopped the car, put on the handbrake, threw his head back and closed his eyes.

I put one hand on his face and the other on the top of his short-cropped head and concentrated. I imagined the stream of power moving through my body and starting to seep out through my palms, soaking into Alisher's head, running along his nerves like cold fire, sparking across the synapses, jolting every neuron . . . No special spells were needed: I was working with pure Power. The most important thing here was a clear understanding of the physiological process.

'That's enough,' Alisher said in a fresher-sounding voice. 'That feels really good. I'd just like a bite to eat.'

'Just a moment.' I leaned back over the seat and reached into the trunk. My instincts had not misled me: there were two boxes of plastic bottles containing cola and several boxes of chocolate bars. 'Will you have some cola?'

'What?' Alisher exclaimed. 'Cola? Sure! And I'll have some of those chocolate bars too! God bless America!'

'Isn't that a bit too much adulation just for inventing a sickly-sweet lemonade substitute and some highly calorific candy?'

Instead of answering, Alisher pressed a button on the in-vehicle music centre. A second later the speakers started playing a rhythmic sequence of chords.

'It's for the rock and roll too,' he said imperturbably.

We sat there for a while, eating chocolate bars and washing them down with cola. All Others have a sweet tooth. Still snoring, Afandi smacked his lips and reached out his fingers that were decorated with the rings. I put a chocolate bar in his hand. Afandi munched it without waking up and carried on snoring.

'We'll be there at three o'clock,' Alisher told me. 'Are we going to wait until morning?'

'The night is our time,' I replied. 'We'll wake old man Rustam up. He doesn't work very hard anyway.'

'It's strange,' said Alisher. 'Odd. Does he live there like a hermit, in a cave?'

'Why do you think that . . .' I started to ask. Then I pondered for a moment. 'Maybe he grazes goats or sheep. Or he keeps bees up in the mountains. Or he has a weather station.'

'Or an observatory for watching the stars . . . What was that strange ring you put on Afandi's hand?'

'You mean the one with the ruby? Protection against a vacuum.'

'Very exotic,' said Alisher, sucking on his plastic bottle. 'I can't remember a case of an Other being killed in a vacuum.'

'I can.'

Alisher said nothing for a few seconds. Then he nodded and said: 'I'm sorry. I didn't think. Does it still bother you?'

'We were friends . . . almost. As far as a Light One and a Dark One can be.'

'Not just a Dark One. Kostya was a vampire.'

'He never killed anyone,' I said simply. 'And it wasn't his fault that he didn't grow up as a human being. Gennady made him a vampire.'

'Who's that?'

'His father.'

'What a bastard.'

'Don't be so quick to judge. The boy wasn't even a year old when he ended up in hospital. Double pneumonia and allergies to antibiotics. Basically, the parents were told that their son wouldn't survive. You know, there are some wonderful doctors who shouldn't even be allowed to practise as vets, for the poor cows' sake . . . "Your little boy's going to die, prepare yourselves for that. You're still young, you can have another child . . ." Of course, they didn't have another. Kostya was Gennady's posthumous child. After initiation vampires retain the ability to impregnate and conceive for quite a long time – it's one of nature's strange jokes. But they can only have one child. After that the vampire becomes sterile.'

'Yes, that's what I heard,' Alisher said, nodding.

'So Gennady had a talk with his wife . . . She was a human being. She knew her husband was a vampire . . . there are families like that. But he hadn't killed anyone, he was a very law-abiding vampire, she loved him . . . Anyway, he bit her. Initiated her. Their plan was for the mother to initiate the son. But she was still metamorphosing, and the baby started dying. Gennady bit him too, and Kostya got well. That is, he died, of course. Died as a human being. But he recovered from his pneumonia. The doctor started running around, crowing that it was all due to her remarkable talent. Gennady once admitted to me that he almost went for her throat when she started hinting that the right thing to do would be to reward her for the miraculous recovery.'

Alisher was silent for a while. Then he said: 'All the same, they're vampires. It would have been better if the boy had died.'

'Well, he did die,' I said. I suddenly found this conversation disgusting. Kostya had been a very normal child, except that once a week he had to drink preserved blood. He loved playing football, reading fairy tales and science fiction, and then he had decided to study biology so that he could analyse the nature of vampirism and teach vampires how to manage without human blood.

But Alisher wouldn't understand me. He was a true Watchman. A genuine Light One. But I tried to understand even the Dark Ones. Even vampires. To understand and forgive – or at least to understand. Forgiving was the hardest thing. Sometimes the hardest thing in the whole world.

The phone in my pocket rang and I took it out. Aha. An even grey glow.

'Hi, Edgar,' I said.

After a short pause Edgar asked: 'Has your phone identified my number?'

'No, I guessed.'

'You're powerful,' Edgar replied in a strange voice. 'Anton, I'm already in Samarkand. Where are all of you?'

'All of us?'

'You, Alisher and Afandi.' The Inquisitor clearly hadn't wasted the last hour or so. 'Well, you've created a fine mess here . . .'

'We have?' I protested, outraged.

'All right, maybe not just you,' Edgar acknowledged. 'But you too. Why did you take the car from the director of the market?'

'We didn't take it, we bought it. In accordance with the clauses concerning the need to confiscate means of transport in an emergency. Shall I recite the relevant paragraphs?'

'Anton, cool it,' Edgar said quickly. 'No one's accusing you of anything. But the situation really is pretty bleak. To cover it up, we'll have to put out a story about the elimination of a large gang

of terrorists. And you know how we hate disguising our own . . .
our own failures as human crimes.'

'Edgar, I understand you,' I said. 'But what has this got to do
with us? I have personal business with an Other who doesn't serve
in the Watches. I flew here unofficially and I have a perfect right
to move around the country.'

'By virtue of the emergency situation, only with the knowledge and under the surveillance of a member of a Watch,' Edgar
corrected me.

'Well, Afandi's with us.'

Edgar sighed. I thought I heard someone say something in the
background.

'Okay, Anton. Deal with your personal business . . . which the
Inquisition will have to deal with afterwards. Only don't go driving
through the mountains at night – you'll end up at the bottom of
a precipice.'

To be honest, I was actually touched by his concern.

'Don't worry,' I said. 'We'll rest until morning.'

'Okay, Anton,' Edgar repeated. Then he paused, and muttered
rather awkwardly: 'It was good talking to you . . . despite everything.'

I put the phone away and said: 'He's strange, that Edgar. He was
strange as a Dark One, too. But when he became an Inquisitor,
he changed completely.'

'You know, I think that sooner or later you'll end up as an
Inquisitor yourself,' Alisher said in a very subdued voice.

I thought about what he'd said and shook my head. 'No, there's
no way. My wife and daughter are Higher Light Ones. They don't
take guys like me into the Inquisition.'

'I'm very glad that's the case,' Alisher said seriously. 'Well then,
shall we go?'

And at that very moment the mountains shook. Gently at first,

as if the strength of the rocks was being tested. Then more and
more powerfully.

'An earthquake!' Afandi howled, waking up instantly. 'Out of
the car!'

When he wanted, he could be very serious indeed. We jumped
out of the jeep, walked a bit higher up the track and froze. The
mountains were shuddering violently. Small stones began slith-
ering down the slope and showering onto us. Alisher and I automatically erected a joint protective dome. Afandi did his bit too
– he set one hand above his eyes and started surveying the night
in search of unknown danger.

And he actually spotted something.

'Look over there!' he shouted, jumping up and down and
reaching out his hand. 'That way! That way!'

We turned round, keeping the Shield above our heads: the rocks
bounced off it with a clatter. We followed Afandi's gaze and
enhanced our night vision. (Actually, after the stimulation I'd given
him, Alisher didn't need to do that.)

And we saw the next mountain, covered with thick forest, being
reduced to rubble.

It looked as if mighty hammer blows were being struck from
within its crest. The mountain was repeatedly jolted and water-
falls of small stones, avalanches of boulders and entire groves
of trees showered down off it, rapidly filling up the ravines. In
a few minutes the kilometre-high peak was transformed into a
plateau of crushed stone and woodchips from the shattered tree
trunks.

Then I got the idea of looking at the mountain through the
Twilight.

And I saw a vortex of Power spinning above the disaster zone.

It was either the vortex of a curse that had been put on the
place, or some special kind of spell that caused an earthquake. I

didn't know which. But there was no doubt at all that the catastrophe had been caused by magic.

'They missed,' said Alisher. 'Anton . . . did you talk to Edgar?'

'Yes.'

'Are you sure the Inquisition doesn't have any beefs to settle with you?'

I gulped to swallow the lump that had risen in my throat. Beefs with the Inquisition were very, very bad news.

'The Inquisition wouldn't have missed—' I began and then broke off. I took out my cellphone and looked at it through the Twilight. Inside its cocoon of plastic, metal and silicon, the SIM card was pulsating with a blue light. Typical behaviour for a working amulet

'I think I know what happened,' I said, keying in a number. 'And I don't think it was anything to do with the Inquisition.'

'Hello, Anton,' Geser said, as if I hadn't woken him. But then, it was still evening in Moscow.

'Geser, I need to have a word with someone from the European tribunal. Immediately.'

'With one of the Masters?' Geser asked.

'Well, not the assistant night-watchman!'

'Wait a moment,' Geser said calmly. 'And don't cut the call off afterwards.'

I had to wait for about three minutes. All that time we stood there, watching the vortex of Power calming down. The sight was like something out of a fairy tale. That earthquake had probably used up the energy of some ancient and powerful amulet. Like the ones they held in the special vaults at the Inquisition.

'My name is Eric,' I heard a strong, confident voice say. 'What can I do for you, Light One?'

'Mr Eric,' I said, without bothering to enquire what position he held in the Inquisition: they really don't like revealing their hierarchy. 'At the moment I am close to the city of Samarkand in Uzbekistan. We have an emergency on our hands. Could you tell me if the Inquisition sent its staff member Edgar here?'

'Edgar?' Eric asked thoughtfully. 'Which one?'

'To be quite honest, I never knew his surname,' I admitted. 'A former member of the Moscow Day Watch, he moved to the Inquisition after the trial of Igor Teplov in Prague . . .'

'Yes, yes, yes,' Eric said more brightly. 'Edgar. Of course. No, we haven't sent him to Samarkand.'

'Then who have you sent?'

'I don't know if you are aware of the fact, Anton,' Eric said with undisguised irony, 'but the European Bureau deals with Europe. And also with Russia, owing to its ambivalent geographic location. We have neither the resources nor the desire to take on events in Asia, where the country of Uzbekistan is located. You need to contact the Asian Bureau, which at the moment is located in Beijing. Shall I give you the number?'

'No, thank you,' I replied. 'And where is Edgar now?'

'On leave. For . . .' There was a brief pause. 'For a month already. Is there anything else?'

'A word of advice,' I said, unable to restrain myself. 'Check where Inquisitor Edgar was during the events in Edinburgh that you already know about.'

'Just a moment, Anton,' said Eric, finally losing his cool. 'Are you trying to tell me . . .'

'That's all I have to say,' I blurted into the phone.

Geser – who, of course, had listened to every single word of the conversation – immediately cut Eric off and said: 'Congratulations, Anton. We've figured out who one of the three is. You've figured it out.'

'Thanks for the SIM card,' I replied. 'If it hadn't distorted my location signal, I'd already be dead.'

'It's actually intended to make your voice sound convincing when you talk to people on the phone,' said Geser. 'The location malfunction is a side effect. I just can't seem to get rid of it. All right, carry on the good work! We'll get straight on to Edgar.'

I looked at the phone pensively, then cut the connection and put it in my pocket. Had Geser been joking about making my voice sound convincing, or was it the truth?

'Edgar,' Alisher said in a satisfied voice. 'So it was Edgar! I knew Dark Ones couldn't be trusted. Not even Inquisitors.'

CHAPTER 6

WE DROVE ON to the Plateau of Demons at half past three in the morning. On the way we passed an *aul*, a tiny settlement in the mountains – less than ten small clay-walled houses set back a little way from the road. There was a bonfire on the only small street, with people crowding round it – ten or twenty of them, no more than that. The recent earthquake had evidently frightened the inhabitants of the *aul* and they were afraid to spend the night in their houses.

Alisher was still driving. I was dozing on the back seat and thinking about Edgar.

What had made him go against the Watches and the Inquisition? Why had he broken every possible taboo and involved human beings in his machinations?

I couldn't understand it. Edgar was a careerist, like all Dark Ones, of course he was. He could kill if necessary. He could do absolutely anything at all: Dark Ones had no moral prohibitions. But to do something that set him in opposition to all Others – that could only be explained by insanity or a thirst for power. And then, Edgar had so much Baltic restraint and reserve. Spending decades crawling up the career ladder was easy. But staking everything on a single throw of the dice?

What had he found out about the Crown of All Things? What information had he dug up in the archives of the Inquisition? Who else had he managed to involve? The Dark vampire and the Light Healer – who were they? Where were they from? Why had they conspired with an Inquisitor? What goals could a Dark One, a Light One and an Inquisitor have in common?

But then, the goal wasn't too hard to figure out. The goal was always one and the same. Power. Power in all its forms. You could say that we Light Ones were different. That we didn't need Power for Power's sake, but only in order to help people. And that was probably true. But we still needed Power. Every Other is familiar with that sweet temptation, that delicious sensation of his own strength: the vampire, sucking on a young girl's throat; the healer, saving a dying child with a wave of his hand. What difference did it make what it was for? Every Other would find a way to apply the might that he acquired.

I was far more concerned about another point. Edgar had been involved in the business with the *Fuaran*. He had been in contact with Kostya Saushkin.

And that brought me back to that unfortunate youth, Victor Prokhorov. The boy Vitya, who had been friends with the boy Kostya . . .

Again and again everything pointed to Kostya Saushkin. What if he had managed to survive somehow? If he'd used his final scraps of Power to erect some kind of vampire Shield round himself and lived long enough to set up a portal and disappear from his burning spacesuit? And then he'd got in touch with Edgar?

No, it was impossible, of course. The Inquisition had checked the matter very carefully. But then, what if Edgar had already been playing a double game, even then? And he had falsified the results of the investigation?

But even so, it still didn't add up. Why would he save a vampire he had just been hunting? Save him and then conspire with him? What could Kostya do for him? Without the *Fuaran* – nothing! And the book had been destroyed, that was absolutely certain. It had been observed just as carefully as Kostya. And its destruction had been confirmed by magical means. The discharge of energy when such a powerful and ancient artefact is destroyed is quite impossible to confuse with anything else.

Basically, there was no way that Edgar could have saved Kostya – that was the first conclusion. And he didn't have any need to save him – that was the second.

But even so, even so . . .

Alisher stopped the jeep and switched off the engine. The silence that fell was deafening.

'I think we're here,' he said. He stroked the steering wheel and added: 'A good little vehicle. I didn't think we'd make it.'

I turned back towards Afandi, but he was no longer asleep. He was looking at the freakish stone figures scattered around in front of us. His lips were pressed tightly together.

'Still standing there,' I said.

Afandi glanced at me in genuine fright.

'I know about it,' I explained.

'It was a bad business,' Afandi said, with a sigh. 'Ugly. Not worthy of a Light One.'

'Afandi, are you Rustam?'

Afandi shook his head.

'No, Anton. I'm not Rustam. I'm his pupil.'

He opened the door and climbed out of the jeep. After a pausing for a second, he murmured:

'I am not Rustam, but I will be Rustam . . .'

Alisher and I glanced at each other and got out of the jeep too.

It was quiet and cool – it's always cool in the mountains at night, even in summer. And it was just starting to get light. The plateau that I knew from Geser's memories had changed hardly at all. Except perhaps that the outlines of the stone figures had been softened by the wind and the rare showers of rain: they were less clearly defined but were still recognisable. A group of magicians with their hands raised in invocatory spells, a werewolf, a magician running . . .

I started to shiver.

'What is this . . . ?' Alisher whispered. 'What happened here . . . ?'

He reached into his pocket and took out a pack of cigarettes and a lighter.

'Give me one too,' I said.

We lit up. The air around us was so pure that the sharp smell of tobacco seemed like a memory of home, a reminder of the smog of the city.

'These . . . were they people?' Alisher asked, pointing to the blocks of stone.

'Others,' I told him.

'And they . . .'

'They didn't die. They turned to stone. Lost all their external senses. But their reason remained, attached to the lumps of rock.' I looked at Afandi, but he was still standing there, pensively examining the field of the ancient battle, or watching the eastern horizon where the sky had turned slightly pink.

Then I looked at the plateau through the Twilight.

The sight was genuinely blood-curdling.

What Geser had seen two thousand years ago had made him feel fear and revulsion. But what I saw now made me feel pity and pain.

Almost all the Dark Ones who had been turned to stone by the White Mist were insane. Their reason had not been able to withstand being incarcerated in total isolation from any sense

organs. The fluttering coloured auras around the stones blazed with
the brown and reddish-green fire of madness. If I try to think of
something to compare this sight with, I would say it looked like
a hundred total lunatics whirling around on the spot, or rather
standing there absolutely motionless: screaming, giggling, groaning,
weeping, muttering, drooling, scratching their faces or trying to
poke their own eyes out.

There were only a few auras that retained some remnants of
reason. Their owners were either distinguished by quite incredible willpower, or they were blazing with the thirst for revenge.
There was not much madness in them, but they were overflowing with fury, hatred and the desire to annihilate everyone
and everything.

I stopped looking through the Twilight and looked at Alisher
instead. The young magician was still smoking, and he hadn't
noticed that his cigarette had already burned down to the filter.
He only dropped the butt when it scorched his fingers. And then
he said.

'The Dark Ones got what they deserved.'

'Don't you feel any pity for them?' I asked.

'They abuse our pity.'

'But if you have no pity in you, how do we differ from them?'

'In our colour,' said Alisher. He looked at Afandi and asked:
'Where should we seek the Great Rustam, Afandi?'

'You have found him, Light One with a heart of stone,' Afandi
replied in a quiet voice. And he turned to face us.

He had transformed with the speed of a mature shape-shifter.
He was a whole head taller and much wider in the shoulders –
his shirt had split and the upper button had been torn out, together
with a piece of cloth. To my surprise, his skin had turned lighter,
and his eyes had become bright blue. I had to remind myself that
two thousand years earlier the inhabitants of this part of Asia had

looked quite different from they way they did now. Nowadays a
Russian will smile when someone from Central Asia tells him that
his ancestors had light brown hair and blue eyes. But there is a
lot more truth in these words than modern-day Russians realise.

Rustam's hair, however, was actually black. And of course, his
eastern origins could be seen in the features of his face.

'So you are Rustam after all,' I said, bowing my head. 'Greetings,
Great One! Thank you for responding to our request.'

Beside me Alisher went down on one knee, like a valorous
knight in front of his lord – respectfully, but proudly.

'Afandi is not Rustam,' the ancient magician replied. His gaze
was clouded, as if he were listening to someone else's voice. 'Afandi
is my pupil, my friend, my guardian. I no longer live among people.
My home is the Twilight. If I need to walk among mortals, I
borrow his body.'

So that was it . . . I nodded in acknowledgement of his words
and said:

'You know why we have come here, Great One.'

'I do, and I would prefer not to answer Geser's question.'

'Geser said that you—'

'My debt to Geser is my debt.' A spark of fury glinted in
Rustam's eyes. 'I remember our friendship and I remember our
enmity. I asked him to leave the Watch. I asked him to stop the
war over people. For the people's own sake. But Geser is like this
youth . . .'

He stopped talking and looked at Alisher.

'Will you help us?' I asked.

'I will answer one question,' said Rustam. 'One question. And
then my debt to Geser will be no more. Ask, but do not make
any mistake.'

I almost blurted out: 'Did you really know Merlin?' Oh, these
sly tricks . . . ask one question, make three wishes . . .

'What is the Crown of All Things and what is the easiest way to get it from the seventh level of the Twilight?' I asked.

A smile appeared on Rustam's face.

'You remind me of a certain man from Khorezm. A cunning merchant to whom I owed money . . . and I promised to grant him three wishes. He thought for a long time and said: "I wish to grow young again, be cured of all ailments and become rich – that is one wish." No, young magician. We shall not play that game. I am not granting a wish, I am answering one question. That will be enough. What is it that you wish to know? What the Crown of All Things is, or how to get it?'

'I really don't want to wind up like Pandora by asking "How do I open this box?"' I muttered.

Rustam laughed, and there was a hint of madness in his laugh.

But what else could you expect from a Light One who had dissolved into the Twilight and was living beside the enemies he had once condemned to eternal torment? He had fixed his own punishment, or penance, and it was slowly killing him.

'What is the Crown of All Things?' I asked.

'A spell that pierces through the Twilight and connects it with the human world,' Rustam responded instantly. 'You made the right choice, young magician. The reply to the second question would have confused you.'

'Oh no, if you're answering one question, then answer fair and square!' I exclaimed. 'Explain how this spell works and what it's for!'

'Very well,' Rustam agreed with surprising readiness. 'The strength of an Other lies in the ability to use the human Power flowing through all the levels of the Twilight. Our world is like an immense plain covered with tiny springs that give out Power, but do not know how to use it. We Others are merely the ruts into which this water flows from the hundreds and thousands of springs. We do not provide a drop of water to this world. But we know how to retain and use the water of other people. Our ability to accumulate that Power is the consequence of our ability to immerse ourselves in the Twilight, to break through the barriers between the levels and manipulate ever more powerful energies. The spell that was invented by the Great Merlin erases the barriers between our world and the levels of the Twilight. What do you think would happen as a result of that, young magician?'

'A catastrophe?' I guessed. 'The Twilight world is different from ours. On the third level there are two moons . . .'

'Merlin thought otherwise,' Rustam said. He seemed quite carried away now that he had answered the question and was perfectly willing to talk. 'Merlin believed that each level of the Twilight is something that didn't happen to our world. A possibility that was never realised. A shadow cast on existence. He thought our world would not die, it would destroy the Twilight. Obliterate it, as the sunlight obliterates shadows. Power would flood the entire world, like the waters of the ocean. And under that layer of water, it would make no difference who had once been able to immerse himself in the Twilight and who had not. Others would lose their Power. For ever.'

'Is that certain, Rustam?'

'Who can say?' Rustam asked, spreading his hands wide. 'I answer your second question because I do not know the answer. Perhaps that is what would happen. People would not even notice the change, and Others would become ordinary people. But that is the simplest answer, and is the simple answer always right? Possibly catastrophe would await us. Two small moons colliding with one large one, blue moss starting to grow in the wheat fields . . . who can say, magician, who can say? Perhaps Others would grow weaker, but still retain some of their powers. Or perhaps something absolutely inconceivable would happen. Something we cannot even begin to imagine. Merlin did not take the risk of using the spell. He invented it to amuse himself. He found it pleasant to think that he could change the entire world . . . but he did not intend to do it. And I think Merlin was right. It is not a good idea to touch what he has hidden in the Twilight.'

'But the Crown of All Things is already being hunted,' I said.

'That is bad,' Rustam declared imperturbably. 'I would advise you to cease these attempts.'

'We're not the ones,' I said. 'It's someone quite different. An Inquisitor, a Light One and a Dark One, who have joined forces.'

'Interesting,' Rustam said. 'It is not often that a single goal brings enemies together.'

'Can you help us to stop them?'

'No.'

'But you say yourself that it is bad!'

'There is very much in the world that is bad. But usually the attempt to defeat evil engenders more evil. I advise you to do good – that is the only way to win the victory!'

Alisher snorted indignantly and even I winced at this well-meant but totally useless conclusion. I thought what a victory evil would have won if Rustam and Geser had not used the White Mist! Perhaps I did feel pity for the incarcerated Dark Ones, but I had no doubt at all that if they had destroyed the two Light Ones standing in their way an agonising death would have awaited the Others and the people whom Geser and Rustam were defending . . . Yes, perhaps you couldn't defeat evil with evil. But you couldn't increase the amount of good by using nothing but good.

'Can you at least suggest what they are trying to achieve?' I asked.

'No,' said Rustam, shaking his head. 'I cannot. Erase the difference between people and Others? Why, that is stupid. In that case you ought to erase all the inequality in the world. Between rich and poor, strong and weak, men and women. It would be simpler to kill everyone.' He laughed and I was horrified to realise yet again that the Great Magician was not entirely sane.

But I replied politely:

'You are right, Great Rustam. It is a stupid goal. One Other has already tried to attain it . . . with the help of the book *Fuaran*. Only by another means, by transforming all people into Others.'

'A fine jest,' Rustam replied without any particular interest. 'But I agree, these are two roads that lead to the same goal. No, young magician! It is perhaps more complicated than that.' He screwed up his eyes. 'I think the Inquisitor found something in the archives. An answer to the question of what the Crown of All Things really is.'

'And?' I asked.

'And it proved to be an answer that suited everybody. Dark Ones and Light Ones and the Inquisition that maintains equilibrium. It is remarkable that such a thing has been found in the world. It even makes me feel slightly curious. But I have told you everything that I know. Merlin's spell annihilates the differences between the levels of the Twilight.'

'You live in the Twilight yourself,' I observed. 'You could suggest something! After all, if the Twilight disappears you will die!'

'Or I shall become an ordinary man and live out the remainder of a human life,' Rustam said without any particular emotion.

'Everyone who has withdrawn into the Twilight will die!' I exclaimed. Alisher looked at me in amazement. Of course . . . he didn't know that the path followed by Others ended on the seventh level of the Twilight . . .

'People are mortal. How are we better than them?'

'At least try to suggest something, Rustam!' I implored him. 'You are wiser than I am! What could it be? What could the Inquisitor have found?'

'Ask him yourself,' said Rustam, reaching out his hand. His lips moved and a stream of blinding white light flashed past me towards the Toyota.

I could probably have spotted Edgar myself – if only I had been expecting to see him on the plateau. Or perhaps even the most thorough check would have been useless. He had not concealed himself in the Twilight or by using the common spells available to all Others. Edgar was hidden from our eyes by a magical amulet on his head that reminded me of a skullcap. It was only its size that prevented me from calling it a hat of invisibility. I supposed it could be a skullcap of invisibility, since we were in Uzbekistan after all.

I automatically raised a Shield around myself and noticed that Alisher had done the same.

Only Rustan seemed entirely unconcerned about the Inquisitor's presence. The light he had summoned had taken Edgar by surprise – he was sitting on the hood of the car with his legs dangling, calmly observing us. For a second it looked as if he couldn't understand what had happened. Then the skullcap on his head started smoking and Edgar flung it to the ground, with a muffled curse. That was when he realised that we could see him.

'Hi, Edgar,' I said.

He hadn't changed a bit since the last time we'd seen each other – in the train, when we were doing battle with Kostya Saushkin. Except that now he wasn't dressed in his eternal suit and tie, but in a much freer and more comfortable style: grey linen trousers, a thin white cotton sweater and good leather shoes with thick soles . . . He looked like a svelte, fashionable European – and in the Central Asian wilderness, that made him seem like an amiable coloniser taking a brief respite from the white man's burden, or an English spy from the time of Kipling and the Great Game that Russia and Britain played in this part of the world.

'Hi, Anton,' said Edgar, getting down off the hood. 'Just look at that . . . now I've interrupted your conversation.'

Strangely enough, he seemed embarrassed. But then, who wouldn't be embarrassed after calling down tectonic spells on our heads? Who wouldn't be afraid to look us in the eye?'

'What have you done, Edgar?' I asked.

'It was just the way things worked out,' he said, with a sigh. 'Anton, I won't even try to make excuses! I feel really awkward!'

'And did you feel awkward in Edinburgh too?' I asked 'When you cut the watchmen's throats? When you hired the thugs?'

'Very awkward,' Edgar said, nodding. 'Especially since we didn't manage to break through to the seventh level in any case.'

Afandi-Rustam began laughing and slapping his sides. How much of it was Rustam and how much Afandi, I couldn't tell.

'He felt awkward!' Rustam exclaimed. 'They always feel awkward, but it never means anything.'

Obviously embarrassed by this reaction from Rustam, Edgar waited until the magician had laughed his fill. I took the chance to look the Inquisitor (perhaps I should have said 'former Inquisitor') up and down through the Twilight.

Yes, he was hung all over with amulets, like decorations on a New Year's tree. But there was something else as well as the amulets. Charms. Combinations of the very simplest natural components, which didn't require great effort to saturate them with magic, which acquired their magical properties from light, almost imperceptible touches of Power. In the same way that saltpetre, charcoal and sulphur, almost harmless in themselves, together become gunpowder, which explodes at the slightest spark.

It was no accident that Edgar was dressed completely in cotton, linen and leather. Natural materials have an affinity for magic. You can't charm a nylon jacket.

And these charms that transformed his light clothing into magical armour bothered me. Charms are the weapon of enchantresses and witches. Magicians rarely make use of them. There was no way I could imagine Edgar carefully impregnating his own trousers with herbal infusions.

So was this the work of another member of their criminal gang? The Light Healer? Yes, healers knew how to work with charms, I knew that very well from Svetlana.

'Edgar, you realise that I am obliged to arrest you?'

'And what if you can't?' Edgar asked, but he didn't wait for an answer. The fingers of his left hand began moving, weaving together a spell. I realised which one it was – and I hesitated for just an instant as I made up my mind whether to warn Rustam or not. Strangely enough, it was in my interest for Edgar to get what he wanted . . .

'Rustam, he's working the Confession!' I shouted.

After all, this ancient magician with bats in the belfry was a Light One . . .

Edgar struck instantly with the spell, simultaneously shouting:

'How can I take the Crown of All Things?'

There you go. I hadn't needed to use my four bracelets that compelled an honest answer to any question!

We all gazed at Rustam in silence. He was slowly rubbing his chest where the spell had struck him. He raised his head, looked at Edgar with his cold blue eyes and said:

'With your hands.'

Alisher started laughing. Edgar had been caught out by the ambivalence of his formulation. Even under a powerful spell Rustam had managed to give a perfectly precise and absolutely useless answer.

And then, with a slight movement of his lips, Rustam struck back. And he struck with something entirely unfamiliar to me. No fancy effects, but Edgar was shaken from side to side, and his cheeks swelled up in red botches from slaps delivered by an invisible hand.

'Never try to put pressure on me again,' Rustam warned him when the slapping session was over. 'Do you understand, Inquisitor?'

Before Edgar could decide what to say, if anything, I threw up my hand, feeling absolutely delighted that I hadn't used my set of bracelets against Rustam, and fired off all four tongue-loosening spells against Edgar. The amulets on the Inquisitor's body blazed up brightly, but they couldn't absorb the full force of the blow.

'Who was the vampire with you in Edinburgh?' I shouted.

Edgar's face contorted as he struggled painfully to hold back the word that was rising to his tongue. He failed.

'Saushkin!' he shouted.

Rustam laughed again and said:

'Bye-bye!'

Afandi was suddenly himself again. It was as if a rubber doll had been slightly deflated – he lost height, his shoulders narrowed, wrinkles appeared on his face, his eyes dimmed, the hairs of his beard fell out and scattered.

Edgar and I looked at each other with hatred in our eyes.

And then, without wasting any time on gathering Power or intoning spells, Edgar struck at us. A fiery rain poured down from the sky, seething and bubbling on the Shields that Alisher and I had erected. But there was no fire around Afandi, who was still confused and hadn't yet recovered his wits – evidently one of the protective rings had been activated.

The minute that followed was full of attacks and counter-attacks. Alisher wisely left me to conduct the battle, took a step backwards and fed Power to our Shields, only occasionally allowing himself a brief lunge of attacking magic.

Geser must have involved the finest diviners in the Watch in the preparation of our equipment. After the fire came ice. A blizzard started howling through the air: tiny snowflakes with edges as sharp as razors tested the strength of our Shields and melted impotently as they approached Afandi. Before the storm of ice had even died away, Edgar struck with the Kiss of the Viper and the rocks under our feet were covered with drops of acid. Afandi was protected yet again. Out of the corner of my eye I noticed that the old man wasn't just doing nothing, he was weaving some weak, but very cunning and unusual spell. I didn't really expect him to be successful, but at least he was busy and not getting under our feet.

The fourth spell that Edgar used was a vacuum. I was already expecting exactly that – and when the air pressure around me started falling rapidly I calmly carried on lashing Edgar alternately with Opium and Thanatos. Behind me Alisher was striking out with fireballs and lumps of super-cooled water from the wands. The combination of fireballs and icy shrapnel exploding into viscous blue drops was remarkably effective – I could see the Inquisitor's amulets, confused by the contrast, starting to lose their Power.

But there was more to all this than just the amulets. Edgar, a first-level magician was holding out against both of us and still managing to counter-attack! Either he was pumped right up to the hilt with Power, or he had surpassed the first level. I didn't have the time to make a thorough check on his aura.

The failure of the vacuum seemed to dent Edgar's fervour. It was such a rare spell that our readiness for it bewildered the Inquisitor. He began to back away slowly, circling round the charred Toyota that was smoking from acid and covered in hoar frost. He got snagged on an icicle that had smashed through the car's door and almost fell: as he waved his arms about to keep his balance he almost let my Opium through.

'Edgar, surrender!' I shouted. 'Don't make us kill you!'

Those words stung the Inquisitor to fury. He paused for a second, and then took a strange pendant off his belt – a bundle of small grey feathers tied together with string, like a small twig broom. He tossed it into the air.

The feathers turned into a flock of birds like overgrown sparrows, but with beaks that glittered like bronze. There were twenty or thirty of them – and they came dashing straight for me, manoeuvring like super-modern re-entry vehicles, the pride and joy of the generals in the rocket forces.

The 'chicken god' hanging round my neck broke and fell off its chain. And the flock of birds began fluttering about aimlessly in the air. They didn't try to approach Edgar, but they couldn't attack me – and they carried on fluttering about like that until Edgar swore and waved his hand to make them disappear.

Afandi too cast his spell and seemed to break through Edgar's defences. But there was no visible effect on the Dark Magician. He carried on backing away, occasionally counter-attacking. There was a glow on his chest that kept getting brighter and brighter all the time – an amulet hidden under his clothes had been activated and was preparing to respond. For an instant I even thought that Edgar had equipped himself with a suicide spell, Shahid or Gastello, which would take us to the grave along with him.

'More Power to the Shields!' I ordered, and Alisher gave it everything he had, powering up the Shields around us and one around Afandi.

But Edgar was clearly not in the mood for a dramatic suicide. He launched one more brief attack and then pressed his hands to his chest, where the amulet was glowing. The blue lines of a portal sprang up around him – the magician took a rapid step forward and disappeared.

'He's hopped it,' Alisher said. He sat down on the rocks and immediately swore and jumped back to his feet, his trousers smoking. The Kiss of the Viper was still working.

I stood there, feeling completely drained. Afandi stood beside me, laughing.

'What did you throw at him?' I asked.

'The next seventy-seven times he lies down with a woman he will suffer shameful failure!' Afandi explained triumphantly. 'And no one will be able to remove the spell.'

'Very witty,' I said. 'Very eastern.'

With a few brief spells I cleared away the traces of magic from the ground under our feet. The drops of acid had raised bubbles in the stone, like rising dough.

Saushkin!

So it was Saushkin!

EPILOGUE

GESER DIDN'T ANSWER straight away. In fact, to be quite honest, it was more than two minutes before he answered.

'Anton, do you think you could . . .'

'No, I couldn't,' I said.

The sky above me was gradually growing brighter. The strangely large southern stars were fading. I took another swig of cola out of my bottle and added:

'Thanks for the amulets. They were all spot on. But now pull us out of here. If one more psychopath comes along . . .'

'Anton.' Geser's voice sounded a bit softer now. 'What happened?'

'I had a heated conversation with Edgar.'

Geser paused and asked:

'Is he still alive?'

'He is. He left via a portal. But first he spent a long time trying to finish us all off.'

'Has our friend the Inquisitor completely lost his mind?'

'Possibly.'

Geser hummed something into the phone and I suddenly realised the boss was trying to think of the best way to use this information when he talked to Zabulon. Of how he could most humiliate Zabulon with this story about his former colleague.

'Geser, we're very tired.'

'A helicopter will come to get you,' Geser said. 'Putting up a portal would be very difficult. Wait for a while, I'll get in touch with Tashkent. Are you . . . at Rustam's place?'

'We're on the plateau where you used the White Mist against the Dark Ones.'

It's not often that I manage to embarrass Geser – I couldn't afford to let the chance slip.

'The helicopter will be there soon,' Geser said after a pause. 'Did you talk to Rustam?'

'Yes.'

'And did he answer?'

'Yes. But not all the questions.'

Geser gave a sigh of relief.

'Well, at least he told you something . . . You didn't have to – er – prevail upon him?'

'No. I discharged all four bracelets into Edgar.'

'You did?' asked Geser, growing more cheerful with every word I said. 'And what did you find out?'

'The name of the vampire who's working with Edgar.'

'Well?' Geser said after a moment's pause. 'Who is it?'

'Saushkin.'

'That's impossible!' Geser barked. 'Absolute nonsense!'

'Then the spells failed.'

'My spells couldn't have failed. But you could have missed,' Geser said in a slightly softer voice. 'Anton, we'll have to do without . . . unnecessary delicacy. When you get here, I'll show you something that I didn't want to show you.'

'I'm all agog,' I snorted.

'I'm talking about the remains of Konstantin Saushkin. We keep them here, at the Watch.'

Now it was my turn to pause. But Geser said:

'I really don't want to distress you once again. Charred bones are not a very pretty sight. Konstantin Saushkin is dead. There can be no doubt about it. Not even Higher Vampires can live without a skull. That's all. Now relax and wait for the helicopter.'

I cut off the call and looked at Alisher – he was lying close by, munching on a chocolate bar. I said:

'Geser told me that we have Saushkin's remains.'

'Yes,' Alisher replied calmly. 'I've seen them. A skull with the glass from the spacesuit melted into it. Your Saushkin's dead.'

'Don't be upset,' Afandi put in. 'Sometimes with an effort it's possible to lie under any spell.'

'He couldn't have been lying . . .' I whispered, recalling Edgar's face. 'No, he couldn't have . . .'

I lifted the cellphone up in front of my face, went into the MP3 menu and switched something on at random. When I heard a woman's voice singing to a quiet guitar, I put the phone down beside me. The tiny speaker strained as hard as it could.

> We used to rise with the dawn
> And live for a thousand years.
> Then someone went and stole
> The fire – the flickering light.
> And then some of us started praying
> And others sharpened their fangs,
> But we all drank from the Blue River.
> But then time slipped through our fingers,
> And by winter the river was shallow.
> And those who had always lived here
> Blamed those who had come from afar.

Some had daughters growing,
And others had sons,
But we all drank from the same stream . . .

'Afandi!' I called. 'Do you know that my daughter told me about you? Back in Moscow.'

'Yes?' Afandi asked in surprise. 'Is your daughter an enchantress, then?'

'Yes, she is,' I said. 'But still a little one. Only six years old. She asked if you would give her your beads. The blue ones.'

'What a fine daughter!' Afandi exclaimed in admiration. 'Only six, and already thinking about beads! And turquoise is a fine choice . . . here!'

I didn't see which pocket he took the beads out of before he handed them to me. I looked curiously at the string of sky-blue pieces of turquoise, and asked:

'Afandi, they're magical, aren't they?'

'Only a tiny bit. I charmed the string so that it will never break. But apart from that, they're just beads. Beautiful ones! I chose them for my great-granddaughter, she's getting on a bit, but she still likes her finery. Never mind, I'll buy some more. And these are for your daughter, may she wear them in good health.'

'Thank you, Afandi,' I said, putting the present away.

One rose higher and higher,
Another damaged his wing.
In some fields the grain swelled and ripened,
But in others nothing would grow.
One was died, struck by a bullet,
And the other fired the gun,
But we all drank from the same stream . . .

After the wine or the poison potion,
Some remember their father, some their mother.
One decides it is time to build,
Another that it's time to destroy,
But every day at midnight
He who sits by the Mill of Fate
Resolves all their arguments
And says who must go out on watch.*

Alisher cleared his throat and said quietly:

'Perhaps it's none of my business – after all, musicians are pretty strange people! But I think we ought to hold an official inquiry into that song . . .'

* Zoya Yashchenko, 'Night Watch'.

Part Three

A COMMON
DESTINY

PROLOGUE

THE TUTOR LOOKED round intently at the trainees. He was young himself: not so long ago he had been standing in their place, and now he was desperately lacking in respectability. Or at least, that was what he thought.

'We're about to make our first field trip,' the tutor said. His hand automatically reached up for the bridge of his nose – he was always trying to adjust his spectacles. Why on earth had he cured own his short-sightedness? Spectacles would have added to his respectability! 'Andrei, repeat the assignment.'

A skinny teenage boy took a step forward and recited in a breaking voice:

'We walk along the street. We examine passers-by through the Twilight. If we see any Dark Ones or Light Ones we inform you. But we pay most attention to finding uninitiated Others.'

'What do we do if we discover an uninitiated Other?'

'Nothing,' the boy said firmly. 'We inform you, and then act according to the circumstances. An Other should be initiated at an appropriate moment, when he is most inclined towards the Light.'

'What do we do if we notice a criminal act committed by Dark Ones?'

'Nothing,' the boy replied, with obvious annoyance. 'We inform you and then contact the Watch . . .'

'While maintaining a safe distance,' the tutor added. 'And what if we discover a crime being committed by human beings?'

'Again, we do nothing,' the boy replied, this time in a really sombre voice. 'All we do is watch!'

The other trainees smiled. In addition to the boy there were two adult men and a young woman standing in the line. In the tutor's opinion, they were all destined for the fourth or fifth level. But the boy might possibly get as far as the second, or even the first. He was an excellent prospect for a battle magician.

'Thank you, Andrei. You put everything quite correctly. We watch. We are only learning. Is that clear? Do not enter the Twilight, do not cast any spells. Our basic task is to search for uninitiated Others. And don't go thinking that it's easy. Sometimes a person has to be studied for several minutes to determine if he or she is a potential Other. By the way, Anton Gorodetsky was discovered during a study assignment like this one. Geser himself discovered him.'

The tutor paused for a few seconds and then joked:

'Well, I'm not Geser, but I am planning to become a Higher Other.'

He had absolutely no chance of reaching the Higher level. As a matter of fact, he had less than half an hour left to live. But the tutor couldn't sense that. In the bundle of probability lines that he could have examined, there was only one inconspicuous little line that led to death.

But at that precise moment dozens of coincidences were coming together and that slim thread was swelling up with blood. Unfortunately, the tutor was too busy to study his own destiny every hour.

'We walk along Chistoprudny Boulevard,' he said. 'We don't do anything, we just watch.'

★　　★　　★

One kilometre away, at the very centre of the city, on Lubyanskaya Square, a car was stuck solid in a traffic jam. The Caucasian driver shrugged and glanced guiltily at his passenger, who thrust several banknotes into his hand and climbed out of the car. The driver put the money in his pocket and frowned as he watched his passenger walk away. The man was not very likeable, somehow. He had paid well enough, but . . . The driver looked at the little icon glued to the dashboard of the old Zhiguli, then at the copper plaque with a sura from the Koran. He mentally thanked both the Christian and Muslim gods that the journey had been short. He really hadn't liked that passenger!

The driver was an uninitiated Other, but he didn't know it. Today his destiny could have taken an entirely new direction.

But it hadn't happened. He turned along a side street, where he was almost immediately flagged down by a pushy young woman. They agreed a price and set off to the south-west district.

The tutor halted opposite the Rolan movie theatre and lit a cigarette. He looked at Andrei, the trainee he felt the greatest liking for, and asked:

'Have you read *Denis's Stories*?'

'Uh-huh,' the boy murmured. He was a well-read, bookish boy from a good family.

'What can we say when we recall the story 'The Grand Master's Hat'?'

'That little Denis Korablyov lived in a very prestigious neighbourhood,' the boy replied.

The young female trainee laughed. She hadn't read *Denis's Stories*, she had only seen the TV film a long time ago and then forgotten it, but she understood the irony.

'And what else?' the tutor asked, with a smile. He never smoked as he walked along, because he had read in a fashionable magazine that it wasn't a respectable thing to do. And now every time he inhaled he brought his death closer – but it wasn't the nicotine that was to blame.

The boy thought about the question. He liked the young woman magician, and he also liked the semi-conscious awareness that he was cleverer than she was.

'We can also say that chess grand masters are very careless people. His hat was carried away by the wind and he didn't notice.'

'I suppose so,' the tutor agreed. 'But for us Others, the main moral of this story is not to get involved in petty human problems. You are likely to be misunderstood or even become an object of aggression.'

'But Denis made up with the grand master. When he offered to play him at chess.'

'And another wise thought!' the tutor continued. 'You don't need any magic to order to establish relations with a human being. You don't even need to try to help him or her. The important thing is to share the other individual's interests.'

They listened to the tutor attentively. He liked to take some fairy tale or children's book as an example and draw lots of interesting comparisons. The trainees always found that amusing.

Half a kilometre away from them the former taxi passenger was walking along Myasnitskaya Street. He stopped at a kiosk, found some change in his pocket and bought the *Komsomolskaya* newspaper.

The tutor looked around for the nearest rubbish bin. It was a long way away. He was about to throw his cigarette butt in the pond, to delight the swans, but he caught Andrei's eye and changed his mind. This was terrible – three whole years as a Light Other and his nasty little human habits were still as strong as ever . . . The tutor walked briskly over to the bin, dropped his butt into it and came back to the trainees.

'Let's move on now. And watch, watch, watch!'

By now his death was almost inevitable.

A middle-aged man holding a newspaper approached the Chistoprudnoe metro station. He hesitated before walking down the steps. On the one hand, he was in a hurry. On the other, the day was much too fine. A clear sky, a warm breeze . . . the borderline between summer and autumn, that season of romantics and poets.

The man strolled as far as the pond, sat on a bench and opened his newspaper. He took a small flask out of the pocket of his jacket and sipped from it. A hobo carrying a plastic bag full of empty bottles stared at the man and licked his lips at the sight of that gulp. Not expecting anything, but unable to overcome his habit of begging, he asked in a hoarse voice:

'Will you give me a drop, brother?'

'You wouldn't like it,' the man replied calmly, without the slightest sign of malice or irritation. It was simply a statement.

The homeless man hobbled on. Three more empty bottles, and he would be able to buy a full one. Number Nine. Strong, sweet, tasty 'Number Nine' . . . damn all these bourgeois types with their newspapers, there were people here suffering from hangovers . . .

That was the very day when the hobo's cirrhosis of the liver would develop into cancer. He had less than three months left to live. But that had nothing to do with what was happening on the boulevard.

'A man with a plastic bag, an ordinary human being,' said the woman trainee. 'Andriusha, you have the keenest eyes here, can you see anyone?'

'I see a hobo . . . A Light Other by the metro!' the boy cried, with a start. 'Vadim Dmitrievich! A Light Other by the metro! A magician!'

'I see him,' the tutor said. 'Initiated ten years ago. A magician. Fifth level. Not an active member of the Watch.'

The trainees looked at their tutor admiringly. Then Andrei turned his head back and blurted out gleefully:

'Oh! On the bench! A Dark Other! Undead! A vampire! A Higher Vampire! Not registered . . .'

The boy had begun lowering his voice at the word 'undead', and he had pronounced the words 'not registered' almost in a whisper.

But the vampire had heard. He folded his newspaper and stood up. He looked at the boy and shook his head.

'Go,' said the tutor, tugging Andrei by the sleeve and dragging him behind himself. 'Everybody go, quickly!'

The vampire walked towards him, taking long steps, reaching out his right hand as if in greeting.

One of the male trainees took out a phone and pressed the emergency contact button. The vampire growled and started walking faster.

'Halt! Night Watch!' said Vadim Dmitrievich, raising his hand and creating the Magician's Shield. 'Stop – you are under arrest!'

The vampire's silhouette blurred as if from rapid movement. The young woman trainee screamed as she tried to erect her Shield but couldn't manage it. The tutor turned to look at her, and at that instant something struck him in the chest, tightened in a hot, prickly fist – and ripped out his heart. The useless Shield fizzled out, dissipating into space. The tutor swayed, not falling yet, staring helplessly at the bloody, beating lump of flesh lying at his feet. Then he started leaning down, as if to pick up his heart and stuff it back into the ragged, gaping hole in his chest. The world around him turned dark, the asphalt leapt up towards him, and he fell, clutching his own heart in his hand. His teaching career had not been a very long one.

The young woman squealed when the blow descended on her and she was tossed between the trees to the very edge of the roadway. She lay there across the kerb, still squealing and watching a car the same colour as the dirty asphalt driving straight at her.

The car managed to brake in time

The young woman squealed again as she tried to get up, and only then felt the terrible pain at her waist. She lost consciousness.

Andrei was suddenly jerked up into the air, as if someone wanted to look him in the eyes or sink their teeth into his throat. A voice whispered:

'Why did you have to see me, A-student?'

The boy screamed and began struggling in those invisible hands. He could feel a shameful damp patch spreading across his jeans.

'Have you been taught to record auras?' the voice asked out of thin air. 'Remember, I can sense a lie.'

'No!' Andrei shouted, squirming. The invisible vampire's grip slackened slightly.

And just at that moment the boy's eyes were blinded by a bright flash. One of the male trainees had managed to gather enough Power for a battle spell after all. Well, of course, it wasn't only young kids who liked to peep into the next sections of the textbook . . .

Andrei was jerked through the air, the world spun round him – and he landed with a splash right in the middle of the pond, frightening the fat, lazy swans and the sly, brazen ducks. From there he saw the male trainee who had thrown the Shock spell fall, and the other trainee, who was making a phone call, take to his heels.

Andrei swam to the structure meant for the swans and scrambled up onto the wooden platform. The little house smelled of bird droppings. But the boy still preferred to sit there in the middle of the pond until the operations group arrived. The following day his action was described by Geser as the only correct thing that

he could have done in the given situation, and the boy was unofficially requested to think about working in the Watch. As Vadim
Dmitrievich had used to say when he was alive: 'Dead heroes serve
in a different place.'

Considering the nature of the situation, there weren't many casualties. Only the tutor and one of the trainees, a mathematician by
education. Perhaps he hadn't had enough time to calculate what
kind of opposition an untrained fifth-level magician could offer a
Higher Vampire.

Or perhaps he simply hadn't bothered to calculate anything.

CHAPTER 1

I SAID HELLO to Garik, who was discussing something with a
colonel of the militia. The colonel was an ordinary man, but he
was involved in our work – he knew something about the Watches
and helped us to cover up incidents like this one. The bodies had
already been taken away, our specialists had finished fiddling about
with auras and traces of magic, and now the forensic experts from
the militia had started their work.

'In the Gazelle,' Garik told me, with a nod. I walked across to
our operational vehicle and got in.

A young lad wrapped in a blanket and drinking hot tea from
a mug gave me a frightened look.

'My name's Anton Gorodetsky,' I said. 'You're Andrei, right?'

The boy nodded.

'I . . .' the boy began in a remorseful voice. 'I didn't know . . .'

'Calm down. You're not to blame for anything. Nobody could
have foreseen the appearance of a wild vampire in the centre of
Moscow in broad daylight,' I said. But I thought to myself that if
the lad had such a natural ability for reading auras, then this sort
of thing ought to have been foreseen. But I didn't want to criticise the dead tutor. Some day this incident would go into the

teacher-training manuals, on the pages printed in red to indicate that the knowledge in them had been paid for in blood.

'But I shouldn't have shouted like that,' the boy said. He put down the mug of tea. The blanket slid off his shoulder and I saw a massive bruise on his chest. The vampire had hit him really hard. 'If he hadn't heard me . . .'

'He would still have sensed your fright and confusion. Calm down. The most important thing now is to catch this undead monster.'

'And lay him to rest,' the boy said in a firm voice.

'Right. And lay him to rest. Have you been studying with us for long?'

'Three weeks.'

I shook my head. He was a talented young boy, no doubt about it. I just hoped that what had happened wouldn't put him off working in the Watch . . .

'Have you been taught how to record auras?'

'No,' the boy admitted. And he shuddered, as if at some unpleasant memory.

'Then describe the vampire as precisely as you can.'

The boy hesitated and then said:

'We haven't been taught. But I've tried studying it. It's the fourth paragraph in the textbook . . . recording, copying and transmitting an aura.'

'And you studied the subject?'

'Yes.'

'Can you transmit the vampire's aura to me?'

The boy thought for a moment and nodded.

'I can try.'

'Go on. I'm opening myself up.' I closed my eyes and relaxed. Okay, come on, young talent . . .

At first there was a faint sensation of warmth — like a hairdryer blowing into my face from a distance. And then I sensed a clumsy, rather confused transmission. I locked onto it and took a close look. The boy was trying with all his might, transmitting the aura again and again. Gradually I began building up a complete picture out of the isolated fragments.

'Just a little bit more,' I said. 'Repeat that . . .'

The coloured threads flared up more brightly and arranged themselves into an intricate pattern. The basic colours, of course, were black and red, non-life and death, the standard vampire aura. In addition to the colour scheme, which was constantly changing and could be very different at different times, there were fundamental features: the subtle pattern of Power, as individual as fingerprints or the pattern of blood vessels in the iris of the eye.

'Well done,' I said, pleased. 'Thank you. It's a very good impression.'

'Will you be able to find him?' the teenager asked.

'Definitely,' I assured him. 'You've been a great help. And don't be upset. Don't punish yourself . . . your tutor died a hero.'

That was a lie, of course. In the first place, heroes don't die. Heroes don't protect themselves with the Magician's Shield when they see a vampire attacking, they strike to stun him. An ordinary Grey Prayer would have slowed the vampire down and stopped him, at least for a while. Long enough for the trainees to scatter and run, and the tutor could have gathered his thoughts and erected a decent defence.

But there was nothing to be done about it now. There was no point in explaining to the boy that his first tutor had been a kind, sweet guy, but completely unprepared for real work. That was the whole problem – genuine battle magicians with the smell of blood and fire in their nostrils didn't often go in for tutoring. The tutors were more often noble-minded theoreticians . . .

'Garik, do you need me here?' I asked. There was already a Dark

One I didn't know loitering about beside Garik and the colonel. Which was only to be expected. The Day Watch had dropped by to get their guy off the hook, if they could, and if they couldn't, to find out how serious our losses were. Garik shook his head. I ignored the Dark One and walked off casually towards my car, which was parked right under a 'No Parking' sign. Anti-theft spells are used by all Others, but applying a spell that lets you be seen by everyone on the road and park wherever you like is a bit more complicated.

Getting an impression of the vampire's aura was a great stroke of luck. In a situation like that even experienced adult magicians lose their heads. But this kid had managed to do well. I was itching to get back to the office as quickly as possible and pass on the impression for the duty watchmen's information – then everyone who went out on patrol could look for the bloodsucker. A Higher Vampire, unregistered . . . No, I couldn't count on a coincidence like that.

But it was a *Higher* Vampire!

Trying to set aside my excessive hopes, I got into the driving seat and set off for the office.

The city duty officer was Pavel. I flashed him the impression of the aura, and he was delighted to get it. It's always a pleasure to hand the patrolmen something serious instead of highly relevant information such as: 'At Chistye Prudy a wild vampire took out two of our side . . . His appearance? Male, kind of middle-aged . . .'

I sat down in front of the computer in my office, looked at the screen and said:

'This is plain crazy.'

But I launched 'Comparison' anyway. The big problem with comparing auras is that you can't let the system compare them automatically, like you can with fingerprints. The impression of the aura can be passed 'from head to head' but not 'from head to computer' – no computers like that exist. To get an aura into the database, we have an elderly artist who works with us, Leopold Surikov. Despite being the namesake of a famous Russian artist, Leopold had not been a great success as a painter. And he had turned out to be a pretty weak Other too. But he could receive an impression of an aura and then reproduce the intricate pattern in a drawing, working patiently and painstakingly in the manner of a Chinese or Japanese miniaturist. And then that drawing could be entered into the computer for safe keeping and comparison. All the other Watches who can afford to keep an artist Other on the books work in exactly the same way.

Of course, it's slow, laborious work. Two days for even the least intricate aura.

But if the aura was already in the database, you could sidestep the long process, which was what I intended to do. Just to make sure I'd done everything possible – well, how would an unregistered vampire's aura get into the database?

A table appeared on the screen and I started clicking away with the mouse, constantly checking with the traces in my memory as I entered plus and minus signs.

'Is there an upper arc?'

Of course not. How could an undead vampire have an upper arc in his aura?

The figure showing the number of registered auras was immediately cut by a factor of five. There were far fewer undead in the archive than live Others. Several lines also disappeared and the table immediately became shorter as it was targeted on vampires.

'How marked is the first lateral barb?'

I entered two plus signs. I could have entered three – the barb was right on the borderline.

The questions followed each other. I answered about twenty of them before I let myself glance at the right upper corner of the table.

I saw the figure 3 winking at me.

I'd got a result after all. A small figure like that had to refer to a vampire and members of his clan, the ones he had initiated. There are certain differences between their auras, but they are absolutely minimal, it would take hundreds of questions to get a specific identification.

But three candidates suited me just fine.

I clicked on the figure 3.

And I almost fell off my chair. There was Kostya Saushkin's smiling face looking out at me, with the words LAID TO REST written across it in thick red letters.

I stared dully at the screen for a few seconds, remembering the contents of the aluminium container that Geser had shown me the previous week, after I had got back from Samarkand . . .

And then I groaned out loud when it finally hit me.

I clicked again, and shuddered again when I saw Polina, Kostya's mother. But it wasn't the photograph that shocked me, it was the words written across it in red: LAID TO REST.

I started running through her file from the top: 'Born a human being, with no abilities as an Other. Initiated by her husband under paragraph 7 of the agreement, "The right to self-determination of an Other's family . . ."' A little further down I picked out the lines: 'Refused to participate in the lottery, rewarded with a monthly supply of non-preserved donor blood, group 3, rhesus positive'. She was conservative in her feeding habits, did not hunt human beings, always took exactly the same type of fresh blood, unlike some vampires who, once they gave up hunting, started demanding 'virgin's blood, only group 1 or 2 — groups 3 and 4 give me indigestion'.

The final lines made everything clear.

'Voluntarily terminated her existence and laid herself to rest on 12.09.2003, shortly after the death of her son, Higher Vampire Konstantin Gennadievich Saushkin (case No. 9752150). Buried on 14.10.2003, at her own request, with the Christian rites of burial, carried out by the Light Other Father Aristarkh.'

I knew Father Aristarkh – he was one of those very rare cases when an Orthodox priest managed to combine his life as an Other with his faith, and also tried to carry out some kind of missionary work among the Dark Ones. I had been speaking to him only a month earlier. Why hadn't I known about Polina Saushkina's suicide – for that was what it was, if you stripped away the shell of words.

I hadn't wanted to know, so I hadn't. All very simple.

A third click of the mouse – and a third file.

Naturally.

'Gennady Ivanovich Saushkin . . .'

I groaned and clutched my head in my hands.

Fool! Fool! Fool!

It didn't matter that, according to the file, Saushkin senior was a fourth-level vampire, that he didn't hunt, was not a member of the Day Watch and had never been known to break the law.

Edgar had never been listed as a Higher Other, either. But just look at the way he had managed to withstand the influence of four amulets and only tell me part of the truth.

And I had understood the partial truth exactly the way that suited me. The way that suited my own complexes, fears and feelings.

The boy Andrei, who had been fished out of the pond after his close encounter with Gennady Saushkin, was wrong to blame himself. He was not to blame for his teacher and fellow trainee being killed.

I was to blame. I had got stuck on the name 'Saushkin', as if it was some kind of impassable barrier. And I hadn't bothered to take even a single step sideways.

I was just about to print out the page when I realised that I couldn't even wait thirty seconds for the printer to purge its printing heads and make itself ready.

I leapt out of my office and dashed up the stairs.

But then I ran into a dead end – Geser wasn't in. Of course, I realised that he needed to rest sometimes too, but why did it have to be right now? This was really bad luck . . .

'Hi, Anton,' said Olga, coming out of the door of the office. 'Why are you looking so . . . hyped-up?'

'Where's Geser?' I howled.

Olga looked at me thoughtfully for a second. Then she walked up to me, pressed her hand carefully against my lips and said:

'Boris is sleeping. He hasn't gone home even once since the day you got back from Uzbekistan. An hour ago I used all the female wiles in the book to get him to go to bed.'

Olga was looking great. Her hair had obviously been worked on by a good stylist, her skin was covered with a wonderful gold tan, she was wearing a hint of make-up – just enough to empha-sise the beautiful outline of her eyes and the sexy plumpness of her lips. And she smelled of something very expensive: spicy and floral, hot and seductive.

She really had used all her female wiles.

But then, I'd seen her when she looked quite different. And not only seen her – I'd actually been inside that magnificent body myself. The sensation had been instructive, but I couldn't say that I really missed it all that much.

'And if you, Anton, start yelling and phoning Boris and insisting that he has to come to work immediately, I'll turn you into a bunny rabbit,' Olga said. 'I just haven't decided yet if it should be a real one or a stuffed toy.'

'An inflatable one from a sex shop,' I said. 'Don't try to frighten me, it's impossible anyway.'

'You think so?' she asked, narrowing her eyes.

'I do. But if you really want to practise your battle magic that badly – I have someone you can use as a target.'

'Who?'

'A Higher Vampire. The one who's been working with Edgar. The one who took out two Light Ones today at Chistye Prudy.'

'Who?' Olga repeated insistently.

'Saushkin.'

A faint shadow ran across Olga's face. She took me very gently by the elbow and said:

'Anton, we all have tragedies in our lives. Sometimes we lose friends, and sometimes we lose enemies, but we still blame ourselves . . .'

'Save the psychotherapy for Geser!' I barked. 'It's Gennady Saushkin! Saushkin senior! Kostya's father!'

'We checked him, he's fourth level . . .' Olga said, and then stopped.

'Do I have to explain to you how easy it is for a vampire to raise his level?' I asked.

'From fourth level to higher . . .' she said. 'But dozens of people would have disappeared; we ought to have noticed . . .'

'Then we just didn't!' I exclaimed, grabbing her by the hand. 'Olga, it's one chance in a thousand, but what if he's still at home? What if we could take him by surprise?'

'Let's go,' Olga said, with a nod. 'I hope you can still remember your old address?'

'Just two of us?'

'I think two Higher Light Ones can handle one vampire. Everyone in the office right now is too young. We don't want to take cannon fodder with us, do we?'

I looked into her eyes for a few seconds, watching the mischievous sparks dancing in them . . . was Olga bored of sitting in the office and managing things, then?

'Let's go,' I said. 'Just the two of us. Although it's a bit too much like the beginning of a Hollywood action movie.'

'How do you mean?'

'I mean there'll be an ambush waiting for us. Or you'll turn out to be the Light Other who's helping Edgar and Gennady.'

'Fool,' said Olga, not even offended. But while we were walking downstairs, she said spitefully, 'By the way, just to be sure we checked out your Sveta.'

'And what did you find?' I asked.

'It's not her.'

'I'm glad to hear it,' I said. 'And have *you* been checked out?'

'All Higher Light Ones have been checked. In Russia and Europe and the States. I don't know who it was that Foma caught a glimpse of in the Twilight, but all the Higher Ones have hundred-per-cent alibis.'

You should never go back to houses where you once used to live. Never, not for anything – not until you're old and senile, and the sight of the sandpit in the courtyard of the building where you were born brings a sweet smile to your lips.

As I looked at my old front entrance, I thought that not so many years had gone by . . . even by ordinary human standards. Eight years ago I had walked out of these doors to set out on just another vampire hunt. I hadn't known then that I would meet Svetlana, that she would become my wife, that I would become a Higher One . . .

But I was already an Other. And I knew that there were Others living above me – a family of vampires. Good, law-abiding vampires, with whom I managed to remain friends for quite a long time.

Until I killed my first vampire.

Well, there's always a first time for everything.

'Shall we go?' Olga asked.

I was suddenly struck by another painful memory. The boy Egor, who was younger than the trainee Andrei at the time, had copied an aura just as successfully and had also almost become a vampire's victim. And Olga and I, working together for the first time, had set out on his trail . . . And Geser had managed to have Olga released from her terrible punishment of being confined inside a stuffed owl . . .★

'Déjà vu,' I said.

'What's brought that on?' Olga asked absent-mindedly. She had lived in the world for so long that she could easily have forgotten that adventure of ours . . . 'Ah, you remembered us tracking Egor? By the way, I recently found out that he works in a circus, can you imagine? As an illusionist!'

'Let's go,' I urged her.

Olga was right not to be afraid of the shadows of her past. If she did feel a little bit guilty about Egor, at least she was still keeping an eye on him.

We got into the lift, I pressed the button for the tenth floor and we rode up in complete silence. Olga was clearly psyching herself up, gathering Power. I examined my fingers. In the years since I'd left the lift had been changed, replaced by a 'vandal-proof' model with metal walls and buttons. Young punks could no longer burn the plastic buttons with cigarette lighters the way they used to, so the buttons were glued up with chewing gum instead.

I rubbed my fingers together to clean off the sticky muck of polyvinyl acetate, artificial flavours and someone else's spittle.

★ This story is told in the first part of the book *The Night Watch*.

I didn't always manage to love people all the time.

The lift stopped and I said apologetically:

'Tenth floor. The Saushkins . . . Saushkin lives on the eleventh.'

I glanced sideways at the door of my old apartment. They hadn't changed the door . . . even the locks looked the same to me, except that the faceplates were a bit brighter and fresher. When we had walked up half a flight of steps I looked back at my door again, and it opened, as if someone had been waiting for us to move away. A dishevelled woman of an uncertain age stuck her head out. Her face was swollen and she was wearing a dirty housecoat. She looked us up and down with a spiteful expression on her face and started shrieking:

'Have you pissed in the lift again?'

The accusation was so unexpected that I broke into laughter. But Olga pressed her lips together and took a step back down. The woman quickly half closed the door, ready to slam it shut. Olga looked hard at the woman for a while and then said very quietly:

'No. You imagined it.'

'I imagined it,' the woman said in a thick, slow voice.

'And your upstairs neighbour is flooding your apartment,' Olga went on. 'Go upstairs and tell him what you think of him.'

The woman beamed and leapt out onto the landing just as she was – in her filthy, soiled housecoat and tattered slippers with no socks. She ran past us eagerly.

'Why did you do that?' I asked Olga.

'She asked for it,' Olga replied fastidiously. 'Let her serve the cause of the Light. At least once in her life.'

I thought that if there was really a Higher Vampire hiding in Saushkin's apartment, this could actually be the last thing the woman ever did in her life. Vampires really dislike personal insults.

But then, I didn't find the woman at all likeable either.

'Who did you sell the apartment to?' Olga asked. 'Who is this mental patient?'

'I sold it through an agency.'

'And they're not poor people, not if they could buy an apartment,' Olga said, with a shrug. 'How can she neglect herself like that?'

Apparently she was more offended by the woman's dilapidated appearance than by her rudeness. Olga was almost obsessively strict about such matters, no doubt as a result of the hardships of the war years and her subsequent imprisonment.

The woman whom Olga had recruited so swiftly was already pounding on Saushkin's door with her hands and feet and screeching:

'Open up! Open up, you bloodsucker! You've flooded me out! You've filled my whole apartment with hot water, you bastard!'

'I'm always touched by these accidental insights that human beings have,' Olga remarked. 'Tell me, why does a neighbour who has flooded her apartment, even if it is with hot water, suddenly become a bloodsucker?'

Meanwhile the woman upstairs had launched into a list of her property that had be soaked and ruined. The list was so colourful that I couldn't help glancing round to make sure there was no steam escaping from the open door of the apartment.

'A Czech piano, a Japanese television, an Italian three-piece suite, a brown mink coat!'

'A chestnut Arab stallion,' Olga said derisively.

'A chestnut Arab stallion,' the woman shrieked obediently.

A little girl slightly older than Nadya came out of my old apartment. Seven or eight years old, a pretty face, with a sad, frightened expression. Unlike her mother, she was dressed like a doll – in a smart dress, white socks and shiny lacquered shoes. She gave us a frightened glance, and looked at her mother with an expression of weary, exhausted sympathy.

'Sweety pie!' the woman exclaimed, jumping away from Saushkin's door. With a panic-stricken glance at Olga, she went dashing down to her daughter, or perhaps back to her apartment, 'Go home,' Olga said in a quiet voice. 'There's no more water flooding your apartment. We'll deal with your neighbour. And tomorrow morning go to the hairdresser's, have a manicure and get your hair done.'

The woman seized the girl by the hand and skipped in through the doorway, with a frightened backward glance at us.

'What is it that makes people the way they are?' Olga asked thoughtfully as she looked at the mother and daughter.

As she closed the door, the woman yapped:

'And don't you . . . pee in the lift any more! I'll call the militia!'

The word 'pee', softened for the daughter, somehow seemed especially horrible. As if there were switches inside the woman's head, clicking away as they tried to return her thoughts to normal.

'Is she sick?' I asked Olga.

'That's just it, she isn't,' Olga said in annoyance. 'She's psychologically healthy! Let's go on through the Twilight . . .'

I glanced down, found my shadow and stepped into it.

Olga appeared beside me.

We looked round and I couldn't help whistling.

The entire stairway was overgrown with lumpy blue garbage. The moss was dangling from the ceiling and the banisters like an ultramarine beard, it was spread out across the floor in a cerulean carpet, and around the light bulbs it was woven into honeycombed sky-blue balls that could have inspired any designer to invent a new style of lampshade.

'The staircase has been neglected,' Olga said, vaguely surprised. 'But then, a rabid vampire and a hysterical woman . . .'

We walked up to the door. I pushed on it – it was locked, of course. Even weak Others know how to lock their doors on the first level of the Twilight. I asked:

'Shall we go deeper?'

Instead of answering, Olga took a step back, twisted round and kicked the door hard just beside the lock. It swung open.

'Why do things the hard way?' Olga laughed. 'I've been wanting to try out that kick for a long time.'

I didn't ask who had taught her to break down doors like that. Despite Olga's confidence, I was by no means certain that the apartment was empty. We went into the entrance hall (the blue moss was still there all around us) and both of us spontaneously left the Twilight.

It was such a long time since I had been here . . .

And it was a long time since anyone else had been here. The apartment was full of that heavy, musty smell that you only find in rooms that have been closed up and abandoned. You'd think that even though no one had been breathing there, fresh air would at least have entered through the ventilation system and the small cracks, but no. The air had died anyway, turning sour, like yesterday's tea.

'There's no smell,' Olga said with relief.

I understood what she meant. There were smells, of course — smells of musty damp and accumulated dust. But there wasn't that particular smell we had been expecting, the one we had been afraid to find — the sickly-sweet smell of bodies that had been drained of blood by a vampire. Like that time in Mytishchi, where the serial killer Alexei Sapozhnikov had been arrested in his apartment. He was a petty vampire, and weak-minded too, which was precisely why he had evaded the attention of the Watches for so long . . .

'Nobody's lived here for at least a month,' I agreed. I looked at the coat rack — a winter jacket, a fur cap . . . a pair of dirty heavy fur-lined boots on the floor. It wasn't just a month, it was a lot longer than that. The owner of the flat had been missing since winter at least. I didn't remove the defensive spells that I had applied to myself in the car, but I relaxed. 'Right then, let's see how he lived . . . so to speak.'

We started our inspection in the kitchen. Like the rest of the apartment, the windows in here were covered with heavy curtains. The tulle that was now grey with dust was no doubt supposed to have given the apartment a cosy atmosphere. It hadn't been washed for perhaps two years, not since Polina had died.

Behind my back Olga clicked a light switch, making me start. She said:

'Why are we walking around in the dark, like Scully and Mulder? Check the refrigerator.'

I was already opening the door of the Korean refrigerator that was churring away smugly to itself. Kitchen technology is the kind that gets along best without any human supervision. But a computer left unattended for six months will very often start to malfunction. I don't know what the reason for that is, but it isn't magic, that's for sure. There isn't any magic in hardware.

There was nothing horrible in the refrigerator, either. That was something I had hardly dared to hope for. A suspicious-looking three-litre glass jar covered with white mould contained sour tomato juice – you could have made home brew out of it. Of course, it wasn't good that the tomatoes had been allowed to go to waste, but the Tomato Watch from Greenpeace could deal with that particular crime. There were two-hundred- and five-hundred-gram thick glass bottles standing in the door of the refrigerator. Each bottle had a Night Watch mark that glowed feebly through the Twilight – it was licensed donor blood.

'He didn't even drink his allowance,' I said.

There were also sausages, eggs and salami in the fridge, and in the freezer compartment there was a piece of meat (beef) and *pelmeni* (mostly soya). Basically the usual range of foods for a man living on his own. Only the vodka was missing, but that was inevitable. All vampires are non-drinkers by necessity: alcohol immediately disrupts their strange metabolism – it's a powerful poison for them.

After the kitchen I glanced into the toilet. The water in the toilet bowl had almost competely evaporated and there was quite a smell from the drains. I flushed the toilet and walked out.

'A good time to choose,' said Olga. I stared at her in confusion, until I realised that she was joking. The Great Enchantress was smiling. She had been expecting to see something terrible too, but now she had relaxed.

'Any time's good for that,' I replied. 'It stank in there, so I flushed the toilet.'

'Yes, I realised.'

When I opened the bathroom door I discovered that the light bulb had burned out. Maybe he had left it switched on when he'd left. I couldn't be bothered to search my pockets for a flashlight, so I called on the Primordial Power and lit up a magical light above my head. What I saw made me shudder.

No, it wasn't any kind of horror. A bath, a sink, a tap slowly dripping, towels, soap, a toothbrush, toothpaste . . .

'Look,' I said, making the light brighter.

Olga walked up and glanced over my shoulder. She said thoughtfully:

'That is curious.'

There was writing on the mirror. Not in blood, but in three-coloured toothpaste, so that the words naturally reminded me of the Russian flag. Someone's finger – and somehow I was sure that it was Gennady Saushkin's – had traced out three words in large capital letters on the glass surface of the mirror:

THE LAST WATCH

'No mystery story ever manages without words on the walls or the mirror,' said Olga. 'Although the writing ought to be in blood, of course . . .'

'This toothpaste suits the purpose too,' I replied. 'Red, blue and white. The traditional colours of the Inquisition are grey and blue.'

'I know,' Olga said thoughtfully. 'Do you think it was deliberate? Vampire, Inquisitor, Healer?'

'I can't see the line between deliberate intention and coincidence,' I admitted.

I walked along the short corridor and glanced into the sitting room. The light worked there.

'It's very nice,' said Olga. 'The house is so run-down, but they did a nice repair job in here.'

'Gennady's a builder by profession,' I explained. 'He did everything at home himself, and he helped me out once . . . well, I didn't know who he was then. He was very well thought of at work.'

'Of course he was, as a non-drinker,' Olga agreed and walked into the bedroom.

'He's a perfectionist too,' I said, continuing to praise Gennady as if we hadn't come here to lay the vampire to rest, and as though I was recommending him to Olga to refurbish her apartment.

I heard a muffled sound behind my back and turned round.

Olga was being sick. She was slumped against the doorpost, with her face turned away from the bedroom, and was puking straight onto the wall. Then she looked up at me, wiped her mouth with her hand and said:

'A perfectionist . . . Yes, so I just saw.'

I definitely didn't want to see what Olga had taken such a violent dislike to. But I walked to the door of the bedroom anyway, on legs that had turned to rubber in advance.

'Wait, I'll get out of the way,' Olga muttered, moving aside for me.

I glanced into the bedroom. It took me several seconds to make sense of what I saw.

Olga needn't have bothered to move. I didn't even have time to turn round, I just puked up my lunch straight into the bedroom, through the doorway. If shaking hands through a doorway is bad luck, then what about puking through one?

CHAPTER 2

GESER WAS STANDING at the window, watching the city deck itself out in its evening lights. Standing there silently, with only his hands, which were clasped behind his back, moving – as if he were weaving some kind of cunning spell.

Olga and I didn't say anything either. Anyone might have thought that it was all our fault . . .

Garik came in and lingered just inside the door.

'Well?' Geser asked without turning round.

'Fifty-two,' Garik said.

'What do the specialists say?'

'They've examined three. They all have the same injuries. The throat has been bitten and the blood has been drunk. Boris Ignatievich, can we carry on with this somewhere else? The stench is so terrible that the spells can't handle it . . . And it's all around the house already . . . as if a sewer had burst . . .'

'Have you called a truck?'

'A van.'

'All right, take them away,' said Geser. 'To some waste ground, well away from the city. Let them be inspected there.'

'And then?'

'And then . . .' Geser said pensively. 'Then bury them.'

'Are we not going to send them back to their families?'

Geser thought it over. Then suddenly he turned to me.

'Anton, what do you think?'

'I don't know,' I replied honestly. 'Disappeared without trace or killed . . . I don't know which is better for the families.'

'Bury them,' Geser ordered. 'When the time comes we'll think about it. Perhaps we'll start quietly exhuming them and sending them back to their families. Invent a story for each one. Do they all have documents?'

'Yes, they were lying in a separate pile. All neat and tidy, the work of a perfectionist.'

Yes, Gennady had always been neat and tidy. He used to lay down polythene sheeting when he drilled holes in the wall, and then carefully cleaned the floor after himself . . .

'How could we have failed to notice him?' Geser asked in a voice filled with pain. 'How did we fluff it? A vampire killed more than fifty people right under our very noses!'

'Well, none of them are Moscow locals,' Garik said. 'They're from Tajikistan, Moldova, Ukraine . . .' He sighed. 'Working men who came to Moscow looking for a job. Not registered in Moscow, of course. They lived here illegally. They have places along the main roads, where they stand for a day or two, waiting to be hired. And he's a builder, right? He knew everyone and they knew him. He just drove up and said he needed five men for a job. And he chose them himself, too, the bastard. Then he drove them away. And a week later he came back for some more . . .'

'Are people really still so sloppy?' Geser asked. 'Even now? Fifty men died, and nobody missed them?'

'Nobody,' Garik said, with a sigh. 'That dead piece of filth . . . he probably didn't kill them all straight away . . . he killed one and the others waited for their turn – for a day, two, three. In this room. And he put the ones he'd drunk in two polythene bags so they wouldn't stink and stacked them in the corner. The radiators on that side are even switched off. He must have started in the winter . . .'

'I really feel like killing someone,' Geser hissed through his teeth. 'Preferably a vampire. But any Dark One would do.'

'Then try me,' said Zabulon, casually moving Garik aside as he entered the Saushkin family's sitting room. He yawned and sat down on the divan.

'Don't provoke me,' Geser said quietly. 'I might just take it as an official challenge to a duel.'

A deadly silence fell in the apartment. Zabulon screwed up his eyes and gathered himself. As usual, he was wearing a suit, but without a tie. And for some reason I got the idea that he had chosen the black suit and white shirt deliberately, as a sign of mourning.

Olga and I waited, watching these two Others who were responsible for what happened on a sixth of the world's land surface.

'Geser, it was a figure of speech,' Zabulon said in a conciliatory tone of voice. He leaned back on the divan. 'You don't think I was aware of this . . . excess, do you?'

'I don't know,' Geser snapped. But from the tone of his voice it was clear that he knew perfectly well that Zabulon had nothing to do with this business.

'Well, let me tell you,' Zabulon said just as peaceably, 'that I am every bit as outraged as you are, or perhaps even more so. And the entire community of Moscow vampires is outraged and demands the execution of this criminal.'

Geser snorted. And Zabulon finally couldn't resist making a jibe.

'You know, they don't like the idea of their food base being undermined . . .'

'I'll give them a food base,' Geser declared in a low, grave voice. 'I'll keep a lid on the conserved blood for five years.'

'Do you think the Inquisition will support you?' Zabulon asked.

'I think so,' said Geser, finally turning round and looking him in the eye. 'I think so. And you will support my request.'

Zabulon lost the game of stare-me-down. The Dark One sighed, turned away, looked at me and shrugged, as if to say: 'What am I to do with him, eh?' He took out a long, frivolous pink cigarette and lit it. Then he said:

'They've gone completely wild . . .'

'Then you make sure they *don't* go wild.'

'Their children can't grow up without this, you know that. Without fresh blood they never reach sexual maturity.'

Naturally, Zabulon was not in the least concerned for the fate of vampire children. He just wanted to make fun of Geser. As far as that was at all possible.

'Children? We'll allow the children fresh blood,' Geser said after thinking for a moment. 'We wouldn't want thirty . . . er . . . Anton?'

'Thirty-two.'

'We wouldn't want thirty-two bloodsucking teenagers. Fresh blood. But donor blood! We are suspending the issue of licences for five years.'

Zabulon sighed and said, 'All right. I've been thinking it was time to tighten their rein myself. I asked the secretary of the community to keep an eye on the Saushkins . . . they proved to be a rotten little family.'

'I ought to have insisted on seven years,' said Geser. 'You agreed to five too easily.'

'But what's to be done now? We've already agreed,' said Zabulon, puffing out a cloud of smoke. He turned to me. 'Anton, did you come to see Gennady after Kostya was killed?'

'No,' I answered.

'But why didn't you? As an old friend and neighbour . . . ai-ai–ai . . .'

I didn't answer. Eight years earlier I would have blown my top.

'We've decided this matter,' said Geser. He frowned as he looked out into the corridor, where they had started carrying out the bodies. The whole entrance and stairway had been put under a light spell that completely removed any desire the inhabitants of the building might have had to glance out of their doors or look out of their windows. But then, in view of the fact that no one had come to see what the woman from my old apartment had been screeching about, people around here must all have been exceptionally incurious anyway.

It kept getting harder and harder for me to love them. I had to do something about that.

'What else?' Zabulon asked. 'As far as help in catching Saushkin is concerned, there's no problem. My watchmen are already out hunting for him. Only I'm afraid they might not deliver him in one piece . . .'

'You're not looking too good, Zabulon,' Geser suddenly said. 'Why don't you go to the bathroom and wash your hands and face?'

'Really?' Zabulon asked curiously. 'Well, since you ask . . .'

He got up and then halted in the doorway for a moment to make way for two watchmen who were carrying a half-decomposed corpse in a plastic sack. Apart from blood, there's a lot of water in a human body. If you leave a bloodless body to rot inside a plastic cocoon, the result is extremely unpleasant.

Zabulon, however, was not appalled by the sight.

'I beg your pardon, madam,' he said, letting the remains past. Then he strode cheerfully off to the bathroom.

'Were there women as well?' Geser asked.

'Yes,' Olga replied briefly.

Geser didn't ask any more questions. Apparently even our iron boss's nerves had given way.

That night the lads who were carrying out the bodies would get totally juiced. And although it was a breach of the rules, I wouldn't try to stop them. I'd sooner go out on patrol duty myself.

Zabulon came back a minute later. His face was wet.

'The towel's dirty, I'll dry off like this,' he said, with a smile. 'Well?'

'Your opinion?' Geser asked.

'I had this friend once, she liked to draw a New Year's tree on the mirror with toothpaste for the festive season. And the words "Happy New Year", and little numbers.'

'Very funny,' Geser said fastidiously. 'Have you heard anything about such an organisation?'

'About a "Last Watch"?' Zabulon asked, clearly emphasising the capital letters in his intonation. 'My dear enemy, even among the Dark Ones there are any number of sects, groups and mere clubs that I have never even heard of. But there are some that I *have* heard of. And the names that you come across! "Children of the Night!", "Watchmen of the Full Moon", "Sons of the Wind". And, by the way, I recall one group of children – human children, not Others – who love to play at vampires. Perhaps we ought to bring them here? To make them realise that a vampire is not really an imposing gentleman in a black cloak who lures maidens into an ancient castle? It's not that Gothic at all . . .'

'Zabulon, have you heard anything about the "Last Watch"?'

'No.'

'Gorodetsky has suggested' – Geser paused and looked at me – 'that it's what the three Others who tried to get their hands on the artefact in Edinburgh call themselves. The Dark One, the Inquisitor and the Light One.'

'The Dark One is Saushkin, the Inquisitor is Edgar,' Zabulon said, nodding. 'But who is the Light One?'

'I don't know. We've checked all the Higher Ones, they're clean.'

'Well, Saushkin wasn't a Higher One . . .' Zabulon said with a shrug. 'Although . . . it's easier for vampires. And then, what about Edgar? Gorodetsky?'

'I didn't have time to study his aura thoroughly,' I replied. 'There was a battle going on . . . and he was also hung with amulets from head to toe. Give me five minutes in a quiet situation, and I'll know everything there is to know about him . . .'

'Nonetheless,' Zabulon insisted, 'I know what happened on the Plateau of Demons. In general terms. So tell us about it.'

'In battle he behaved like a Higher One,' I stated after seeing Geser nod reluctantly in consent. 'There were three of us . . . well, two, if you don't count Afandi, although he tried his best too. We had a set of protective amulets from Geser, all very well chosen. But he was almost a match for us. I even think that he might have been able to continue the fight and have a chance of winning. But when Rustam left, Edgar had no reason to carry on fighting.'

'And so we have an Other who has managed to raise his level,' said Zabulon. 'My dear Geser, don't you think that the Inquisition did get hold of the *Fuaran* after all?'

'No,' Geser said firmly.

'If Kostya had survived,' Zabulon said, thinking out loud, 'then we might have hypothesised that he had memorised the formulas in the *Fuaran*. And managed to create some − er − copy of the book. Perhaps not as powerful, but still capable of raising Edgar to the Higher level. And then a Light One could have been subjected to the same procedure.'

'And then we could suspect any Light One,' Geser summed up. 'But fortunately for us, Kostya is dead and he wasn't able to reveal the secret of the *Fuaran* to anyone.'

'Did he not have time to share the contents of the book with his father?'

'No,' Geser replied firmly. 'It's a book of enchantment. You can't retell it over the phone, you can't photograph it.'

'What a shame, that would be such a good idea,' Zabulon said, clicking his fingers. 'A little witch showed me just recently that there's this thing in cellphones, it's called MMS messaging! You can send a photograph over the phone.'

At first I thought Zabulon was being witty again. Talking with a straight face about the MMS messages that little kids cheerfully send each other in class, he looked very comical.

And then I realised he was being serious. Sometimes I forget just how old they are. To Zabulon a cellphone is like magic.

'Fortunately it's not possible,' said Geser. 'He could have memorised something and reproduced it . . . but no, that's nonsense. Even that's impossible. The nature of a vampire is different from the nature of a witch. Only an experienced witch could recreate the *Fuaran*, even in a weaker form . . .'

I looked at Geser and asked:

'Tell me, Boris Ignatievich . . . can a witch become a Light One?'

The happiest moments in the life of the parents of a small child are from a quarter to nine until nine o'clock in the evening. Fifteen minutes of happiness while the child joyfully watches adverts for yogurt and chocolate (even though that is a bad thing) and then his or her eyes are glued to Piggy, Crow, Stepashka and the other characters in the programme *Good Night, Kiddies*.

If only the people who allocate time for children's programmes on TV sat with their own children in the evening, instead of dumping them on highly trained nannies, then *Good Night* would last half an hour. Or an hour.

And by the way, that would be great for improving the birth rate. Fifteen minutes is not very long, whichever way you look at it. At least there would be time to drink a cup of tea in peace.

I didn't tell Svetlana the details of what we had seen in Saushkin's flat. But she understood everything perfectly well, even from a very brief account. No, it didn't spoil her appetite, she carried on drinking tea. We had seen plenty of worse things in the Watch. But, of course, she turned a bit gloomy.

'We have a theory about the Light One,' I said, trying to lead the conversation on to a different subject. 'Geser checked out all the Higher Ones, no one's under suspicion there. Well, Edgar had a lot of charms on him. That's the work of a witch. So I thought . . .'

'That Arina had changed colour?' Svetlana asked, looking at me. 'Maybe.'

'You squeezed her pretty hard that time,' I said. 'You must have felt her mind. Do you think she could have become a Light One?'

'For an ordinary Other, it's impossible,' Svetlana said. 'Or almost impossible . . . For a Higher One . . . for Arina . . .'

She paused, remembering. I waited, glancing now and then at the TV screen, where a sad little girl was dragging a mitten along on a string and imagining that it was a puppy. How terrible! That would be the end of all our mittens and gloves. Nadya wouldn't actually turn them into dogs, of course – any magic has its limits. But there would be more toy dogs in the apartment from now on.

It was time to buy her a puppy, before life became unbearable.

'She could,' Svetlana said. 'She could have become a Light One. Her soul is very strange, everything's mixed up together inside it . . . there weren't any particular atrocities, though. But Arina swore an oath to me that she would live for a hundred years without killing a single human being or Other. She can't go against that.'

'And she hasn't killed anyone,' I observed. 'But as for supplying Edgar with amulets and raising his level of Power . . . nothing was said about that. Arina has enough wisdom to interpret your prohibition like that.'

'Anton, we're talking about the wrong thing,' Svetlana said, putting down her cup. 'Arina, who has become a Light One, or some other enchantress – that's not the point at all. The important question to ask is: What are they trying to achieve? What has united them? The ambition to destroy the entire world? Nonsense! You only find people who want to destroy the world just for the sake of it in stupid films. Power? But that's stupid too, Anton! They have enough Power already. No artefact, not even one made by a crazy magician fifteen hundred years ago, will allow them to achieve absolute Power. Until we understand what they are trying to achieve, what they want to find at the bottom of the Twilight, then it's completely irrelevant whether it is Arina or not, if she has become a Light One, or disguised herself so that Thomas couldn't recognise her.'

'Sveta, do you have any hunches?' I pretended not to notice that she had said 'we'. It's true what they say – you never really leave the Watch completely.

'The Crown of All Things erases the barriers between the levels of the Twilight . . .' Svetlana said and paused.

'Mama, the cartoon's over!' Nadya shouted.

'Try comparing it with the White Mist. The spells obviously have a single root . . .' Svetlana said, getting up and walking towards Nadya. 'Time for bed.'

'A story!' Nadya demanded.

'Not today. Daddy and I have to talk.'

Nadya looked at me resentfully, fiddling with the thin string of turquoise beads round her neck. She muttered:

'You're always talking . . . And Daddy's always going away.'

'That's Daddy's job,' Svetlana explained calmly, grabbing hold of her daughter's hand. 'You know he fights against the forces of darkness.'

'Like Harry Potter,' Nadya said rather doubtfully, looking at me. I suppose I didn't have the spectacles or the scar on my forehead that were needed to match up to the image.

'Yes, like Harry Potter, Fat Frumos and Luke Skywalker.'

'Like Luke Skywalker,' Nadya decided and gave me a smile. Obviously that was the character she thought I resembled most of all. Well, that was better than nothing.

'I'll be straight back . . .' said Svetlana, and the two of them went to the nursery. I sat there, looking at a chocolate sweet with a bite taken out of it. It had alternate layers of dark chocolate and white chocolate. When I counted seven layers, I laughed. It was a graphic illustration of the structure of the Twilight. The White Mist folded all the layers together, turning any Others who got in the way into stone. Okay, let's sidestep the effect of the spell in battle. What happened afterwards? I closed my eyes, trying to remember.

Afterwards the Twilight straightened out again. The levels of the Twilight returned to their old places.

Why had we decided that the Crown of All Things would join the Twilight and the real world together for ever? Simply because we believed what Rustam had said? But how did he know . . . The Twilight would fold up – and then expand again. As it left our world the Twilight would spread out its layers again. It was like a stiff spring – you could compress it, but it would straighten back out.

And that was interesting. I didn't believe in a Merlin who had created a magical bomb to destroy the entire world simply for the fun of it. He wasn't that kind of Other. But I could easily believe in Merlin as an experimenter who had invented a new amusement but had decided not to try it out.

What might happen if all the levels of the Twilight were united with the real world for a short time?

Would all Others die out?

Hardly.

In that case Merlin would surely have boasted of his power.

But he had thought up a kind of allegorical riddle for his message . . .

I recited the verse in a low voice as I watched Svetlana walking back quietly into the kitchen.

'The Crown of All Things is here concealed. Only one step is left.
But this is a legacy for the strong or the wise –
You shall receive all and nothing, when you are able to take it.
Proceed, if you are as strong as I;
*   Or go back, if you are as wise as I.*
Beginning and end, head and tail, all is fused in one,
In the Crown of All Things. Thus are life and death inseparable.'

'Trying to understand it?' Svetlana asked as she sat down beside me. 'You know what I was thinking – why did we decide that the Twilight would come together with the world for ever? Most probably it would move back out again.'

'That's what I was thinking too,' I agreed. 'Like with the White Mist. But what would that lead to? Blue moss starting to grow in our world?'

Svetlana laughed.

'Wouldn't the botanists have a field day! A new form of plant life, and one that reacts to human emotions. They'd write millions of doctoral theses . . .'

'They'd open factories for processing blue moss,' I added. 'Start spinning threads out of it, making blue jeans . . .'

Svetlana suddenly turned serious.

'And what would happen to those who live in the Twilight?'

'The disembodied Others?' I asked.

Svetlana nodded.

'Life and death,' I said, and nodded too. 'I don't know. Do you suppose they might be . . . resurrected? Come to life again in our world?'

'Why not? We know they live there. I even saw one on the fifth level, when I was fighting Arina . . .'

'And you didn't tell me,' I commented.

'You know it's best not to talk about these things. It's best not to know about it if you can't get there yourself. I'm not at all sure that everybody ends up there, perhaps it's only the most powerful. The Higher Ones, for example. Why should all the rest know that they won't have any existence after death?'

'Thomas the Rhymer said that down there on the lower levels of the Twilight there are magical cities, dragons and unicorns – all the things that don't exist in our world, but could have done.'

Svetlana shook her head

'Thomas seems like a very good man to me. But he's a bard. A poet. You can't cure that, Anton. You talked to him when he was in his Twilight Form, dreaming about unicorns and fairies, and magical cities, Others who have built a world of their own and don't live as parasites on the human world. I wouldn't count too much on all that being true. Perhaps there are only little huts and wooden houses there. And no fairies and unicorns.'

'That's still not too bad,' I said. 'Very many people would gladly swap the heaven they desperately hope to get to some day for eternal life in a hut out in the countryside. There are certainly trees there.'

'The Other I saw didn't look very happy,' Svetlana said. 'Of course, he was . . . well, kind of blurred, not very clear. But that's only natural, if his usual habitat is the seventh level of the Twilight. But he looked so . . . creased and rumpled. And he ran towards me, as if he wanted to tell me something. But I had other things on my mind at the time, you understand.'

'And I saw a former Other on the first level,' I recalled. 'When I was hunting that wild White One, Maxim.* He even gave me a bit of help, told me which way I should go.'

'It happens sometimes,' Svetlana agreed. 'Not often, but I've heard a few stories. And you already told me . . .'

Neither of us said anything for a while.

'Maybe they really would be brought back into our world,' Svetlana said. 'And that might be enough to make Edgar, Gennady and Arina work together. They must all have lost loved ones, not just Saushkin. And probably anyone who has lost loved ones would be thrown off balance by an opportunity like this.'

'It would throw anyone at all off balance,' I said.

We looked at each in alarm. It was good that now we were guarded round the clock. It was bad that our potential enemies were three Higher Ones.

'I'll put up a few more protective spells for the night,' said Svetlana. 'Don't think me a coward.'

'The Crown of All Things can be reached by force,' I said. 'By breaking through to the seventh level of the Twilight. But I couldn't do it. Probably Nadya could. If only I knew how to get through by using my wits . . . by cunning. I'd use that artefact myself. There'd be about the same number of Light and Dark magicians down there — we'd manage.'

'And what if we're wrong, and it's nothing but a bomb that will destroy the world?'

---

* This story is told in the second part of the book *The Night Watch*.

'That's why I prefer not even to think about how to reach the artefact. I'll leave that headache to Geser and Zabulon.'

'Let's go to bed and sleep on it,' Svetlana said. 'Tomorrow's a new day.'

But we didn't go to bed straight away. First Svetlana put up several new protective spells around the apartment, and then I did the same.

CHAPTER 3

THE MORNING TURNED out so fresh and clear that all of the previous day's doom and gloom seemed to have evaporated into thin air. Nadya meekly ate the rice porridge that she didn't like, and Svetlana didn't say a word when I casually told her that I was thinking of going to work early. But she did suggest that I should come back home early too, so that all of us could go to watch some family movie that her friends had told her was really great. I imagined the Dark Ones who were guarding Nadya being forced to watch a romantic fairy tale in which, naturally, good defeats evil, and I smiled.

'Definitely. I just want to find out how things are going. Maybe there's been some kind of breakthrough.'

'They would have called you,' said Svetlana, scattering my idle dreams like smoke.

But that didn't spoil my mood. I got ready quickly and grabbed my suitcase full of papers (oh, yes, even Light Magicians have to do their paperwork), then kissed my daughter and my wife and walked out of the apartment.

On the next floor down Roma, an amiable young lummox who had been working in our Watch for about two years, was making lively conversation with a thin, pretty young woman, one of the Dark Ones that Zabulon had assigned to guard us.

I greeted them both and walked on, shaking my head.

That was the way romances with unhappy endings got started. The way it had happened with Alisa and Igor . . .

The weather was so good that for a second I hesitated, standing outside the door of the building and wondering if I ought to walk to the metro. On the other hand, I really didn't want to go into the metro at all. Those hot trains, those jostling crowds – the rush hour in Moscow ends at somewhere around midnight.

No, the car would be better. Svetlana wasn't planning on going anywhere. And if I checked the probability lines, I could skip past the traffic jams and be at work in just twenty minutes.

I removed the protective spells that wouldn't have done me any harm but would have made sensitive drivers give my car a wide berth. I got into the driving seat, turned the key in the ignition and closed my eyes to check the best route for me to drive. The result was rather discouraging. For some reason all the probabilities were centred on Sheremetievo Airport, which was crazy since I had no intention of going there!

I felt something fluffy twine round my neck, and an amiable voice with a slight drawl asked:

'Does the king have a long journey to make today?'

I looked in the rear-view mirror and didn't like what I saw.

I didn't see Edgar. But I did see the thing that he had thrown round my neck – a silvery strip of fur. It didn't look much like a decorative neckpiece, there was something predatory about it . . . as if there were lots of tiny teeth hidden under that grey fur.

And I also saw Gennady Saushkin, sitting on the right side of the back seat. The vampire's face was composed and impassive.

'What's on your mind, Edgar?' I asked.

'That's none of your business,' Edgar replied, with an ominous laugh. 'Don't even think of withdrawing into the Twilight and don't try any spells. That little ribbon round your neck exists at every level of the Twilight . . . at least as far down as the sixth. And it will rip your head off if you use even a trace of magic.'

'I won't test it,' I said. 'So now what?'

'Maybe you'd like to invite us back home?' the invisible Edgar asked.

'Surely you don't think that I'd give you Nadya?' I asked. I didn't feel afraid, I was simply astonished by the question. 'You can kill me.'

'I wasn't really counting on it,' Edgar said. 'But Gennady insisted on the question being asked — he's very keen to make use of your little daughter.'

'The way he made use of his own son?' I asked, unable to resist, and was rewarded with a vicious scowl that wiped away everything human in the vampire's face.

'Quiet now,' said Edgar, nudging my shoulder. 'Don't get carried away, or I won't be able to hold Gennady off. He's very upset with you — can you guess why?'

'Yes. Why don't you make yourself visible? It's not a pleasant sensation talking to empty space.'

'Drive out of the yard,' Edgar said, laughing. 'I wouldn't like your bodyguards to notice us . . . We'd finish them off before they even knew what hit them. But Svetlana's a different matter, I'm afraid she might prove too hot to handle.'

Gennady scowled again, demonstrating that he had a full set of teeth and that his four canines were larger than the average human size.

'I'm sure she would,' I said quite sincerely. I stepped on the gas and drove the car gently out of the parking lot. Maybe I should crash into a lamp-post? No, that wouldn't catch them out, they were prepared for tricks like that . . . 'For Nadya she'd grind you into the dust.'

'That's what I think too,' Edgar said as politely and peaceably as ever. 'The last thing we need is a rampaging woman on our trail. And whether or not your daughter can get through to the seventh level of the Twilight still remains to be seen. The chances are no better than if we give you a good shaking-up.'

I snorted.

'I'm afraid I'll disappoint you there. I can't do what's beyond me. I'm a Higher Magician, but not a zero-point one. You have to be Merlin to get through to the seventh level.'

'I told you we have to take the girl,' Gennady said in a quiet voice. 'I told you he couldn't do it!'

'Cool it!' Edgar reassured him. 'He can. He's just not motivated enough yet, but we'll help him, and he'll manage just fine.'

'Try it,' I said. 'But where should I drive?'

'Sheremetievo 2, where else?' Edgar laughed. His invisibility was gradually peeling away and he was appearing by stages, first as a transparent outline, then acquiring colours. Gennady still hadn't revealed himself and I could only see him in the mirror. 'I think the quickest way will be round the ring road, right? And try not to waste any time. We have a flight to Edinburgh in an hour – I think we'll get there before anyone misses you. I don't really want to waste the last charge in my Minoan Sphere on a portal to Scotland. But bear in mind that if you're late for the plane, we will go through a portal.'

'I assume that Arina's waiting for you in Edinburgh?' I asked.

'You just drive,' laughed Edgar. 'And in the meantime I'll explain why you're going to help us.'

'Very interesting,' I said. There was a cold sensation spreading through my chest, but there was no way I was going to show any fear. But what difference did that make? Vampires can sense fear instinctively. It's hard to shield yourself from their perceptions even with magic.

'You're going to do your best for your daughter's sake, of course,' said Edgar. 'For your daughter's and your wife's. That wouldn't work with a Dark One, but it's just the trick for Light Ones.'

'You'd never get to my family.'

'Perhaps I wouldn't – on my own. Geser and Zabulon would give it everything they've got. I counted six bodyguards. How many do you know about? The two young fools on the staircase?'

I didn't answer.

'I expect there are at least eight, or even twelve,' Edgar said thoughtfully. 'There's no point in guessing, both the old farts have decided to play safe. But if there was an explosion beside your house – not an ordinary explosion, but a nuclear one – then even any Higher Magicians there would be killed. Hiroshima demonstrated that quite clearly.'

'You wouldn't go that far, Edgar,' I said. 'You're a Dark One, but you're not a psychopath. An atomic bomb in the centre of Moscow? Just to kill my wife and daughter? How many people would be killed? And what if somebody panics and decides it's a nuclear attack, and it starts a world war?'

'Right! That's the most important point.' Edgar laughed again. 'Even if Geser senses that something's wrong and moves your family far away from Moscow, to some secure vault in Ufa, for example, that won't fundamentally change the situation. Your actions will still decide the fate of hundreds of thousands or even millions of people. Not bad bait for a Light One, is it?'

'Edgar,' I asked, 'what's happened to you?'

'Nothing,' said Edgar, with a nervous, unnatural laugh. 'I'm just fine!'

'Have you lost someone, Edgar?'

The question was a shot in the dark. But when Edgar didn't answer, I knew I'd hit the target. That I'd finally begun to understand something about what was going on.

'My wife,' he said eventually. 'Annabel.'

'You said you were in Crete with her,' I recalled.

'I was. Exactly a year ago. We were walking to the beach from the hotel . . . There was a truck driving past us. The driver lost control and ran into her at eighty kilometres an hour. There was no time for me to do anything.'

'You loved her,' I said, amazed.

'Yes,' Edgar said, nodding. 'I loved her. I'm not Zabulon, I can love. Or I could.'

'I'm very sorry,' I said.

'Thank you, Anton,' Edgar replied in a perfectly normally voice. 'I know you really mean that. But it still doesn't change anything . . . in the way things are between us.'

'Why did you go against everyone? Why did you involve people?'

'People? What difference does it make how we use them, Anton? We live off their energy. Why shouldn't we use them as cannon fodder too? And as for why I went against everyone . . . that's the wrong way of putting the question. I'm not against them, I'm for them. For all Others, if you like. Dark Ones and Light Ones. When we achieve our goal, you'll understand. Even you will understand.'

'That's not what we agreed,' said Gennady.

'I remember what we agreed,' Edgar snapped. 'We do what we planned. And then you challenge Anton to fight. That's right, isn't it? You wanted an honest duel?'

'Yes,' Gennady said rather doubtfully.

'Well, if you're so certain that I'll understand,' I said as I turned onto the ring road, struggling with the temptation to swing the steering wheel hard and throw the car off the overpass, 'then you could tell me what it is you've planned. And then maybe I'll help you voluntarily.'

'I thought about that,' Edgar said, nodding. 'From the very beginning, I thought that of all the Light Ones I know you were the sanest. But I happened to find myself working with Gennady here. And he was absolutely against it. He doesn't like you. And you know why – you killed his son. His wife laid herself to rest because of you. So how could we take you into the Last Watch?'

'A very romantic name.'

'That's Gennady, he's a great romantic.' Edgar chuckled. 'No, we weren't going to touch you. Revenge is a fine thing, but only if you've got nothing else left . . . but Geser had to go and send you to Edinburgh!'

'Did you kill Victor because he recognised Gennady?'

'Yes,' said Edgar. 'It was an improvised move. Gennady got nervous: he thought Kostya's old school friend couldn't have turned up by accident, that we were being followed. It was a mistake, of course. But we did discover how to open the barrier on the third level. We didn't have precise information about that before then.'

'But you did about the golem on the fifth level?'

'Oh yes!' said Edgar, laughing again. 'After Annabel was killed I was transferred to work in the in the secure archive. You know . . . to settle down and get over my pain in a quiet job . . . If only you knew, Light One, what they have hidden away in the strong-rooms at the Inquisition! I had never even suspected that things like that could be created. I tell you honestly, in the last hundred years, the quality of magic has actually deteriorated. We've been spoiled by using human things. But we used to have things that were like telephones and cars and aeroplanes . . . they weren't just like them, they were better. We could have founded a civilisation based entirely on magic!'

'Except that we produce less Power than we consume,' I said. 'We can't live without people.'

'I thought about that too,' said Edgar, brightening up. 'We could have – Hey, don't slow down! Take the left lane, it's free now . . .

So, I've thought about that subject. I picture the ideal society as something close to the medieval model. People living a simple, healthy, uncomplicated life, working in the open air, pursuing the arts and crafts. No centralised state would be needed: a feudal system with barons and nominal kings would be quite good enough. And we Others would live partly separately and partly among the people. Without hiding from them! And everyone would know about us. Of course, under this arrangement even people could challenge a magician or a vampire. Let them! There has to be an effective mechanism of natural selection to weed out the weak and excessively cruel Others. A world like that would be far more pleasant than the one we have now, for Others and for people. Have you ever read any fantasy?'

'What?'

'Haven't you read any of those books? *The Lord of the Rings*? *Conan*? *A Wizard of Earthsea*? *Harry Potter*?'

'I've read a few,' I said. 'Some are a bit naive, but some are interesting. Quite passable as escapist literature, even for us.'

'And it's far more popular with people than science fiction is,' Edgar said confidently. 'That's the paradox: people aren't interested in reading about settling on Mars or flying to the stars – all the things that people really can achieve, but we can't. But they dream about becoming magicians, rushing into battle with a big sharp sword . . . if only they knew what the wounds from a real sword look like . . . What does all that mean? That a medieval world in which magic exists is the one most attractive to people!'

'Well, yes,' I said. 'Of course. Because no one thinks about how delightful it is to relieve yourself into a cesspit at twenty degrees below zero, or the stench those pits give out when it's forty degrees in the shade. Because the heroes in the books don't get colds in the head, indigestion, appendicitis or malaria and if they do there's a Light Healer right there on hand. Because everyone sees themselves sitting on the throne, wearing a magician's cloak or, at the very least, in the retinue of a brave and jolly baron. Not out in a parched field with a wooden hoe in their hands, watching the baron's retinue ride off after they've just trampled their pitiful harvest, half of which belongs to the brave and jolly baron anyway.'

'That's a different matter,' Edgar said peaceably. 'There are pluses and minuses to everything. But there wouldn't be any advertising, politicians, lawyers, genetically modified food . . .'

'It's time you joined Greenpeace. There would be plenty of children who were jinxed in their mothers' wombs. And even more perfectly normal children dying during birth because of incorrect presentation or lack of medicines. Edgar, are you really planning to throw the world back into the Middle Ages?'

Edgar sighed.

'No, Anton. That's a very, very unlikely outcome. I can tell you honestly, that's what I'm hoping for. But the chances aren't great.'

'I'm thinking very seriously about turning the wheel and crashing into a pillar,' I said. 'See that pedestrian bridge over the ring road? It has these very tempting concrete piers . . .'

'We wouldn't be hurt,' Edgar replied. 'And I don't think you would, either. You've got a good car, air bags, safety belts – you could survive. Don't be silly. If you want to kill yourself, try working a bit of magic.'

'What did you dig up in the archives? What are you hoping for?'

'Don't tell him,' Gennady said morosely. But his words seemed to have the opposite effect from what he intended. After all, Edgar was a primordial Dark One, used to regarding vampires with disdain. Even those that were his allies.

'The Inquisition has always taken a great interest in artefacts that lie out of its reach,' Edgar said. 'And particularly in the artefacts created by Merlin – for perfectly understandable reasons. Not much was known about the Crown of All Things. Only that it was in Scotland and was potentially one of the most powerful magical objects in existence. If not the most powerful. But it was believed that no information about the Crown existed. Fortunately, several years ago the Inquisition began compiling a comprehensive catalogue and putting everything in the computer system. This included the translation into electronic form of the results of medieval interrogations of witches and reports by agents and scholars that had been forgotten by everybody. I searched for everything to do with Merlin and discovered a few lines that had been forgotten for a long, long time. A certain thirteenth-century first-level Light Enchantress . . . let's say that she came into possession of information above and beyond her rank . . . This enchantress was questioned about a dust-up in Glasgow, which was still a small provincial town at the time. And during the interrogation, she mentioned the "last artefact" created by Merlin. They asked her to say what this artefact did and she replied, to translate literally: "The Crown is what all the Others who have left us dream about, what they wait for in the Twilight, what will bring them happiness and restore their freedom . . ." Nobody attached any significance to her words at the time, and they just lay in the archives for centuries. Until that sheet of parchment was put into a scanner and I started a search with the key word "Merlin".'

'Am I to assume that this information is no longer in the Inquisition's database?' I asked.

Edgar laughed.

'You want to bring dead Others back to life?'

'Departed,' Gennady hissed. 'Departed, but not dead!'

'It's not that simple,' said Edgar. 'We think that the Crown of All Things will fuse the Twilight world and the human worlds, eliminate the barriers between the levels. At present the departed ones cannot – or *effectively* cannot – return to our world, and we are not strong enough to stay in the lower levels of the Twilight for any length of time. But the Crown will change all that. Our departed ones will be with us.'

'Edgar, you don't know anything for certain,' I said. 'You can't know anything. This is all nothing but guesswork. What if the different levels really do fuse with our world? That will be a catastrophe!'

'We know that the departed Others want this,' Edgar said firmly.

'All based on a single phrase spoken by an enchantress in the thirteenth century?'

'She was Merlin's mistress. She knew for certain.'

I didn't argue any more.

What could I oppose to their faith? Nothing. Faith can only be opposed by another faith, not by facts, let alone hypotheses.

'Edgar, if I knew definitely that the Crown would bring back the departed Others, then I would help you. But I'm not sure it will.' I turned onto the Leningrad Chaussee. 'That's the first thing.'

'Carry on,' Edgar said politely.

'But even if I wanted to help you, the guard on the artefact in Edinburgh has been strengthened. Everyone knows that you'll go back in there again. And I think they've already figured out what magic you stole from the repository and how much, so your amulets won't come as a surprise any longer. We won't get through that easily. That's the second thing.'

'Believe me, I did a thorough job,' Edgar said proudly. 'Right now in the Inquisition they have no idea of what they had, what they didn't have and how much is left. The Inquisition is a very highly bureaucratised structure, which is probably the inevitable fate of any supranational organisation, whether it's human or ours. It will be hard, but we'll get through. Even if you don't help us . . . I expect it's almost impossible to make you kill Light Ones.'

'We should have taken the girl, then he would have helped us,' Gennady rumbled from behind me.

'Calm down,' Edgar told him. 'What kind of monster are you anyway? You should be more humane, Gennady!'

'I was humane when I was alive,' said the vampire. 'And I held out until they killed Kostya. And until Polina left me. I can't take any more!'

'But even so we have to try to overcome our differences of opinion, since we're going to be in the same team for a little while at least,' Edgar stated reasonably. 'Avoid insults, don't threaten his family . . . there's no point. Is that all you have to say, Anton?'

'No, there's one more little comment. I can't get through to the seventh level. When I got to the sixth, I was hyped up, the adrenalin was flowing. But the next barrier is too strong for me to break through. And the Watches have also evaluated the strength of the barrier — no input of Power from outside will help.'

'Why?'

'Because it's not a case of Power as such! There's more of it pouring down the vortex above the Dungeons of Scotland than you could possibly use. But you have to work with it, pass it through yourself. And what if you do supply Power artificially? Pump it out of people, out of artefacts . . . what then? You can't keep raising the voltage in the mains for ever, the wires will melt! What's needed is a superconductor, do you understand? And that superconductor is a *zero-point* Other, someone who produces absolutely no magical energy!'

'Oh, these technical explanations,' Edgar sighed. 'Gennady, did you understand that?'

'I did. I told you—'

'All right, be quiet. Anton, I understand that you can't jump over your own head. And neither can I . . .'

'Edgar, when did you become a Higher One?'

The former Inquisitor laughed.

'Just recently. Don't pay any attention to that.'

'Okay, so you removed Gennady's registration seal,' I said, thinking out loud. 'That's fine, I know they taught you fancier tricks than that in the Inquisition. But you can only raise your level of Power with the *Fuaran*. The book was burnt up . . .'

'Don't try to blind me with science,' Edgar said. 'Tell it to Gennady, he likes that stuff. Nobody's expecting any miracles from you. What's expected is a bit of savvy. Find the way round the barrier.'

'I'm sure Thomas the Rhymer has been searching for that for hundreds of years.'

'But he didn't have a wife and a daughter sitting on a nuclear bomb all set to blow,' said Edgar, glancing at his watch. 'We're on time. Well done, you're a good driver. And now listen – don't go into the parking lot, we don't want to leave any unnecessary tracks. There's a young guy waiting for us at the entrance to the departures hall, give him the keys. He has been paid to drive your car to a parking lot and pay for three days. If you come back, you can pick it up.'

'If you come back,' Gennady growled.

'I'm sorry, but I think his chances are better than you do,' Edgar snapped. 'So, we'll slip through passport control quickly, and you won't try to attract the attention of the Others at customs. A Light One wouldn't want any unnecessary casualties, right? We'll get into the plane and you'll have a cup of coffee, even a sip of brandy is permissible. And you'll think. Think hard. So hard that I can hear your brains creaking. And it will be very good if by the time we reach Edinburgh you already know how to get the Crown of All Things. Because we don't have any time to spare. Only twelve hours until the bomb goes off.'

'You bastard,' I said.

'No, I'm a highly effective personnel manager,' Edgar said, with a smile.

CHAPTER 4

THERE ARE SOME words that can send a man into a trance without using any magic.

For example: 'Tell me something funny.' Even if you've just watched the final of *Smart-Alecs Club*' on TV, read the latest Terry Pratchett book and dug up ten really funny, fresh jokes on the internet – that will all fly right out of your head in an instant.

The words 'Sit and think' are pretty effective too. They immediately remind me of an algebra test or some quarterly essay at school, and the weary face of the teacher who no longer expects anything good from his pupils.

This time we were flying directly to Edinburgh, on Aeroflot. If this had been a standard assignment, I wouldn't have minded at all – I liked what I'd seen of Scotland. And particularly since Edgar, of course, had taken seats in business class. Three infuriated compatriots of ours, who between them could obviously have bought the Boeing 767 we were flying in, were left fuming at check-in when their tickets proved to be invalid. I didn't say anything, but I felt hope beginning to warm my chest. Most human problems with double bookings or invalid tickets are caused by the machinations of certain light-fingered Others, most often Dark Ones but sometimes Light Ones too. That's why all such incidents are investigated by the Watches. Well, in theory all, but in practice only the ones that cause serious scandals. In this case it looked as if a really large-scale scandal was in the offing . . .

But I was afraid that the investigation still wouldn't be as prompt as I needed it to be. Especially right then, when everyone all the way across Moscow was hunting for Saushkin.

The customs post at departures had also been reinforced. Instead of two Others on duty, there were four – in such cases parity is strictly observed. I had been hoping that perhaps they might use some of our lads for the reinforcements and they would spot me, but all of the Others were from Moscow District, not the city. And before check-in Edgar had given us false passports and applied high-quality masks that fourth- and fifth-level Others wouldn't be able to penetrate. So I walked past my colleagues under the name of Alexander Peterson, resident of St Petersburg. Gennady became Konstantin Arbenin, but what Edgar called himself I didn't hear.

Once I was in the plane and the flight attendant had brought the coffee and cognac that Edgar had promised I realised that I had lost the game all hands up. Every now and then the furry noose on my neck, which had attracted glances of puzzlement at customs, squeezed a little bit tighter, or scratched at my skin with its tiny little claws . . . or teeth. Just about the only thing it didn't do was purr while it waited for me to use any magic. I even remembered what the thing was called. Schrödinger's Cat. Evidently because nobody had ever been able to decide whether this piece of trash was alive or dead. In the Inquisition they used Schrödinger's Cat for transporting the most dangerous criminals. The lousy son of a bitch had never failed. And by the way, unless I was getting things confused, it was the only one of its kind. Edgar had stolen some truly unique artefacts.

'Drink your coffee,' Edgar said amiably. I had been put in the window seat, with Gennady beside me. Edgar sat behind us, and he made sure there was no one in the seat beside him: the perplexed but unprotesting passenger was moved to somewhere in economy class, with showers of apologies and promises of countless bonuses in compensation. All in all, Aeroflot made a quite remarkably pleasant impression. No worse than the western carriers, or even a bit better. It was just a pity I wouldn't be able to enjoy the flight. I was in the wrong company for that.

I drank coffee and brandy by turns, watching as the plane rolled out onto the runway. Edgar whispered something behind my back – and the roar of the engines disappeared. A Sphere of Silence. Well, it made sense: now no one would bother us, and no one would hear us. It was a good thing that, unlike the wizard Khottabich in the fairy tale, Edgar had other ways of combating the noise apart from stopping the engines . . .

Proceed, if you are as strong as I;
Or go back, if you are as wise as I.

He was mocking. Of course he was – mocking the hapless treasure hunters. But he still believed that he had to give a hint. That was in the unwritten rules of the game in those days. So there had to be a way.

Proceed–go back. Forwards–backwards . . .

Perhaps you had to pump up the momentum, by swinging backwards and forwards, like trying to free a car that's got stuck in the mud – an art completely forgotten by the masses in this era of automatic transmissions. Reach the sixth level, jump back, then back to sixth and take a run straight through . . .

Absolute drivel. I had just barely managed to get as far as the sixth level once, pausing to catch my breath after every breakthrough.

Even assuming that I could jump straight out of the depths of the Twilight, like Geser, I still wouldn't be able to pump up my speed like that.

Let's repeat the argument from the beginning.

The Crown of All Things is here concealed. Only one step is left.

That was all clear enough. The inscription was on the sixth level. The Crown of All Things was hidden on the seventh. The cunning Merlin had left the signpost where only the most powerful and skilful magician could reach it . . . it felt really good that I had managed to get there!

But we weren't told anything special in this line. It was a kind of preamble. An introduction. We could only hope that Thomas the Rhymer's translation was adequate . . . but then it ought to be, coming from a great bard and an ancestor of Lermontov.

But this is a legacy for the strong or the wise—

This was more or less clear too. Merlin had left the decision about whether to use the artefact or not up to those who would be his equal. In Power or wisdom – it didn't matter which.

You shall receive all and nothing, when you are able to take it.

Right, now this was a bit more interesting. It looked as though Merlin believed that using the Crown might cause a global catastrophe. *You shall receive all and nothing* – you shall receive everything, but not for yourself.

Or was I like Edgar and Gennady, only seeing what I wanted to see?

What if 'you shall receive all and nothing' meant that the whole world would be in your power, but it would be destroyed?

I didn't know. I couldn't understand. If only I could have read it in the original . . .

'Edgar, I have to make one phone call,' I said.

'What?' Edgar chortled. 'Who to, Geser? We've already been warned to switch our phones off.'

'Do you want me to produce a result? I have to ask Foma Lermont about something.'

Edgar didn't hesitate for long. He closed his eyes, then nodded.

'Call. You have three minutes before we start to take off. But remember, I'm listening very carefully.'

It was a good thing that I hadn't erased Lermont's number. I took out my phone and called. One ring, two . . .

'Anton?'

There was a clear note of curiosity in Lermont's voice.

'How does that third line go? You translated it as "You shall receive all and nothing, when you are able to take it" – remember? What's the point here – "you shall receive everything and lose everything" or "you shall receive everything, but you don't need it"?'

Thomas grunted and recited the line in Old English:

'With it thou shalt acquire all – and nothing shalt thou get . . .'

Well, thanks a bunch for not saying it in Welsh . . .

'That means . . .' I began, determined to get it clear.

'It means that if you get it, you will receive something that you personally don't need, although it is very important, global, universal.'

'Thank you, Foma!'

'Brainstorming?' Lermont enquired. 'Good luck. We're not wasting our time here either, we're working . . .'

I cut the connection. I wondered if Edgar and Gennady had heard our conversation and was suddenly surprised to realise that I was enthralled by the task. Despite the noose on my neck. Despite the blackmail. Despite the vampire and the crazed Inquisitor sitting there with me. I wanted to understand. I wanted to solve Merlin's riddle. I could never be as powerful as him, but maybe I could at least rival him intellectually.

I wanted to believe that I could.

THE LAST WATCH 349

Proceed, if you are as strong as I;
Or go back, if you are as wise as I.

Right, then. We'd come back to that phrase. The meaning was more or less clear. The strong could proceed and attain the goal by following Merlin's route. The wise would go back and choose the other way round.

Beginning and end, head and tail, all is fused in one . . .

That was probably just fine words. Alpha and omega, the beginning and the end. Head and tail? Maybe that was a hint at the golem on the fifth level of the Twilight.

Right, this line had to be thought about seriously.

In the Crown of All Things. Thus are life and death inseparable.

This bit probably referred to the application of the spell. Life and death are inseparable. The Others who have withdrawn into the Twilight will come to life again, return to our world . . . I wondered if that was what they wanted. I'd almost had to drag Thomas the Rhymer out of there, he'd wanted to stay so much, to taste the joys of the magical heaven.

I imagined the resurrected Kostya yelling at his father: 'Did I ask you to resurrect me?' Was that a possibility?

I didn't know. I couldn't understand a thing. Oh, but Thomas could hardly be right. He was caught in the trap of his own dream, just as Edgar and Gennady were blinded by theirs. That inhabitant of the Twilight who had managed to reach the first level and had even saved me, you could say, by showing me the way to the Dark Ones' headquarters such a long time ago, hadn't looked very happy with things. I wondered who he was and why he had helped me. How had he ever found out about what was happening from down there in the spectral Twilight depths of the creation?

Questions, questions and no answers to them . . .

Beginning and end, head and tail, all is fused in one . . .

There seemed to be something in this, though. Head and tail
– that was the bit that I couldn't get out of my mind. Whose head
was fused with his tail down there? That was if I didn't take the
golem–monster with teeth in both tails seriously as a candidate . . .

And by the way, why not take it *almost* seriously?

Not for myself, of course. For our own dear Last Watch.

So, the Crown of All Things was concealed in the body of this
miserable two–headed beast. Somewhere in the middle, where one
part ended and the other began. Where head and tail were indis-
tinguishable . . . Go back, that is, to the fifth level, and you'll find
it there!

Well, that sounded very convincing. If it was said with a straight
face. They didn't have the Rune, and Edgar wasn't likely to be able
to get it. Just let them try to destroy a golem created by Merlin!

Of course, if the Crown of All Things really was found in the
belly of that creeping horror, then that would be . . . that would
be very annoying.

But I doubted that would be the outcome.

'You're smiling,' said Gennady. 'What have you come up with?'

'Quiet,' I said. 'I'm soaring on the wings of inspiration. Better
give me some cognac.'

Gennady pursed his lips and said nothing.

Absorbed in my thoughts and surrounded by a cocoon of total
silence, I completely missed the moment of take–off. When I
looked out of the window we were already high up above the
first layer of clouds, the first level. Aagh, now I was seeing levels
that had to be broken through everywhere!

Yes, there was definitely something about that line that stuck
in my mind. Head and tail, right? I'd heard about that somewhere.
In magic? No, more likely in folklore. In some beliefs or other . . .
yes, of course! Egyptian myths and, later, European ones. Alchemical
treatises. Buddhism, in the form of the wheel of Samsara, rebirth . . .

Uroboros.

The snake devouring its own tail.

I felt goose pimples rising on my skin. It was no accident that Merlin had set a two-headed snake to guard the fifth level . . . The Crown wasn't in it, of course.

But it was a hint, and a very clear one!

The beginning and the end. It gives birth to itself, fertilises itself and kills itself. An eternal and unchanging force that is dissolved in space and then restored again, the eternal circle of time, a defence against chaos and darkness, safeguarding the Universe, enclosing and supporting the world, bringing life into death and death into life, simultaneously motionless and moving . . .

Death and resurrection.

An eternal stream of Power, dying and being reborn . . .

I understood.

I understood everything.

My fingers started trembling and I grabbed hold of the armrests tightly. I caught Gennady's suspicion glance and said:

'I'm afraid of flying. Get me some cognac, okay? Be a real man, even if not for very long.'

Gennady got up without saying a word and beckoned to the stewardess.

Uroboros.

The beginning and the end. Life and death. The circle of Power maintaining the Universe.

I understood it all. I was the first since Merlin. Now I had something to be proud of, if only I could manage to stay alive!

'You've thought of something,' said Edgar. Half-standing, he leaned forward over the back of my seat and looked into my eyes curiously. 'Ah, Anton! I was right. You do have an idea.'

'I do,' I said, not trying to deny anything. 'Edgar, I want to ask you one more time – are you sure that bringing out those who have withdrawn is safe? You know what the Shade of the Masters is, don't you?'

'I know,' said Edgar, and his face darkened. 'It summons magicians who have withdrawn back from the fifth level, where they can exist for a fairly long time. Torn out of their natural surroundings, pumped full of Power, absolutely insane . . . destroying everything around them with appalling ferocity. Anton, don't confuse the forcible extraction and exploitation of the withdrawn with their resurrection. You know, if someone woke you up in the middle of the night, hit you on the head, poured shit all over you and started yelling in your ear, you'd go on the rampage too.'

'So you've definitely made your mind up . . .' I said and paused. I ought not to 'surrender' straight away. Edgar couldn't read my thoughts – I was a Higher One, after all – but he could sense a lie in my intonation or the expression on my face. And so could Gennady. 'Edgar, what guarantees do I have?'

'What guarantees do you mean?' he asked in amazement.

'Guarantees that when I explain everything to you, you won't give orders for the bomb in Moscow to be detonated. And that you'll take Schrödinger's Cat off my neck.'

Edgar laughed.

'Anything else you'd like?'

'I'm giving you a lot,' I answered.

'Will the Oath of the Light and the Dark satisfy you?'

'Edgar!' Gennady said in a chilly voice. 'There are limits to everything!'

'I swear on the Light and the Dark and the equilibrium between them,' Edgar said in a steady voice, 'that if you help us to obtain the Crown of All Things, I will remove Schrödinger's Cat from your neck, will not give orders for the bomb in Moscow to be detonated and will allow you to fight Gennady one against one. If you win, I shall cause no further hindrance to you and your family, provided that I am not attacked by you. If you lose, I undertake not to undertake any measures against Svetlana and Nadya. Again provided that they do not attack me themselves. I do so swear!'

A small sphere appeared on the palm of his hand. One half of it glowed brightly and the other half was black, as if it was sucking the light into itself. The sphere revolved slowly, with light flowing into darkness and darkness flowing into light.

'One clarification,' I said. 'What does "If I help you to obtain" mean? When's that?'

'When we have the Crown in our hands.'

'I don't agree,' I said, shaking my head. 'There's a serious chance that you'll be killed trying to obtain the Crown. But the Cat can only be removed by the person who put it on. I don't fancy the prospect of spending the rest of my life with no magic and this piece of garbage round my neck.'

Edgar thought about it. Or, more likely, he pretended to think about it. He had probably decided long ago just how far he was willing to move.

'Let me clarify,' he said, looking at the sphere of Light and Dark spinning on his palm. 'I shall order the bomb in Moscow not to be detonated just as soon as we all believe that what you tell us is the truth. I will remove the Cat before we set out to obtain the Crown. But you will be with us, bound by an oath not to obstruct us. That is as far as I can go.'

Now it was my turn to demonstrate the workings of my thoughts. Was I or wasn't I prepared to accept such conditions? If I was going to tell the truth, then I probably ought to do a bit more haggling . . .

'Another clarification,' I said. 'You will not only remove the Cat, you will also allow me to withdraw to a safe distance. I do not wish to be obliged to join battle on your side against my own will!'

'Battle?' Edgar repeatedly curiously. 'You probably don't mean against the members of Lermont's Watch?'

'No, I don't,' I said, with a smile. 'You'll have enough problems without them, believe me.'

'All right,' said Edgar. 'I will allow you to withdraw to a safe distance before we set out to obtain the Crown. But afterwards you will be obliged to come back and do battle with Gennady. He . . . wants that very much.'

'Agreed.' I held out my hand and said, 'I swear on the Light.'

A sphere of fire appeared on my hand and immediately disappeared again. The Cat round my neck tightened in annoyance – and relaxed again. It wasn't my magic: the Primordial Power itself decided whether or not to affirm a magician's words.

'Gennady, do you confirm Edgar's commitments?' I asked.

'Yes.' He didn't swear on the Dark. The Primordial Power only rarely descends to vampires. But I believed him. After all, the most important thing for Gennady was to get his son and wife back. Revenge was secondary now.

Suddenly realising that the Sphere of Silence would not prevent passengers from observing the strange lights, I glanced around.

No, everything was in order. The passenger on the other side of the aisle was sleeping. His neighbour by the window was working on his laptop. What fine fellows these businessmen were . . .

'It is not possible to get through to the seventh level,' I said. 'There is no way. Only a *zero-point* magician can do it . . . or an Other who has dematerialised and withdrawn into the Twilight.'

Gennady tensed up. Edgar asked in an icy voice:

'And is that your advice?'

'No,' I said, shaking my head. 'Merlin explained everything quite marvellously. You simply got hung up on your own idea about the seventh level of the Twilight! Well, not only you,' I added self-critically. 'Merlin didn't simply give instructions on how to obtain the Crown! He was writing about the problem in general! About how it was possible to meet one who had withdrawn!'

Edgar and Gennady exchanged glances.

Yes, that had been meant to hook them. And it had.

'Proceed, if you are as strong as I,' I declaimed. 'What's that about? It's about travelling to the seventh level, where those who have withdrawn live! But if you don't happen to be a *zero-point* magician, what then? Then you need the artefact created by Merlin. The Crown of All Things. And where do you get it? The inscription on the sixth level reads: "Go back, if you are as wise as I"! And what do we have on the fifth level?'

'The guard. A golem in the form of a double-headed snake,' said Edgar, screwing up his eyes.

'Head and tail, all is fused in one!' I exclaimed triumphantly. 'It's not just a guard, you idiots! It's the artefact's wrapping, its protection. Did you read fairy stories when you were children? The death of Kashchei is in the egg, the egg is in the duck, the duck is in the trunk . . . It's the same principle. And by the way,' I added in a sudden access of inspiration, 'I wouldn't be surprised if, when you rip the golem in half, some other vile beast crawls out of it. Or even flies out of it. It will probably try to get away, so be prepared to take down a fast-moving flying target!'

'Thus are life and death inseparable,' Edgar said and started thinking.

'The death of the golem is a new life for the withdrawn,' Gennady whispered. 'Edgar, could this be true?'

Edgar thought. He was trying to remember something.

'By the way, the Crown is probably the golem's activator. Merlin inclined towards simple and elegant solutions.'

'There have been two cases in history when a golem-guard also served as the casing for what it was guarding,' Edgar said. 'And the first to use this cunning trick was one of Merlin's pupils.'

In my own mind I gave thanks to this unknown magician for so aptly confirming what I had said. But outwardly all I did was to nod pensively.

'There, you see. Merlin probably told him about his own idea. Or perhaps he helped his teacher to make the snake-golem.'

Edgar nodded and said:

'If only we had the Rune . . . It was the simplest thing in the world to neutralise the golem with it.'

He believed me.

'It's your own fault,' I said. 'Instead of organising secret societies, you should have opened up your ideas for general discussion. All Others have lost someone at some time . . .'

'You have no idea how strong the bureaucracy is,' Edgar said in disgust. 'The discussion would have gone on for a hundred years. And in the end they would have decided not to do anything.'

'That can't be right,' I blurted out.

'You're simply too young . . . and too remote from the administrative structures. Geser and Zabulon would agree with me.'

I shrugged. Perhaps they would.

I wondered if Geser had anyone to grieve for. He loved Olga, and now she was with him. He had even managed to make his son an Other. But surely, over thousands of years the Great Geser must have lost loved ones, friends, children. And some of them must have been Others, not ordinary people. Others who had withdrawn into the Twilight.

And Zabulon? Of course, as he now was, Zabulon didn't love anyone. But could that always have been the case? He had been a child once, the same as all other children, except that he had been a potential Other. He happened to have taken the path of Darkness. But it wasn't possible that he had never loved anyone! Even Dark Ones can love . . . even malicious and heartless ones like Alisa Donnikova . . .

An interesting little situation. In principle, the activities of the 'Last Watch' worked to Geser's and Zabulon's advantage! Any Other of any serious age had to be delighted by the idea of bringing back the withdrawn.

Although, of course, they could never admit it openly.

CHAPTER 5

THE FLIGHT ATTENDANT handed out the lunches. I was offered cognac again, but I refused. Enough already. I had to be in good form in Edinburgh.

Behind me Edgar ate with a hearty appetite. Gennady prodded pensively with his fork, picking out the pieces of meat. When his gaze fell on me I completely lost all desire to eat my meat. It even cost me an effort to get the salad and a piece of cheese down. It was really rather annoying that everything tasted so good. I ought to have ordered the vegetarian lunch.

Saushkin took a flask out of his pocket. He unscrewed the top and took a gulp, then he put the flask away, ostentatiously licking his dark-stained lips.

'You know, Edgar, there's one thing that surprises me,' I said in a quiet voice. 'I thought you always had a dislike for bloodsuckers. Not to mention vampires who violated the Treaty . . . And you removed a criminal's registration seal?'

'Calm down, Anton,' Edgar said soothingly. 'When Gennady killed those Light Ones on the boulevard, it was only self-defence. And in Edinburgh . . . well, that was unfortunate. But it was self-defence too in a certain sense. Gennady didn't even drink the boy.

He didn't like the idea of drinking one of Kostya's friends, so he poured all the blood away . . .'

'And how did he reach the Higher level?' I asked, looking at Gennady.

The vampire opened his mouth just a crack, extending his fangs. He shook his head.

'His son left the recipe for "Saushkin's Cocktail" in his notes,' Edgar said coolly. 'Sure, Gennady increased his level illegally. But he didn't have to kill any people to do it . . .'

'Are you sure about that?' I asked, looking at Gennady. His fangs were moving further and further out. I wondered what Schrödinger's Cat would do if someone tried to bite me though its fluffy body.

'It's true, isn't it?' Edgar asked, reaching out one hand and taking Gennady firmly by the shoulder. 'Or is there something I don't know about my comrade-in-arms?'

'He's lying,' said Gennady. 'He's trying to set us against each other.'

'I don't think so,' said Edgar, still holding the vampire's shoulder, and perhaps even applying a little pressure to it now. 'You're very agitated, Gennady. Calm down.'

'I'm perfectly calm,' the vampire hissed.

'Have you killed people?' Edgar asked imperturbably. 'There wasn't any recipe for a cocktail e-mailed to you by your son, was there?'

'Yes, I've killed some,' Gennady said. He took the flask out again and shook it. 'But there *was* a cocktail! This is it, Kostya's cocktail. I didn't check the mail, I had too many things on my mind! So I only read the letter in the spring, and by then it was too late . . . So what now?'

'They found fifty-two bodies drained of blood in his apartment. Perhaps you were wondering what had got the Watches so het up? His own kind are ready to tear Gennady to pieces now. They've been left without licences for five years!'

'That's Geser being too modest again,' Edgar commented. 'In his place I would have demanded ten. It's outrageous. I had my own suspicions on the matter. Outrageous! Gennady, that's not the way to do things! We're all one team!'

'Are we still one team?' Gennady asked.

Edgar sighed.

'Yes. What's done can't be undone . . . But why did you do it?'

'How was I to know that you would come and find me?' the vampire asked. 'I wanted my revenge on Anton. And how can a weak vampire take his revenge on a Higher One? I had to build myself up. It's all his fault!'

This was an excuse that would never go out of fashion, I thought. Not only among the sons of Darkness, but among the most ordinary of human scum.

'It was all his fault! He had an apartment, a car and an expensive cellphone, and all I had was three roubles, chronic alcoholism and a hangover every morning. That was why I waited for him in the gateway with a brick . . .' 'She had long legs, she was seventeen and she had a handsome boyfriend, and I had impotence, a porn magazine under my pillow and a face like a gorilla's. I just had to attack her in the hallway when she walked in, humming to herself, with her lips still hot from kisses . . .' 'He had an interesting job, work assignments all over the world and a good reputation, and I had a degree diploma that I'd bought, a petty job working under him and chronic idleness. That was the reason I fixed things so that he would be accused of embezzlement and kicked out of the firm . . .'

They're all the same, these people and these Others who are desperate for glory, money or blood and have discovered that the shortest path is always the Dark one.

There's always somebody who was getting in their way and somebody who was to blame . . .

Probably when Gennady Saushkin wanted to save his little son he really was trying to do good. He didn't have a soul, but in his mind and his heart he simply couldn't accept Kostya's death. Just as he didn't want to accept it now. And the Dark way had proved so simple and so short . . .

For a long time he had teetered on the very brink, if a vampire still has that option open to him. He hadn't killed people. He had even tried to be honest and kind, and he had managed it. He had even managed to bring Kostya up almost as a human being.

But what makes the short roads different is that you have to pay a levy for using them. And on the Dark roads they like to announce the charge at the end of the journey.

'Are you satisfied with his explanations?' I asked.

'I'm disappointed,' Edgar replied. 'But there's nothing to be done about it now.'

'There are some things that you can't put right,' I agreed.

But to myself I added: 'And there are some that you can.'

The Twilight customs counter at Edinburgh was empty. There were some forms lying there, and even a search amulet, glowing an even, milky-white colour. The last Other to pass this way had been a Light One. There were no Others on duty.

Edgar pulled me into the Twilight. I still couldn't use magic, with that damned Schrödinger's Cat squirming on my neck and occasionally sticking its claws out. I took one look at Gennady and turned away. He was an appalling sight. What was it that Zabulon had said about human children playing at vampires? They ought to be shown what a vampire really looked like. Cheeks eaten away by ulcers; earthen-grey skin; vacant, cloudy-white eyes like hard-boiled eggs with the shell removed.

We walked past the counter and through a door that was closed in the real world, into some kind of service corridor. We went into a small room that was either a poorly furnished janitor's office or a store for lumber that was already worn out but not yet written off. Chairs with their backs torn off and broken legs, shelves full of dusty boxes and jars, rolls of murky-coloured flooring material.

Edgar jerked me by the shoulder and pulled me back into the real world. I sneezed. It was definitely a temporary store for junk. I blinked as my eyes grew accustomed to the dim lighting – the windows were completely shut off by blinds. I laughed. Well now, I could award myself another point in this game.

Sitting in a chair that was better preserved than all the others was a beautiful woman with black hair. The simple everyday clothes – trousers and a blouse – seemed entirely inappropriate on her. She ought to have had a long dress that emphasised her femininity, or something light and airy, white and transparent, or nothing at all.

But she would have made any clothes look good. Even a hobo's old suit.

I admired her once again. Like that first time when our paths had crossed.

'Hello, Arina,' I said.

'Hello, sorcerer.' She held out her hand, and I pressed my lips to the palm.

Even though I had seen her in her Twilight form.

Even though I knew that this magnificent body, so healthy and overflowing with vitality, only existed in the human world.

'You're not surprised,' said Arina.

'Not a bit,' I said, shaking my head.

'He knew,' Edgar put in. And from the way he spoke I suddenly realised that he was not the most important member of the trio.

Maybe Edgar was the one who had stirred everything up in the first place, and he had supplied the Last Watch's battle magic, but he wasn't the most important one there.

'Svetlana guessed?' Arina surmised.

'We decided together,' I said. 'By the way, you're a Light One now, aren't you? Pardon me, but I won't risk looking at your aura – I've got this little kitten dozing round my neck . . .'

'Yes, I am,' Arina said calmly. 'But you already knew that Great Ones can change colour, didn't you?'

'Merlin changed,' I said casually. 'I have a question for you, witch, or whatever you are now. Healer?'

Arina didn't answer.

'You gave a promise to my wife. Swore an oath. That for a hundred years . . .'

'I would not cause harm to anyone, neither Others, nor people, except in self-defence,' Arina continued.

'Surely changing your colour hasn't released you from your oath.'

'But I haven't killed anyone, Anton. I fitted out Edgar and Gennady, but that's a different matter altogether. That didn't violate the oath.'

'Svetlana took pity on you,' I said. 'She took pity on you.'

'Perhaps she was right to, Anton,' Arina said, smiling. 'Look, I've become a Light One. And I haven't harmed your wife and daughter, have I?'

'And what about the nuclear weapon that Edgar is threatening to explode beside our house? In how many hours' time?' I asked, looking at the former Inquisitor.

Edgar raised one hand and looked at his watch. He said:

'The thing is, Anton, that to be really interested in the success of our venture, you had to feel a real personal involvement.'

Before he had even finished speaking, I felt a heavy throbbing in my temples and a mist seemed to obscure my vision.

'The explosion took place five minutes ago,' Edgar said dispassionately. 'I haven't broken my oath – the time was set yesterday . . . And don't get emotional, please. If Schrödinger's Cat finishes you off, you won't be able to help your wife and daughter.'

I had no intention of using magic.

The dead always have trouble with taking revenge. Especially dead Others. I didn't need that kind of trouble.

I kicked Edgar. Maybe not as elegantly as Olga kicked open the lock on Saushkin's door. But I think I kicked harder.

Edgar flew back against the wall, struck it hard with the back of his head and slowly slid down it, catching at his crotch with his hands.

Then Gennady jumped me. He grabbed me across the chest with superhuman strength, pulled my head back with his free hand and bared his teeth . . .

'Gena!' Arina only said a single word, but the vampire's fangs were instantly withdrawn. 'Edgar asked for what he got. Calm down, Anton. Our grey friend was mistaken.'

Edgar groaned as he rolled around the floor, clutching his crotch. I'd hit the right spot.

'There hasn't been any explosion,' Arina continued. She got up and came towards us, then looked into my face. 'Hey, Anton! Calm down. There hasn't been any explosion!'

I looked into her eyes. And nodded.

She was telling the truth

'What do you mean . . . there hasn't . . .' Edgar groaned from the corner.

'I told you I didn't like the idea,' Arina said. 'Even if I was still a Dark One, I wouldn't have liked it! There hasn't been any explosion. The criminals who stole a tactical nuclear warhead have repented and have returned it to the authorities. They are being interrogated at this very moment.' She sighed. 'And not very humanely, I'm afraid. There hasn't been any explosion and there won't be.'

'Arina!' Edgar had even stopped groaning. 'Why? You could have just delayed it . . . for a guarantee . . .'

'I can't do things like that now,' Arina explained, with a sweet smile. 'Unfortunately, I just can't. I told you at the beginning that I would cut out any acts of mass destruction with massive human casualties.'

'Then why . . . did you let me start all this anyway . . .' Edgar said, straightening up with difficulty. He gave me a glance filled with hate. 'Bastard! You've . . . smashed everything up!'

'You won't need any of it for the next seventy-seven times,' I replied spitefully. 'Didn't you notice the spell that Afandi flung at you?'

Arina laughed.

'So that's it. That old joker Afandi. Yes, the next seventy-five times you can pester someone else, Edgar.'

'Why did you do this?' Edgar asked with pain in his voice.

'So that what you said would sound convincing. Anton could have spotted a lie, even with the Cat on his neck. Saushkin, please let our guest go. He won't fight any more. Boys always try to settle their disagreements by the most primitive methods . . .'

Gennady reluctantly moved away from me and sat down on the floor with his legs crossed under him. I looked round for a chair that wasn't a total wreck and sat down, deliberately not asking for permission. Arina went back to her own chair. Suddenly realising that he was the only one standing, and that he was clutching his own private parts, Edgar also took a seat.

'All right, now everyone's settled down and we can talk calmly,' Arina said in the voice of the hostess at a literary salon who has just watched one poet pulling another's curly hair. 'Peace, peace and more peace! Anton, let me explain things to you. You understand that it's far more difficult for me to lie than it is for Gennady or Edgar. We don't want any atrocities, we're not trying to destroy the world. We're not trying to exterminate all human beings. All we're doing is bringing the withdrawn back to life.'

'Arina, what did they hook you with?' I asked. 'Someone you loved? A child?'

For a moment I clearly saw sadness in Arina's eyes.

'A loved one . . . Yes, there was someone I loved, sorcerer. He was here for a while, and then gone. He didn't even live out his human lifetime, he was killed . . . And I had a daughter. Earlier, before him. She died too. When she was only four . . . from plague. I wasn't there with her, I arrived too late to save her. But not even the Crown will bring them back – they were people. Wherever they might have gone, there's no way for us to reach them and no way back for them to come back.'

'Then why . . .' The question was left unfinished, hanging in the air.

Gennady gave a quiet, hoarse laugh.

'She's got ideals! She's a Light One now, like you. She only kills for noble reasons . . .'

'Hush, bloodsucker!' said Arina, and her eyes flashed. Then she immediately continued in a steady voice: 'He's telling the truth, Anton. I became a Light One by my own deliberate choice. On the dictates of my reason, not my heart, you might say. I'm sick of the Dark Ones. I've never seen anything good come of them. I was thinking of joining the Inquisition, but I had too many old charges to answer. And I don't like them anyway, the smug hypocrites . . . I beg your pardon, Edgar, that doesn't apply to you, of course. I went straight to Siberia that time. And I lived in Tomsk, a nice quiet town. It inclines you towards the Light. I worked for a living the way I used to, as a local witch. I put an advertisement in the newspaper, and when they came from the Watch to check me I pretended to be a quack. It's not hard for me to wind the average watchman round my little finger. And then I realised that I was only doing good deeds. I only sent husbands back to their wives if I could see their love was still alive, that it would be better for everyone. I healed sicknesses. I found people who were lost. I made people younger again . . . just a little bit. The important thing there was to use just a little bit of magic: all the rest is making people believe in themselves, making them live a healthy life. And not a single hex, not a single potion to send someone back to a woman he didn't love . . . So I decided I'd had enough of playing Dark games. But do you know what it takes for a Dark One to change colour?'

I shook my head.

'You have to think of something immense, something really important. It not as simple as "If you've done good deeds for a year, you become a Light One; if you've worked evil, you become a Dark One." No. You have to do something that turns everything in you upside down. Something that will bleach white everything that came before, everything you did with your life . . . or simply cancel it out.'

'Was Merlin caught out by his massacre of innocent children?' I asked.

'Yes, I think so,' Arina said, nodding. 'What else? He wanted so badly to create a kingdom of justice and nobility here on Earth, that was what he nurtured Arthur for. How can you be choosy about your methods in the cause of such a great idea? And suddenly the probability lines showed a child who would grow up and destroy the entire kingdom . . . I wasn't alive then, so I don't know what Merlin was thinking and what he wanted. But the very moment that Merlin decided to murder the innocent for the sake of his dream, the Great Light Magician died and the Great Dark Magician was born.'

Uroboros again. Life in death and death in life.

Could it all really have been so very simple for Arina? She was tired of being a Dark One, she was drawn to do good deeds – and so she became a Light One? She reformed, like the old woman Shapoklyak in the story, and changed sides . . .

Or was there something else involved? For instance, the long and complicated relationship that bound her to Geser? Those joint intrigues of theirs, when the Light Magician and the Dark Witch pursued the same goals? Had Geser inclined her towards the Light, or had Arina realised that there wasn't that much difference between her Darkness and Geser's Light?

I didn't know, and she wouldn't answer me if I asked. Just as she wouldn't answer if I asked whether Geser and Zabulon had known her plans in advance and were playing their own game, allowing the 'Last Watch' to get closer to Merlin's legacy.

'But how did you and Edgar get together? If it's not a secret, that is.'

Edgar didn't say anything. He was whispering – obviously trying to heal his injuries as best he could.

'Why should it be a secret?' said Arina, looking at her comrade-in-arms and, apparently, lover. 'He managed to track me down after all. It had become a matter of principle for him. Well, he tracked me down, but by that time he wasn't interested in his career any more. His wife had been killed, he had found out about Merlin's last artefact and he wanted to get his hands on it. And the quickest way to do that was to become a Higher One, and not simply a Higher One but a *zero-point* magician, like Merlin. Edgar thought I could reconstruct the *Fuaran*. He overestimated my abilities a little there. But I liked what he told me about the Crown. So the two of us joined forces.'

I nodded. That sounded like the way it must have happened. Edgar, already obsessed by the idea of reaching the artefact, had found Arina. Together they had co-opted Saushkin, who was thirsting for vengeance, into their 'Last Watch'. And they had set to work. An Inquisitor who had access to an absolutely vast repository of magical amulets; a highly intelligent witch who had become a Light One; a Higher Vampire who was going insane with grief for his son and his wife . . .

A sorry sort of crew they made.

But a terrible one.

'Aren't you afraid that the Crown will become your mistake, Arina? In the same way that Mordred was Merlin's?'

'Yes,' she said. 'I am a bit afraid of that . . . Well then, did we make a mistake by taking you prisoner? Have you found a way to get hold of the Crown of All Things?'

'Yes,' I said. 'Merlin deliberately confused the question of the seventh level. Only a *zero-point* Other can enter the kingdom of the dead.'

'The withdrawn,' Gennady corrected me without any malice in his voice. 'Not the dead, the withdrawn.'

Why was that such a sore point with him? Because he wasn't alive?

'I think it's impossible too,' Arina said, nodding. 'If I had the *Fuaran*, I could have raised Edgar to the *zero-point* level. But without the book it's difficult. I remembered some things, I managed to rewrite a few others, and somehow or other I raised him to the Higher level. But I obviously don't have the skill to rival the *Fuaran* . . . So what were your thoughts?'

'The Crown of All Things is on the fifth level,' I said. 'You could have taken it two weeks ago!'

Arina screwed up her eyes and peered at me. And I started telling her all the nonsense I'd fed to Edgar and Gennady in the plane. About taking a step back. About the head and the tail. About the golem.

'You're probably lying, I suppose,' Arina said pensively. 'It all fits so well . . . But it's a bit simple for old Merlin, don't you think? Well?'

'I think he's lying too,' Gennady suddenly put in, backing her up. He hadn't shown any sign of trusting me in the plane either. 'We ought to have taken the daughter . . .'

'Gena, don't you dream even in your worst nightmare of ever touching that little girl!' Arina said in a quiet voice. 'Is that clear?'

'Of course,' said Gennady, suddenly changing his tune.

'Well then, sorcerer, are you telling the truth or lying?' Arina asked, looking into my eyes. 'Eh?'

'The truth?' I said, leaning forward. The only thing that could save me now was fury . . . and frankness, of course. 'Who do you take me for? Merlin? How should I know the truth? They hung this brute round my neck, threatened to blow up my wife and daughter, together with half of Moscow, and then ordered me to tell them how to get the artefact! How do I know if I'm right or not? I thought about it. It seems to me that this could be the right answer! But nobody, including me, can give you any guarantees!'

'Just what do want from me, my darling cut-throats . . . maybe I should play "Murka" for you?' Edgar said suddenly.

I didn't immediately realise that it was a joke. He didn't often manage that.

'But there is something to this lie of his, after all,' Edgar added, giving me a hostile look. 'It sounds like the truth.'

Arina sighed. She spread her hands and said:

'Well then, all we can do now is check it. Let's go.'

'Stop,' I said. 'Edgar promised to take the Cat off me.'

'If you promised, then take it off,' Arina told him after a moment's thought. 'But don't forget, Anton, that you may be powerful now but there are three of us, and we're as strong as you are. Don't even think about pulling any tricks.'

CHAPTER 6

GENNADY WAS DRIVING. Apparently Edgar and Arina thought that they could restrain me better than he could if I attempted to escape or attack them. I was sitting on the back seat with Edgar on my left and Arina on my right.

But I didn't attempt to attack or to escape – they had too many trump cards up their sleeves. Now that they had taken the Cat off my neck, the skin where the fluffy strap had been was scratched and itchy.

'They're guarding the Crown much more seriously now,' I said. 'Aren't you afraid of a massacre, Arina? Will your conscience be able to handle it?'

'We'll manage without bloodshed,' Arina replied confidently. 'As far as that's possible.'

I doubted very much that it *was* possible, but I didn't try to argue. I looked out in silence at the suburbs we were driving through, as if I was hoping to see Lermont or his black deputy and at least be able to warn them with a look or a gesture . . .

If I tried to get away, they would almost certainly catch me. I had to wait.

★   ★   ★

The day was just declining into evening. It was the busiest time for tourists, but today Edinburgh seemed quite different from two weeks earlier. The people on the streets seemed somehow muted and joyless, the sky was obscured by a light haze and the birds circling overhead seemed alarmed by something.

So apparently everything in the world could sense the approaching cataclysm, including people and birds . . .

The cellphone in my pocket jangled. Edgar started and tensed up. I looked enquiringly at Arina.

'Answer it, but be discreet,' she said.

I looked at the phone. It was Svetlana.

'Hello.'

As ill luck would have it, the connection was excellent. You would never have suspected that we were thousands of kilometres apart.

'Are you still working, Anton?'

'Yes,' I said. 'I'm driving in the car.'

Arina was watching me closely. She was bound to be able to hear every word that Svetlana said.

'I deliberately didn't ring. They told me something had happened – some terrorists or other, pumped full of magic – is that why you're late?'

A faint spark of hope began to glimmer in my breast. I wasn't late yet! Svetlana couldn't have been expecting me home from work so early.

'Yes, of course that's why,' I said.

Come on now, guess! Use magic! You can find out where I am now. Raise the alarm. Warn Geser, and he'll get in touch with Lermont. If the Edinburgh Night Watch are expecting an attack, that will be the end of the 'Last Watch'.

'Make sure you don't get stuck for too long,' Svetlana told me.

'Surely you have enough people working for you to manage all these things? Don't take everything on yourself. Okay?'

'Of course I won't,' I said.

'Is Semyon with you?' Svetlana asked casually.

Before I could answer, Arina shook her head. Of course, if Svetlana suspected something, she could phone Semyon after I said yes.

'No,' I said, 'I'm on my own. I've got a separate job to do.'

'Do you want me to help? I'm getting a bit bored sitting at home,' Svetlana said and laughed.

Arina was alarmed and tense now.

'Don't be silly, this is nothing special,' I said. 'Just an inspection visit.'

'As long as you're sure,' said Svetlana, sounding a bit disappointed. 'Call me if you get completely stuck. Oi, Nadya's trundling something around, bye . . .'

She cut off the call and I started putting the phone away in my pocket. Looking straight into Arina's relaxed face, I pressed three buttons on the phone: Incoming calls – Call last number – Off.

That was all. I couldn't risk leaving the phone switched on. Arina might hear the ringing tone from inside my pocket. Had the call gone through, had the international telephone network managed to process it before it was cancelled? I didn't know. I could only put my hope in the greed of the cellphone network operators – it was more profitable for them to put the call through and take the money for it from my account.

And also, of course, I put my hope in Svetlana's common sense. When her phone rang and then stopped again, she had to use magic, not try calling back. Arina and Edgar were far older than me. But for them a cellphone would always be a portable version of a cumbersome apparatus into which you had to shout: 'Young lady! Young lady! Give me the Smolny Institute!'

'She suspected something,' Edgar said. 'You shouldn't have done that with the bomb . . . it didn't have to be detonated, but at least we would have had a trump card in reserve!'

'Never mind,' said Arina. 'Even if she did suspect something, they don't have any time. Anton, give me that phone.'

A glint of suspicion had appeared in her eyes. I gave her the cell without saying anything, handing it to her fastidiously with the tips of my fingers without touching the keys.

Arina looked at the phone and saw that it was in waiting mode. She shrugged and switched it off completely.

'Let's do without any calls, all right? If you need to call anyone, you can ask me for my phone.'

'I won't bankrupt you?'

'No, you won't.' Arina took out her own phone and dialled a number – not from the phone book, but the old way, pressing every key. She raised the phone to her ear and waited for an answer. When it came she said quietly: 'It's time. Go to work.'

'Still haven't run out of accomplices, then?'

'They're not accomplices, Anton, they're hired hands. People can be perfectly effective allies if you equip them with a small number of amulets. Especially the kind that Edgar has.'

I looked at the royal castle towering up in state above the city, crowning the remains of an ancient volcano now for ever extinct. Well, well, this was the second time I'd ended up in Edinburgh, and I still didn't have time to visit its main tourist attraction . . .

'And what have you prepared this time?' I asked

There was an idea flickering on the edge of my conscious-ness, scratching away at it like Schrödinger's Cat. Something very important.

'Funnily enough, I've actually prepared one of Merlin's artefacts,' Edgar said. He had already recovered from my ungentlemanly blow. 'It's called Merlin's Sleep.'

'Ah, yes, he was rather uninventive with his names for things,' I said, nodding. 'Sleep?'

'Just sleep,' Edgar said, shrugging. 'Arina was very upset about the high number of casualties the last time. This time it will all be very . . . cultured.'

'Ah, and there's the first little spark of culture,' I said, looking at the smoke rising from a taxi in front of us. The driver had clearly fallen asleep as he took a bend, and his car had run up onto the sidewalk and crashed into an old building. But the most terrible thing was not the smoke coming from under the taxi's hood, or the motionless bodies inside it. The sidewalks were covered with the corpses of local people and tourists – one young woman had clearly been knocked aside by the taxi's radiator and then crushed against the wall by its old-fashioned black box of a body. She was probably dying. The only thing I could be glad about was that she was dying in her sleep.

This was not the humane Morpheus that we learned in the Night Watch, the spell that gave people several seconds before they lost consciousness. Merlin's Sleep acted instantly. And it was very precisely localised – I could see the boundary line of the artefact's influence. Two adults stepped inside it and fell to the ground, instantly overcome by sleep. But the seven- or eight-year-old boy who was walking a few steps behind them was still awake and he cried as he shook his motionless parents. He had little prospect of help – those people who had not entered the zone of sleep were running away from it with remarkable alacrity. I could understand why. To someone who didn't know the truth it all looked like the effect of some highly poisonous gas. And somehow the sight of this little boy trying to get his parents to their feet on the other side of the scattering crowd was almost as tragic as the sight of the young woman killed in the crash.

Edgar continued gazing fixedly at the smoking taxi after we

had driven past it. That would probably have been a good moment to escape . . . if I had been intending to escape.

'Does that remind you of something?' I asked.

'Incidental casualties are inevitable,' Edgar said in a voice that had turned flat and hoarse. 'I knew what I was getting into.'

'What a pity they didn't,' I said. And I looked at Edgar through the Twilight.

This was bad, very bad. He was hung all over with amulets: dozens of charms had been applied to him and there were spells trembling on the ends of his fingers, ready to dart off at any moment. He was positively glowing with Power waiting to be used. Arina and Gennady looked exactly the same. Even the vampire had not scorned the magical trinkets.

I wouldn't be able to manage by using force.

We drove to the Dungeons in total silence, past sidewalks strewn with bodies and motionless vehicles (I saw three that were burning). We got out of the car.

On Princess Street, on the other side of the ravine, everything had stopped dead too, but I could already hear a siren howling somewhere. People always recover from a panic. Even if they don't know what it is that they're up against.

'Let's go,' said Edgar, pushing me gently in the back.

We set off down the stairs. I looked back for a moment at the stone crown of the castle above the roofs of the buildings.

Why yes. Of course. You only had to think for a moment and put it all together. Merlin had been most magnanimous when he'd composed his little verse . . .

'What are you dawdling for?' Edgar shouted at me. His nerves were on edge, and no wonder. He was anticipating a meeting with the one he loved.

We walked past motionless bodies. There were people and Others – Merlin's Sleep didn't differentiate between them. I noticed several sleeping Inquisitors. Behind the fake dividing walls everything was lit up brightly by the glow of auras. They had been waiting, and the ambush could not have been prepared better.

Only no one had known the full Power of the artefact that had been used.

'You haven't forgotten about the barrier on the third level, I suppose?' I asked.

'No,' said Arina.

I noticed that as we walked along first Edgar and then Arina left perfectly innocent-looking objects charged with magic on the floor and the walls: scraps of paper, sticks of chewing gum, bits of string. In one place Edgar rapidly sketched several strange symbols on the wall in red chalk – the chalk crumbled into dust as soon as he had traced out the final sign. In another place Arina smiled as she scattered a box of matches across the floor. The 'Last Watch' was clearly afraid of pursuit.

Eventually we entered the room with the guillotine, which for some reason the 'Last Watch' had chosen as its point of entry into the Twilight. This was probably the exact centre of the vortex, the precise focus of Power.

And here, as well as two first-level magicians who were asleep, there was one person who was wide awake.

He was a young man, short and plump, wearing spectacles on his cultured-looking face. He looked very peaceful and unaggressive in his jeans and bright-coloured shirt. In the corner of the room I noticed a girl about ten years old, sleeping with her head resting on a bag that had considerately been placed under it. Had they decided to open the way through with the blood of a child, then?

'My daughter fell asleep,' the man said, correcting my mistaken assumption. 'An extremely interesting device, I must say . . .' He took a small sphere woven from strips of metal out of his pocket. 'The lever shifted and it won't move back again.'

'That's the way it should be,' said Edgar. 'It won't move back again for seventy-something years. So the device is useless to you – leave it here. Take this!'

He tossed a wad of money to the man, who caught it and casually ran his finger over the ends of the notes. But I noticed that he was keeping his left hand behind his back. Oh-oh . . .

'All correct,' the man said with a nod. 'But I'm a little concerned about the scale of the event . . . and the devices that you employ. It seems to me that the deal was clearly made on unequal terms.'

'I told you this would happen,' Edgar said to Arina. He turned back to the man and asked, 'What do you want? More money?'

The man shook his head.

'Take the money and your daughter, and go. That's my advice to you,' said Arina.

The man licked his lips and then unbuttoned his shirt.

He turned out not to be fat at all. His torso was encased in something that looked like an orthopaedic corset. Except that it had wires protruding from it.

'A kilogramme of plastic explosive. The switch works on the "dead hand" principle,' said the man, raising his left hand. 'I'm going to take that sphere, all the strange trinkets that I found on these guys' – he prodded one of the sleeping Others with his foot – 'and everything you have in your pockets. Is that clear?'

'As clear as day,' said Edgar. 'I said right at the beginning that this would happen. I made the right choice with you.'

I suddenly noticed that Gennady was no longer there with us.

'And this resolves a certain number of moral difficulties,' Edgar said, turning away.

The explosives belt suddenly flew into little pieces. It wasn't an explosion: it looked like the work of a clawed hand moving with unnatural speed – out of the Twilight, for example. Totally confused, the man opened his left hand, and a small switch with an absurd little tail of wire fell out of it. He'd been telling the truth.

The next moment the man screamed, and I too chose to turn away.

'An exceptionally loathsome character,' said Edgar. 'His threat was serious, even though the little girl is his own daughter. But now we have the blood we need, with none of the killing of innocent people that upsets Arina so much.'

'You're no better than him,' I replied.

'I don't pretend to be,' Edgar said, with a shrug. 'Let's go. It's not the first time we've entered the Twilight together, is it?'

He even took hold of my hand. I didn't protest. I found my own shadow on the floor and stepped into it. Through the gust of icy-cold wind, into the frozen, hungry space of the Twilight . . .

The first level.

We moved on without delay. The second level. The space around us was seething, agitated either by the fresh blood or by the hole that Merlin had made here in the fabric of creation.

Edgar and Arina were still beside me. Intensely focused. A moment later Gennady too appeared, with blood on his lips. On the second level I could barely recognise Saushkin senior, his face was so badly distorted by hideous malice and insane hatred.

The third level. The final eddies of the vortex of Power that had been blocking our way so recently were still raging here. Edgar started looking round and said:

'Someone's following us . . . one of the signs has been activated.'

'Successfully?' A cloud of steam escaped from between Arina's lips as she asked.

'I don't know. Let's go lower!'

The fourth level greeted us with its pink sky and coloured sand. I pulled my hand out of Edgar's grasp and said:

'We agreed! I won't join the fight against the golem!'

'And nobody's forcing you to,' Edgar said, with a toothy grimace. 'Don't worry, you can keep out of it. Forward!'

This was the point at which I had planned to start an argument. To drag things out and then run for it, or even stay here and send the 'Last Watch' on to a pointless battle against the monster.

But something seemed to urge me on. Something like the insane obsession that had possessed Arina, Edgar and Gennady seemed to take possession of me too. I had to go down to the fifth level . . . I had to!

If only to lull their vigilance . . .

'All right, but I don't intend to lay my life down for your sake!' I shouted and stepped down to the fifth level under Edgar's watchful eye.

They appeared beside me almost instantly. Yes, they had certainly pumped themselves full of Power. Gennady was the only one who was slightly delayed. He had obviously got through at the second attempt.

And this level of the Twilight was so much nicer than the ones above it! Cool, even chilly, but already without that icy wind that sucked the life out of you. And the colours here looked almost natural . . .

I looked round, trying to spot the golem, and I saw it about two hundred metres away – there were two snakes' heads sticking up out of the grass, turning this way and that like submarines' periscopes. Then the golem spotted us. The heads shuddered and reached up higher. There was a loud hissing sound, very much like a real snake's hiss, except that it was coming from such a long distance away . . .

A moment later the snake was already slipping towards us, managing to keep both of its heads above the grass at the same time.

'Head and tail,' Arina said pensively. 'I don't know, I don't know . . . Edgar, release Kong.'

I understood what she meant when Edgar took a small jade figurine out of his pocket – it was a long-armed monkey with short pointed horns protruding from its head. The Inquisitor breathed on the figurine and then carefully screwed its head off – the figurine turned out to be hollow – and carefully set it down in the grass. We barely had time to jump back before the vessel started giving out green smoke that coiled into the form of a monster.

The deva that had hunted Alisher in Samarkand was nothing like King Kong. He didn't have the height for that, since he only stood about three metres at the withers. But the toothy, gaping jaw, muscular limbs with sharp claws, coarse dark green fur and brutish, flaming-orange eyes impressed me far more than the sentimental giant from the old movies.

And King Kong probably never had such a repulsive acrid smell either. How could a golem stink, when it consisted of concentrated Power, not flesh, or even clay, and it had been stored in a magical vessel? I didn't know. Maybe it was an accidental side effect. Or maybe it was a joke by the deva's creator?

'Go and kill it!' Edgar shouted, pointing to the snake. Kong roared and went dashing towards the snake in huge bounds. The snake slithered towards him, not at all frightened by his sudden appearance, even seeming to liven up at the prospect of a worthy opponent. The earth shuddered under the impact of their feet and coils; the monkey's thunderous roar and the snake's deafening hiss fused together into a single mighty rumble.

Now was the time! While they were entranced by the prospect of the forthcoming battle.

I turned round – and froze. Standing behind me was a short old man with a beard, dressed in white. At some moments he looked absolutely real – I could count every last hair in the grey beard and gaze into the weary face furrowed with wrinkles; at others he became a hazy white shadow, through which I could see the grass and the sky.

The old man pointed slowly to the ground at his feet. Then he repeated the gesture.

Did he want me to go down to the sixth level?

I jabbed my hand downwards. The old man nodded, and an expression of relief appeared on his face.

He began melting away into the air.

There was no time to hesitate. At any moment one of the 'Last Watch' might look round and realise that I was preparing to make my escape.

The Power is within me! I can go down to the sixth level.

The Power is within me! I can see it always.

I must do this! Therefore I will do it.

I felt a blast of icy wind.

As I stepped through the barrier I heard Arina's voice:

'Somebody really is—'

The voice fell silent, cut off at the border of the sixth level. At the border that protected the world of Others who had withdrawn.

'Thank you for coming,' the old man said. And he smiled.

Before I answered, I looked around me.

Daytime. A blue sky with white fluffy clouds and a sun. A meadow of green grass. Birds twittering in the trees.

An ancient grey-haired man standing in front of me. His clothes had probably never been white – the coarse greyish sackcloth had only appeared to be white at first glance. And he was barefoot too . . . but the effect was not a pastoral, sentimental closeness to nature. He was simply a man who went barefoot, who didn't think it was worth wasting time on making shoes.

'I greet you, Great One,' I said, bowing my head. 'It is an honour for me . . . to see the Great Merlin.'

The old man looked into my face curiously. As if this wasn't the first time he had seen me but he'd never had a chance to look at me properly before.

'An honour? How much do you know of my life, Light One?'

'I know about some things,' I said, shrugging. 'I know about the ship with the little children.'

'And even so it is "an honour"?'

'It seems to me that you have already paid for many things. And, in addition, for millions of people you are a wise defender of good and justice. That also counts for something.'

'There were only nine of them . . .' Merlin muttered. 'Legends – they always exaggerate. The bad things, and the good things . . .'

'But they did exist.'

'They did,' Merlin confirmed. 'Why do you think that I have already paid? Do you not like the heaven that awaits Others after death?'

Instead of answering I bent down and plucked a stalk of grass. I put it in my mouth and bit it. The juice was bitter . . . only not quite bitter enough. I screwed my eyes up and looked at the sun. It was shining in the sky, but its light was not blinding. I clapped my hands – the sound was very slightly muted. I breathed in, filling my lungs with air – the air was fresh . . . and yet there was something lacking in it. It left a slight musty odour, like the one in Saushkin's apartment . . .

'Everything here is not quite genuine,' I said. 'It lacks life.'

'Well done,' said Merlin, nodding. 'Many do not notice that straight away. Many live here for years – or centuries – before they realise that they have been deceived.'

'Can't you get used to it?' I asked.

Merlin smiled.

'No. It is impossible to get used to this.'

'Remember the joke about the fake New Year's tree decorations, Anton?' someone asked behind me. I looked round.

Tiger Cub was standing just five steps away.

There were many of them. Very many of them, standing there and listening to my conversation with Merlin. Igor Teplov and Alisa Donnikova – they were together, holding each other by the hand, but there was no happiness in their faces. The girl–werewolf Galya was hiding her eyes. Murat from the Samarkand Watch gave me an embarrassed wave. A Dark One I had once killed by throwing him off the Ostankino Television Tower looked at me with no malice or resentment in his eyes.

There were so many. The trees prevented me from seeing just how many of them were standing there. If not for the forest, they would have stretched all the way back to the horizon. They had let the ones I had known come through to the front.

'Yes, Tiger Club, I remember,' I said.

I didn't feel any more fear or anger. Only sadness – a calm, weary sadness.

'They look so real,' Tiger Cub said and smiled. 'But they bring no joy at all . . .'

'You're looking good,' I muttered, for the sake of saying something at least.

Tiger Cub pensively examined her tiger-skin cape. She nodded.

'I made an effort. For the sake of this meeting.'

'Hi, Igor!' I said. 'Hi, Alisa!'

They nodded. Then Alisa said:

'Good for you, Anton, You're powerful. But don't get too big-headed, Light One! Merlin himself has been helping you.'

I looked round at the old man.

'Sometimes,' Merlin said tactfully. 'Well . . . beside that outlandish tower of yours. And then when you were fighting that werewolf in the forest . . . And only just a little bit . . .'

I wasn't listening to him any longer. I was gazing round, trying to find the one whose words were most important of all to me.

Kostya pushed aside the Other he had been standing behind and came forward towards me. Of everyone there, he probably looked the best and the most absurd at the same time – he was wearing a tattered spacesuit that had once been white but was now blackened and burned through in several places.

'Hello, neighbour,' he said.

'Hi, Kostya,' I replied. 'I . . . I've been wanting to say something to you for a long time. Forgive me.'

He frowned.

'Will you drop those Light affectations of yours? What is there to forgive? We fought honestly, and you won honestly. Everything's fine. I ought to have realised that you weren't erecting the Shield because you were afraid . . .'

'Even so,' I said. 'You know that I hate my job. I've turned into a small screw . . . a tiny part of a machine that gives no quarter and shows any mercy!'

'And how else could it be, between us?' Kostya suddenly smiled. 'Drop that . . . And you . . . forgive my father. If you can. He never used to be like that.'

I nodded.

'I'll try. I really will.'

'Tell him that Mom and I are waiting for him.' Kostya paused and then added firmly: 'Here.'

'I'll tell him,' I promised, trying to spot Polina.

Kostya suddenly took a step forward, shook me awkwardly by the hand – and stepped away again.

And in that brief instant when our hands touched I felt his cold hand turn warm, saw his skin flush pink and his eyes gleam once again. Kostya stood there swaying, looking at his hand.

But my hand was seared by an icy chill . . .

The ranks of Others shuddered. Slowly, involuntarily, they began moving towards me. There was hunger and envy in their eyes – in all of their eyes, even Tiger Cub's, even Igor's, even Murat's . . .'

'Stop!' Merlin shouted. He darted forward and stood between me and the withdrawn Others, raising his hands high in the air. I noticed that he carefully skirted round me to avoid touching me.

'Stop, you mad fools! A few minutes of life . . . that is not what we want, not what we have been waiting for!'

They stopped and looked at each other in embarrassment. Then they moved back. But the hungry fire was still blazing in their eyes.

'Leave now, Anton,' Merlin said. 'You understand everything and you know what you have to do. Go!'

'I can't get through, the "Last Watch" is up there,' I said. 'Unless your golem has stopped them . . .'

Merlin looked straight through me at something. Then he sighed.

'The golem is dead. Both golems are dead. A pity – I used to go up to the fifth level sometimes and play with the snake. But it was sad and lonely too.'

'Can you take me through?' I asked.

Merlin shook his head,

'Not many of us are capable of going to the fifth level. Only very few can reach the first level, and even so we are powerless there.'

'I won't be able to get past them,' I said. 'And I can't go straight forward to the seventh level either.'

We smiled at each other.

'You will be helped,' Merlin said. 'Only do everything right, I beg of you.'

I nodded.

I didn't know if it would work. All I could do was try.

The next moment the air around me started to vibrate as if

something seething with an huge excess of Power had broken through the Twilight. What levels, what distances? What did these mean in the face of this Power resonating in awareness of its own self?

Little Nadya stepped down onto the grass. She waved her arms about, but couldn't keep her balance and plumped down onto her bottom, looking up at me.

'Get up,' I said sternly. 'It's damp!'

Nadya jumped to her feet, dusted off her velvet jumpsuit and jabbered:

'Mommy taught me how to walk into the shadow! That's one! And there was a monkey and snake fighting, and they both beat each other. That's two! Two men and a woman were watching the snake and saying very bad words. That's three! And Mommy told me to bring you straight back home for supper! That's four!'

She gulped when she saw the huge crowd around her, then lowered her eyes in embarrassment and said in a polite little girl's voice:

'Hello . . .'

'Hello,' said Merlin, squatting down in front of her. 'Are you Nadezhda?'

'Yes,' Nadya said proudly.

'I'm glad I've seen you,' said Merlin. 'Take your daddy home. Only not straight home – first go back to the people. And then home.'

'Backwards means forwards?' Nadya asked

'That's right.'

'You look like a wizard from a cartoon,' Nadya said suspiciously. Just to be on the safe side, she took hold of my hand, and that clearly made her feel more confident.

'I used to be a wizard,' Merlin confessed.

'A good one or a bad one?'

'All kinds,' he said, with a sad smile. 'Go now, Nadezhda.'

Nadya cast a wary look at Merlin and asked me:

'Shall we go, Daddy?'

'Yes, let's go,' I said.

I looked round and nodded to Merlin, who was watching us silently. In sad anticipation. The first to raise her hand and wave goodbye was Tiger Cub. Then Alisa. And then they were all waving to us . . . waving goodbye for ever.

And when my daughter, the newly initiated Absolute Enchantress, took a step forward, I stepped after her, holding her hand in order not to lose my way in the swirling vortex of Power that had completed its circle and was returning us to our world.

Because the Twilight, of course, has no end, just as no ring has an end.

Because the warmth of human love and the cold of human hate, the running of beasts and the singing of birds, the fluttering of a butterfly's wings and the sprouting of a grain through the earth do not pass away, leaving no trace. Because the universal stream of living Power out of which parasites like the blue moss and the Others greedily snatch their crumbs does not disappear without trace – it returns to the world that is awaiting rebirth.

Because we all live on the seventh level of the Twilight.

EPILOGUE

'How! lovely! it is! Here!' Nadya exclaimed.

I picked her up in my arms. We were standing on a cobbled street in Edinburgh, surrounded by hundreds and thousands of sleeping people. The sirens were drawing closer and closer as the time of the Others was coming to an end.

'Yes,' I agreed. 'Everything here is real.'

'Only everyone's sleeping,' Nadya observed sadly. 'Like in the fairy story about the sleeping princess. Can I wake them up?'

She could . . . She could do anything at all now – if she was taught.

'But aren't you tired?' I asked. My legs were buckling under me and I was feeling a bit dizzy.

'What from?' Nadya asked in surprise

'In a little while,' I said. 'Just a little while, we'll wake everyone up . . . all those we can. Daddy just has to do one thing that's very important first. Will you help me?'

'How?'

'Just hold onto me,' I said. I closed my eyes and flung out my arms. I held my breath.

I had to feel this city. The stones and the walls that remembered

Merlin and Arthur. People might have forgotten, but the stones remembered. The ancient fortress, set above the city like a crown, remembered too, and it was waiting.

Why were we so stupid sometimes? Why did we expect magic to be hidden in something we could hold in our hands, when it could be everywhere all around us?

Of course, Merlin hadn't hidden his most important creation in the Twilight, he hadn't put his trust in the strength of the golem, but he hadn't put it in the strength of oak chests either. This ancient fortress had stood on the cliff for fifteen hundred years, it had been defended and captured, it had been destroyed and rebuilt, the proud kings of Scotland had kept their treasures in it — and the stones covered with runes that Merlin had laid in the deepest foundations had been waiting for their time to come.

I only had to reach out to them. Touch them. Feel them . . .

'Light One!' someone roared behind me. I looked round, emerging from my trance.

Edgar and Arina were standing there, just looking at me — and I was astonished to realise that their eyes were full of fear. Gennady was running at me. Running and shouting. Surely he didn't think that the power of magic depended on how loud you shouted? He came rushing towards me, taking immense bounds, transforming as he advanced, looking less and less like a human being. His fangs were growing, his skin was turning the colour of death, the hair on his head was falling out in tangled grey skeins.

I raised my hand, gathering Power for the Grey Prayer.

But just then Nadya stepped forward and shrieked in the vampire's face:

'Don't shout at my daddy!'

Gennady staggered. What had struck him was more powerful

than hate. But he couldn't stop, he kept moving forward, as if he was running against a hurricane. And he collapsed at our feet. Nadya squealed and hid behind me.

I squatted down and looked into Gennady Saushkin's eyes. He looked at me and asked:

'Can't they come?'

'No, they can't come. And they would never have been able to. But I will do what they asked me to. Go, while there is still time.'

'Help me, Anton,' he said in an almost normal voice.

'Nadya, look the other way!' I ordered.

'I'm not looking, I'm not!' my daughter mumbled, turning away and putting her hands over her eyes to make quite sure.

I raised my hand, with Gennady watching my movements as if he were already spellbound. And the Grey Prayer dispatched the vampire to the sixth level of the Twilight.

I got up and looked at Edgar and Arina. 'A *zero-point* Other,' Arina said in delight. 'An Absolute Enchantress . . .'

'For five minutes I'll be much too busy too be concerned with you,' I said, looking at them. 'But afterwards . . .'

'We have the Minoan Sphere,' Edgar said pleadingly. 'Can we?'

'They'll search for you,' I said. 'And so will I, remember that. But just now you have five minutes. And only because they asked me to forgive.'

'What are you going to do?' Arina asked.

'What those who have withdrawn have been dreaming of. Grant them death. Because without death resurrection is impossible.'

Edgar narrowed his eyes. He opened a bag hanging at his waist, took out a small ivory sphere and handed it to Arina. She took it without saying a word.

'Help me too, Light One,' Edgar said. 'What's it to you?'

'You've got protective charms draped all over you like garlands on a New Year's tree. How can I help you?'

'I'll help him,' Arina suddenly said. 'Don't you get sidetracked. Do what you've got to do.'

I didn't understand exactly what it was that she did. She seemed just to move her lips. Edgar smiled, and for an instant his face was handsome and almost young. Then his legs buckled and he collapsed onto the cobblestones of the street.

'But you're not planning to dematerialise,' I remarked. 'What kind of a Light One are you?'

'Well, one way or another the goal has been achieved now,' Arina declared. 'The withdrawn will get what they were longing for!'

I shook my head. Then I looked at the castle and closed my eyes again.

'I'm returning your phone . . .' Arina said. 'I don't want anybody else's things.'

I heard the Minoan Sphere burst quietly behind my back, opening up a portal for Arina, one that would be impossible to trace. Oh, she had been a strange Dark One, and she had turned into a strange Light One.

Suddenly I heard the faint sound of music. Arina had switched on the player built into the phone. By chance?

Or to show that her grasp of technology was a lot better than I thought?

They seem to have left the *nigredo* like you and I
And they walk in the light, knowing nothing.
They spit in the mirror and laugh at themselves – yes,
They have left the *nigredo*, knowing nothing.

The dark one will be punished, his brow smeared with chalk,
The light one will be caught and rolled in soot,
But what can you do?

Like you and I they seem to have left the *nigredo*,
Knowing nothing.

On the capricious hand there are eight lifelines,
And so when they meet they maul each other,
But what can you do?
Like you and I they seem to have left the *nigredo*,
Knowing nothing.*

Well now, that's already a blessing. When you manage to get out of the *nigredo*, whether you're a Dark One or a Light One, you have a chance to continue your journey. You can only move on via the *nigredo*, decay and dissolution. Move on to synthesis. To the creation of the new. To *albedo*.

The ancient stones on the top of the cliff were waiting.

I reached out to them. No spells, words or rituals were required here. I only had to know what to reach out towards and what to ask for.

Merlin had always left himself a loophole. Even as he was about to set out for the Others' heaven he had suspected that this stolen heaven might turn out to be hell.

'Release them,' I pleaded, without even knowing whom I meant. 'Release them, please. They have done evil that was evil, and good that turned into evil. But for all things the time comes for forgiveness. Release them . . .'

The fortress towering over the city seemed to sigh. The birds circling in the sky started moving lower. The dense gloom in the air began to dissipate. The final ray of the setting sun fell on the city in a promise to return with the dawn.

And I felt all the levels of creation shrink together and tremble.

---

* Translator's note: *Nigredo* and *Albedo* are alchemical terms for 'Blackness' and 'Whiteness'.

I saw the stone idols on the Plateau of Demons in Uzbekistan collapse and crumble, as if it were happening in front of my very eyes. I saw the Others who had withdrawn into the Twilight after dematerialising dissolve into it – with a feeling of relief and tremulous hope.

It became easier to breathe.

'Daddy, can I look now?' Nadya asked. 'Just peep with one eye?'

'Yes,' I answered. I squatted down – my legs wouldn't hold me up any longer. 'Daddy's just going to have a little rest, and then we'll go home . . . will you take me the short way?'

'All right,' Nadya agreed.

'No, you know what, let's not take the short road,' I said, changing my mind abruptly. 'I don't really like short roads. Why don't we fly in an aeroplane?'

'Hooray!' Nadya shrieked. 'In an aeroplane! And will we come back here sometime?'

I looked at her and smiled. Maybe I'd manage to teach her always to be wary of simple answers and short roads.

'Definitely,' I said. 'You didn't think this was the Last Watch, did you?'